Rhinelander Pavillion

By Barbara Harrison

ZEBRA BOOKS
KENSINGTON PUBLISHING CORP.

ZEBRA BOOKS

are published by

KENSINGTON PUBLISHING CORP.
21 East 40th Street
New York, N.Y. 10016

Copyright© 1979 Barbara Harrison
Second Printing: March 1980
Third Printing: April, 1980

All rights reserved. No part of this book may be reproduced in any form or by any means without the prior written consent of the Publisher, excepting brief quotes used in reviews.

Printed in the United States of America

DIAGNOSIS: CRITICAL CONDITION

David took a small leather notebook from his pocket. He tore off a sheet of paper and handed it to Patrick.

"Here's a list of our problem students. You'll want to read their files very carefully."

Patrick glanced at the list. "One name's underlined in red."

"That's O'Hara. If you can bring him into line, you can bring any of them into line."

Patrick sat back, sighing softly. "Rhinelander Pavillion has so *many* problems, David. I wish you'd told me before this."

"If I had, you'd have run, and time is running out—for Rhinelander and for you. It's now or never, Patrick, and these next months will determine if the hospital makes it or not . . . if *you* make it or not. That can't wait any longer."

"You make too much of everything," Patrick said impatiently.

"No. These next months are make or break—maybe for all of us. Now," David said, leaning over the desk to the folders, "there are a few things I want to review with you . . ."

BESTSELLERS FOR TODAY'S WOMAN

ALL THE WAY (571, $2.25)
by Felice Buckvar
After over twenty years of devotion to another man, Phyllis finds herself helplessly in love, once again, with that same tall, handsome high school sweetheart who had loved her . . . ALL THE WAY.

HAPPILY EVER AFTER (595, $2.25)
by Felice Buckvar
Disillusioned with her husband, her children and her life, Dorothy Fine begins to search for her own identity . . . and discovers that it's not too late to love and live again.

SO LITTLE TIME (585, $2.50)
by Sharon M. Combes
Darcey must put her love and courage to the test when she learns that her fiance has only months to live. Destined to become this year's *Love Story*.

RHINELANDER PAVILLION (572, $2.50)
by Barbara Harrison
A powerful novel that captures the real-life drama of a big city hospital and its dedicated staff who become caught up in their own passions and desires.

THE BUTTERFLY SECRET (394, $2.50)
by Toni Tucci
Every woman's fantasy comes to life in Toni Tucci's guide to new life for the mature woman. Learn the secret of love, happiness and excitement, and how to fulfill your own needs while satisfying your mate's.

Available wherever paperbacks are sold, or order direct from the Publisher. Send cover price plus 50¢ per copy for mailing and handling to Zebra Books, 21 East 40th Street, New York, N.Y. 10016. DO NOT SEND CASH!

*Lovingly, to the memory of my mother
Ann Harrison*

1

Catherine's portrait hung above the mantel in the large, elegant drawing room of the Dain duplex on Fifth Avenue, dominating the room. It demanded attention much as Catherine had throughout her life, and as it had been impossible to turn away from her, so it was to turn from her likeness. There was a singular radiance about it, but more compelling than that was the extraordinary, turbulent beauty — the beauty which had brought happiness, and then grief, to so many.

The face in the portrait was indeed exquisite, oval and delicately boned, framed by a mass of tumbling hair the exact color of well polished gold. The eyes were provocative, several shades of gray, the complexion rosy porcelain. All of the features were soft and gently rounded but none more so than the mouth, which was intensely, profoundly sensual. Catherine had worn the magnificent Dain emeralds for her portrait yet their fabled beauty was no match for her own. She was, it had been said, perfection.

Patrick Dain stood very still, staring at the portrait of his wife, studying it, searching it, as if looking for an answer, a clue, to a deep, elusive mystery. He stood that way for some time, not moving, hardly breathing, his eyes never leaving Catherine's face. Finally, almost grudgingly, he stepped away from the portrait and sat down on a small damask sofa. He let his glance wander around the room, feeling its splendor as clearly as he felt his own discomfort.

It was a square, spacious room, its windows tall and narrow, covered with gold draperies hung in formal, careful folds. The walls were antique *boiseries*, white and gold. In the center of the gleaming, burnished floor was an Aubusson rug, off-white, with pale rose and blue flowers. Silk and brocade chairs and sofas in shades of primrose and ivory and plum were placed in formal groupings around the room. Several differently shaped rosewood tables held Catherine's collection of old, miniature music boxes. The room was high above Fifth Avenue and there was no errant sound, no noise to disturb the infinite stillness.

For just one moment Patrick Dain had a terrible desire to take one of the precious old music boxes and smash it to the floor; in that moment he could have smashed it all, every treasure in the room—starting, he thought grimly, with Catherine's portrait. A dark, angry look came into his eyes and then was gone, replaced by an expression of utter weariness. He sighed and leaned back, throwing his arms over the top of the sofa. He tilted his face upward, staring at the ceiling, at nothing in particular, lost in some old reverie.

Patrick was a handsome man, with very dark hair and deep, brooding, dark blue eyes, thickly, blackly lashed. His features were strong and sure, with a firm jaw and chin, though his mouth was gentle, even vulnerable. His skin was very fair, in sharp contrast to all the rich darkness of his hair and brows and eyes, and in the pale light of the room he looked considerably younger than his forty years. A tall man, over six feet, there was an authority and yet a grace about him. He had broad, muscular shoulders and a trim, lean body, in the manner of all the Dain men.

The American branch of the Dain family had been founded more than a hundred and fifty years before by Edwin Dain, a robust, brashly charming man who'd believed in the young country and in the power of his own hard work and had built a vast fortune while still in his thirties. This he'd passed on to succeeding generations, along with a strong, indomitable character. Patrick had never known his great-great-grandfather, but he'd inherited his character as surely as he'd inherited his dark blue eyes. It was evident in everything about him, in his bearing and his honest, direct gaze, in his unwavering sense of duty and honor. He'd inherited his ancestor's charm as well, his gift for laughter, though this, like much else about Patrick, had been greatly subdued in the past few years.

Patrick sighed once more. His eyes returned to the portrait and again he was lost in it, far away in some other time and place. So absorbed was he that he didn't hear his housekeeper enter the room.

Delia Woodlow, small and spare, her gray hair drawn back neatly, her dark dress immaculate, took several steps into the drawing room and then stopped. Her mouth opened in surprise as she saw Patrick Dain sitting there, for it had been Patrick Dain, in as vehement a tone as he'd ever used, who'd ordered the drawing room closed and locked five months before. Exactly five months before, she remembered, on the day of Catherine Dain's funeral. Since that time the room had been opened only for cleaning and airing, and that as quickly as possible. Delia knew he hadn't set foot inside the room in all that time; privately she'd doubted he ever would. She turned quickly to leave but as she did so a ring of keys dropped from her hand and fell to the floor. Patrick looked around. He smiled very slightly, thoughtfully.

"I've never liked this room . . . did you know that, Delia?"

Delia said nothing though her heart went out to him, for she was one of the few who knew about the real despair of the last few years, about the cruelties Patrick Dain had been made to suffer.

"Well," he said quietly, "it doesn't matter now."

Delia clasped her hands together uneasily. "I was looking for you, Dr. Dain. I couldn't think where you might be. And then I saw the light coming out of here. I'm sorry, sir."

"No need. What may I do for you?"

"Dr. Murdock called, sir. He said he'd be here at eight."

Patrick glanced at his watch. "That's fine."

"There's all that good roast left. I could make up a nice plate for the doctor. With the little bitty peas he likes so much."

"Thank you," Patrick smiled, "but I'm sure he'll have eaten," he said, standing up. He walked to where his housekeeper stood and bent swiftly, picking up the keys and handing them to her. "Where's Hollis?"

"Putting some things away, Doctor. Do you want him?"

"Tell him, please, that I'll be in the library. I'll see Dr. Murdock in there. And tell him we won't be needing anything." Patrick walked a few steps and turned around. "Why are you here so late, Delia?"

"It was the big monthly cleaning today, sir. The girls are just now leaving."

"Well, you work too hard," he said, walking toward the big double doors. "Go home. I don't want you overdoing." Patrick reached the doors and looked back. He hesitated for a moment and then spoke. "We'll continue to keep this room locked," he said softly, "at least until Tony comes home for the holidays." He smiled briefly though there was no smile in his dark blue eyes. "That's still a way off, we'll think about it later."

"Yes, Doctor, as you say."

"Goodnight, Delia."

"Sir," she said, watching him walk off, a tall, erect figure in fawn-colored slacks and a blue shirt, the collar open, the sleeves rolled to the elbow.

Patrick strode through the doors and through the broad center hall, walking quickly until he reached a door to the right of the central staircase. He opened the door and entered his library. Almost immediately he felt the familiar peace of the room come over him. Patrick loved his library; it was, in fact, one of only a few rooms in the huge apartment in which he felt at home.

Warm, hospitable, with a slightly unkempt look, it was a handsome room. Panelled in rich, dark mahogany, one end was lined with floor-to-ceiling mahogany bookcases, the shelves tightly packed with the books he'd gathered and loved over the years.

Near the tall windows was the beautiful old Hepplewhite desk which had belonged to his grandfather, its red leather surface now covered with papers and reports. There was a fireplace on one side of the room, handsome bronze pokers at its side. In front of it were two overstuffed wing chairs in a soft tan, black and red plaid, the colors picking up the colors of the rugs scattered throughout the room. There were several small, circular tables, their tops nearly obscured by dozens of photographs, each in silver frames. Near Patrick's desk was a larger table holding a silver tray, three crystal decanters, glasses and a small crystal ice bucket, freshly filled by Delia.

Patrick turned a small dial on the wall, dimming the lights slightly, and then went to his desk. He switched on a chunky pewter desk lamp and sat down, moving around in the old brown leather chair until he was comfortable. He reached for one of the reports marked RHINELANDER PAVILLION and then searched around the desk until he found his pen. Patrick read steadily, a youthful earnestness on his face as he made small checkmarks here and there, occasionally emitting small, disapproving sounds and making larger, slashing checkmarks. He continued on the reports for some forty minutes. He was almost finished when the door opened and David Murdock walked into the room.

"Hollis said to come right in. Am I interrupting?"

"No, of course not," Patrick smiled. He came around the side of the desk and shook hands with David, genuinely glad to see him, for the two were very old friends.

Patrick Dain and David Murdock had been childhood friends, roommates at prep school and at Yale, both eagerly heading toward medical careers. They went through medical school together, interning at the same hospital and often assigned to the same shifts. They'd shared the grueling competition and study and work of those years, coming away from them with a deep respect for each other, with a bond as strong as any that might bind brothers together.

They'd shared good times; it was David who'd introduced his cousin Catherine to Patrick and later was best man at their wedding—a favor Patrick returned a year after when David married. And they'd shared bad times; it was Patrick who'd helped David through the death of his little girl and the subsequent crumbling of his marriage; it was David who'd tried to help the Dains through all their many troubles.

The years had strengthened their friendship, their fondness for each other. This was true despite the very real differences between them. Patrick was easygoing,

David intense; Patrick preferred a certain disarray, David was rigorously organized; Patrick was a casual man, David meticulous.

David Murdock had dark wavy hair, always neatly, precisely barbered. He had dark brown eyes and a good looking, regularly featured face which he was careful to shave twice, sometimes three times a day, whether he needed it or not. He was not as tall as Patrick but he carried himself well, in expensive clothing, perfectly cut and tailored; the shine on his shoes had the sharp clarity of ice.

"Sit down, make yourself comfortable," Patrick said now. "Have you had dinner? Delia offered to make up a tray."

"I ate at the hospital," David said, settling himself into the big leather armchair by Patrick's desk. He spoke crisply and distinctly, decisiveness in every syllable.

"Brandy?"

David nodded, watching Patrick closely as he stood at the liquor tray. "I'm surprised you recognized me. It's been a while," he teased.

"It hasn't been that long. What's it been, a month, two?"

"Three," David said, taking his drink. "How are you?"

Patrick returned to his chair and sat down. "Fine, I'm fine. And you?"

"Not a hair out of place."

Patrick smiled. "Was there ever? David, has it really been three months?"

"Three months," David said, sipping his drink. "Just before I left on vacation."

"I got your cards. How was it?"

"Quiet. Nice. I buried myself in Maine and did a lot of fishing and hiking. Blissful serenity. I needed it."

"And since then? Bring me up to date."

David smiled, a brief flash of white, though his eyes still studied Patrick. "I've been overworking, thanks to you. I've hardly left the hospital."

"What? I don't believe it. Not you. Not man-about-town-Murdock."

"Believe it. I'm doing two jobs, yours and mine. I'm teaching two sets of classes. Throw in some sleep and there's very little time left over. If you think I'm blaming you for all of this, you're right."

"Hard work builds character," Patrick laughed.

"Easy for you to say. Particularly since you're not doing any of the hard work." David paused for a moment, concern clear in his eyes. "Patrick, small talk is all very well and good, but not now. I'd hoped your call meant you were ready to go to work again. I'd hoped you'd decided to stop being such a damned hermit."

Patrick looked at David. "A hermit? Is that what you think?"

"What am I supposed to think? Your friends have hardly seen you since the funeral. You don't return phone calls or invitations. You were due to begin work at Rhinelander Pavillion a month ago and didn't. Some people are beginning to think you're a figment of my imagination."

Patrick looked down at his drink and smiled. "I've put you on the spot, haven't I?" he looked up again. "I'm sorry, but I've had a lot to do, things coming at me from all sides. Slowly but surely the air is starting to clear."

"Is it?"

"I think so, yes. I found a good young doctor to take over my practice; that's out of the way. Tony's settled back up at school. Those were my main concerns. And Rhinelander, of course," he added, smiling.

"Of course. Any second thoughts?"

"I suppose. A few. And when I read the hospital reports, friend, quite a few more. But it's the right thing to do. I don't want to go back to the routine of private practice. I had very healthy patients. Very little challenge and too much free time. That's not for me anymore, not after Catherine . . ." Patrick's dark blue eyes grew quiet. "I need work that will keep me interested and busy. I want to get back the feeling of commitment I once had. I remember when medicine was the most important thing in my life. I want that back."

David said nothing. He stared at Patrick, at the abstract, closed look on his face. It was a look he'd seen more and more in the last few years and it disturbed him.

"You mean you don't want time to think," David said finally.

"All right. I don't want time to think. I'm tired, I'm tired of thinking."

"You intend to lose yourself in your work."

"I do."

David shook his head. "It won't work."

"Perhaps not for you. It will work for me. I've made up my mind," he said firmly and David saw the stubborn determination in his eyes.

He'd seen that look before, in Patrick and Patrick's father, and in the eyes of the Dain ancestors whose portraits hung in the upper gallery. He knew the strength of Dain resolve when tested, knew there was no fighting it.

"If that's what you really want," David said, "Rhinelander Pavillion has a lot to offer. I will gladly give you twenty-four hour shifts seven days a week. Better you than me," he smiled. "All you have to do is show up. And I hope that's soon; the boys and girls are getting restless."

Patrick leaned back in his chair and laughed abruptly. "Are you saying the Chief of Services of all of Rhinelander Pavillion can't handle a few students and interns?"

"Yes. They're not so few and they're running everyone a merry chase. Especially me, the famous Chief of Services. We haven't had a student-intern director since Dr. Stein left last month. It's been one solid month of chaos, thanks to you." He laughed suddenly, shaking his head. "It's bad, Patrick. They're running amok."

"*Panem et circenses*. Give them bread and circuses."

"I'd rather give them you. The question is when do we get you? It's time, Patrick, past time. And I don't just mean Rhinelander, though that's a start. It's time to start living your life again. You know the old expression—you can run, but you can't hide." He spoke with an unusual intensity, for he was concerned about Patrick, a concern shared by many of Patrick's friends; it seemed to them that with each passing month his distance, his inaccessibility, was the more complete. "Don't *talk* about going back to work. *Do* it."

Patrick looked at David, a small frown crossing his brow. "I haven't been running away," he said quietly. "Well, maybe I have. In part. There's quite a lot to run from." He looked away and was silent for a moment, his eyes thoughtful. After a while he looked back at David and smiled. "I'll be starting at the hospital on Monday, the proverbial bright and early. There, does that make you happy?"

David nodded but said nothing. He wasn't deceived by the laughter and the smiles, for they'd held no mirth, no real cheer. He knew Patrick well and he could see beyond the easy manner, beyond to the hurt and the pain, to the thousand punishing memories he carried with him.

"Do I have your word?" he asked.

"You do. You know, David, I'm not sure I like being treated like a wayward child. Bad Patrick, papa spank."

"You bring it on yourself."

Patrick finished his drink and put the glass down, looking at David. "The delays were unavoidable, and I think you know that. Tony decided he wanted to work in Dad's office again this summer. All right, but that meant that if I wanted to spend time with him—and I did—I had to be in Washington. Then there was his interview at Yale. Then I had to drive him back up to St. Botolphs. In between there was my practice to settle and patients to notify and a million financial details to be arranged. And there was this place," Patrick said with a sweep of his arm. "The household staff had to be reorganized. Catherine loaded this place with servants. Everytime I turned around I bumped into somebody in uniform."

"Did you cut back?"

"To Delia and Hollis and some daily cleaning women. But I had to help the others find new jobs. And there was the matter of Catherine's things. They had to be sorted and packed and . . . removed. Her jewelry had to be catalogued and packed off to the vault. Wills and insurance matters had to be adjusted, with lawyers and insurance people chattering at me all the time," he said, annoyed. "Catherine's will. It was a nightmare."

"I heard something about that," David said.

"Did you? It was incredible, bequests totaling millions. To her retinue, her hangers-on, her—protegés. Well, I paid all her bills and she got ten thousand a month on top of it. So at first we thought maybe she *had* millions put away. She had *nothing* put away. She'd bequeathed *my* money and some of the

Dain jewels . . . things which have been in the family for a hundred years."

"She was never so charitable in life," David said tersely.

"It was a lark, I'm sure. She was having fun."

"At someone else's expense. As usual."

"That's not the point. The point was we had to figure out what to do about it."

"You couldn't have been held to it. Why do anything at all?"

"I started thinking about it," Patrick sighed. "Those people were parasites but they were *her* parasites. They were loyal, they gave her undivided attention. I thought she would probably want them to have something. We settled with each one of them. We traded down, and held on to the Dain jewels, but we did settle."

"Well, you're a fool."

"I . . . I probably owed her that much," Patrick said softly.

"You owed her nothing!"

"You know what really bothered me about her will? There was not a mention of Tony in it. Not one. Huge bequests and nothing, *nothing,* to her son."

"That surprised you?"

Patrick looked up sharply. "I tell you all of this only to explain that I've been legitimately busy. It's been work and effort. I haven't been partying every night."

"Some partying would do you some good."

Patrick shook his head. "I've told you, I've told everybody, I plan to do my work and then I want to be left alone. I don't want to be entertained, to be dragged here and there. I don't want a bunch of women being thrown at my head. I'm not in the market, David. I don't want any involvements or responsibilities beyond those I already have. And they are considerable," he added, his mouth tightening slightly.

"Like Tony?"

Patrick rubbed his eyes wearily and then stood up. He walked to the broad double windows and stared outside, seeing nothing. "Sixteen is a difficult age," he said finally, though what he thought was, Tony blames me for Catherine's death.

Patrick remembered back to the afternoon of the funeral; he remembered standing in the drawing room with his parents when Tony, red-eyed, tearful, burst in upon them and the terrible, accusing words had come. "You're glad Mother's dead!" Tony had shouted. And then, "It's your fault, it's your fault Mother's dead!"

Patrick remembered the hours it had taken to calm the boy, the sedative that hadn't worked, the anguished sleeplessness of that long, long night. He remembered Tony's genuine apology the next morning; he remembered how it had been with Tony since that day—his son, once so naturally boisterous and loving, was now sometimes cool and often too quiet.

He clasped his hands together, rubbing the whitened band of skin where his wedding ring had been. He looked down at the pale circle and he knew the specter of Catherine hung over this house, over him, haunting him, as once she'd promised to do.

"Patrick . . . Patrick?" David's voice came to him from far away. He'd forgotten the presence of his friend, forgotten everything but the memory of that time, and he felt suddenly relieved that David was there, that he was not alone. He turned, sitting on the window seat.

"Sorry, I was daydreaming."

"That's all you've done for the past few years," David said quietly. "You moon around here, staring at things without seeing them. It's over, Patrick, let it go."

"A little psychiatry on the side?"

"Why not? Look what you're doing to yourself."

Patrick crossed his long legs in front of him. He smiled.

"Stop huffing and puffing at me. I'm not doing anything to myself. There are problems, I admit that, but they'll work themselves out in time."

"Problems never work *themselves* out. You of all people should know that by now."

"Low blow, friend. You'd prefer bold, vigorous action I suppose. Behold the man of action," he said, pointing at David. "It took you, man of action that you are, six months to decide what kind of *car* to buy last year."

"I'm—deliberate—about some things," David laughed.

"So am I. Now stop being so disagreeable. You're in one of your 'I'm right' moods tonight. If I said white, you'd say black. If I said rain, you'd say sunshine."

Patrick rose and went to his desk. He sat down, staring at the stack of hospital folders.

"Nervous about joining the staff?" David asked.

"Of course. I feel as if I'm starting out all over again."

"You're starting *fresh*. And it's in the nick of time."

"I'm not so sure."

"Patrick, the hospital's in bad shape. You're in bad shape. You can help Rhinelander and Rhinelander can help you."

"Help me? How?"

"Use the hospital as a nucleus. To meet new people, to build a new life for yourself. My reasons for wanting you at the hospital are not entirely selfish. This is an opportunity for you to bury the past. Take it. *Use* it."

Patrick stared at David for a moment. "I'm beginning to think you cooked up this job as therapy for me."

"You know better than that. The student-intern program is the foundation of Rhinelander. If it goes down the hospital goes down."

"And I'm supposed to keep the ship afloat," Patrick smiled.

"More than afloat. Sailing merrily along. And you'll do it. You're the right man for the job."

"I wish I were as certain as you are."

David took a small leather notebook from his pocket. He tore off a sheet of paper and handed it to Patrick.

"This is a list of our problem students. You'll want to read their files very carefully."

Patrick glanced at the list. "One name is underlined in red."

"That's O'Hara. If you can bring him into line, you can bring any of them into line."

Patrick sat back, sighing softly. "Rhinelander Pavillion has so *many* problems, David. I wish you'd told me in front."

"If I had, you'd have run."

"Don't you think I had the right to make that choice?"

"No. Time is running out. On Rhinelander and on you. It's now or never. These next months will tell the story. These next months will determine if the hospital makes it or not, if you make it or not. That can't wait any longer."

"You make too much of everything," Patrick said impatiently.

"No. These next months are make or break. Maybe for all of us. Now," David said, leaning over the desk to the folders, "there are a few things I want to review with you."

2

The graceful, gray stone facade of Rhinelander Pavillion occupied a square block of the pretty, tree-lined East Eighties near Fifth Avenue. The clean, elegant lines of the hospital matched those of the neighborhood, an area of lovely old townhouses and handsome, if somber, apartment buildings. Set back from the sidewalk behind a sloping, curved driveway, its only identification was a small bronze plaque marked RHINELANDER PAVILLION; farther down the street was another entrance and another small plaque marked CLINIC. At the end of the hospital's structure was an unobtrusive underpass, used by ambulance drivers instructed to silence their sirens a full three blocks before entering or leaving, so as to disturb neither neighbors nor patients. The hospital's main entrance was tended, night and day, by neatly groomed doormen, their shiny taxi whistles resting on the cloth of their proper gray livery.

The lobby of Rhinelander Pavillion was similarly decorous. It was a large room, and well cared for. The marble floors and columns glowed with the careful attention of the staff. The couches and chairs in the waiting area were comfortably arranged, their rich brown and burgandy upholsteries clean and unmarked. Rosy beige walls, smooth as velvet, gave off a soft, pearly light, in keeping with the low-key overhead lighting system. The deep brown draperies were spotless, as were the surfaces of the dark wood tables.

High above all, staring down at the morning calm, was a portrait of August Rhinelander, founder and patron of the hospital. Bewhiskered, with rheumy eyes and a sharp, beakish nose, the old man was smiling. It was a sly, ugly smile; there was triumph in it, and behind the triumph, malice.

David Murdock walked briskly across the lobby, his heels clicking rhythmically against the marble floor. He paused, as he often did, to stare at the portrait, scowling as he did so. David was not a man given to hate, but he hated that portrait—hated in fact, August Rhinelander, though the founder had been dead more than sixty years. David scowled again, again reminded that all these years later the intricacies of the old man's will still dictated a few of the hospital's policies. All the familiar irritations bubbled up in him and then, with a slight smile, he turned away, feeling newly invigorated.

He walked toward the recess which housed the information desk, nodding at the gray-uniformed volunteers as he passed. They smiled; they'd observed David's odd little ritual often and they sensed, as did David, that he used that brief angry communion as an impetus, the sharp sword of resolution, to take into each day's battles.

To the left of the information desk David turned into a long corridor of self-service elevators and entered a waiting car, pressing the button for the second floor, the administrative floor. He checked his watch and took a black leather notebook from his pocket. Impatiently, he flipped some pages and then read carefully, his eyes on his notes as he left the elevator.

He turned right, past a long row of doors, walking to his office. Halfway down the corridor he stopped, opening the door to his outer office. It was a wide, deep room, with offices to the right and left. He crossed it quickly, still reading, waving absently at his secretary.

"Good morning, Grace. Come in, will you," he said, as he walked by.

David's office was even wider and deeper than the room before and beautifully decorated. There was a lot of mahogany panelling and one entire wall of books. His desk was oakwood, massive and very neat; his papers were evenly arranged in tidy stacks, small crystal weights atop each in perfect alignment. There were two long, dark tweed couches in the room and on the tan walls a collection of framed English sporting prints.

Grace Evins, notepad in hand, walked across the thick, dark carpeting and sat in one of the two chairs by his desk. She was a pretty woman in her early thirties, very blond, with an easy, sunny smile. She looked at David for a moment and a twinkle came into her brown eyes. She had worked for David for five years and was fond of him. More than that, she enjoyed working for him, for he was cheerful and his precision, rather than annoying her, amused her.

It was not yet seven-thirty in the morning, she thought to herself, and there was David, immaculately dressed and combed, looking not unlike some mens' fashion advertisement. She smiled, recalling her own morning—she and her husband stumbling sleepily around for a half hour before they could even face a mirror, still stumbling as they left their apartment, showered, dressed, but hardly awake and certainly not very well combed.

"Thank you for coming in early," David said, standing behind his desk.

"Sure. Do you want your messages?"

"Messages this early?"

"They're standing in line for meetings with Patrick. This is the day, isn't it?"

"Pray," David smiled. "I went to the phone a dozen times this morning, but I didn't call him. I don't want him to think I doubt his word. Though I do." David tore a sheet from his notebook and handed it to Grace. "These are the meetings I want Patrick to have today. The moment he comes in, if he comes in, set them up."

"Right," she said, looking over the list. "David, you have to put Stuart Claven on this list. He called four times between seven and seven-twenty, very anxious."

"Damn! I'd hoped to put him off. Get him in first. He won't take long. A little bowing and scraping, a little hand wringing. He'll be a happy man."

Grace made a notation on the list. "Okay, what else?"

David held up his hand. "One minute," he said. He turned to the telephone and dialed a number. "Dr. Murdock here, how is Mr. Riley this morning? When I left last night he . . . I see. Has Dr. Shay been informed? . . . I see . . . No, that's fine, thank you." He looked at Grace and shook his head. "Three o'clock this morning," he said, rapidly dialing another number. "Never regained consciousness. Tough one to lose," he shook his head. "Hello, Dr. Murdock here. How is Miss Parrish this morning? When I left last night she . . . good . . . very good . . . check that with Dr. Venable when he comes by . . . yes, that's correct." David hung up the phone and walked around the side of his desk. "I'm going to see Dr. Shay and then I'll be in Julie Carlson's office. Call me if Patrick comes in."

"Will do."

"There's a list of things on my desk, when you get a

chance. Also, I'll need a Xerox of the new Larrimer budget figures." David paused, smiling. "Patrick hasn't seen them yet, lucky fellow. And two extra sets of schedules—clinic, intern, student, the lot."

Grace nodded. "That it?"

"You work too hard, Grace," he said, walking to the door.

Grace took the lists from the desk and put them together with her notes. She returned to her desk and spread all the papers out before her, quickly assembling them in order of importance. That done, she turned to the telephone and dialed a number, drumming her fingers while she waited.

"Julie, it's Grace. David's on his way, should be there in ten minutes or so. It's tight schedule time today, so *please* have the material ready for him. Okay?"

Julie Carlson didn't like getting instructions, no matter how polite, from secretaries. Had it been any other day she would have made a fuss, but as it was Monday, the fifteenth of September, the day Patrick Dain was joining the staff, she'd let the impertinence go. She'd been sweet with Grace, Julie said to herself, sweeter than she'd deserved, she thought, and then put the thought out of her mind.

Indeed, Julie's mind was spinning with so many thoughts there was little room for minor inconveniences. This was a special day; it seemed to Julie that this was the day she'd been waiting for, preparing for, most of her life. Patrick Dain! She was almost giddy with anticipation. She smiled, remembering the one brief time she'd met him, remembering the many secret hours she'd spent learning all she could about him.

Patrick Dain was everything Julie had ever wanted: rich, handsome, from an old, distinguished family—

the kind of man she'd dreamed of as a girl of fifteen. Now, twelve years later, he was the man she was determined to have. She was radiant with confidence for she'd thought it out very carefully. Unlike David Murdock, whom she'd once considered, Patrick Dain would be vulnerable; his wife's death, the circumstances of it, had seen to that. The past, the scars it left, would be very useful to her now. Of that she was certain.

Julie took a mirror from her desk drawer. She stared at her image, examining it critically, impersonally. After some moments she relaxed, pleased with what she saw, having every reason to be pleased for she was a very beautiful woman. She had lustrous coal-black hair falling softly to her shoulders from a side part. Her skin was creamy and very fair, with a slight rose blush at the cheeks. She had a delicate mouth, a deeper shade of rose, and large hazel eyes flecked with an exquisite green.

Julie gave a last satisfied pat to her hair and put the mirror away. She sat forward in her chair, carefully smoothing the soft pleats of her skirt as she considered what she had to do that day. One slim, manicured finger reached out and poked at the waiting correspondence. Julie had little enthusiasm for it; she decided to postpone it to later in the day . . . later, when she had less on her mind.

Julie Carlson had come to Rhinelander Pavillion five years before as an assistant in the Patient Relations department. Within a year, moving subtly but with sure purpose, she'd replaced the head of the department. Within weeks of her appointment she'd reorganized the department, altering its character to suit her own personal priorities. Old staff members had been dismissed, a new, smaller staff hired. She'd selected three young assistants and a middle-aged woman to serve as secretary. The women were neither very pretty nor very bright and they had in common the absolute lack of ambition that Julie found reassuring. They worked in modest, plain cubbyholes in the outer office; Julie paid little attention to them.

The work, Julie knew, was not hard, nor was there very much of it, though she was paid extravagantly. Her salary was as extravagant as her office and all of these generosities came from the hospital board. She'd thoroughly charmed the board members and in so doing had secured her position, free to pursue her ambitions.

Julie's ambitions had been clear in her mind from the beginning. She'd planned to ingratiate herself with the wealthy patients of Larrimer Wing, and there she had succeeded. She'd been attendant to their whims and solicitous of their problems; she'd been available always. Presenting herself as a friend, showing an occasional, calculated deference, she'd won the favor of many. Her reward had been invitations.

Invitations to parties, to lunches and dinners, to weekends in Southhampton and Maine, had come her way. She'd been a frequent guest at the homes of the rich, her lovely hazel eyes alert to the rich men she met. Many of them had courted her enthusiastically, yet in one way or another each had fallen short of her expectation. Until, one day, not at a party or a dinner, but in the corridors of Rhinelander Pavillion, she'd met Patrick Dain.

Julie sat back in her chair. A slow, nearly smug smile spread across her beautiful mouth. She'd been right to come to Rhinelander, she thought; it had taken five years, but she'd been right.

"Julie?"

David Murdock stood in the doorway, staring thoughtfully at her. Julie confused him; she always had. She was so beautiful, so correct, and there was a becoming modesty about her, yet he'd always sensed that she was not entirely what she seemed. Without knowing why, he sensed another side to her, one that was perhaps not so pleasant. He knew she reminded him of someone, but in five years he hadn't been able to decide who that was.

"David, please come in," Julie said. She felt flustered for a moment, as if he'd been reading her thoughts, but she quickly composed herself, smiling. "I'm afraid I was daydreaming. Trying to forget all I have to do today."

"Heavy schedule?"

"We have nine new admissions to Larrimer this week."

David sat down. "Anything I should know about?"

She shook her head, her soft black hair moving prettily about her shoulders. "I've taken care of all the special requests. The medical side is all yours. Here are the lists, the files will be sent on later today."

David glanced over the notated list and then folded it, slipping it into his notebook. "Some new names."

"Three. Isn't that wonderful?"

"That's a matter of opinion."

"Spoilsport," Julie smiled. "We need new business, it keeps the momentum going."

"What we need is to close Larrimer Wing. Or scale it down. It eats money faster than we can pour it in."

"Now, now. It's a showplace."

"Did you have some reports for me?"

Julie handed a manila folder across her desk. "Complaints, I'm sorry to say. Two complaints about Buddy O'Hara over the weekend. On top of the complaints we had last week, David. Can't you keep him out of Larrimer? Most of the patients don't like him at all. He's so abrupt."

David frowned. Buddy O'Hara. Again. They would

have to do something about that young man, though just what it would be he didn't know. He only knew that O'Hara was the most promising student to come along in a very long while and he didn't want to lose him.

"I could, but I won't," David said firmly. "He's the best, his attitude aside. I can't blame him. He's here to learn, to practice his knowledge, to perfect it. So what do we do? We bar students from Larrimer Wing at the discretion of the patients. And the few patients who allow them in don't help much. Larrimer Wing is turning into a damned rest home for the rich and O'Hara knows that. Most of the patients up there are no sicker than I am. He resents a hospital being used that way and I can't blame him. Not when there's such disparity between Larrimer and the other hospital services."

"That's politics, David," Julie said. "You know I never get involved in politics."

"It's not politics; it questions what we are as a hospital. And I wish you would get involved. The board's crazy about you. If anyone could influence them, you could. My influence doesn't seem to go very far."

Julie smiled brightly. "You underestimate yourself."

"Julie, Larrimer has the newest equipment. It's almost never needed. The wards have equipment so old it creaks. They have a respirator—"

"I wouldn't know a respirator from a bandaid," Julie tossed her head, laughing. "I just do my little job and leave the medical things to you and the other doctors. David, you're tired. After all, you're doing two jobs. It'll be easier for all of us when we get a new student-intern director."

"Ah, now that you mention it," David said, looking at his watch, "I'm hoping to hear the pitter-patter of Dr. Dain's feet any minute."

"Oh, is it today?"

"With any luck at all. You know, you should discuss your Buddy O'Hara problems with Dr. Dain. He'll be in charge. O'Hara will be his responsibility."

"I'd rather you handle it, David. Dr. Dain is going to be very busy. I'd hate to intrude."

"He has to know these things. The sooner the better." David opened his notebook, writing hastily.

"I hate to make a pest of myself," Julie protested.

"You'll be helping. This way he'll have an idea about O'Hara before he meets him."

"*If* it'll help, I'll take it up with Dr. Dain."

"Good. The schedule for today is tight, perhaps I can set something up at the end of the day. We can all have a drink and you can tell your sad tale. Have you met Dr. Dain?"

"I'm not sure. I may have. There are so many doctors around here, it's not easy to keep track."

"I hope you'll make him feel at home here, Julie. It's a whole new world for him. It won't be easy."

"I'll do anything I can. Call on me anytime."

David stood up. "Fine," he said, going to the door. "I'll have Grace call you. See you later."

"Yes, later," Julie smiled.

David walked through the outer office into the corridor, turning back to his office. He thought about Julie, about how especially lovely she'd looked. He smiled to himself. They'd dated several times a couple of years before. He'd been interested in her and she'd seemed interested in him, yet they'd soon stopped seeing each other. He couldn't recall who'd stopped it or why; it had been smooth, he remembered, but then everything about Julie Carlson was smooth.

David stopped outside his office as another thought took shape in his mind; smoothly, effortlessly, Julie had avoided any comment when he'd asked her help with the board. It hadn't been the first time. It was a request he'd made, in one form or another, at least a dozen times before. Each time, he realized now with some surprise, Julie had adroitly led into another subject. His eyes darkened a little. He found himself thinking again that there was a side of Julie he didn't know. He found himself wondering if under all that feline cream and silk there wasn't a sly bundle of street cat.

"Patrick come in?" he asked, walking into the office.

"Not yet. And the phone calls are driving me crazy. You look pretty gloomy," Grace said, watching him. "Don't give up so soon."

"What? No, I was thinking about Julie."

"What about her?"

"She confuses me sometimes."

"Only sometimes?"

"You've never liked her. Why?"

"She's a sneak."

"She speaks very highly of you," David laughed.

"I bet."

David looked at his watch. "It's past eight. Patrick should have been here by now. What do you think?"

"I think you worry too much."

"Worrying is my hobby. Almost a second career," David said, going into his office.

3

Patrick Dain paused, took a deep breath, and walked into the lobby of Rhinelander Pavillion. He was tired and edgy after a fitful night which had brought little sleep. Preparing himself to return to work had been hard, for he wasn't at all sure he was ready. People, demands, responsibilities—all these he had avoided as much as possible in the past year; now, he knew, people and demands and responsibilities would be part of his daily routine.

He was uneasy at the thought. He'd had to force himself out of bed, force himself through the motions of the morning, force himself to come to Rhinelander. Now, crossing the lobby, he felt as if his legs were made of lead. He clutched at his briefcase as if for strength, for reassurance, gripping it so hard his knuckles were white. He hesitated a few steps away from the information desk, wondering if he should leave, if he should forget the whole thing. Instead, his jaw set in determination, he propelled himself forward.

One of the information clerks looked at him. "May I help you, sir? . . . Oh, it's Dr. Dain, isn't it?"

"It is. Nice of you to remember."

"I heard you were coming to work for us. Johnny," she called to her deskmate, "this here is Dr. Dain. He's coming to work for us."

"Hello, Doctor."

Patrick nodded, smiling slightly. "Has Dr. Murdock come in yet?"

"He was our early bird today," she chuckled. "Not even a quarter after seven and he was on his way upstairs."

"I might have known," Patrick shook his head. "I'd better be on my way then. Thank you."

"Welcome to Rhinelander Pavillion, Doctor."

"Thank you," he called over his shoulder, "nice to be here."

Patrick walked to the elevators and stood there for a moment, staring at the large clock on the wall. He sighed and entered the elevator, absently pressing the button for the second floor. The door opened on two but Patrick stayed where he was, riding instead to the fourth floor.

The fourth floor was the first semi-private patient floor in the hospital and Patrick knew it well. Through the years, though most of his patients had been admitted to Larrimer Wing, many had also been admitted to the semi-private floors and he'd spent much of his time there. He'd enjoyed it. There was a certain brisk energy on these floors that was missing from Larrimer Wing. There was constant activity, doctors and nurses, visitors and patients going back and forth. There was noise, the comfortable hum of conversations and occasional laughter, of radios and television sets. It was in sharp contrast to Larrimer Wing, Patrick thought, looking around, for Larrimer was as quiet as a church, the comings and goings of staff and visitors muffled behind the closed doors of patients who seldom left their suites.

Patrick walked leisurely down the long, tan corridors, stopping here and there to watch the interns and residents assembling for morning rounds. He felt suddenly nostalgic, thinking back to his own days as an intern. Happy times, he thought, those were the happy times; long before it all went wrong, long before he knew it would.

"Well, Dr. Dain!" A nurse stopped in front of him, smiling broadly. "It's been so long. Too long! Where've you been keeping yourself? We heard you were joining the staff. Welcome."

"Thank you very much," Patrick smiled back, amused. "Where do you find such enthusiasm so early in the morning?"

"I meditate."

"Good for you."

"I meant it, welcome to our hospital. I'll tell all the girls you're part of the family now. You need any help with anything, you just come on down to 4," she said, walking off, little white cap bobbing as she went.

Patrick looked after her for a moment and then continued on down the corridor to the Doctor's Room. He walked inside, tossing his briefcase on a chair. Patrick relaxed slightly, for the lounge, like every other staff lounge in the hospital was pleasant and serene. It was very quiet, a long narrow room with pale green walls and dark green carpeting. There was an ample number of comfortable chairs, several tables, and a wide selection of medical journals.

"You a doctor? This room is for doctors."

The voice came from the other end of the lounge and it startled Patrick. He swung around to see a young man — blond, broad-shouldered, square-jawed — seated at a table, a book open in front of him. He wore a white hospital jacket over his shirt; judging by his youth, Patrick thought, he was probably a student.

"Yes," Patrick said, going to the coffee machine. "I'm a doctor."

"Okay," the young man said, returning his attention to his book.

Patrick poured a cup of coffee and carried it to a chair not far from where the young man sat. "Are you a student?"

"Yeah, I am. Second year."

"Don't you have morning rounds? I saw them getting ready out there."

"They'll be getting ready for another ten minutes," he snapped. "Why should I waste my time?"

Patrick looked closely at the young man. He interested him. The impatience, the gruffness in his voice had been unmistakable, but Patrick thought he'd heard more than that; he thought he'd heard anger. Patrick didn't doubt that this young man had a formidable temper. Indeed, everything about him seemed made for temper.

He was big and raw-boned, with large strong hands. His eyes were blue but they were a *hard* blue, piercing. They held an odd expression that was at once defiant and defensive. The young man seemed troubled and it was with a start that Patrick realized that now this young man, and all the others like him, were his responsibility.

Patrick glanced at his watch. It was almost eight-thirty and David would be frantic, he thought, though he made no move to leave. "What's your name?" he asked.

"What's it to you?"

"Are you always so rude?"

The young man looked up very slowly, assessing Patrick before he answered. "I don't have time for *manners*. I leave *manners* to all the big shots in the five-hundred-dollar suits," he said, staring pointedly at Patrick's dark, custom-made jacket.

Patrick suppressed a smile. The young man's intensity, his sturdy self-righteousness made him seem very young, very vulnerable. "I hate to think what your bedside manner is like."

"When I need one, I have one."

"You probably do. The expedience of youth."

"Anything wrong with it?"

"I'm not sure." Patrick leaned forward in his chair. "What's your name?"

"O'Hara. Buddy O'Hara."

Of course, Patrick thought to himself, he should have known. Buddy O'Hara, a difficult young man, but the best student they'd had in many years. "Why are you so rude, Buddy O'Hara?"

"I'm whatever I have to be," he slammed the book shut. "Look, I've had three hours sleep in the last thirty, I have rounds coming up and a lab exam in two hours. If that's not enough we have to hang around to meet the new student-intern director. I could be sleeping, but instead I have to hang around here to meet some rich bastard who has as much interest in medicine as—"

"Before you finish that," Patrick smiled, "you ought to know I'm that rich bastard. I'm Dr. Dain. Patrick Dain."

"As my Aunt Fanny," Buddy O'Hara finished implacably.

"I haven't even begun and you've made up your mind."

"There's a grapevine around here. Everybody knows everything. I know you got more money than God. You're bored, probably, so you're going to fool around here for a while. What do you care, it's not serious to you."

"What makes you so sure?"

"Call it an educated guess."

"Call it arrogance, Mr. O'Hara," Patrick said, his dark blue eyes steady on the young man. "And while I have you here, let me tell you a couple of things," he said evenly. "One, is that I spent the weekend reading your files. After a brilliant first year, your work this term is disgraceful. So is your behavior. Complaints an inch thick. There'll be no meeting today, but there will be a meeting soon. We are going to discuss these matters. In detail.

"Two, is that I have a low tolerance for tough-guys, punks and *provocateurs*. I think if you stop pretending you're in a James Cagney movie, we'll get on very well. I'm here to help you and that I intend to do, whether you like it or not."

"I didn't have your *help* last year and I did okay."

"This is a new year. And you will learn, Mr. O'Hara that I don't—as you put it—fool around." Patrick stood up, tucking his briefcase under his arm. "Go on to rounds now. I'll let you know about the meeting."

Buddy O'Hara swept his books from the table and stood up. He went to the door and paused, looking back at Patrick. "I give you a week before you get Larrimer-Syndrome."

"What?"

"Larrimer Wing-Syndrome. All the top brass around here have it. It means everything's for Larrimer. Time, money, attention, interest. Larrimer's all anybody cares about. You're talking big now. In a week's time you won't give a damn about anything but Larrimer. Well, I want to be a doctor. I want that more than anything and you guys aren't going to stand in my way."

"I repeat, I am here to help you. If you are worth helping—and that remains to be seen."

Buddy O'Hara stared at Patrick, about to speak. He turned then and left abruptly, slamming the door behind him. Patrick smiled after him. He had, he thought, gained a head start on his maneuverings with

O'Hara, possibly an advantage. It was an advantage he was certain he would need, for he'd sensed the conflict in the young man, the obstinance.

Time and time again he'd read the word "superior" in O'Hara's evaluation reports; David Murdock's assessment had been a flat "brilliant potential, needs careful handling." Patrick knew that the careful handling was now up to him and, to his surprise, he felt a small surge of confidence. The unexpected run-in with O'Hara had given him a certain assurance; it was not great but it was more than he'd begun with and he thought it a good sign.

It was past nine when Patrick reached the second floor. He strode purposefully down the corridor, the sound of his footsteps obscured by the poundings of a dozen different typewriters in the dozen different offices around him. He stopped at David's office and peered inside, putting his finger to his lips to silence Grace. Grace laughed softly, holding her hands out to Patrick as he entered the room.

"How are you?" he smiled at her.

"Great. It's so good to see you again. How are you, are you okay?"

"Fine. I'm fine. Tell the truth, you didn't expect to see me here today, did you?"

"I'm a believer," she grinned, "but . . ." she inclined her head in the direction of David's office.

"Tearing his hair out? I suppose he's suffered enough. I'll go right in."

"Wait, I'll tell him you're here."

"Never mind," Patrick said, throwing open David's door.

David looked up, annoyed by the sudden interruption. His annoyance disappeared when he saw Patrick. He sat back and smiled.

"Is it really you?"

"O ye of little faith."

"You're late."

"But I'm here," Patrick said. He threw his briefcase on a chair and walked over to David's desk. He sat down. "I'm not really late either. I was here on time. I wandered around for a while, getting my bearings. I haven't been here in a while."

"There have been some changes, but mostly in Larrimer Wing."

"I walked around the fourth floor. The first patient I ever admitted to a hospital was admitted to the fourth floor here. It seems like a hundred years ago. Where has the time gone, David? I'm forty, you're forty, where has the time gone?"

"I try not to think about it," David smiled.

"I stopped for coffee and ran into one of the students. So young. So young and so earnest. Us, fifteen years ago."

"Which student?"

"A volatile, angry, opinionated young man. I liked him."

David nodded. "Say no more. You met our *enfant terrible*, O'Hara. He is all the things you described, and more. Still, he has his admirers among the instructors, the patients, and some of the staff. He has his detractors, too. And they are loud and determined. A distinct anti-O'Hara bloc. There have been times when I was ready to join it; he's so difficult. There's a chip on his shoulder the size of an oak tree. If that's not enough, something's been bothering him lately. I don't know what. He's been distracted, faraway. So what we have is a young man who's either in another world, or snarling at the world he's in."

"Do you get along with him?" Patrick asked.

"Nobody really gets along with him. The people who admire him admire him in spite of himself. I think they admire his honesty. There's no guile in him." David leaned forward, smiling. "That's not something I can say for all, or even most, of our young Galens. It's refreshing. On the other hand, he's so honest he's often rude. Inexcusably rude. That upsets a lot of people. I haven't been able to give him the time he needs. It's up to you now."

"I read all the reports on him. He shows great promise."

"O'Hara has unlimited potential," David nodded. "Or he started out that way. I never saw the kind of first year he had. He led everybody in everything. He could do no wrong. But this term is a different story. His work is way, way down. Soon, the question will be, is keeping him in the program worth all the trouble? I want him in the program but not at any cost."

Patrick looked at David. "That's short-sighted. If O'Hara really has potential we ought to be ready to go the extra mile with him. I've read the files of the other students and they're nothing much."

"There's a lot of mediocrity here, I know that. And I'd forgive a lot of trouble from any student who showed brilliance. I've done just that with O'Hara. But now his work is declining badly and we still have the trouble. Patrick, the whole program, the whole hospital has to be considered. It's a tricky situation."

"I want time to try and work it out."

"You'll have time. How much, I don't know. The medical school is beginning to make noises." David shook his head. "His instructors like him because they sense he's something special. The patients like him because he's authoritative. The staff likes him because he's honest. Fine, but there's nothing personal in all that. He doesn't have friends, he has fans. So when he starts to slip, as he's slipping now, he has no allies. His instructors start to reassess, the patients see his distraction, the staff figures he's on his way out. No allies."

"Are you trying to discourage me?"

David smiled. "Get his work up and his temper down. That's all you have to do."

"Thanks."

"Julie Carlson, the woman who handles patient relations, was complaining about O'Hara just this morning. She's had her problems with him in Larrimer Wing. I told her I'd set up a meeting with you this afternoon. She can give you an idea of what you're dealing with."

"Thank you," Patrick said, "but no thank you. I want to hear about Buddy O'Hara from Buddy O'Hara. I thought about it on my way down here, David. I want to handle him in my own way. Everything direct and cards-on-the-table." Patrick smiled briefly. "I heard him on the subject of Larrimer Wing. I can imagine that he and the Larrimer patients aren't chums, but first things first."

"I'll cancel the meeting with Julie," David agreed. He was surprised to hear Patrick speak with such surety. He wondered if Buddy O'Hara, immovable object that he was, would turn out to be the motivation Patrick needed. "I promised you a free hand," he said. "I intend to keep my word. We may come to disagree about O'Hara, but I won't get in your way. Grace is setting up other meetings for today—things to get out of the way—and after that your schedule is your own to make."

"My schedule. I haven't had anything as formal as a schedule in a long time."

"You'll get used to it."

"I wonder."

"Don't wonder. Give yourself a chance." David stood. "I'll show you your office."

Patrick followed David to the door which connected

their offices. David opened the door and stepped back as Patrick entered the room which had been waiting for him for weeks. Patrick silently surveyed it and then looked at David.

"It's an awful lot of office."

"It's the same size as mine. You'll be spending so much time here, you'll find the space useful. I certainly do."

Patrick was not convinced. He walked slowly around the room, getting the feel of it, looking at everything very closely. It was carpeted in a deep gray and furnished with comfortable, dark tweed couches and chairs. Mahogany panelling and cabinetwork ran around one wall, opposite a wall of medical texts and reference books. The desk was polished rosewood, the walls, hung with several fine watercolors from Patrick's private collection, were a buff color. A soft morning sunlight spilled through the windows, falling on a bowl of creamy daisies.

Patrick bent to the flowers, gently touching the white petals, and David stiffened. For a moment, seeing Patrick's dark head near the pale flower, he was reminded of the day of Catherine's funeral, of Patrick, placing one ashen rose on the dark casket, of the terrible, ravaged look on his face. David felt a chill and he hastily put the memory from his mind.

"It's really a very hospitable office," he said.

Patrick straightened up, looking around. "What did I do with my briefcase?"

"It's in my office. I'll get it."

Patrick went to his desk and sat down, bouncing around in the big leather chair until he felt comfortable. David returned and Patrick took the briefcase from him. He put it on the desk top and opened it, removing a small, square object wrapped in flannel. He undid the cloth and removed a double silver picture

43

frame, placing it on the desk. He stared at the two photographs of his son: Tony, aged ten, with his pony in the stables of their Connecticut estate; Tony, aged sixteen, on the soccer fields at St. Botholphs.

"I miss him," he said quietly.

"He'll be back."

Patrick glanced up as the door opened. He stood up.

"Hello, Stuart," David said. "Dr. Patrick Dain, Stuart Claven, the hospital director."

"How do you do," Patrick said and the two men shook hands. Stuart Claven was a tall, reedy man with thin silver hair and bright, dark brown eyes. He had a nervous, fluttery manner about him; he seemed to be in motion even when he was standing still.

"Dr. Dain, I can't tell you what an honor it is to have you with us. I have heard of you, of course, and I have also had the pleasure of meeting your distinguished father." He spoke rapidly, smiling all the while, a big, toothy smile. "I have the pleasure of serving on a charity committee with your father."

"Stuart," David said, "we have a lot of meetings today, so perhaps we could keep this short."

"Of course, of course. I want only to welcome you, Dr. Dain. We need you here. A man of your reputation will be a great benefit to our hospital."

"Thank you," Patrick said, "for such a nice welcome." Patrick found himself fascinated by Stuart Claven's hands: he rubbed them together, clenching and unclenching them, wringing them in what seemed to be an enormous desire to please. Patrick forced his eyes away. "And thank you for all the kind words. I look forward to working with you."

"After you are settled I hope to have the pleasure of introducing you to our board. Distinguished men all, you may know some of them."

"Yes," Patrick nodded.

"This is a wonderful day for Rhinelander Pavillion," Stuart said to David.

"Wonderful," David echoed tiredly.

Stuart looked back at Patrick. He smiled nervously, lacing and unlacing his fingers. "I will leave you two men of medicine to your work now. Anything you need, anything at all," he said, hurrying to the door, "I am right down the hall. My door is always open."

Patrick nodded again, watching as he rushed out. When he was gone, Patrick turned to David. "Men of medicine? Is that what he said?"

"In another life he was Uriah Heep."

Patrick laughed. "Why is he so—overwrought?" he asked, sitting down.

"It's his way. Especially when he's impressed by somebody." David perched at the edge of Patrick's desk. "I gather his family was poor and he married a very wealthy woman. He's impressed by money, by people who have it. Especially by old money. Put him around old money and he practically salivates."

"Don't be cruel."

"Don't you make the mistake of feeling sorry for him. Many have, and had their legs cut out from under them. He's an incompetent, often venal, man. And he has a *lot* of power with the board. He and Max Rhinelander, particularly, are very big pals."

"Max Rhinelander? Does he still practice here? I went to the student-intern Christmas party two years ago," Patrick smiled. "There were little gifts for everyone, but the box for Max was very big. Enormous. All done up in gold paper, a huge gold bow. Max was delighted. There he was ripping off the paper, great big smile on his face. Well, inside the box were dozens of rubber ducks. The students and interns had enclosed a card—'Quacks to the Quack.'"

David chuckled. "He's still here. Still a quack. But

he's a Rhinelander so Stuart looks out for him. Max owes him a lot. Stuart finds a way to blame Max's mistakes on any unsuspecting intern or resident who happens to be in the vicinity. And Max goes on playing doctor, playing at being a board member."

"What about the other members?"

"They're good men, mostly. But they owe Stuart, too. He flatters them and they're grateful. Their wives, their mistresses, their children, their own servants tell them to go to hell. Not Stuart. Stuart builds up their egos. Stuart tells them they are distinguished men." David shrugged. "Stuart Claven is Big Man on Campus around here. Because he knows how to keep the apple polished. And polished. And polished."

"That's the politics you were talking about."

"Only part of it. He'll polish your apple forever, but cross him—even once—and you'll have applesauce. He's extremely sly. He's centered a lot of power in himself and he intends to keep it. He'll willingly be the butt of any joke. He'll take personal abuse. But cross him on a matter of policy and he turns into cold, blue steel."

"You're still walking and you've tangled with him."

"Not on Larrimer Wing. And that's the biggie."

Patrick sat back, a frown creasing his forehead. "Patrick Dain, welcome to Rhinelander Pavillion."

4

"Sorry to interrupt again," Grace said, walking into Patrick's office. "I know you had a rough morning."

"The first day is always the hardest. I keep repeating that, it gives me strength," Patrick smiled. "What now?"

"Dr. DeWitt's outside. He insists on seeing you."

"Andrew DeWitt? Sure, send him in."

"You'll be sorry."

"She's right," Andrew DeWitt's hearty voice filled the room. "Because I'm here to raise hell. Leave us, please, Grace."

"My pleasure," Grace said, closing the door behind her.

"Hello, Andrew. Good to see you again."

"Hello, Patrick. This isn't a social call."

"I gathered that. You were a little short with Grace."

"I'm short with everyone. I'm at the end of my patience."

"Sit down, tell me about it."

"I haven't much time; I'm due at my office," Andrew DeWitt said, glancing at his watch. "To get straight to the point, you have to do something about one of your interns."

"Do you have a complaint?"

"*A* complaint? I have dozens of them. This intern,

Laura Ferris, seems to take particular pleasure in interfering with *my* patients."

"I see."

"No, you don't. Ferris is constantly sticking her nose where it doesn't belong. This time she's gone too far. I have a patient in Coronary Care Unit. He's had all the tests, and I was going to schedule him for bypass surgery."

"So?"

"So, Laura Ferris has somehow managed to talk him out of it. One talk with a damn fool intern and my patient informs me he wants to think it over."

Patrick made a notation on a long yellow pad. "I'll look into it."

"Is that all you have to say?"

"What do you expect me to say, Andrew? I've only been in this job a few hours. I don't even know Dr. Ferris. Give me a chance to talk to her."

Patrick stared at Andrew DeWitt. He was a dark, square-jawed man in his early fifties. Patrick knew him as a calm man, a man of even, careful temper, but now his eyes were bright with anger, his face taut with strain.

"What's got into you, Andrew?" Patrick frowned. "You're rude to Grace, you're rude to me. The first time I've seen you in months and you bite my head off. I thought we were friends."

"I apologize for being abrupt. This Ferris girl is getting me crazy."

"All right, all right. I said I'd look into it and I will. I'll do it today. I'll do it now. Take it easy."

Andrew DeWitt took a handkerchief from his pocket and wiped at his brow. "I really am sorry, Patrick. I've been under a lot of pressure lately."

"You always thrived on pressure. Most surgeons do."

"It gets harder. Some days are harder than others."

"Granted."

"But that doesn't excuse my behavior. I should have congratulated you on the new job."

Patrick smiled. "With irate doctors storming into my office I'm not sure congratulations are in order."

"It won't happen again. Just take care of the Ferris girl. Please."

"Have you talked to her?"

"There's no point in that. She won't listen to reason. Perkins, her supervising resident, talked to her. It solved nothing; she continues to interfere."

"Well, I'll see what she has to say."

"What *she* has to say? What does it matter what she has to say?"

"She's a doctor, Andrew. She deserves a hearing."

"A doctor! Good God, Patrick, she's been a doctor for all of *two months!* Who cares what she has to say?"

Patrick stared again at Andrew DeWitt. "This isn't like you at all. You don't sound like yourself," Patrick shook his head. "You don't even look like yourself."

"You noticed," Andrew said, smiling for the first time.

"I notice the tension."

"Underneath the tension, look, look closely," he said, leaning across Patrick's desk. "I had an eye job. Got rid of the pouches and the wrinkles."

Patrick studied Andrew's face. "Of course . . . it looks fine. It's a good job. But . . . you always joked about cosmetic surgery."

"One jokes less at my age. Also I . . . I'm married again." Andrew crumpled his handkerchief in his hand, dabbing again at his forehead. "My wife is . . . younger than I."

"Congratulations, Andrew. I hope you'll be very happy."

"She's really a wonderful girl."

49

"I'm sure she is."

"We'll get together soon," Andrew said. "We have a lot of catching up to do." He rose, looking at his watch. "I have to get to my office. You'll take care of the Ferris girl for me? I have your word?"

Patrick stood. "I'll see her now. There's a favor you can do for me, by the way."

"What's that?"

"Stop calling her 'the Ferris girl'. She's a doctor."

A small smile played about Andrew DeWitt's mouth as he stared down at the floor. "It's not like the good old days," he said quietly. "I remember when students and interns were seen but not heard. They knew their place, they kept their place."

"I think we remember those days more fondly than we should."

Andrew looked sharply at Patrick. "You talk like a renegade. Don't knock the system. The system worked. It worked a damn sight better than it does now with a bunch of green kids contradicting everything we say."

"Andrew," Patrick laughed softly, "I'm not knocking the system. I'm merely suggesting that give and take can be useful sometimes."

"I'm late."

"I'll walk out with you," Patrick said, following Andrew to the outer office.

Grace handed a file folder to Patrick. "The evaluation report on Laura Ferris," she said.

"Are you listening at keyholes, Grace, or are you psychic?" Andrew asked with a wink.

"When you burst in here screaming about 'that damn Ferris' I know what file to pull."

"Andrew," Patrick said, looking up from the file, "Dr. Ferris is planning a residency in cardiology. Maybe that's—"

"Not if I have anything to say about it," Andrew

snapped, going quickly to the door. "And I will have a *lot* to say about it."

Patrick stared after Andrew DeWitt, then returned his attention to the file. He read through it, then gave it back to Grace.

"Has this argument between Dr. DeWitt and Dr. Ferris been going on long?" he asked. "You know all the gossip."

"It's more than gossip. DeWitt's been up here several times. He tried to get David to discipline Dr. Ferris."

"And?"

"David was very busy. He was also determined to stay out of it."

"Very well," Patrick said, striding to the door. "Call CCU. Tell them I'm on my way up. Tell them to round up Dr. Ferris and the senior resident . . . Perkins, I think his name is."

"Patrick, wait."

"Yes?"

"Dr. DeWitt admits a lot of patients to Larrimer Wing."

"What if he does?"

"That makes him . . . important, to Stuart Claven."

"Are you warning me?" Patrick laughed.

"DeWitt expects you to settle the argument in his favor. Stuart would expect the same thing."

"I know it's an old-fashioned idea, but I expect to settle the argument in favor of the patient."

Patrick hurried through the corridor to the stairway. He rushed up the stairs, feeling a sudden irritation stir in him. He was bothered by the change in Andrew DeWitt. He was bothered by the implied politics in the DeWitt-Ferris situation. He found himself wondering if all hospital decisions would stand or fall on politics, on the politics of Stuart Claven.

Patrick reached the Coronary Care Unit just as

lunch trays were being taken away. He dodged the phalanx of oncoming lunchtime carts and then walked slowly up the corridor, looking around.

CCU was divided into two sections, one for patients undergoing intensive testing, the other for those recovering from illness or surgery. The entire Unit was painted a serene beige, the walls decorated with inexpensive prints of peaceful country scenes. It was a quiet floor, the quiet underscored by the constant, low hum of medical machinery which stood at almost every bedside.

Patrick stopped at the nurses' station, a large formica and chrome island located midway between the two CCU sections. Several nurses were huddled over medication orders, another was busy with charts, and yet another was standing at one of the duplicate heart monitors, pounding at it with her fist.

"I'm Dr. Dain," Patrick said to the nurse at the monitor. "What are you doing?"

"This is the monitor that feeds out of 302. It doesn't work unless you smack it."

"That's a dangerous way to monitor a patient. Why don't you put in for a replacement?"

"Hah! You want replacements, you want new equipment, go to Larrimer Wing. Here we have to do our best with what we have."

"But surely—"

"Doctor, we had falling plaster in 313 and 314 for six months. We complained, we wrote memos, we begged for a plasterer. Finally, after a hunk of ceiling fell into a patient's oatmeal, we got our plasterer. Nothing comes easy, unless it's for Larrimer." She gave the monitor a last slap, then smiled, satisfied. "Dr. Ferris is waiting in the doctor's lounge."

"I take it you are the no-nonsense head nurse on this floor," Patrick smiled.

"You got it," she smiled back. "And Rhinelander Pavillion needs me more than I need Rhinelander Pavillion."

"In other words, don't tell you your job."

"In those words. Friends?"

"Friends. I like your style." Patrick laughed, walking off.

He was amused, yet he was embarrassed, for he realized how much he had to learn. The words "Larrimer Wing" rang in his head. It seemed to him that sooner or later, everything always came back to Larrimer.

Patrick reached the doctor's lounge. He paused, then quietly opened the door and stepped inside. The room was littered with the debris of the morning. Dirty coffee cups and half-eaten danish and doughnuts were strewn across the table. Newspapers were scattered about. The wastebasket was crammed with paper towels and napkins, with plastic spoons and soggy teabags.

Patrick turned and then stopped. He saw Laura Ferris sitting at a small table, her eyes fast on the book open before her. He was struck at once by her beauty, struck, too, by her obvious attempt to mask that beauty.

Laura Ferris had thick chestnut hair, brushed away from her face into a severe knot at the back of her head. She had a long, graceful neck, all but hidden beneath the high collar of a drab tan shirt. Her eyes were dark brown and huge, her complexion, her features, perfect. She wore no makeup, for even the slightest touch of makeup would have made her beauty spectacular. She had a full, round figure, almost obscured by a white hospital coat a size too big.

Patrick realized instantly how hard it must have been for this lovely young woman in medical school.

Certainly, he thought, she must have been the punch line to every silly, lewd joke made by the male student majority.

"Dr. Ferris?"

Laura Ferris stood up. "How do you do, Dr. Dain."

"Please sit down," Patrick said, sitting opposite her. "Dr. Perkins will be here as soon as he can. He's with a patient."

"That's fine. I wanted to talk with you alone."

"You came to chew me out. I'm ready," she had a clear, firm voice, with more than a trace of Boston in it.

"No, I came to hear you out."

"Oh?" Laura's eyes opened wider. "That's hard to believe. Dr. DeWitt wants to ride me out of town on a rail."

"He tells me you've been interfering with his patients. If true, that's a serious matter."

"It's not true. Not the way he means it. He has a patient here, Mr. Dagget. He was all set to schedule Mr. Dagget for a bypass."

"And you disagree with that?"

"I told Mr. Dagget he has the right to a second opinion. I told him that in cases like this a second opinion is a good idea."

"That's all?"

"Mr. Dagget didn't ask my advice. I volunteered it. I strongly volunteered it."

"Dr. Ferris, patients are aware of their right to a second opinion. Why—"

"Excuse me, but you'd be surprised at how many patients aren't informed of their rights. And if they are, many of them are reluctant to do it, they're afraid of offending their doctors. When you put your life in a doctor's hands, you don't want to offend that doctor."

"This second opinion. Are you talking about a

routine matter of procedure, or are you questioning the validity of Mr. Dagget's bypass?"

Laura stood up. She walked back and forth across the room, her hands jammed into the pockets of her coat. "Can I talk to you, Dr. Dain? Can I *really* talk to you?"

"Of course you can, that's why I'm here."

"Okay, I'm questioning the bypass. I didn't tell that to Mr. Dagget," she said quickly, "but Dr. DeWitt knew what I meant. I've seen Dagget's tests. There's every possibility that less drastic treatment is indicated. Plus, Dagget's a bad surgical risk. He's twenty-five pounds overweight. His blood pressure's in the danger area. He's a very nervous man."

Patrick was silent for a moment. "Dr. DeWitt has been a cardiovascular surgeon for a good many years. A brilliant surgeon."

"I know that. Dr. DeWitt was a guest lecturer when I was pre-med at college. He's part of the reason I decided to go into cardiology. I have great respect for him."

"You don't sound like you have great respect for him."

"There's nobody better in an operating room than Dr. DeWitt. He's a master. Outside of the operating room . . . what I question is his judgement, not his skill."

Patrick frowned. "His diagnostic judgement?" he asked slowly.

"Yes," Laura said intently.

"Let's understand each other, Dr. Ferris. Are you talking about unnecessary surgery? Are you saying Dr. DeWitt operates when he doesn't have to?"

"I'm not saying he takes a perfectly healthy person and cuts into him, no. I'm saying . . . well, there are marginal cases. Patients who don't need surgery but who get surgery nevertheless."

"Dr. Ferris, I've known Andrew DeWitt a long time. He is an honorable man, an honest man, of that there is no question."

"I've known honorable, honest people who've been ground up by the success trap. Start chasing money and the next—"

"Dr. Ferris!" Patrick said warningly. "It is one thing to question Dr. DeWitt's judgement, quite another to suggest he operates willy-nilly to fatten his bank account."

Laura was silent as Patrick went to the coffee machine. He took his time at the machine, his mind on what Dr. Ferris had said. It wasn't possible, he thought. There were certain doctors he knew who might be suspect in that area, but Andrew DeWitt had never been one of them. He walked back across the room, setting two cups of coffee on the table.

"Why do you suggest such a thing?" he demanded.

"There's no one answer to that question."

"You'd better find an answer."

"Dr. DeWitt's stepped up his operating schedule in the last few years. There's been talk that some of his operations could have been avoided."

"Talk!" Patrick scoffed.

"He lost three members of his surgical team. Part of the argument was overheard. It was after a woman died on the table. The argument was that she shouldn't have been there in the first place."

"Andrew DeWitt has earned a lot of money for a lot of years."

"There's a grapevine, Dr. Dain. We all hear things."

"Go on."

"Dr. DeWitt has a large suite of offices on Park Avenue. He has four children in graduate schools. He's on his third wife. He's the brand new owner of a Sutton

Place townhouse. Do you know how much all of that costs? When you're locked into a standard of living, I mean *locked in,* you're stuck. I'm not saying it's a conscious thing on his part . . . but unconsciously one's judgement can be affected."

"If you have these suspicions, why haven't you gone to the Surgical Review Committee?"

"Dr. Dain," Laura laughed mirthlessly, "who's going to listen to me? One intern, a woman at that, questioning the judgement of an established, respected surgeon."

"What about the three members of his surgical team? The ones who left him? Why didn't they go to the Committee?"

"Probably because they wanted to work at other hospitals."

"I see. Everyone's afraid. Why aren't you afraid?"

Laura stared down into her coffee cup. "I don't know," she said quietly. "I am afraid . . . the question is why didn't I keep my mouth shut? Why don't I keep my mouth shut now? I've asked myself that. I'm asking myself that now."

"What's the answer?"

"I guess because I haven't walked through hell to wind up a robot . . . a doctor who does what she does because that's the way it is." Laura sipped her coffee. She put the cup down and stared up at Patrick. "When I talk about hell, I mean it. I haven't had one bit of help from anyone. It'll be ten years or more before I pay off my debts from college and med school. My mother keeps telling me I'm crazy to be a doctor. My father keeps telling me he liked the world better when women knew their place. My fiancé broke our engagement because he didn't want to be married to someone who would earn more money than he did. I've been the object of pranks and dirty jokes and condescension from my male peers. I have no social life. I can't remember the last time I had a real, sit-down meal, or a real night's sleep."

Laura went to the coffee machine and refilled her cup. She walked slowly back to Patrick. She looked hard at him, the urgency clear in her eyes.

"Maybe that's every doctor's story, I don't know. I do know that only one thing kept me going . . . when it was all over I was going to be a doctor, a good doctor, the best damn doctor I knew how to be. And I was going to do that because helping people, sick people, people who need you, rely on you, was the greatest thing anyone could be. There would a joy in that . . . and no matter what happened, no one could touch that joy. It would be there, inside me."

Patrick sat back. He'd been touched by her words, by her absolute sincerity. The feelings she'd expressed were the feelings felt by almost every young doctor; some of them lost them along the way, but Patrick didn't think Laura Ferris would be one of them.

"When I see a great doctor like Andrew DeWitt . . . doing what he's doing . . . I can't stand it."

Patrick tried to find the right words. He knew he couldn't encourage her thinking on Andrew DeWitt until he'd looked into the records himself. He knew, too, that he couldn't discourage such spirit as he'd seen . . . felt . . . in her.

"For the time being, I'll say this much," he began carefully. "You have every right to explain a patient's options to him. Suggesting a second opinion is good for everybody. That is, or will be, hospital policy. In the particular case of Mr. Dagget," Patrick said, making a note in his book, "I'm going up to the film lab to look at the angiogram. Until I do, and until I form an opinion, I want you to steer clear of Dr. DeWitt on the subject. Understood?"

"Yes, sir."

"As for Dr. DeWitt . . . in general. I will check into the recent records. Until I do, and until I form an opinion, you are to steer clear of . . . damaging statements of any kind. Understood?"

"Thank you, Dr. Dain. I . . . I really didn't expect to find a sympathetic ear."

"You haven't, not entirely, not yet. Dr. DeWitt is a surgeon of long experience; you're an intern. What you think you see you may not see at all. You have my promise to look into it, and I have your promise to be . . . discreet and fair."

Laura Ferris nodded agreement. She smiled then, a vast bright smile that was part relief, part gratitude.

"Dr. Dain? You wanted to see me, sir?"

Patrick turned to see a young man standing at the door.

"Dr. Perkins? I'll be right with you." Patrick stood up, walking with Laura to the door. "By the way, do you know the more you try to disguise your good looks, the more obvious they are?"

Laura looked quickly at Patrick. "Would you say something like that to a male doctor?" she asked, not exactly angry, but surprised.

"I wouldn't have to," Patrick laughed. "Good-looking male doctors milk their looks for all they're worth. All I'm saying is, don't let a few idiots intimidate you. Be yourself, you'll feel better."

"Thank you," she said, laughing, too. "It's been an interesting meeting. I think."

"We'll talk again, Meanwhile . . ."

"I keep my promises," she said.

"Laura, they can use you in 319," Dr. Perkins said.

"On my way."

"Hurry it up." Dr. Perkins turned to Patrick. "Did you want to speak to me, Doctor?"

"Walk with me to the stairs," Patrick said, organizing his thoughts. "You're the supervising resident on this floor?"

"Yes."

"You've been working with Laura Ferris then?"

"Oh, yes."

"What's your opinion?"

"Laura Ferris is a pain in the ass."

"Is that your professional opinion?" Patrick asked shortly.

"Sorry. I mean that she mixes into things that are none of her business."

"She's here for medical training. This is a hospital. What isn't her business?"

"That's the point, this *is* a hospital. It's not some dream world, it's a hospital. Like most hospitals, we're understaffed and underequipped. We move 'em in and move 'em out. There's no time to haggle over every point."

"Then you believe her . . . situation . . . with Dr. DeWitt is haggling, nothing more?"

"I believe it's none of her business. She's an intern, a new intern. Who is she to question him? She has to earn her rights, just as we did. I tried to explain that to her, but it didn't sink in. Maybe you can straighten her out."

"Indeed," Patrick said quietly as they reached the stairway.

Lloyd Perkins stared at Patrick for a moment. "I know what you're thinking," he said. "You're thinking I'm a cynical, cold-hearted son of a bitch. Well, you're wrong. Look," he said, opening the door to the stairway, "can we step inside, out of earshot?"

"Fine," Patrick said.

Dr. Perkins checked his watch, then settled himself on a step. "I'm in my fourth year of residency. That means four years of front-line duty. I know what the pressures are. On one hand, we're expected to investigate every aspect of a patient's condition before deciding on treatment. On the other hand, insurance companies, the government, and hospital administrators tell us we're spending too much money, to cut costs to the bone. Meanwhile, patients expect miracles, and if they don't get them they're all too happy to sue for malpractice. Surgeons are pulled in every direction. 'Medical Science' gets the credit if an operation is successful . . . the surgeon gets the blame if an operation fails."

"I don't disagree with what you say."

"But you're not persuaded either. You want to know about Mr. Dagget. Personally, I wouldn't operate. I'd put him on a diet, on an exercise program, on drugs. *If* he followed the diet, and the exercise program, and took the drugs, he'd get by. He will ultimately need bypass surgery. I would rather take my chances later than now, but I'm a cautious man. Put Dagget in a room with five surgeons, three would elect to wait, two would say go ahead, operate. It's that close."

"Dr. DeWitt was always a cautious man."

"True. He's taking chances now he wouldn't have taken a couple of years ago. I don't know why, maybe his philosophy has changed. I only know he's been successful. He hasn't lost a patient to haste, or error, or miscalculation."

"Are you certain of that?" Patrick asked carefully.

"Laura told you about the woman who died during surgery."

"I understood several members of the operating team quit."

"The woman was in a bad way. She was practically an invalid, she had only a few months at best. There was one chance in a few thousand that surgery would help her. She knew the odds, she knew everything. She chose surgery. She didn't make it. It was courageous of DeWitt to try it. Eight out of ten surgeons would have refused."

Patrick stared into Lloyd Perkins' bright, cool blue eyes. He saw no hesitation, no guile. This was not a routine defense of another surgeon; it was the truth as he knew it.

"As for the team . . ." Dr. Perkins went on, "the woman's daughter went to one of the attending surgeons. She was hysterical, threatening a malpractice suit. The surgeon panicked. He panicked the anesthesiologist. Who panicked another attending physician. They walked out. The next day there were a dozen guys anxious to get on DeWitt's operating teams."

"Were you one of them?"

"No. I told you I'm a cautious man. DeWitt's not my style. But that doesn't mean I don't respect him, it means I don't want hassles. Medicine's an art, not a science, and we all have our different interpretations."

"Dr. Ferris is as sure of what she says as you are of what you say."

"Why not? DeWitt's new style is admired by some, opposed by others. That's what makes horseracing. Dr. Dain, Laura's a good kid, she'll be a good doctor, but she's still a pain in the ass. The grapevine around here is always active, it isn't always accurate. She should learn to get her facts straight."

"There you are," David Murdock's voice called up the stairway. "We've been looking all over for you. You're supposed to take your beeper when you leave your office."

Lloyd Perkins stood up. "I know you're going to stand behind your students and interns," he said, "but right doesn't lie exclusively with Laura Ferris or with

Andrew DeWitt. It lies somewhere in between. If you ask me, they're both taking too many chances."

"Thank you, Dr. Perkins. I appreciate your candor."

"I'll be getting back to work," he said, returning to the corridor.

"Why didn't you let Grace know where you were?" David asked.

"I've been learning," Patrick said.

"Learning what?"

"Learning what it's like on the front lines. David," Patrick said, as they walked down the stairs. "What's the scoop on Andrew DeWitt?"

David hesitated. "Why ask me, you know him as well as I do."

"I've been out of touch."

"I don't know what I can tell you."

"I know that tone of voice. It means you can tell me a lot. He spoke to me about Laura Ferris. I spoke to her. Then I spoke to the senior resident."

"Damn! I knew DeWitt was going to involve you in this, and I knew you were going to involve me."

"According to Ferris, Andrew's gone knife-happy. That could be the rash judgement of inexperience, probably is . . . but even according to Perkins, Andrew is taking chances."

"Well," David sighed, "he is. Don't misunderstand me," he said as they entered the corridor. "He's still one of the best there is. But he is taking chances and he's going to get burned."

"Have you talked to him?"

"Ferris has him so shook up, nobody can talk to him."

"Have you talked to anyone?"

"To whom? The Surgical Committee? Andrew's done nothing wrong."

"They might encourage him to go easy."

"The Surgical Committee is made up of six surgeons. They would split down the middle, three to three, the way they do on almost every decision. Anyway, this is a sensitive time for surgeons. Ninety-five percent of all surgeons are beyond reproach . . . the trouble is they all take the flack for the five percent who are suspect. Andrew's taking chances but they're not unethical chances. I'm uncomfortable about it, but it's his choice."

"What about the patient's choice?"

"Don't worry about that. On these close calls, I make damn sure the patient knows the score. Andrew's changed, that much is certain."

"Why?"

"How should I know?"

Patrick stopped at the door to the outer office. "David, level with me."

David shook his head. "Obviously you've heard gossip about Andrew needing money."

"Is it true?"

"I don't know."

"The truth."

"I'll say this much. There's no such thing as a poor surgeon . . . but there is such a thing as a man living beyond his means. Andrew's living high. Whether he can afford it or not I don't know. And that's as far as I go. Period. The end."

"I know Andrew. I can't believe that's the reason."

"Forget Andrew for a moment. What are you going to do about Dr. Ferris? This feud can't go on."

"Over the next few weeks Dr. Ferris and I are going to spend a lot of time in the film lab. We're going to review angiograms and O.R. videotapes together."

"That might help."

"She's so new, so young. Without dampening her spirit I want to expose her to a wide variety of diagnoses and treatments. What I really want her to learn is that there are few absolutes. After that, we'll see."

"Patrick," David said as they entered the office, "DeWitt's going to expect more than that. Something on the order of a vote of confidence."

"We'll see."

"You can do better than that."

"My first responsibility is to the students and interns. Votes of confidence can come later, if they come at all."

5

Buddy O'Hara stepped off the Second Avenue bus into a brisk early evening wind. He walked south from Thirty-third Street, walking quickly, a heavy canvas book bag slung over his shoulder. The wind caught at his blond hair, ruffling it around his face, but he hardly noticed. He was tired after thirty-six hours of work and classes. He was distracted by thoughts of that day's laboratory exams, exams in which he knew he'd not done well.

His eyes were downcast as he walked along. He cursed himself, for he'd known the test material as well as anyone, but when it had come to put that knowledge on paper his concentration had failed; he'd become confused, skipping some questions and then running out of time. His concentration had failed often in the last few months. Thinking about it, he began to perspire, thick beads of moisture breaking out on his forehead despite the chill temperature.

Buddy turned into his block, his mouth curled tightly in anger and frustration. He reached his building and ran up the four steps of the stoop, shoving the door open, letting it slam shut behind him. He hurried through the dingy foyer and then took the stairs of the three flights several at a time, pounding down the dirty hallway to his door.

He jammed his key into the door, twisting it roughly. "I'm home," he called.

"In here, Buddy."

He dropped his book bag on a chair and crossed a small living room to the kitchen. "Hi, Ma."

"Hi. Dinner's almost ready." Ann O'Hara turned away from the stove and looked at her son. "You look tired."

"Not as tired as you look."

"Don't change the subject," she smiled. "Didn't you get any sleep at all?"

"Sure I did. Here and there, you know how it is."

"How were the exams?"

"Okay."

"You stayed up studying when you should have been sleeping," she shook her head. "You don't always have to be first in your class, Buddy. Other things are just as important."

"Stop worrying," he said quickly. "I'm okay. I'm going to wash up."

Buddy left the kitchen and Ann O'Hara turned back to the stove, frowning slightly as she stirred the stew.

Ann O'Hara was a lovely woman with proud, high cheekbones and the same soft, pale blond hair she'd had as a child. She had lively, pretty blue eyes and a smile that dimpled her cheeks. Tall, erect, she'd always been slim, but lately her slimness had seemed too pronounced and her figure had taken on a certain angularity.

That, along with her fatigue, the dusty shadows which sometimes appeared beneath her eyes, had not gone unnoticed by her son. Ann herself paid little attention to such things. The past ten years had been difficult and she had come to take it for granted that that was the way it was supposed to be, that she was not one of the people upon whom life bestowed favors.

She'd married at seventeen. Brendan O'Hara, only two years older, was moody, restless, unpredictable, but Ann had loved him with all her heart. She'd loved him through the noisy times when Brendan's voice led theirs in old Irish songs or the laughter of silly, oft-told jokes; through the quiet times when Brendan, drink in hand, bent over the worn pages of a book of poetry, tears in his eyes; through the silent times when Brendan, without a word, disappeared for days at a time.

She'd loved him the rainy November night when some sharp, sure, instinct told her he'd finally left them for good. And she'd continued to love him. She'd loved him right up to the time when, weeks later, she'd looked into the confused, stricken faces of her children and felt the raging fire of her love burn itself out and die.

Brendan had taken his insurance policy and the meager contents of their savings account, leaving only the few dollars of "emergency money" in the old tin coffee can. Ann set about making a new life for her family, and this she did not with bitterness but with determination. Doggedly she sought and found jobs—any jobs—for herself, taking as many as she could handle at one time. What little free time she had was spent on household chores, or on mending and altering her childrens' clothing to make it do another week, another month, or walking blocks out of her way to find the best bargains on groceries. All of this became the pattern of Ann's life and all of this she accepted, sometimes in the spirit of adventure, more often in the spirit of a cause of which she was wholly devoted.

Now, all these years later, though still working hard and burdened by debt, Ann felt a quiet pride in her accomplishment. Her family had survived, her children were being educated, and she allowed herself to think of better times ahead. Her daughter Jill was a scholarship student at a small college in California and was, in addition, a spunky, light-hearted young woman who would have no trouble making her way in the world. Buddy, after a scholastic career marked by first place honors, was studying medicine and indeed, that had been all he'd ever talked about, dreamed about.

Ann frowned again, thinking about Buddy. He'd been deeply hurt, deeply angry, when his father left them and he seemed to carry that anger with him still. There was a palpable tension about him, a tension Ann feared would one day explode.

"Mae coming for dinner?" Buddy's voice was sharp as he surveyed the neatly set table.

"It's Monday, you know Aunt Mae always comes over on Monday."

"It wouldn't kill her to miss a week. Why should you be cooking for her all the time?"

It was an old argument and Ann shook her head. "Buddy, she's lonely and she has so little money. Have some compassion."

"Compassion! Who ever had any compassion for us?"

Buddy's blue eyes were narrowed in annoyance, though it was an annoyance stirred by his concern for his mother. She looked so tired, so thin; he worried all the time, worried even more when so many symptoms in his medical texts seemed to be her symptoms. Time and time again he'd asked her to see a doctor; she'd agreed but somehow never got around to it and her reluctance frightened him.

"I wish you wouldn't talk that way, Buddy. Aunt Mae's a nice woman and she enjoys spending time with us. And she's my friend."

Ann took a small taste of the stew and then lowered the flame. She turned away from the stove and sat down opposite Buddy.

"Ma, I heard about a job today." He spoke hesitantly for she was adamantly opposed to his working. "It's only part-time; I can work it around my schedule. The man who owns the place likes to hire students. He makes allowances for their schedules."

"No."

"Ma, it's too much for you this way. Two jobs, cooking, cleaning, shopping, all the rest of it."

This, too, was an old argument, but one for which Ann had little patience. Her tone was firm when she spoke. "You make it sound like I'm out chopping rocks or loading freight. My work is not that hard, and this apartment is not that hard to take care of."

"You're always tired."

"So are you. A lot of people are always tired. A lot of people work two jobs, harder jobs than mine. When people have a goal they work for it. My goal is seeing my children educated and doing the work they want to do."

"And I say I should help."

"You worked all through college and that was a big help. But medical school is not college. Buddy, it's so hard getting into medical school, so hard staying in. You can't take chances with that. Not with such a short time to go. In a couple of years you'll be an intern. I can manage very well until then."

"Ma, I'm just talking about a part-time job."

"You have all you can handle with your studies and your schedule. You're doing so well, you can't take a chance. I won't let you. The dean of your own medical school told me he doesn't approve of students working." Ann smiled. "In a few years you and Jill will be on your own. You can buy me a yacht," she said, standing. She removed her apron and draped it over the refrigerator. "Okay?"

"I shouldn't even talk to you about this. I should just go and get the job. It's my business if I do."

Ann turned around quickly. "It's not just *your* business. It's my business. I haven't worked and planned all this time to see you throw it away over a few dollars a week. What difference will a few dollars make? We've got loans, thousands of dollars of education loans, medical school loans. Making hamburgers a few hours a week won't get them paid off. When you start making money I'll expect your help. In the meantime I expect you to be sensible. The subject is *closed*, Buddy." Ann banged the metal cover back on the stew and then took a deep breath, calming herself.

Buddy went over to her, kissing the top of her head. "I'm sorry, Ma."

"Okay." She turned back to the stove as the sharp sound of the doorbell rang through the apartment. "Get the door, Buddy, please."

"Sure, Ma," he said, hurrying from the kitchen.

Ann began putting the food on the table, straightening plates and glasses as she moved busily about. She set out a large loaf of bread and then stepped back, checking the table. She was smiling when Mae O'Hara, Buddy behind her, came in.

"Everybody's on time today," Ann said, kissing Mae on the cheek. "I've been looking forward to your pie all day," she smiled, taking the package from her.

"I made peach this time. It's the last of the peaches but they looked pretty good. Not too expensive, either."

"You go to too much trouble, Mae," Ann said.

"I like baking. Gives me something to do. I was always good at it, you know? I was always good at baking."

"The best," Ann agreed.

Mae O'Hara, nearing fifty, was a small, plump woman with broad features and a happy, child-like smile. She had short, over-curled, over-bleached hair and a shy, wounded look in her small eyes. Ann could remember the days when Mae's eyes had sparkled and danced, but that was many years in the past.

It was in the years before one fiancé left her only days before their wedding, and another died in a subway accident. It was in the years before her beloved brother Brendan disappeared and her mother decided suddenly to return to Ireland, where she died, just as suddenly, a year later. It was in the years before Mae started talking about the curse on the O'Hara family.

Ann sat down, ladling out large portions of stew and salad. She ate slowly but Buddy and Mae went at their food hungrily. For Buddy it was the first decent meal he'd had in two days; for Mae, who liked to eat and ate heartily, it was the first meal she'd had since a snack an hour before.

Ann drank two glasses of Chianti and refused a third. "That's enough for me, you go ahead, Mae."

Mae nodded gratefully, refilling her glass. "It takes the edge off, you know?"

"I know," Ann said, though she knew that too many of Mae's nights were filled with too much wine.

Now she watched as Mae stuffed large forkfuls of food into her mouth, washing them down with big gulps of wine, and the familiar, genuine sympathy welled within her. Mae had few friends and no interests, save for television and newspapers, which she devoured as hungrily as she devoured food. She'd started as a clerk at Macy's thirty years ago, was still a clerk at Macy's, and would continue being a clerk at Macy's until she died or was retired.

"Buddy, you're real quiet tonight," Mae said between swallows.

Buddy looked up from his plate. "Sorry, Aunt Mae, I guess my mind's on school."

"It's not good, worrying all the time. It's not healthy."

"I wasn't worrying, I was thinking."

"Same thing."

"It's not the same thing," Buddy said shortly.

He wanted to tell his aunt to be quiet, to mind her own business, but Ann's pleading look silenced him.

"Buddy's a very hard worker, Mae," Ann smiled, dividing the last of the stew between Mae and Buddy.

"He gets that from your side of the family," Mae nodded. "Our side was always dreamers. My old grandma, she was the practical one. She had ambition, you could say. But she didn't pass it on. She was always at her kids, and then her grandkids, to do more, to work harder. 'Poetry don't feed the bulldog.' She must've said that a thousand times." Mae laughed and for a moment she looked very young. "But it went in one ear and out the other. My old grandma, she thought anyone coming to this country should become a millionaire. Some did, but not the O'Haras. Not 'til now anyways," she added, looking at Buddy. "Maybe your generation."

"I don't plan to be poor."

"That's good, I suppose," Mae nodded again. "I suppose it's how you got to think."

Ann looked closely at her son. "There's more to being a good doctor than making money."

"It's a capitalistic society, Ma. When you swim with sharks you either get eaten or you become a shark."

"You're swimming with sharks?" Ann asked, unsmiling.

"Listen, Ma, medicine isn't all noble intentions and pretty dreams. Far from it. It's a billion dollar industry. Controlled by the rich. For the purpose of making the rich richer. There's a lot of money to be made. A *lot*. I want my share."

Ann said nothing, though she was disturbed by the tough tone, the beligerence that so often crept into

Buddy's voice. She didn't know—had never known—if it was real or merely his defense against the world; she wondered if she would ever know.

"Speaking of the rich," Mae said, "did you meet that big muckymuck you were worried about?"

"The student director," Buddy said. "I ran into him today."

"Why were you worried?" Ann asked.

"I wasn't worried, exactly. You know, a new guy, and a guy like that to boot."

"Like what?" she asked.

"Rich. Super-rich. Aristocratic. I looked him up. He is quote—'heir to a great timber and railroad fortune.' And that family! He has ambassadors and senators and cabinet members on his family tree. And Wall Street—the market would collapse if the Dains pulled out. His father has a big deal Washington law firm. He pleads cases before the *Supreme Court*. Dain is supposed to be worth millions and millions from his trust funds, *besides* what he'll inherit one day. There are *towns* named after them."

Ann O'Hara sat back, thinking about what Buddy said. She knew, of course, that there were such people in the world, people who were worth millions, but she found it difficult to comprehend. She wondered what it would be like to have so much money.

"Millions and millions," Mae whispered. "Imagine that. And he works, too. My old grandma would have liked him," she said, laughing at her little joke. "What would you do if you had all that money, Ann?"

"Me? . . . Oh, I don't know. I think I'd like to take a trip somewhere. Anywhere, the place wouldn't matter. I've never been out of New York. Not once in my life."

"I'd buy a shop," Mae said. "A bakery shop. But I'd only make pies, and it would be the best pie shop in the city."

Ann smiled. "A trip. A pie shop. What small imaginations we have. What small dreams."

"What else are we used to, Ann?" Mae wiped her plate clean with a chunk of bread and popped the bread into her mouth. She pushed her plate away and glanced at Buddy. "So what's he like, this guy?"

Buddy shrugged. "He speaks his mind. Some of them don't say boo, you know," he grinned at Ann, "afraid of offending the lower classes. Not Patrick Grayson Dain. I only saw him a little while, but he's nobody's fool."

"Patrick Grayson Dain," Mae repeated, her small eyes narrowed in concentration.

"What's the matter, Aunt Mae?"

"Now I know who he is. Now you said his whole name, it came to me. It was in the papers. He's the man they thought maybe he killed his wife."

"What?" Buddy's head snapped up.

"They didn't come right out and say it, but it was in the papers, if you read between the lines. They thought maybe he wasn't so innocent, maybe he wasn't telling all he knew."

Ann and Buddy stared at Mae. "That's crazy," Buddy said finally.

"Maybe, maybe not. Didn't you read about it? It was maybe six months ago, around there somewhere."

Ann shook her head. She had no time for newspapers; what news she got, she got from television and from quick glances at headlines as she passed newsstands on her way to work. Buddy, she was sure, hadn't read a newspaper since he'd begun medical school.

"What happened?" Ann asked.

"I don't remember too good anymore. But I remember it was him, all right. Something about his wife dying after an accident, and how some said the investigation was too quick. How maybe it wasn't such an accident. I guess it never came to anything, cause all of a sudden the stories stopped and there was never another word about it. She was a beautiful woman, his wife. The papers called her the 'Belle of New York.' She had all this golden hair and great big eyes, and she had this expression on her face like—I don't know how to explain it—like she was giving somebody a dare. Her face I remember like it was yesterday."

"That's crazy," Buddy said again, his eyes still wide with surprise.

"There's investigations and there's investigations," Mae said. "Maybe he wouldn't be the first big shot to get away with murder. Who's to say?"

"I agree with Buddy," Ann said. "If he'd done anything wrong, they'd have found out about it."

"Who's to say?"

"You've seen too many movies, Aunt Mae," Buddy said, standing.

"I was just telling what I read," Mae said apologetically.

"We know that," Ann smiled. "But it's gossip. Let's forget it."

Ann was very weary. Already exhausted from a long day, the conversation, with its talk of millionaires and murderers, had taken her last energy. When Buddy offered to clean up in the kitchen she agreed without argument.

"C'mon, Mae, let's see what's on television."

Mae took her glass and the wine bottle and followed Ann into the living room. They settled themselves on the couch, Mae thumbing through the *TV Guide*. Ann reached for her sewing basket, expertly threading a needle, setting to work. She worked at a quick pace, her mind on the things she had still to do that night. There was an overdue letter to Jill and there was laundry to sort and her yellow blouse to iron. She looked around the room, thinking it could use some tidying, but then decided it could wait another day.

Her living room was comfortable and plain, with simple, sturdy furniture in pleasant, if faded, colors. It was spare but it was not severe for there were dozens of pretty green plants and hundreds of paperback books in neat, vivid stacks. Ann had covered the cracks in the walls with inexpensive, colorful posters and bright rag rugs covered the worn spots in the linoleum. The windows, which faced a bleak brick wall, were covered with bamboo shades.

Ann had moved them into this apartment after Jill left for college, three years before. By Ann's standards—and considering the apartment's small size and the three flights of stairs—it was too expensive by far. She'd taken it because it had two bedrooms—tiny, it was true, for they'd once been closets—because it was quiet and close to transportation, and because after one full month of walking the city, it had been the cheapest apartment she could find.

"There's a good Joan Crawford on," Mae said. "*Flamingo Road*. What she doesn't go through in that one."

"Okay," Ann smiled at Mae. "*Flamingo Road*."

Mae went to the television set. She slipped the dial and then spend another minute carefully adjusting the antennae before she returned to her seat.

"*Flamingo Road*," she explained to Buddy as he came into the room.

"Good, Aunt Mae. Ma, it's all done and the coffee's on. Anything you want before I hit the books?"

"No, thanks, I'll bring some pie into you. I'm writing to Jill tonight. Anything you want to say?"

"Tell her I said hi."

"I'll tell her how well you're doing," Ann beamed at

77

him. "You're so modest about it."

Buddy was quiet for a moment, staring down at the floor. There was so much pride in her eyes, in her voice, he felt ashamed of himself. He wouldn't be able to stand it, he thought, if she found out the truth.

"Yeah, Ma," he said after a while. "Tell her that."

"Good night, Buddy."

"Night, Aunt Mae."

Ann watched him leave and then glanced at the televison set. A big closeup of Joan Crawford filled the small black and white screen.

"Look how she's suffering, Ann. I never saw anyone like her for suffering."

6

Patrick Dain, in his shirtsleeves, closed his pen and tossed it on the desk. He stretched his arms high above his head and then looked at his watch.

"Had enough?" David asked. He rose and went to the cabinets at the side of the room. He opened a door to a compact, well-stocked bar. "Join me?"

"A small scotch, thanks."

David fixed the drinks while Patrick sat back, kneading the muscles of his neck. He'd been sitting at his desk for hours and he felt stiff and sore all over. He took the drink David handed him and sipped it.

"That's good."

"Do you feel like some dinner?" David asked. "The dining room's still open. Or there are a couple of good restaurants in the neighborhood."

Patrick thought about it and then shook his head. "I don't think so. I'd wanted to tour the hospital tonight. Top to bottom, to refresh my memory."

"It's a little late. Past ten."

"I know. Perhaps just a few floors. I'll start at the top and work my way down."

"Then we'll start with Larrimer Wing. Get it out of the way. They keep their own hours up there, so we'll be able to look in on a patient or two. I'd planned to do that anyway."

"I hate to keep you here. I hate to keep the Playboy of the Western World from his appointed rounds," Patrick smiled.

David was quiet, as if he were considering something. "I'm not much of a playboy anymore."

"No? The black crepe must be up all over town. Shot down in his prime," Patrick joked. "Why aren't you much of a playboy anymore?" He stared at David. "Don't tell me you've been treed. Is it time to polish up the orange blossoms?"

"No."

"Then?"

Again, David hesitated. "I'm just not much of a playboy anymore. That's all."

Patrick looked at David with some interest. Throughout the day he'd noticed slight, subtle changes in him, a certain amiable reserve when they'd strayed into the subject of his personal life. It was unlike him and Patrick was curious.

David was beginning to look ill at ease and Patrick quickly decided to change the subject. He finished his drink and stood up. "If we're going, let's go."

He went to the closet and took his jacket from a hanger, slipping it on. He straightened his tie and buttoned the top button of his vest. "Do I pass inspection?"

"You do."

David put his glass on a small cork coaster and walked to the door. Patrick followed, flipping the light switch off as they left the office. The corridor was silent, the office staff long gone, and they got an elevator right away.

Riding upstairs, David turned to Patrick. "It's changed quite a lot since you last saw it."

"Larrimer? I heard about the renovation. I contributed, as a matter of fact."

David nodded. "It cost a fortune. I don't think

there's anything like it anywhere."

"Is that good or bad?"

"Bad. In my opinion."

The elevator doors opened on Larrimer Wing and Patrick was immediately struck by the deep, almost sepulchral quiet of the place. He looked around and drew in his breath, for it was unlike any hospital facility he'd ever seen.

The walls were clear, pristine white, decorated at intervals with huge, pastel murals. Scattered thoughout the vast space were smooth, glove-leather benches, soft, indirect lighting built into the ceiling above them. Towering metal sculptures stood at both ends of the main corridor. Black slate wall consoles held crystal vases, their bowls laden with fresh flowers.

Patrick stared at David. "I hardly know what to say."

"Not an unusual reaction. What all this has to do with a hospital I don't know. I will *never* know."

David led Patrick to the reception area, introducing him to the nurses on duty. David wandered behind the nurses' station, glancing at the patient charts in their shiny metal holders. He selected one and read it carefully before rejoining Patrick.

"Most of the Larrimer patients are here for things like cosmetic surgery, or rest, or tests," David explained as they walked down the corridor. "For nothing very serious. It varies, of course, but this week we have only three patients who legitimately belong in a hospital."

David stopped at a door and knocked. He got no response and so he opened the door a crack and peered inside.

"Sleeping," he said, closing the door.

They continued on, crossing into a narrow, longer corridor. David knocked at another door. He waited a moment and knocked again.

"Come in," a voice called and they went inside.

It was a two-room suite, graciously, lavishly, appointed and Patrick was once again taken aback. The sitting room had pale ivory walls and large, cheery prints in polished metal frames. A small sofa and several chairs were covered in a pretty floral chintz. A large bowl of fresh flowers sat on a low glass coffee table. There was a writing desk in one corner, and in another, a color television set. A small portable refrigerator nestled at the edge of the room.

David gestured at the refrigerator. "For the champagne," he said wryly.

"Of course."

They crossed the threshold into the patient room and Patrick looked around. The bed and the cabinet at its side were standard hospital design, but there the institutional similarity ended. The walls were painted a soft, pearly pink, the bed linen was patterned with roses, and the closets were large, with built-in shelves, luggage racks, and padded hangers.

"This is Miss Parrish," David was saying and Patrick turned to look at the patient. She sat up in bed, using the remote control to silence the color television screen on the opposite wall. "One of the three I mentioned."

Patrick smiled at her. "You certainly don't look sick."

"Miss Parrish doesn't look it," David said, "but she's becoming one of our regulars." He took up her wrist, checking her pulse against his watch, and Patrick looked more closely at her.

She was a handsome woman who he supposed was in her early thirties. Everything about her bespoke clean, shining good health. Her hair was short and a deep brown, glossy with a thousand coppery highlights. Her fair skin, free of makeup, was smooth and clear and rosy, like the skin of a child. She had neat, classic features, with large brown eyes under graceful dark brows. She was as fresh and crisp as an autumn day and Patrick thought it had been a long time since he had seen such an entirely attractive woman.

David finished his brief examination and looked at Patrick. "Duodenal ulcer. We were getting some tricky hematocrits last week. Miss Parrish is stabilized now." He turned to her. "Did you see Dr. Venable today?"

"He says if everything stays the way it is I can be discharged in four or five days."

"Good," David said. "But you know what that means. Lots of rest, no cheating on the diet, taking your medication. All of it."

"I know. Dr. Venable's done everything but stamp instructions on my forehead."

"We'll do that next, if you don't cooperate."

She laughed. "You can see I don't get away with much around here, Doctor. I'm sorry, I didn't get your name."

"This is Dr. Dain," David said. "He's our student-intern director. He's responsible now for all the young hooligans sticking you with needles and punching you in the stomach." David smiled at Patrick. "Miss Parrish is one of the Larrimer patients who lets our students practice on her."

"Do they give you a hard time?" Patrick asked.

"Not at all. I like the company. I like the comfort of Larrimer Wing, but I hate the quiet. The students clatter and clunk around here and I feel less forgotten."

"In your case the quiet is useful," David said. "Rest is what you need. And lots of it."

"It's so boring," she groaned, looking at Patrick.

He smiled. "I sympathize, but Dr. Murdock is right. How long have you had the ulcer?"

"Off and on since I was sixteen. It comes and goes as it pleases. I have nothing to say about it."

"You have quite a lot to say about it," David chided. "If we haven't convinced you of that by now, I give up."

"I've promised to reform," she said to Patrick. "I don't want to go through this again. Now when all the guys in the white coats start talking about surgery."

David looked at his watch. "I think that's enough for tonight. Ring for your pill and get some sleep." He took the remote control box from her hand and put it on the bedside cabinet. "No more of this either. Your pill and then to sleep."

"You're so mean."

"That's right," David nodded.

"I'll keep an eye on the hooligans, Miss Parrish," Patrick said. "Goodnight."

"Goodnight."

They left quietly, turning out the lights in the sitting room before entering the corridor.

"One of your students," David said, "Brenner, Phil Brenner, I think it is, seems to be particularly interested in ulcer management. I understand he spends a lot of time with our ulcer patients. Especially Miss Parrish, because of the long history. He can give you chapter and verse on this case. He's going for a cardiac specialization. I think you might want to change his mind."

"I'll talk to him. Meanwhile, what about her? She's had this since she was sixteen?"

"Apparently. There was one very long remission. It's flared badly in the last year or so. This time was the worst."

"Have all the new wonder drugs been tried?"

"Yes, but the ulcer finds all of them resistible."

"Does she understand how serious this can be?" Patrick asked.

"I don't know. I don't know what she understands. There is a part of her she keeps to herself," he said thoughtfully, "no-trespassing signs all around. You saw how cheerful she was. She is always cheerful. She jokes about the hole in her stomach but it could kill her one day."

Patrick shook his head. "It's very frustrating, I know. I've seen it time and time again. We treat the symptoms of the illness with medicine and milk and bland food, while the *cause* of the illness goes unchecked. She's a classic case. What's her problem, do you know?"

"No."

"What does she do?"

"She's a model. Fashion, I think."

"Obviously successful, if she can afford Charlie Venable and Larrimer Wing. So she's successful, bright, attractive. What could be disturbing a woman like that so badly?" Patrick asked as they turned into another corridor.

"I'm not a detective, Patrick. Merely a doctor." David's tone was brusque and Patrick glanced at him.

"All right, but sometimes doctors have to be detectives. Is she seeing a psychiatrist?"

"Refuses. Venable's tried. I've tried. The Brenner kid had a long talk with her about it. No dice. Perhaps you can try. It's not part of your job, but there are times I can use help with some of our patients."

"Somebody ought to find out what problem is eating a hole in her stomach. A psychiatrist—"

"Changing a person's life is not an easy thing, Patrick," David interrupted. "You don't just wave a wand."

David sounded distracted and Patrick looked at him again. "Why do I suddenly have the feeling we're talking about two different things?"

David offered no reply and they walked along in silence for several moments. It was Patrick who broke the silence. "I plan to work with the patients. I didn't come here just to sit behind a desk. I can start with Miss Parrish."

"Go to it. I thought you'd be interested. Hoped you'd be. But there are complications in everything, remember that."

Patrick wasn't sure he'd understood David's remark, but as he was about to question him, his attention was diverted by a door halfway down the corridor. Standing there, at either side of the door, were two burly men, their arms crossed over their chests, their eyes staring straight ahead. They were almost identically dressed in dark suits and ties and plain white shirts.

"Who are those men?" he asked. "They look dangerous."

"They probably are," David said, lowering his voice. "They're bodyguards. The patient in that suite is J. J. Caldwel. The name familiar?"

"The billionaire?"

"The same. He had a mild heart attack. He's been here a week. And what a week! I really think he scared himself into the attack. Talk about psychiatric problems. Caldwel ought to buy Menningers for his personal use. Our hero, it turns out, is one solid mass of fears. He's afraid of being kidnapped, of being poisoned, of being drugged, of being murdered in his bed."

Patrick and David neared the doorway and the two guards sprang to life. They moved together, their combined width blocking the entrance; in one smooth movement they opened their jackets and brought their arms to their sides. Patrick was not surprised to see the bulge of metal under their arms.

"This is Dr. Dain," David said. "He's on our staff.

It's all right." The two men nodded in unison, all the while studying Patrick's face. "Everything all right in there tonight?" he asked.

"Dr. Brent's in there. As usual."

"Good night," David said as he and Patrick walked away. "Those two men," he explained to Patrick, "or others exactly like them, guard his door at all times. There's another one of them in his room at all times. He has private nurses and his personal physician is always with him. His only visitors are his business associates, and I don't think he trusts them either."

"What about the hospital staff? Don't they get in there?"

"Rounds, morning and evening. Period." David looked at Patrick and laughed. "Larrimer gets all the loonies. There we are, a beacon in the long night of *dementia praecox*."

"None of which you told me before I signed on for this trip."

"I am not a fool. Here," David said, leading Patrick through another doorway, "you have to see this. A big chunk of the renovation money went on this. The solarium and it's Stuart's pride and joy."

"I'm not surprised," Patrick said, gazing around. "It's spectacular."

The solarium was very large, divided into a glass-walled roofed indoor section and a terraced, open-air section. The canvas furniture throughout was sleek and comfortable, awash in bright, clean colors. There were dozens and dozens of cactus plants, each in jaunty white pots, and on the terrace was a group of young trees, lush with the last of their summer foliage. Encircling the whole of the solarium was a sweeping view of the city below. To the west was the grandeur of a hushed Central Park and to the south and north, a thousand different twinkling lights in a thousand different windows; capping it all was the panorama of endless sky, a sliver of moon shimmering among the stars.

Patrick came in from the terrace and sat down on a bright blue couch. "All right," he said, "I'm impressed."

"We aim to please."

"I didn't say I was pleased. All this," Patrick said, waving his arm around the room, "and all that," he added, gesturing toward the corridor and patient suites beyond, "is ridiculous extravagance. Hospitals are scrambling to afford their basic needs and here I sit in Xanadu. It gives me an uneasy feeling."

"I know," David said, sinking into a chair. "I put up a fight at first. I was indignant, then angry, then irate. All for nothing, of course. Stuart did his tap dance for the board. He prevailed, as he always prevails. It's disturbing," David said slowly, "because it's so disproportionate. We spend a fortune here while other, normal, hospital services are hurting. We spend only what we have to on the semi-private floors and practically nothing on the wards.

"I thought about quitting. David Murdock's protest," he said scornfully. "But I've been here a long time. I'm comfortable, settled in." He looked down at the floor. "You know David Murdock, not a man for the big battle. I fight the little battles. I fight them every day and I win more than I lose. But this," he shook his head. "I like a neat, orderly life, Patrick. Not too many complications, not too many hard decisions. So I play the game, staying just close enough to the rules not to get thrown out."

Patrick looked thoughtfully at his friend. He knew what he'd said was true. David could be persistent when he believed in something but, more often than not, he'd back away when that persistence threatened to overwhelm the symmetry of his life."

"So you brought in new blood," he said softly.

"Not just new blood, *stubborn* blood. I'm a sprinter, you're a long distance man."

A high-pitched, staccato sound echoed suddenly in the room and David reached into his pocket for a small plastic receiver. He pressed a button and stood up, going to the telephone at the side of the room. Patrick rose, returning to the terrace. He stared out at the park and thought about David, about the years of their friendship, about how different they were.

David had always been quick to pick up a challenge and quick to drop it, whereas he was slow to a challenge but dogged once the challenge was accepted. He smiled slightly, looking at the park with all its old memories of softball games and cycling and rowing on the lake. It had always been David who'd organized the activities, who'd forced him to join in; and it had always been David who'd quit halfway through while he wound up pitching or pedalling or rowing to the end.

Patrick's eye was caught by a kite stuck in the upper branches of a tree and the smile slowly left his face. A sad, quiet look came into his eyes as remembered Tony's huge red kite Victoria, remembered the perfect Saturday mornings when he and his son flew Victoria higher and higher in the sky. He remembered those days with a clarity so sharply etched it was painful; those days when they were all young and brave and sure and thought nothing bad could ever happen to them.

"Sorry," David said, joining him on the terrace. "That was Julie Carlson. She's still here. Wondered if you'd like to have a drink after all. I said we'd do it later in the week."

"Julie Carlson?"

"Patient relations. She's a very beautiful woman. She—"

"God save me from very beautiful women," Patrick said, his voice almost a whisper.

Davis was silent for a moment, looking at Patrick. "If you keep living in the past, the past is going to eat you whole."

A small, hollow sound escaped Patrick's throat. It was not quite a laugh, not quite a groan. but an odd, tired combination of both.

"Past, present, future, it's all the same. It doesn't go away. Perhaps it shouldn't. At least not until I've thought it all through." Patrick turned his back on the park, leaning against the terrace rail. "I think I've had enough for today, though."

"How about some dinner?"

"I don't think so. I'll have something at home. If I know Delia, she'll have left something. You're welcome to come."

"It's been a long day for me, too. I'll scramble some eggs at home."

They left the terrace and walked through the solarium. "You seemed to enjoy today, most of it," David said. "Did you?"

Patrick ran a hand through his dark hair, considering David's question. "It wasn't as difficult as I thought it would be. Everybody was very kind. It's hard to say, David, the real test is still ahead. A test of commitment, of wills. The problems here are more than I had anticipated. But I have to admit I'm relieved."

"Relieved?"

Patrick shrugged. "I didn't see any fishy looks, I didn't hear any whispering. I didn't expect anybody to come up to me and say 'Hey, fella, did you really do in your wife?', but I did expect some murmurings. There was none of that. So far."

"You need a good, swift kick," David said as they turned into an elevator.

Patrick grinned and pressed the button for two. "I have to stop at the office and pick up my homework. I hear the schoolbells calling."

David glanced at a page in his notebook and then put it away." Aside from the obvious problems, what did you think of her?"

"Who?"

"Miss Parrish."

"She's bright, attractive."

"You like her?"

"I suppose." Patrick looked warily at David. "If you're cooking up a romance in that little mind of yours, I advise you to forget it. I told you I'm not in the market."

"You're entirely too suspicious."

"And you're entirely too crafty."

"No such thing," David smiled. "I was curious, that's all."

"Sure. Now tell me the one about the Three Bears."

7

"That's all, ladies and gentlemen, thank you for coming," Patrick Dain said, smiling at the earnest young faces in his audience.

For most of the assembled students, interns and staff, this Wednesday meeting was the first opportunity they'd had to scrutinize the new student-intern director and they'd given him their full attention. For the fifteen minutes of Patrick's talk his deep, calm voice had been the only sound heard in the cavernous auditorium. The young people had hunched forward in their chairs, intent on every word. They'd taken notes, they'd smiled at his occasional humor; they'd grown serious as he'd discussed, in steady, deliberate tones, his goals, his plans, his rules.

Patrick understood the importance of this first meeting, of their first impression of him, and he'd prepared his remarks carefully. Now, watching as they prepared to leave, he allowed himself a satisfied smile, for he felt it had gone well. He was about to return his notes to the pocket of his hospital jacket when he looked up and hastily returned to the microphone.

"Sorry," he said, "two things more. One, is that I will be joining your rounds from time to time. I will expect you to proceed as you normally would. Two, is that I hope to have reviewed your records by the end of the week, and I will be arranging individual conferences with each of you. Thank you." He folded his notes and turned away from the podium, making his way to the side of the stage.

At the rear of the auditorium, a pretty, dark-haired woman, a white hospital jacket over her gray wool dress, gazed around the room. After some searching, she located the young man she'd come to see.

"Henry? . . . Henry, over here," she called, but in the sudden babble of voices her own voice was lost.

She walked into the center aisle, edging her way past the clusters of young people oblivious to all but their talk of Patrick Dain. She waved but the young man didn't see her and she continued down the aisle. She stopped a few rows behind him and tried again.

"Henry . . . Henry? . . . Dr. Henry Potter, over here."

The young man, slender, very tall and straight, looked around and smiled. "Dr. Shay," he said, hurrying to her. "Did you want to see me, ma'am?"

"I want you to meet Dr. Dain," Lola Shay said, leading him though a row of metal chairs to the side of the auditorium. "It'll only take a minute. Okay, Henry?"

"Yes, ma'am."

Lola Shay smiled fondly at the young man, for indeed, Henry Potter had been a favorite of hers since his student days. He was a self-effacing, uncertain young man of great ability and great good nature. There was a kind of innocence about him and this, coupled with a deep shyness, often made him seem inarticulate, inept. Her heart had gone out to him.

In the rowdy world of the medical students he'd stood apart, an observer of their activities and camaraderie, never a participant. Too often he'd been the butt of clumsy hospital jokes and almost everyone, students and staff alike, used him to do the work they didn't want to do themselves.

Lola Shay realized he needed special help and she'd become his chief supporter. She'd encouraged him, she'd praised him; above all, and unlike her colleagues, she'd paid attention to him. She was not surprised to discover in Henry Potter a young doctor of great gentleness and talent.

She was awed by his rapport with patients. With them his awkwardness, his reserve, disappeared; he was sure and soothing and they trusted him. They spoke to him as they might a friend, telling him their fears and their sadnesses, confiding the secrets they'd confide to no one else. Often it was Henry Potter who sat up through the night with a gravely ill patient, speaking softly, his hand offered in comfort.

At such times his very appearance seemed to change. Henry Potter was an unattractive young man. He had wide brown eyes, an overlarge nose and thick, indifferently cut brown hair. His mouth was narrow, his chin too square. Taken together, his features seemed mismatched, even comical, yet in those small dark hours of the night, bent over a patient, he had a certain beauty of expression that was as hard to explain as it was startling.

Lola Shay had seen this expression many times, just as she'd seen his thoughtfulness, his goodness, and she was determined that it not all be lost to the callousness of a large hospital. He needed guidance; more, he needed friendship, and Lola was counting on Patrick Dain to provide both to him.

"Wait here a moment, Henry," she said, rushing to catch Patrick.

She reached him as he was going through a side door. She grabbed at his sleeve and he turned around.

"Lola," he smiled, "how good to see you," he kissed

her cheek. "I thought we were going to meet in the cafeteria."

"I wanted you to meet someone first. Wait," she said, grasping his arms, taking a step back. "Let me look at you. You look well, are you?"

"Tip top."

"I'm glad, I really am. All right if I make an introduction?"

"Of course."

She waved at Henry Potter to join them and then looked back at Patrick. "He's an intern, so he's one of yours," she said as the young man came up to them. She introduced them and they shook hands.

"How are you enjoying your intern year, Dr. Potter?" Patrick asked, smiling.

"I'm managing to hang in there, sir," Henry said. He was nervous, embarrassed by the attention, and bright pink color flooded his cheeks.

"He's doing better than that," Lola said impatiently. "He doesn't appreciate himself enough, but that's going to change." She looked at Patrick. "You've yet to visit my bailiwick, the wards and clinic. When you do, I think Dr. Potter will make an excellent guide. He knows the set-up inside and out."

"Very well, I'd appreciate the help. I'll check my schedule—and yours, Dr. Potter—and let you know when."

"Really, Dr. Dain?" Henry Potter beamed, surprised. "Thank you very much, sir, I'd like that." He stood there, shifting from foot to foot, not knowing what else to say. Finally he looked at Lola. "Is that all, ma'am?"

She nodded. "You can go back to your service now."

"Thank you, Dr. Shay. Thanks a lot, Dr. Dain." After one quick, backward glance, he hurried away.

Patrick opened the big side door and he and Lola

walked into the corridor. They walked along quietly for a moment and then Patrick smiled.

"Confess, Lola Shay, what was that all about?"

"Do you see through me so easily?" she laughed.

"I sensed a certain urgency. And he's as jumpy as a flea. What's going on?"

"I'm worried about him. Patrick, I need your help."

"Of course, if I can."

"You can," Lola said as they stepped into an elevator. "He's a fine young man and he'll be a fine doctor, given half a chance. He has—personality problems. You saw how shy he is, ungainly. Well, he's gone through four years of hell here. The students make fun of him. They call him Dr. Banana Nose, Dr. Goofy, any mean thing they can think of. Every stupid joke in the world has been directed at him."

Patrick winced. "Hospital humor. You know how cruel it is. We all went through it. The old joke—'How many medical students does it take to change a lightbulb? Two. One to stand on the chair and put the bulb in. The other to knock him off the chair.'"

"Patrick, we all went through it for a year or so. He's had it for *four years,* and *this* year's no better. His confidence has been destroyed."

They got off the elevator and walked down a long corridor to the cafeteria. Patrick glanced at Lola.

"Medical school is a tough world. It's tough, competitive, cruel. The intern year is just as bad. There's a survival of the fittest theory there, and I'm not sure it's a bad theory."

Lola was silent as they walked into the cafeteria. It was a big, square, yellow room, crowded with formica tables and metal chairs. There was a steam table for hot dishes, a counter for sandwiches and salads, rows of coffee machines, and several juice and soft-drink dispensers.

Patrick took Lola to a table in the corner of the room. "What would you like?"

"Coffee."

Patrick stared at Lola for a moment and then walked off. When he returned minutes later, Lola was staring glumly into space, her mouth a tight line. He put cups on the table and sat down. He sipped his coffee, smiling then at Lola's strained expression.

"I'm up to my neck in problems. Drowning in them. You're about to hand me another one, aren't you?"

"It's important, Patrick. And I don't need any lectures about survival of the fittest."

"I apologize. Tell me what's on your mind."

"His future is in the balance. He's hinted more than once that he might not finish out the year. His ego—what little he has—is in shreds. His self-respect is gone."

Patrick looked closely at Lola, his blue eyes steady. "You know, I know—we all know—medicine isn't for the faint-hearted. Every good doctor I know—and that includes you and me—has some small core of steel in his character. Has to, because that's where the tough decisions are made. And ego. Because how else would we have the temerity to interfere in life and death? Call it toughness, but you cannot be a doctor without it."

Lola opened her mouth to speak but Patrick held up his hand. "Hear me out. We've all seen students and interns call it quits. It's been my experience that when they find it too tough, when they want to quit—*really* want to quit—they probably should. Because it won't ever get any easier. It will only get tougher."

"You wouldn't say that if you saw him with our patients," Lola said heatedly. "He has the kind of toughness the rest of us envy. The kind of toughness that makes him sit with a dying patient long after the attending physician has conveniently stepped out of the room. Death is all around and he *stays,* giving that patient more comfort, more strength, than one would have thought possible," she argued, her brown eyes blazing. "They call him Dr. Death around here, too, but they do it very nervously, because they know they haven't got the guts to see it through themselves. *Time* after *time, patient* after *patient,*" she said, her hands waving furiously.

"The nurses get a little lax about sponging off a decaying body," she continued, "the residents don't look too closely at festering bedsores and withered skin, so it's Henry Potter who brings in a basin of soapy water, or some cream for that cracked skin. He cares, Patrick, when most of the others are finding excuses to be elsewhere."

"Calm down," Patrick said, taking her hand, "you're going to need a bed yourself."

"I'm sorry, Patrick," she said, taking a deep breath, "but I'm dead serious about this. And it's so damned unfair. Henry Potter isn't like the ones who quit because they can't cut it — the grades, the work, the hours, the pain, the little shocks along the way. What Henry can't cut is being everybody's buffoon, everybody's horse's ass.

"Rhinelander Pavillion is a teaching hospital," she stared at him, "or so it says in all the brochures. You wouldn't hesitate to help a student who was having problems with his classes, or an intern who needed help with diagnostic technique. Well, Henry has a different kind of problem, but we're obligated to help him just the same."

"I have a list of problem children. I can't be everybody's psychiatrist, everybody's parent."

"It comes with the territory. You don't take a job supervising students and interns unless you're willing to be psychiatrist and parent along with all the other things you have to be. They're young, still developing, and sometimes the state of their heads, their hearts, is more important than the state of their performance reports."

Patrick smiled. "What do you expect me to do with this young man, Lola? What do you think I can do?"

"Pay attention to him, for a start. Involve yourself. If I'm wrong about him, okay, I'll drop it. But I won't drop it until you've given the situation a long, hard look. I was wrong to tell you he was thinking of quitting. *God*, how men hate that. It's not *macho* enough for them. John Wayne wouldn't quit."

Patrick laughed. "Well, now I suppose I have to help, if only for the honor of my sex."

Lola looked down at the table. "I don't mean to be so belligerent, but it's so frustrating. This whole damn hospital is frustrating. I was a student here. An intern. A resident. Then staff. Now I'm a department head and that's fourteen years of observing this place. I hate what's happening to it. It's been a long time since we got the cream of the student crop—or interns or residents. We get so many jerks around here that when I see quality I want to nurture it. Can you understand that?"

"Of course I can. One of the things I want to do is upgrade the quality of the program. We've become a third-choice place for many young people. Last choice for some. I'm aware of that, Lola, and I don't like it any more than you do. I'm sorry I was brusque about Potter. I'll stand on what I said about medicine and the faint-hearted, but I will certainly take a long look at him—and his work. If he's worth it, I'll do everything I can. You have my word."

"Thank you," she sat back. "That's all I wanted. He hasn't had an easy life," she said slowly. "His father is Don Potter—the golden boy of all those MGM musicals of the fifties."

"Don Potter? Are you sure?"

"Oh, yes, I'm sure. His mother is Melanie Lawrence."

Patrick's mouth opened in surprise. "One of the loveliest ladies in Hollywood. Still. He is . . . their child?"

"Don't think Henry doesn't wonder how someone who looks like him could be the child of such parents. Don't think Mr. and Mrs. Potter don't wonder. They packed him off to military school at the age of seven. Though I understand they're very kind at Christmas," she said dryly.

Patrick thought suddenly of Catherine. Tony had barely turned seven when she'd wanted to send him away to school; he made her feel old, she'd said.

"I am beginning to understand Potter's problem," Patrick nodded.

"He needs a friend. If it's a friend in high places, all the better."

Patrick smiled. "Lola, you're getting very sly."

"That's survival around here." She took up her cup, sipping the coffee slowly. After a moment she smiled. "It's been months since I've seen you and the first thing I do is bite your head off. It wasn't much of a welcome. I apologize."

"Accepted."

"To prove how sorry I am, I'm not going to lay my other problems on you today. I'll wait a decent period of time."

"Other problems?"

"Oh, my son, the stories I could tell." Lola paused. "You haven't seen the wards yet, I guarantee you won't like what you see. But I'll hold off on that, give you a chance to catch your breath."

"How very kind," he smiled at her. "Considering the awesome burdens you carry on your shoulders, you're looking very well. What's your secret?"

"Clean living," she laughed.

Lola had a bubbly, vivacious laugh and it was heard often, for she was as quick to laughter as she was to anger. Her eyes were luminous with the enthusiasms and passions she brought to her work, to her life.

Now, Patrick and Lola heard the sharp beeping of the page and they reached into their pockets for their receivers.

"You or me?" Patrick asked, holding his receiver to his ear.

"Me," Lola said, rushing away from the table.

Patrick watched her admiringly. She was a pretty woman grown prettier each year, he thought. Her step was light and quick and the hundreds of miles she walked in the hospital each month kept her figure lithe and trim. During the course of her career at Rhinelander she'd argued with almost everyone, sometimes bitterly; yet for all that, Patrick thought, smiling, she had the unqualified affection of all her associates, their unqualified respect.

Patrick returned the receiver to his pocket. He removed his notebook and spread it open before him. It was already crowded with names and questions and dates, and with a resigned sigh, he added another notation—the name Henry Potter and a large question mark. He put the small leather book away and stared straight ahead, thinking of all that lay ahead of him that day. It was a long list of activity and he had to force himself to concentrate on all the things to be done.

For one long moment Patrick wanted to run, to flee Rhinelander Pavillion for the solitude of his library, of any quiet place. His mouth tightened as he recounted all the responsibilities he'd taken on; it was more than he'd bargained for, more than he'd wanted. At that moment he thought longingly of his big Connecticut house, of the private, endless woods stretching out in all directions. He closed his eyes and he could see the stream that ran through his property, the clear, rippling water splashing at the shiny, speckled rocks.

"Patrick? Anything wrong?" Lola asked.

Patrick stood. "I alternate between wanting to be busy and wanting to be left alone," he said as they walked to the door.

"Give yourself a few days to settle into the routine. You'll see, after a while you'll love it."

"Promise?"

"You're a doctor. No matter what else happens you can't shut that off. Catherine never understood that," Lola said, starring at him. "You do, so make the most of it."

"That sounds like an order," Patrick smiled.

"Advice. I give very good advice."

Patrick settled himself behind his desk and pressed the intercom button. "Grace, what do I have now?"

"You have a free half hour. Your next appointment isn't until nine. Dr. Rusher of the medical school."

"Thank you."

"Want some coffee?"

"No thanks."

Patrick looked around at the many papers on his desk, stopping when he saw a new report from the medical school. It was a list of grades on the first laboratory exams of the term. He glanced at the first page and then turned several pages until he came to the second year group. He read until he found the name he was looking for: *O'Hara, Dennis M. (Buddy)*. Patrick ran his finger across the page and scowled, banging his fist on the desk.

"What?" David asked, coming into the office.

"The lab scores," Patrick flipped the stapled sheets across the desk. "Take a look. O'Hara, Dennis M."

David read the notations and returned the report to the desk. "He's on the thin edge. I don't know how much more of this can be tolerated."

"I spent an hour last night checking his first year grades. Brilliant. So I went back and checked his pre-med grades. Brilliant. So I went back and checked his college entrance scores. Brilliant. I simply don't understand it. He's had a magnificent scholastic career. This term he's lucky if he gets the date right. Dr. Rusher is coming over; I hope he has some answers."

"Don't count on it. This is about the time he starts preparing warnings. There's a grace period but it's not long. O'Hara's been on the verge of failing since July. Now he *has* failed. Rusher may want to skip the grace period and chuck him out."

"I'm going to call O'Hara in. See if I can get to the bottom of this."

"I'd *hate* to lose him," David said. "But the numbers speak for themselves. Get too partial and the other students start thinking they can let down, too." David sat down. "How did your talk go?"

"I was satisfied. I'm going to repeat it tomorrow for those who weren't on schedule today. I had coffee with Lola afterwards. She's upset about one of the interns. Potter. Henry Potter."

"Potter? . . . Potter . . . Oh, yes. He's a nice young man. Much too skittish."

"He's a cause with her."

"Well, Lola has her causes," David said slowly. "Always has had. She's our resident firebrand. Sometimes I think she's our resident conscience. Hell of a woman."

"You were seeing quite a lot of her. I had high hopes."

David glanced away. "I don't see much of her anymore. Outside the hospital." He paused, as if thinking about something, and then looked back at Patrick. "Julie Carlson's on my back. She wants a meeting with you. Can you arrange something?"

"Who?"

David sighed impatiently. "Patient relations. And something of a wheel around here because the board loves her. Can you arrange something?" he repeated.

"The end of the week, not before. I don't want to get bogged down with silly departments like patient relations."

"She keeps people happy. If they're happy they don't complain. If they don't complain we have more time for important things."

"All right, but what does she want with me?"

"Patrick, as a *favor* to me, will you *please* arrange something?"

"The end of the week."

"*Thank* you," David said, rising, walking to his office.

Patrick pressed the intercom button. "Grace, I'd like you to arrange a meeting, please."

"Sure, go ahead."

"Buddy O'Hara. He's a second year. He's working the . . . let's see," Patrick said, consulting a student chart, "the fourth floor service through the end of this week. As soon as possible, and I'd like to have about forty-five minutes. All right?"

"Sure thing."

Patrick removed his white jacket and draped it over the back of his chair. He looked at his watch; he had fifteen minutes until his appointment with Dr. Rusher. Again, he pressed the intercom.

"And let me have the files on Henry Potter. He's an intern."

8

The taunting, derisive laughter began slowly, growing and growing in intensity until Patrick sat upright in his bed. His heart thundering, his hands cold, damp, he searched wildly about the room for the source of the terrible sound. It was not the first time he'd heard it. It had come several times in the last few months, always in the black, early hours of morning, and always without any direction he could follow.

He threw the covers back and jumped out of bed, stumbling around, switching on lights, his eyes darting left and right, up and down. He saw nothing, but still the laughter came. Great waves, great tides of laughter came at him, buffeting him from every side until he thought his head would split in two. He ran across the large bedroom to the suite of rooms that had been Catherine's. His fingers trembling, he pulled the door open and reached for the light switch.

Again, he saw nothing. The room was as she had left it. The big canopy bed was undisturbed, piled with cream-colored satin comforters and pillows with ruffled lace edges. The delicate silk-covered chairs were in place, and the dressing table, laden with crystal bottles and jars of every size and shape, with silver brushes and combs and mirrors, was untouched. The doors of the long wall of closets were closed; the rose-tinged, white silk draperies were still. He crossed into the sitting room and it, too, was as it had been, the graceful, antique-filled room serene and quiet.

Patrick ran back to his bedroom, the ugly, mocking laughter pounding in his ears. He poured a brandy from a crystal decanter at his bedside and drank the dark liquid down in a single swallow. He lit a cigarette, the red-gold flame flickering with his unsteady hand. His brow was shiny with perspiration as he went to a cabinet above his desk, opening a door to a small, closed circuit television monitor.

He pushed a button and a picture of the staircase and the center hall below came into focus. It was empty and he manipulated another dial, tuning in pictures of the connecting hallways and of a tall, deep closet. The closet—containing the priceless Dain collection of silver, gold, and vermeil flatware, plates and candelabra—was securely locked. Patrick sat down, massaging his temples, his eyes shut tight. Then slowly, as slowly as it had begun, the laughter began to die away. Finally it was gone and Patrick looked around.

The room was peaceful once more and he exhaled a great breath. He drew deeply on his cigarette and then stubbed it out, quickly lighting another one. His handsome face was drawn and very pale as he considered the last few minutes, considered the times before this time.

The first time the laughter had come, he'd ascribed it to a nightmare, a bad dream which had taken unusually long to awaken from. The next couple of times he was no longer certain, and now he knew that what he'd heard had nothing to do with dreams. It was a real voice. It was Catherine's voice. And it was pursuing him. He shook his head once, twice, three times, but still the terrifying notion would not go away. His heart beat furiously, for he wondered if he might be going mad. He smiled wanly, for he didn't know which would be worse—to be suffering hallucinations, or to be suffering a real presence come to haunt him in the night. But no, Patrick slammed at the desk, it had not been hallucination; it had been real. He knew that laugh; he would never forget that laugh.

Patrick rose slowly and walked back to his late wife's bedroom. He sat at the edge of a silken chaise lounge and stared around the room. It was a beautiful room, pale and romantic, ruffled, beribboned, a perfectly conceived setting for Catherine's extraordinary beauty. And how skillfully she'd used that setting, he thought bitterly. It was her stage, her showcase, and she'd used it to mirror her moods, her many whims.

He remembered those moods. Catherine in cool, pure white silk; Catherine in girlish, flower-sprigged cotton; Catherine, a seductress in black chiffon, and how especially well she'd played that part. He remembered how it had been. Catherine, in the midst of all the pale, soft, pink light, of all the pale, soft silks and satins, emerging from her dressing room in stark, sheer black lace.

Her golden hair tumbling about her shoulders, she would stand in a circle of light, the light shining through the lace to outline her body. She would turn slightly and the light would catch her firm, full breasts, the smooth, round curve of waist and hips, her bare, shapely legs. Taking her time, she would open the first button of her gown, and the next and the next until the swell of her breasts was exposed.

Patrick buried his head in his hands; that was all a very long time ago, for he had other memories of this room—of dreams shattered, of hurt, and pain, and at the end, of hatred and ugly, mocking laughter.

He stood and dimmed the lights, returning to his bedroom. He put on his robe and slippers and dropped some keys into his pocket. He left the bedroom and walked into the long hallway to the staircase. He descended slowly, tiredly.

Patrick walked through the center hall, hesitating at the door of the drawing room. He unlocked the door, turning on a single light as he went inside. He stared up at Catherine's portrait. Anger burned brightly in his eyes. The portrait captured all of her beauty, he thought, but none of her evil. He remembered how she'd loved the portrait, how she'd seemed to draw strength from it, and again he felt an urge to destroy it, to tear it apart, to burn it to black ash. He turned quickly and left the room, locking the door behind him.

Patrick walked down a hallway to the kitchen. He turned on a bright overhead light and went to the stove. He reached for the kettle and it went crashing to the floor. Cursing, he kicked it across the room. He filled a small pot with water and slammed it on the burner, turning up the flame. He watched it for a moment and then slumped wearily into a chair.

"Oh, it's you, Dr. Dain, sir."

Patrick looked up. "I'm sorry I woke you, Hollis," he said to the plump, cheerful man who'd been the Dain butler for the last ten years. He smiled slightly. "You can put the baseball bat down."

"Can't be too careful, sir. Things as they are these days. Bad night again, sir?"

Patrick glanced at the wall clock. "I'd be getting up soon anyway. But you needn't be up; go back to bed."

"You know me, sir, up with the birds."

Hollis stood the bat in the corner and walked to the round oak table, tying his robe tightly across his broad middle.

"A good breakfast is what you need, sir. Won't take a minute," he said, moving toward the refrigerator.

"Don't trouble yourself, Hollis. All I want is coffee."

"No trouble, Dr. Dain. I can cook for two as easy as one. Save old Delia some work when she gets here, eh sir?"

"All right. Perhaps some eggs?"

"Very good, sir. Scrambled?"

"Fine . . . Hollis, did you hear any . . . noises around here before? And—sounds?"

"Well, sir, I was brushing my teeth when I heard a door closing. I heard footsteps and I heard something crash down. I got my bat, all prepared to fight it out, I was. Then I saw it was you. It *was* you, sir?"

"Yes. I meant before that. Did you hear anything unusual before that?"

"Can't say as I did, sir," he shook his head. "Did you hear something, Dr. Dain? Do you think we had an intruder?"

Hollis' round, rosy face was alight with excitement and Patrick couldn't help but smile. "No, I'm sure we didn't have an intruder," he said, though he thought to himself that "intruder" was the proper word for it, perhaps the only word.

Hollis put oranges, eggs, milk and butter on a tray which he took to the counter at the side of the stove. He paused, looking over his shoulder at Patrick.

"Of course, sir, if there was somebody upstairs, I wouldn't hear it down here. Good sound construction, not like some of those new buildings. Would you like me to have a look around, Dr. Dain?"

"No, that won't be necessary. Let's forget it. Can I give you a hand with that?"

"Oh, no, sir. Too many cooks and all that, eh, sir?"

Hollis turned back to his work, adroitly slicing the oranges in two and putting the halves into the juicer. He poured the fresh juice into a pitcher and placed it in the refrigerator, then turned to the eggs, cracking them against the side of a glass bowl.

"Hollis, I've been thinking about clearing out Mrs. Dain's rooms."

"Clearing them out, sir?"

"I don't see any reason to keep them as they are. They're not used. It only makes more work for Delia. I think you might start making an inventory of the rooms. We can decide later what to keep and what to send out."

"And close off the rooms, sir?"

"I don't know what I'll do with the rooms. We have too many rooms as it is. But we can at least get the things out. What do you think?"

"Very good idea, sir. And Delia will be pleased, I'm sure. She and the women have to be so careful in there. So many delicate things, you know. I'll get at that inventory first thing."

"Thank you, Hollis."

Patrick felt relief at his decision. He'd wanted to clear those rooms out months before but he'd postponed doing it. Now he was glad her things would finally be gone, would be someplace away from him, someplace far away.

Hollis put a glass of juice in front of Patrick. "Thank you," he said, sipping it.

He sat back, enjoying the peace of the kitchen. It was a friendly room, with copper pans and molds decorating the tan walls and lots of hanging plants above. There was one whole wall of small appliances; the refrigerator and stove were double size—recalling the time of Catherine's French chef, and the lavish, incessant dinner parties she'd given. Every counter top was decorated with herbs growing in pretty yellow pots.

Hollis set a plate of eggs and another of buttered muffins on the table.

"Join me," Patrick said, "while it's still hot."

"Thank you, sir, I'll take you up on that." He served Patrick first and then filled his own plate before sitting down. "Coffee in a minute, sir."

"This is very good," Patrick said between bites. "I'm glad you talked me into it."

"Nothing like a good breakfast to set up the day, Dr. Dain. It was always the biggest meal of the day when I was a lad. But Americans, with their doughnuts and danish," he shook his head, "on the run. I can't say as I understand it, sir, for all I've been in this country."

"Everybody doesn't have you and Delia to cook for them."

"What does it take, sir, a few minutes? It takes no longer than that queueing up to buy a doughnut. Yes, sir, at home it was eggs and sausages and pots of cream and jam and bread hot from the oven. Until the war, of course, sir. Then it was many a year before we saw an egg again. My mum used to say she'd give her gold tooth for an egg," he laughed heartily. "An egg, such a simple thing as that. But time passes and we forget how it was, eh, sir? No matter how bad it was, we forget, and that's as it should be."

Patrick smiled. Hollis often told him little stories of his life and they, like Uncle Remus tales, often had appropriate little morals at the end—things about forgetting, or forgiving, or patience, or courage. Patrick always wondered if they were deliberate or merely an accidental turn of Hollis' mind. He was fond of him and he knew him to be shrewder than he appeared; he wondered if the little stories weren't Hollis' discreet way of offering advice or help.

"Speaking of home," he said, "you never did take your holiday. When do you want your vacation, Hollis?"

Hollis rose and unplugged the coffeepot. He brought it to the table and filled Patrick's cup and his own. He returned to his chair.

"Well, sir, it would be nice to have a few days at Christmas. I'd like to see my sister and her lads in New Jersey. But as for a long holiday, I'd just as soon pass it by this year."

"But why?"

"There's still too much to see to here, Dr. Dain. I wouldn't feel right in leaving. I wouldn't have much of a time for myself if I was worrying about other things, eh, sir?"

"That's very kind of you, but you mustn't cheat yourself. I can manage."

"That you can, sir. But with Master Tony going off to Yale next year, and with your new job—there's a lot to see to."

Patrick was touched by Hollis' concern. He wanted to tell him so but dared not for fear of embarrassing him. "I'm very grateful," he said instead.

"Thank you, sir." Hollis stood and began taking the breakfast dishes to the sink. "I'll leave these for the women. I'll be up in a minute to draw your bath."

"Please don't bother. I'll have a shower."

"Very good, sir. I'll lay out your things straight away."

Patrick lingered over a last sip of coffee, thinking about the morning ahead. He had a meeting with Buddy O'Hara directly after rounds and he wasn't looking forward to it. He hoped the young man was in a better mood than the one of their first meeting, for his own patience, after the turmoil of this Friday morning, would be short. He put his cup down and then turned his head to the sound of a key at the service door.

Delia, struggling with a heavy shopping bag, walked into the kitchen. She stopped, surprised to see Patrick. "Good morning, Dr. Dain."

He drew his robe closer around him and hurried to her, taking the bag from her hands. "Good morning, Delia. Why do you carry such heavy things? The elevator man would be happy to help you."

"By the time you get somebody to do something, you're better off doing it yourself." She took off her coat and scarf and draped them on a counter top. "It's cold out there, sir. You'll need a heavy coat. It feels like winter."

"Delia, the coffee is made. Sit down and relax a while."

"Did Hollis make breakfast?"

"Yes, and very good, too."

"I hope you ate, Dr. Dain. It's not good to go into the cold on an empty stomach."

Patrick smiled. "With you and Hollis looking after me, I have nothing to fear."

"Yes, sir."

Patrick went to the door, patting her shoulder as he passed. "Have that coffee now."

Patrick nodded a greeting to the doorman on duty in the large, ornate, downstairs lobby.

"Taxi, sir? Or did you call for your car?"

"I'm walking, thank you."

"It's cold out there."

"So I hear," Patrick smiled, stepping out of the lobby onto Fifth Avenue.

He walked rapidly up the avenue, one hand jammed in his pocket, the other holding both his medical bag and his briefcase. He stopped at the corner for a traffic light, his mind on Buddy O'Hara. Staring straight ahead, he didn't see the beautiful, elegantly dressed woman leave the shelter of a doorway and hurry toward him. As he stepped off the curb he felt a light tap on his arm. He turned around.

"Aren't you Dr. Dain?" she asked.

"Yes."

"I'm Julie Carlson, and this *is* a stroke of luck."

"It is?" he smiled, taking her elbow as they crossed the street.

"I work at Rhinelander Pavillion," she laughed prettily. "I have the patient relations department. David Murdock has been promising me a meeting with you. Of course," she smiled up at him, "I didn't expect we would meet in the street. I'm glad I kept my dressmaker appointment this morning."

"I'm sorry, Miss Carlson, David did mention you several times, but my schedule's been so tight. I should have recognized you," he grinned, "David said you were very beautiful, and so you are. Beautiful women don't usually accost me in the street. I, too, am glad you kept your appointment."

"Thank you," Julie said, modestly lowering her eyes. "Then I may walk along with you?"

"I would be honored," Patrick said, as all around him he saw heads turning for second looks at Julie Carlson.

Patrick had been honest in his compliment, for indeed, Julie looked especially beautiful. Dressed entirely in dove-gray, her glossy black hair fluttering gently about her face, the half hour she'd waited in the cold had brought a special glow to her skin, an extra shine to her hazel eyes.

"Tell me about your department, Miss Carlson."

"Please call me Julie," she said and Patrick nodded. "It's not only my department I wanted to talk about. I wanted to talk about one of your students, Buddy O'Hara."

"I'm not surprised," he laughed shortly. "Go ahead, I'm all ears," he said, slowing his pace to accommodate hers as they walked along.

Julie first explained the workings of her department, emphasizing the various ways she assisted patients during their hospital stays. Her summary was accompanied by graceful gestures and graceful anecdotes, and Julie was encouraged by the fact that Patrick gazed appreciatively at her throughout her recitation.

"So you can see," she said as they crossed another street, "my department is more than window dressing."

Patrick nodded again and she went on, changing to the subject of Buddy O'Hara. These comments she accompanied with fluttering eye lashes and astonished little smiles and the lovely, low laugh she knew to be charming.

"There's more," she said as they turned off Fifth Avenue to Rhinelander Pavillion. "I'd like to talk to you in greater detail, when your schedule is easier."

"You've given me a very clear picture, I don't think I need to hear more."

Julie was annoyed; she'd spent two days planning this encounter, planning it to lead to other encounters, and now she felt she'd failed.

"I'm glad I could help," she forced herself to say.

"I'm meeting with O'Hara this morning, as a matter of fact. I'll let you know the results."

"I'd appreciate that," Julie smiled.

She hadn't failed after all, she thought gleefully; she'd opened the door a crack and that was all she needed.

They walked into Rhinelander Pavillion and hurried to a waiting elevator, pressing themselves into the crowded car. Patrick greeted several doctors, exchanging a few brief words, all the while aware of the soft, pretty scent of lilac as Julie leaned close to him.

They got out of the elevator and Patrick walked Julie to her office. "Pleasure meeting you," he said.

"And you, Patrick," Julie purred.

Patrick continued down the corridor, unbuttoning his coat as he went.

"Good morning, Grace," he said, entering the outer office.

"Morning, Patrick. Coffee?"

"Thanks," he said, going into his office. He hung up his coat and jacket and went to his desk, turning as David entered through the side door.

"Morning," David said. "Revised budget figures," he added, putting a folder on the desk.

"Thank you," Patrick said, flipping through the pages before he sat down.

"You look tired."

"I am. But I'm almost caught up on the old paper work, and that's something. Oh, and I finally met your Julie Carlson and heard her problems. You were right. She's something to look at and then some."

"Yes, she's . . . you met her? Where did you meet her?" David asked.

"On the way here. I was walking over and so was she."

"Walking over from home?" David frowned.

"I suppose," Patrick looked up. "Why?"

"Julie doesn't live anywhere near you."

Patrick shrugged. "She said something about a dressmaker appointment. Anyway, I told her I was having a meeting with O'Hara. I promised her all my cooperation. Satisfied?"

David was silent for a moment and then suddenly a tiny smile turned up his mouth. "A dressmaker appointment," he said slowly. "What luck."

"That's what she said. David, O'Hara will be here any minute."

"I'm going."

David crossed to the door and then stopped, looking back over his shoulder at Patrick. He considered him for a moment and then entered his own office. He stood behind his desk, drumming his finger tips on the polished wood; only a few days ago he'd wondered about Julie and now he wondered again. He laughed out loud; she would bear some watching, he thought.

9

"Sit down, Mr. O'Hara," Patrick said. "Would you care for some coffee?"

"We can skip the amenities. Let's get down to business, whatever it is. Flat out," Buddy said, his chin set in defiance.

Patrick stared coolly at him. "Very well," he said. "You failed your laboratory exams. Is that flat out enough for you?"

Buddy's lips parted in surprise. "Failed? I knew I'd done badly, but I didn't think that bad."

"Yes."

"Failed?"

"Yes."

Buddy pushed a hand through his thick blond hair, his eyes blinking rapidly, trying to blink away the panic he felt. A picture of his mother flashed through his mind; she would find out now, he thought, she would find out the truth. He felt the perspiration start on his forehead and he wiped at it impatiently before looking again at Patrick.

"I don't understand. I got a warning notice. A lot of guys did. But I didn't get anything about a failure."

Patrick had been watching him carefully. He'd seen some of the defiance go out of his manner and he considered that a hopeful sign.

"I spoke with Dr. Rusher and we decided I would handle it. I have some questions, Mr. O'Hara, and I want some answers."

"I don't understand," Buddy repeated, almost to himself, "I knew I wasn't doing that well, but—"

"That well?" Patrick asked incredulously. "Your work has been *appalling*. You've been near the failing mark the whole quarter. The whole quarter, Mr. O'Hara. I could boot you out of the program right now."

Buddy swung around. "Now, hold on. I was the best student in the program last year. The best! And you know it."

"That was last year. Past tense. Faded glory. You've completed a quarter of *this* year and it's been a disaster. That happens sometimes," Patrick said slowly. "The hot shots get cooled down."

"Bull!" Buddy yelled. "You've got it all wrong."

"Have I? How?"

"I know the class work as well as anyone. Better."

"Then why doesn't it show on the test scores?"

Buddy looked away, his nails digging into the palms of his hands. He remembered every examination he'd had in the past months—the quick, informal quizzes, and the long, printed tests, the oral exams and the written exams. He remembered that each time he'd been confronted with a set of symptoms, or a sick laboratory animal, or a set of slides, he froze; an image of his mother, too pale, too thin, hollow-eyed, overwhelmed him until his concentration was gone. He'd become nervous and disoriented, often unable even to complete the examination.

His work on rounds had suffered too; he'd become indecisive, trying to hide in the group of medical personnel around him. He was not surprised it had come to this, he thought, digging his nails deeper and deeper into the flesh of his palms.

Patrick hadn't taken his eyes off Buddy. He'd watched as the young man struggled with his emotions, and now he decided to try a different tack.

"I've read your files back through college," he said quietly. "You've always been an A, A+, student. That fact alone is buying you some time."

Buddy looked up, his expression guarded. "I've always been the best."

"Which brings us to an interesting point. With your scores you could have gone to Bellevue, to City. Why did you choose Rhinelander Pavillion?"

"Why? Because this is where the money is. I'm making a connection or two here that I wouldn't make anyplace else. I'm not looking to be any ghetto doctor. My practice is going to be for rich people, people who can pay, pay through the nose."

Patrick leaned back in his chair. He frowned. "Among other things, you're inconsistent. If treating rich people is your plan, why do you abuse them in Larrimer Wing?"

Buddy laughed, some of the swagger returning. "That's part of my training, too. You got to know how far you can go—how much the bastards'll take. I'm going to treat 'em but I'm not going to kow-tow. I never saw a rich person in my life before I came here. Now I'm seeing a lot of 'em. I'm *learning* them, you could say."

Patrick was quiet for a moment, watching Buddy. The young man was filled with a kind of turmoil he didn't understand. "So you are here by choice, not because you were afraid of the competition at other hospitals?"

"Afraid? Me? No way." Buddy looked around the office, his eyes running over the fine furnishings, the prints, the crystal and leather accessories. "This one room," he said, "is probably larger than our whole apartment. It sure as hell has better stuff. One of those things on the wall probably cost more than all our stuff at home. This place says money. Everywhere you go around here says money. Except the wards. And that's the difference. The rich get, the poor bleed. I'm no bleeder."

"All right. We have established that money is your objective."

"That's everybody's objective in this country."

"Not only in this country, Mr. O'Hara," Patrick smiled.

"And I'll do anything I have to to get it."

"Which brings us back to the subject of your failing grades. How do you expect to make your millions if you are kicked out of here?"

Buddy said nothing, his mouth clamped shut, his eyes averted.

"Well?" Patrick demanded.

"It's going to be okay. You said I bought some time, I'll straighten it out."

"No, no, Mr. O'Hara. You're not going to bluff me out of this. You've bought some time, but at my discretion. If you are going to be stubborn, then the time has just run out."

"I said I'll straighten it out."

"Not good enough. Your work is a disgrace and you're certainly not getting by on your charm. I want to know what's gone wrong."

"I . . . I got a problem. Personal," he snapped the word out. "I'll take care of it."

"Not good enough."

"What do you want from me?" Buddy shouted. "My life story?"

"If that's what it takes."

"Listen . . . you wouldn't understand . . . and anyway—"

"Try me."

"For God's sake! It's none of your damn business! Can't you get that through your head?" Buddy shouted again, his blue eyes hard and cold.

Patrick took a deep breath. "All right, Mr. O'Hara," he said in a quiet, firm voice. "As of today you are cancelled. I will send the appropriate notice to Dr. Rusher and to the head of your service. You may leave the program upon written notification. That will take a day, perhaps two. In the meantime, you are not to return to classes or rounds. You may use the time to get your things together, and to arrange for the return of any fees we may owe you. That's all, Mr. O'Hara," Patrick said, turning to the papers on his desk. "Good morning."

Buddy stared open-mouthed at Patrick. The words began to sink in and his hands clenched into tight, white fists. He jumped up, kicking the chair away.

"Okay," he yelled. "*Okay!*" He threw the word at Patrick and then stomped to the door. He walked out, slamming the door so hard that the door knob rattled.

The side door opened and David poked his head inside. "What in the —"

"Get out of here, David," Patrick said quietly, his eyes fast on the closed door.

David withdrew and Patrick glanced quickly at his watch. Seconds passed and then minutes, while Patrick continued to stare at the door, his lips pressed tightly together. Ten minutes later there was a soft click at the door and Buddy O'Hara, ashen, trembling, reentered the room.

"Yes?" Patrick asked. "Did you forget something?"

"Can I . . . can I talk to you for a minute?"

"Of course," Patrick gestured at the chair. "What is it?"

Buddy walked slowly back to the desk. He pulled the

chair back into place and sat down. "Look, I . . . I got a little hot just now . . . I . . . what I'm trying to say is I want to stay in the program. I *have* to stay in the program," he said, looking directly at Patrick for the first time since he'd come back. "What you said, it doesn't have to be final, does it?"

"No. But you must understand a few things, Mr. O'Hara. I'm here to help you, and I want to keep you in the program if it's at all possible. But I won't be toyed with, or bluffed. I certainly won't be intimidated. I would be sorry to lose you, but don't think you can use that as leverage, because I won't hesitate to cut you if this . . . poor . . . behavior continues. And I'm not going to make this especially easy for you either, because you must learn there are consequences to all actions. Good consequences *and* bad. Unfortunately for you, it's the latter."

"Can I stay?" Buddy asked impatiently.

"I go back to my original subject: your failing grades. You say you have a problem. I want to hear it."

"It's personal."

"I'm aware of that." Patrick sighed. "Mr. O'Hara, I've not gone through life without experiencing personal problems. Some of them quite serious."

Buddy heard the last quiet words and suddenly he was reminded of his Aunt Mai, of what she'd said about Patrick Dain. He looked up quickly, a brief, startled recognition in his eyes.

"I'm waiting," Patrick said.

"Sorry," Buddy said, remembering where he was and why, dismissing his aunt from his mind. "It's . . . look, it sounds stupid. I don't like to make an ass of myself, okay?"

"Mr. O'Hara, *SPIT IT OUT.*"

"Okay, okay. It's about my mother. I'm worried about her," he said, looking down at the floor, hugging his arms around him. "I worry all the time." He looked back at Patrick. "If that makes me sound like a kid, or a mama's boy, okay, but that's what it is. I haven't been able to concentrate for months. Everytime I pick up a textbook or look at a path slide, I think about her. If that makes me sound like a kid, okay."

"On the contrary," Patrick smiled slightly, "I am encouraged to learn you have a heart after all. What is your mother's problem?"

"That's just it, I don't know. She's lost a lot of weight lately. She's pale—she gets these big dark circles under her eyes. Her appetite is bad. She takes a lot of aspirin, so maybe she's in pain. She . . . she works very hard, maybe she's just plain tired. But she has the look of a sick person. I'm beginning to recognize that look and I see it in her."

Patrick leaned forward, crossing his hands on the desk. "Why hasn't she seen a doctor?"

"She promises and promises. She never does it. Or maybe she did, and doesn't want me to know what he said. I worry about that too."

"So you're assuming the worst," Patrick said. "You've been taught better than that. Those are nonspecific symptoms. They could mean something or nothing."

"This isn't a hypothetical case in class, it's my mother I'm talking about. It's not so non-specific. There's a leukemia patient in the wards right now who started out like that. When he first came in there was a little weight loss, a little pallor, bad appetite, headache. I've seen Hodgkins' start like that."

"You're getting way ahead of yourself. And speculation is useless. I'll arrange an appointment in the clinic and I'll do the examination myself. Try not to worry, Mr. O'Hara, things are rarely as serious as they seem. I've yet to meet a student who didn't think he or his wife or parent had every disease in the book. It's easier than you think to make symptoms fit a disease—the worse it is, the easier it is."

Buddy's eyes flashed. "I'm not that stupid."

"It has nothing to do with stupidity. You are all surrounded by illness day in and day out. Every class, every book, every lecture, every video tape, is about illness. Every minute on rounds is about illness. The perfectly natural result is to begin to think you, or people close to you, are ill."

Buddy got up and walked around the room. He wandered over to the side of the office and stared at the watercolors of Cape Cod.

"I don't know why we're talking about this," he said finally. "She won't come in. She'll find an excuse, like she always does. And she doesn't like to be told what to do. She's proud, my mother," Buddy said, looking back at Patrick. "That's where I get it from."

"It's for her good and yours. If she won't do it for the sake of her health, then she will do it for the sake of your tenure here. You can't go around in a fog; we've seen the results of that. You must explain."

Buddy stared at Patrick. "I can't tell her—about what's happening. She thinks . . . well, she thinks . . ." Buddy looked away, leaving the sentence unfinished.

"She thinks you're still her fair-haired boy. Straight A's and honors. I'm sorry," Patrick shook his head, "but she must be told the truth. You're not a boy anymore, you're a man. It's time you started acting like one and take the responsibility."

"Look, you don't know her—what this would do to her. Not because she's ever pushed me, but because *I've* made her expect the best."

"I'm a parent, and parents are not so very different. We would prefer the truth, whatever it is."

"She won't come in."

"She must. If you wish to remain here. And if you are really concerned about her health, you will put your pride aside and make her come in."

"This isn't fifth grade, you know. I mess up and the teacher sends a note home to mama."

"I don't know what my predecessor did, but I'm in charge now and I make the rules. You have no choice. She comes in or you go out. Now come back here and sit down," Patrick ordered and Buddy complied. Patrick opened a folder and glanced at the top page. "I see several numbers for Mrs. O'Hara. I take it two are business numbers?"

"Yeah," Buddy pouted.

"She has a busy schedule then. When is she free?"

"She has a couple of evenings off, and Saturday afternoons."

"I can see her tomorrow at 4 or . . . next week at 2."

"If you give her a choice she'll wiggle out of it."

"Tomorrow at 4," Patrick nodded, writing her name in his book.

"*What* am I going to tell her?"

"The truth," Patrick said quietly. He looked at Buddy and then laughed softly. "Children grow up a little and immediately decide their parents must be treated like delicate old fools a step away from the home. I assure you we're capable of withstanding a nasty shock now and then." Buddy's expression was unchanged and Patrick smiled. "It's not so terrible. You haven't murdered anyone, you haven't run off with the minister's wife. Square your shoulders, take a deep breath, and tell her the truth."

"Man, she's not going to like it one bit. I don't even have off tonight. I'm going to tell her all this on the *phone?*"

"You're on duty where?" Patrick asked, looking at his chart.

"Fourth floor. It's my last night, I go on wards tomorrow morning. But I'm also on for the E.R. in case they get busy."

"I can't do anything about that, I'm sorry. The E.R. is short. Telephone her on one of your breaks and do the best you can. I will explain it more fully tomorrow."

"Oh, brother."

"That's all, Mr. O'Hara."

"Look, could I . . . could I be there?"

"You know better than that. Now go along, I have problems aside from you."

Buddy stood up. He looked at Patrick, about to speak, and then changed his mind. He walked slowly to the door, his hands deep in his pockets, his broad shoulders hunched forward.

"I *hate* this," he said at the door.

"Mr. O'Hara?"

"Yeah?"

"Don't misunderstand—this is a reprieve, not a pardon. I'll be expecting drastic improvement."

"Yeah," Buddy said, pushing his way through the door.

Patrick leaned back and smiled broadly; this round had been his. The intercom buzzed and he bent to it.

"Yes, Grace?"

"Can I put your calls through now?"

"Anything urgent?"

"No, but they're piling up."

"Give me a couple of minutes, will you?"

"Okay."

The side door opened and David entered the room. "I tried to listen at the door, but the damned thing's so thick I could only hear when there was shouting. Tell me."

"There may be hope for him."

"He's a con artist, you know. That's a polite way of putting it."

"He's been worried about his mother. He thinks she's ill."

"That's the problem? Is she?"

"I don't know. I'm seeing her at the clinic tomorrow. It's probably student-syndrome. They see too much illness all at once."

The intercom buzzed again and Patrick reached to answer it.

"Yes, Grace?"

"You better take this one. It's something about an intern and Larrimer Wing. There's all kinds of screaming and carrying on up there."

"Thanks," Patrick said, taking up the telephone. "Dr. Dain here . . . yes . . . I see . . . yes, all right . . . all right, I'll be right there."

"What is it?" David asked.

Patrick slipped into his white jacket. "Something about an intern and J. J. Caldwel."

"I'll go with you."

Patrick stopped, looking at David. "Oh?"

David smiled. "I didn't mean . . . go ahead, I won't go clucking over your shoulder. It's all yours."

Patrick smiled, giving David a small salute as he hurried from the office.

10

Patrick got off the elevator at Larrimer Wing and hurried to the nurse's station. Several nurses and doctors and two of the Caldwel guards were gathered there, shouting, gesturing angrily. Some of the Larrimer patients stood in their doorways watching the unusual scene and Patrick directed them back into their rooms before joining the argument.

"What is this all about?" he demanded, raising his voice to be heard above the noise. "Get back now," he ordered, moving the participants away from each other, "and tell me what this is all about."

They all began to speak at once and Patrick held up a hand for silence. "Who is the floor doctor in charge?"

"I am," a tall, thin resident spoke. "I'm Dr. Parker and it was all a mistake. An honest mistake, that's all."

"Suppose you tell me about it. Quietly."

"Dr. Waverly tried to get a blood sample from Mr. Caldwel and—"

"Dr. Parker, Dr. Waverly," Patrick interrupted, "come with me. May I see you, too?" he asked the guards. "The rest of you go back to work."

Patrick led the four men away from the desk to a corner.

"I remind you this is a hospital," he said, glancing at each of them. "Now, quietly, start from the beginning. Dr. Parker?"

"There was an order for a CBC on Waverly's work sheet. He's been on vacation, he didn't know about the—setup in Mr. Caldwel's suite. The guards were inside, there was no one at the door. Waverly walked inside. They ordered him out and he protested. That's all of it, Dr. Dain."

"It was your responsibility to inform Dr. Waverly of the Caldwel arrangements. I'll talk to you later; you may leave. Dr. Waverly, do you have anything to add?"

"No, sir."

"I do," the taller of the guards said. "This man came in waving a hypodermic around. Mr. Caldwel's doctor was out of the room at the time, so we asked this man to leave. He refused, trying to force his way into Mr. Caldwel. We restrained him, but Mr. Caldwel is very upset."

"*He's* upset?" Dr. Waverly asked. "You gorillas practically broke my arm and *he's* upset?"

"That's enough," Patrick warned, turning to the two guards. "I'm sorry for the disturbance. This is a large hospital and communication isn't always perfect. Even so, I will not have members of the staff pushed around."

"I think you better tell that to Mr. Caldwel."

"If you wish. Dr. Waverly, wait for me here. Gentlemen." Patrick said, following them down the corridor.

Patrick entered the suite and a short, gray-haired man stood up.

"This is the kid's boss," one of the guards explained.

"I'm Patrick Dain," he said, extending his hand.

"Peter Brent," the gray-haired man replied. "Mr. Caldwel's physician. This is all very regrettable, Doctor. Mr. Caldwel is very upset."

"Dr. Waverly is upset too. He was only trying to do his job, he meant no harm."

"Would you have a word with Mr. Caldwel?" Dr. Brent asked.

Patrick was shown into J.J. Caldwel's room. It was a spacious corner room, done in soft tans and browns, the draperies closed against the daylight.

"This is Dr. Dain, sir," Dr. Brent explained. "He is the young man's superior."

J.J. Caldwel stared at Patrick for a moment and then waved Peter Brent out of the room.

"Very disturbing, very disturbing," he said in a low, tired monotone.

"I apologize for the trouble. It wasn't intentional," Patrick said, looking closely at J.J. Caldwel.

He was a handsome, well-built man with pale eyes and a ruddy complexion. He was known to be in his early forties though his hair was heavily streaked with gray and the area around his eyes was deeply lined.

"Everybody should understand the rules."

"I will talk with the young man. He was overzealous, perhaps, but so were your—associates. Mr. Caldwel, I won't have the staff of this hospital pushed around."

J.J. Caldwel looked at Patrick with some interest. "Sit down," he said. "I know your father. He handles my anti-trust work when it goes to the Supreme Court. You remind me of him." He looked away. "My men were doing their jobs. I hired them away from Secret Service. All of them. They are well trained."

"Perhaps over-trained," Patrick smiled slightly. "Mr. Caldwel," he said, sitting down, "the staff will be reminded of your security arrangements, but you'd do yourself a favor to relax. You're safe here."

"Am I?" he gazed at Patrick. "Call me John. The name is John James Caldwel. I have always been called John. I prefer it. It was the press that started calling me J.J. Anything to make me sound like a damn fool. The bodyguards, the alarms, they make a lot of that, too," he said, his dark, tired eyes staring straight ahead. "I was kidnapped when I was fourteen. My father paid the ransom. Two million dollars. Even then they left me out in the damn woods. No food, no water. It was three days before I was found. Did you know that story?"

"I'm sorry, I didn't."

"I was twenty-seven when I came into my father's money. He could have left it to my brother. He left it to me. It's increased ten-fold since then. So have the threats. Everybody writes to me asking for money. When they don't get it they write back. Threatening to kill me. They send letters. They call people in my companies. There were three kidnapping attempts in the last five years. Last one almost succeeded. Did you know that story?"

Patrick shook his head, saying nothing. Kidnapping—the very word chilled him for whenever the Dain name had appeared in the newspapers he'd worried that much more about Tony.

"Crackpots. But don't underestimate them. I live behind gates. My men carry guns. Can't walk on my property for all the guard dogs roaming around. I would give it all away. All of it. Keep enough to live on, give the rest away. Lord knows my brother's been trying to get his hands on it for fifteen years. But no one would believe it. I would still be fair game." John Caldwel looked at Patrick. "The average man in the street would say 'I should have such problems.' The average man in the street would be wrong."

Harsh color began to rise in his face and Patrick stood, leaning over him. He took his wrist, timing his pulse, and then took his stethoscope from his pocket, listening to his heart.

"Please try to relax, Mr. Caldwel. Those are terrible worries, I know. But you musn't dwell on them so. You're making yourself sick."

"That is what everybody is hoping for. Call me John.

I prefer it."

"You've had a difficult morning. I'll talk to Dr. Brent about a mild sedative."

"I like to keep a clear head."

"A mild sedative. Now please, John, try to relax."

Patrick left the room, conferring briefly with Dr. Brent on his way out. He walked into the corridor, his mind on John Caldwel, for he'd seen an unhappiness, an unhappiness bordering on despair, in his eyes.

He walked toward Dr. Waverly. The young man was pacing around, his head bent; he jumped when Patrick tapped him on the shoulder.

"It wasn't my fault," Dr. Waverly said, wheeling around.

"No, it wasn't. But when you were asked to leave you should have gone to Dr. Parker for further instructions. When an intern has any question he goes to a senior man for instructions. Is that clear?"

"Yes, Dr. Dain."

"Good, because I will not have staff arguing with patients. Is *that* clear?"

"Yes, sir."

"Very well, go along now." The young man turned to go but Patrick called him back, "Dr. Waverly?"

"Sir?"

"The new rule around here is neatness. Get a haircut. Collar length, no longer. And have those sideburns trimmed."

"Dr. Dain, I feel—"

"I don't want to hear about your constitutional rights, Doctor. Get a haircut."

"Yes, sir," he said curtly, walking away without another word.

Patrick smiled, watching the young man walk off. After a moment he turned, headed toward the elevators but then changed his mind, going instead to the solarium. He was tired; he wanted a few minutes of quiet before he returned to his office.

Patrick selected a chair facing one of the huge windows and sat down.

"Hello there," a bright, female voice called to him.

Patrick looked around. "Hello, Miss Parrish," he said, standing.

She was curled up on a couch, a tiny portable television set on the table before her.

"How are you this morning?" he asked.

"Fine, thank you. Dr. Venable was in and he thoroughly approved."

"I'm glad," Patrick said, sitting down. "It's boring being in a hospital, isn't it?"

"Not always," she laughed. "I heard some of the excitement before. Brought a little life to the place."

"An over-anxious intern and an over-anxious patient. It happens. I hope you weren't disturbed."

"I loved it. I was sure somebody was going to punch somebody in the nose. You broke it up just when it was getting interesting. Caldwel's people?"

"Caldwel?"

"You hear things in a hospital, Dr. Dain. I heard John Caldwel was here."

"No comment," he smiled at her.

She looked fresh and lovely in a peach colored gown and robe, her eyes twinkling in amusement. He noticed again how clear and perfect her skin was, a few light freckles scattered across the bridge of her nose.

"Why does such a pretty, happy, woman have an ulcer, Miss Parrish?" he asked.

"Make it Gail. Why? I don't know," she shook her head, her short dark hair rising and falling about her head. "Mom always said I was high-strung. She said I got it from my Aunt Lucy, who was a spinster lady and fainted a lot."

"Spinsterhood can't possibly be your problem."

"Is that a compliment? Thank you. No, it's not my problem, and I don't faint. But I probably am high-strung. And this is a high-strung town . . ." she said slowly, "about as different from my home town as it can be."

"Where is home?"

"Indiana. Beulah, Indiana. A small, picture-postcard town. Dad has a small insurance agency. Mom makes chicken and dumplings every Sunday. My sister has four kids and lives near a place called Miller's Pond, where everybody ice skates in winter. The big trip each year is the State Fair, the big holiday is Fourth of July," Gail finished, a faraway look in her eyes.

"I didn't think there were places like that left. Why would anyone leave a place like that?"

"You mean why did I leave? Well, it's hard to explain. It wasn't enough. I don't think it was enough for my Aunt Lucy either," she chuckled, "and as you have already heard, she fainted a lot."

"You don't faint, but you get holes in your stomach. What are you going to do about it?"

She laughed. "I am going to obey Dr. Venable. I am going to give up french fries. I am going to take a blue pill every day. I have a whole list of things; you don't want to hear it all."

"You control an ulcer through diet and medication. You don't cure it that way."

Gail looked quickly at him. "Lecture number two thousand and twelve. I know what you're going to say. I've heard it before. I don't want to hear it again."

"Why not?"

"Psychiatry's not for me. Let's say it's not in the tradition of Beulah, Indiana. In Beulah you don't run to a shrink everytime some little thing goes out of kilter."

135

"You left your home town."

"I left it but that doesn't mean it left me."

Gail's tone was growing increasingly sharp and Patrick looked closely at her. "A chronic ulcer isn't some little thing. Something's been eating at you for a lot of years. You may know what it is, you may not, but either way psychiatry has its place."

"I know about psychiatrists. They want to force everybody into nice, neat, little molds. If you don't fit in then you're crazy. Thanks but no thanks. There are a lot of different ways to live. Some shrink's idea of how to live isn't the only way."

"That's a very mysterious answer."

"It means I like my life just fine, just the way it is."

"Psychiatry needn't change that. Gail, somewhere there is conflict. Psychiatry can help you deal with that conflict."

"I don't need anyone pouring through my life. Passing judgement, picking out what's right, what's wrong. I *won't do it*."

Gail heard the hard edge in her voice; she saw the startled expression on Patrick's face and she smiled quickly.

"It's a pretty day, and I feel well, and let's not get all gloomy and serious. It's the french fries. It's no more complicated than that."

"That defense would never hold up in court."

"I'm not in court," she said, staring at him.

Patrick heard the beeping of his page. "Excuse me," he said, standing up, going to the telephone.

Gail watched as he took his call, glancing away when he returned.

"Where were we?" he asked, sitting down.

"I was being nasty. I didn't mean to be. I get this all the time—see a shrink, see a shrink. It gets on my nerves."

"It's only that an ulcer can be a serious thing. Patients don't always understand that. It makes a doctor's job difficult."

"I know that. I've promised to take care of myself, isn't that enough?"

"Your condition is chronic. A condition such as that is caused by some conflict. It will not magically go away."

"Can we change the subject?"

"It bothers you that much?"

"That much."

"All right," Patrick smiled. "For now."

"You mean I can look forward to another of these chats?" she laughed.

"I don't understand why you refuse to help yourself."

"I don't."

"Gail, of course you do. Perhaps you understand it. I don't."

Gail stared at him for a long moment. "Maybe you will, one of these days."

"Ah, more mystery. What does that mean?"

"No more questions," she said lightly. "You've had your limit for the day."

"So much for my powers of persuasion."

"Who put you up to this? Dr. Murdock?"

"It was my own idea."

"With a little help from Dr. Murdock?"

"A little. But our thinking is similar on most things."

"Really? You seem like different types."

"We are," Patrick smiled, "except in our thinking."

Patrick's page sounded again and he stood up. "I'd better be going. I know you will gladly excuse me," he laughed.

"I enjoyed the company. Come talk to me again when you have more time."

"I will. I'll come and badger you."

"No badgering allowed. Nice, soothing conversation. Okay?"

"Okay," he called over his shoulder. "I'll find a soothing way to badger you," he smiled, waving, hurrying through the door.

Gail Parrish stared at the closed door for a time, an odd expression on her face. She glanced away, looking at the television set. She switched it off impatiently, looking back to the door. Her eyes were cold. They were angry.

"Damn," she said. "Damn, damn, damn."

11

Ann O'Hara stepped off the Madison Avenue bus into the cool Saturday afternoon sunshine. Dressed in a plain brown blouse and skirt and a plain, tan raincoat, she turned west, walking in long strides. Her normally calm expression was clouded with a deep irritation, for she couldn't remember the last time she'd been so angry.

Unprepared as she'd been for Buddy's phone call—for the news of his failing grades—she'd been even more unprepared for the news that he'd been lying to her all along. She'd been hurt and then she'd been angry—angrier still to have been *ordered* to Rhinelander Pavillion by Patrick Dain. She would have quite a lot to say to him, she thought furiously, her pretty mouth set in resolution. She would have quite a lot to say to both Patrick Dain *and* Buddy. How dare they treat her that way, her mind ran on, like some child who had to be told what was best for her.

Ann turned into another street and glared at the great gray stone facade of Rhinelander Pavillion. She located the clinic entrance and stood looking at it for a moment before going inside. It was crowded, she saw, but it looked comfortable, with soft beige walls and lots of clean, brightly colored chairs. She spotted the reception area ahead and walked briskly to it, her back straight, her head high.

"Excuse me?" she said to one of the nurses at the desk.

"Yes?"

"I'm Mrs. O'Hara. Mrs. Ann O'Hara."

"Yes?"

"I have an appointment with Dr. Dain. For four o'clock. I'm sorry, I'm a little early."

"Four o'clock?" the nurse asked, running a pencil down a long list of names. "What's the name again?"

"O'Hara. Ann O'Hara. For Dr. Dain."

"Yes, yes, I have it. You're early."

"Yes, I know, I—"

"First time here?"

"Yes, I—"

"Fill this out," the nurse said, handing her a printed form attached to a clipboard, a pencil dangling from a piece of string at the side. "Answer all questions and write *clearly*. You can wait in there, you'll be called when the doctor is ready for you."

"Thank you," Ann said.

She took the questionnaire and walked into the waiting room. She found an empty chair in a corner and sat down, staring down at the form. She read it over once and then took the pencil in hand, writing as clearly as she could. Five minutes later it was completed and she checked it carefully to be sure all the blanks had been filled. She set the clipboard on her lap and glanced around.

There were about fifteen people waiting, most of them women, many of them older women. They were dressed in cheap cotton dresses and pantsuits, though some of the younger women wore bright, splashy colors and prints with scarves and turbans and many necklaces. The few children in the room were uniformly dressed in jeans and tee shirts and played quietly at their mothers' feet. The few men in the room wore slacks and neat white shirts; they all wore ties and some wore old felt hats.

Ann gazed from face to face. Whether the faces were white or black or brown, there was no mistaking the used weary look of their poverty. She felt a part of them, for she remembered those earlier times when she and her children had nothing, living on pasta and potato stews, always weeks behind in the rent; even now it was a struggle, every extra penny spent grudgingly, luxuries unknown to them. Hope had sustained her, she thought to herself, but even that had its limits. All the dark nights of worry, of tears, had left its mark on her, the same mark she saw reflected in all the faces around her.

She sighed softly and then smiled, watching a small black girl draw misshapen animals on a huge blackboard chained to the wall. After a while she glanced away, reading a large printed sign which forbade eating or drinking or defacing clinic property.

A nurse came to the edge of the doorway and looked around the room. "Mr. Williams?" she called out. "This way please," she said as a tall, bony man folded his newspaper and followed her out.

With a jolt, Ann remembered why she was at the clinic and she felt her anger rise again. Silently, she repeated all she would have to say to Patrick Dain. She was impatient to have it over with and when her name was finally called she rose quickly, rushing out of the waiting room. The nurse took the clipboard from her and tore off the top sheet.

"Give this to the doctor," she said, walking Ann past a row of closed doors. "This is it, go right in," she said and Ann turned to see a door with a hastily written sign, Dr. P. Dain.

"Go on, Dr. Dain doesn't have all day," the nurse

added tersely before walking away.

Ann knocked once and then went inside. There was a small outer room with a desk and two chairs. She could see beyond to a larger room, a long examination table covered with paper, the overhead lights bright and cold.

"I'll be with you in just a moment, Mrs. O'Hara," a deep, quiet voice called to her. "It is Mrs. O'Hara, isn't it?"

"Yes it is."

"Make yourself comfortable — as comfortable as you can in that terrible chair."

Ann sat down, putting her handbag beside her on the floor. She heard the sound of water splashing and then the sound of paper crumpling and she looked expectantly at the door. "Don't beat around the bush," she told herself, "tell him what you think in no uncertain terms."

"Good afternoon, Mrs. O'Hara," Patrick smiled, coming into the room. "I apologize for insisting you come in. My reasons were good ones, I assure you."

Patrick sat down. He took the form from her and turned away, reading it over.

Ann said nothing, staring at him, for she had not been prepared for such a man. She'd imagined an older man, cold, stuffy, indistinguishable from those bland men she'd occasionally seen in the society pages. But this man was no older than she was, she thought in surprise, and he was handsome. She thought he was probably the handsomest man she'd ever seen.

Patrick put the form aside and looked at her. "I don't know how much Buddy has explained to you," he began quietly.

"He told me he was in trouble with his grades. Because of me, his worry about me. He told me I had to come today," Ann said, most of her anger already gone, dissipating with her first look at Patrick Dain.

"Did he tell you he failed his lab exams?"

"Failed?" her hand flew to her throat. "He told me he'd been doing badly, that he was in trouble, but he didn't say anything about failing."

Patrick smiled. "I rather imagined he was going to leave the juicy parts to me."

"Buddy's never failed anything in his life."

"He's been a brilliant student up to this term, Mrs. O'Hara. But this term everything seemed to come apart. It happens that way sometimes. When the going gets heavy, as it can at this stage of his training. The truth is he's on the verge of being dismissed from the program."

"No!" she clasped her hands tightly together.

"I think—I hope—it need not come to that," Patrick said gently. "I had a long talk with him. Perhaps," he laughed, "a long *shout* is more like it. I gather it's not the work but his concentration that is giving him trouble. On the strength of his past records, I'm inclined to believe him."

"I'm the problem?"

"He is genuinely worried about you. And that is not an altogether uncommon thing in medical school. The students are surrounded by sickness. It can begin to seem as if everyone in the world is sick. Usually a student will decide he, himself, is ill. Sometimes he decides it is someone close to him. Do you follow me?"

"Yes, Dr. Dain, go on," Ann said intently.

"Buddy has made that conclusion about you. He has also suggested that it's none of my business," he smiled, "but his work *is* my business. It seems to me the only sensible way to clear up his class problems is to clear up his personal problems. And as soon as possible, because I can't carry him for too long. That was the reason for the hurry, and for what must have seemed like inexcusable rudeness."

Ann tried to formulate her thoughts. She was astonished that Buddy could have been brooding for so long without her noticing it; she was grateful for the thoughtful way in which Patrick Dain had explained the problem.

"I was angry, at first," she said, "but I understand now. I appreciate your trying to help Buddy. He's not easy."

Patrick laughed. "World War Two was easier. Mrs. O'Hara, I want to talk further about Buddy, but I would like to get this problem out of the way. I can't compel you to have an examination, but I hope you will agree. It will ease Buddy's mind and it's a good thing to do for yourself. I am an excellent diagnostician," he smiled. "References on demand."

Ann smiled back. She liked him, his easy, comfortable manner. "I'm not sick."

"Buddy mentioned your fatigue."

"I'm tired, yes. I work hard. I have a goal and I work for it."

Patrick saw the pride, the spirit, in her steady blue eyes. He watched her a moment longer and then looked back at his folder.

"He mentioned a weight loss."

"A dollar only goes so far, Doctor. There've been a few extra expenses lately. The meatloaf gets a little smaller and with Buddy's schedule he needs it more than I do."

"I see. In other words you really haven't been taking care of yourself."

"I'm stronger than I look."

"Let's be sure. When's the last time you had a checkup?"

She shrugged. "My people came from Ireland. There's a home remedy for everything."

"Trying to put me out of business?"

"I never get sick. I'm healthy as a horse," she smiled.

"Let's be sure. For Buddy's sake, if not your own."

"Well," she sighed, "I have Blue Cross, I guess it's all right."

"We'll talk about that later."

"I pay my way, Dr. Dain."

"This is a free clinic. I can't change the rules. Not even for an O'Hara," he grinned. "In any case, your son is a student here, so you're entitled to medical care. Are you going to be as obstinate as your son?"

"No one's as obstinate as Buddy," Ann said and then laughed. "Tell me what to do."

"You may undress in there," Patrick nodded to the examination room. "There are robes on the first shelf."

"Thank you, Dr. Dain."

Ann took her purse and walked into the examination room, Patrick watching as she went. She was the kind of woman he admired. Looking at her he'd seen that she had not had an easy time; she was alone, responsible for two children, obviously a woman who worked hard and took little for herself. He'd seen the softness in her eyes and he'd seen the fine, sure spirit that in Buddy was only arrogance. She was a strong woman, he thought, practical, though there were no hard, mean edges about her. He'd liked her honesty, her openness.

"Ready, Dr. Dain," she called and Patrick rose.

"Try to relax, this won't take too long," he said, going to the table.

Patrick noticed that she'd folded her clothing into a neat square, pile and he looked at it, remembering how Catherine had strewn her things about, knowing her maid would attend to them. It was unfair, he thought suddenly; the wrong people have too much.

"Any particular complaints?" he asked, wrapping a

blood pressure cuff around her arm.

"I come from peasant stock. We scare the germs away."

Patrick wrapped the cuff on her other arm. "What do you do?"

"I work for the phone company. I have a part-time job a few evenings a week. In a women's shop near home."

"Two jobs?"

"A son in medical school, a daughter in college. We have loans, scholarship help, but it's not enough."

Patrick put the cuff aside and brought his stethoscope to her chest. "The children could work," he said after a while.

"Jill has a little job. But she's a young girl, I want her to have the things young girls need. Buddy wants to work, but the dean told me he doesn't recommend it."

"That's not a hard and fast rule. When he gets his grades in shape—"

"I want my children to have the best chance," she interrupted in a firm, clear, voice. "If it were your son would you want him to study *and* work?"

Patrick smiled. "No, I suppose I wouldn't. You're pretty scrappy, I see where Buddy gets it from."

He continued the rest of the examination in silence. He checked her carefully, taking his time until he was satisfied. He made frequent notations in her file, walking back and forth between the table and a small desk in a corner of the room. He weighed her, asking a few quick questions for her file, and then drew blood, carefully marking the vial.

"Phase one is over. It wasn't so bad, was it?"

"Phase one?" Ann asked.

Patrick nodded. "I scheduled you for an EKG, a chest X-ray and GYN."

"All that?"

"Why do things half-way? Get dressed now, I'll see you outside."

Patrick returned to the outer office and sat at the desk. He bent over her file, writing rapidly in his large, flowing script, finishing just as she came into the room.

"Do I pass?"

"Your pressure's a little low, nothing to worry about. As for the rest, we'll wait for the tests to come back. I think we'll find you're rundown, anemic, perhaps. We'll see."

Ann hesitated for a moment and then spoke. "About Buddy."

Patrick leaned back, toying absently with a pencil. "Well, I'd like to talk about him. There are some things I'd like to know. Things which would help me to help him." He looked at his watch. "You have an hour or so down here and I have some things to see to in my office. Why don't we talk over a drink when we're finished?"

"A drink?"

"We might as well be comfortable. The dining room is on the twelfth floor. Go right up when you're finished. I'll be waiting."

"I . . . couldn't trouble you that way. It's Saturday, you must have better things . . . " she broke off, coloring slightly. "I mean I don't want to put you out."

"Not at all. Please say yes."

"If you're—sure."

"I'm sure. All settled?"

She nodded. "Thank you."

"I'll take you to the nurse," Patrick said, standing.

They walked into the corridor and he took her arm, guiding her to the desk.

"Claire, this is Mrs. O'Hara. Take good care of her. Don't leave her sitting in a corner somewhere."

"Thank you, Dr. Dain," Ann said, "for everything."

"Twelfth floor," Patrick said, walking off.

He turned into the long corridor connecting the clinic with the main hospital. He nodded to a couple of passing residents but his mind was on Ann O'Hara; he'd liked her, he had the odd feeling he'd known her a long time.

A woman's voice called to him and he turned. "Hello, Lola."

"I've been looking for you."

"Here I am. What may I do for you?"

She looked at him. "You sound chipper today."

"I'm enjoying my work."

"That's what I wanted to talk to you about. You shouldn't have added a patient to the clinic rolls without checking with me first. It's a tight operation, we're jammed as it is. This throws everything out of whack."

"Where was I supposed to examine her?"

"How do I know? Who is she anyway?"

"Buddy O'Hara's mother. It's a long story, but she needed an examination and I gave it to her. She's finishing the rest of the tests now. Don't worry," he smiled, "I saw my scheduled patients first."

"It's not that," Lola said, her hands waving in the air. "We're tightly budgeted. Even one extra patient puts bumps in the budget. We work from a waiting list, Patrick. When a patient drops out of the clinic we take an applicant from the list. Mrs. O'Hara probably doesn't even qualify for the clinic."

"She qualifies for next-of-kin care." Patrick said evenly. "Was I supposed to examine her on my office couch?"

"You should have let me know. I'm really very upset with you, Patrick."

He laughed. "Tell me, are you the Dr. Shay who asked me for a favor a few days ago?"

A slow smile spread across her face. 'Yes," she grinned.

"And tell me, *how* upset are you with me?"

"You're learning how to play the game."

"It's a stupid game when Larrimer Wing has fresh flowers all over the place but one extra clinic patient strains the budget."

"Exactly. Wait until you see the wards."

"I plan to do that Monday. And I think I may have an idea about Dr. Potter. I'll explain another time, I have to get going."

"I'll go along with you," she said as they headed for the elevators. "I wanted to see David. Is he upstairs?"

"He was." Patrick was quiet for a moment, thinking about something. "Lola, you used to see him away from the hospital. If it's none of my business say so, but do you still?"

"No. I don't know why. He just stopped asking," Lola said quietly, looking away. They entered the elevator and she looked at Patrick. "He's had something on his mind, I don't know what. I haven't pressed him. Have you?"

"David's a cagey fellow. If there's something to tell me, he'll tell me, but in his own time."

"Well, you have that in common. If there . . . *is* something — with David — will you let me know?"

They walked into the corridor. Patrick smiled at her. "Of course. It's probably nothing at all. I've had so many problems thrown at me in the past week I'm beginning to see problems everywhere."

"Get below the surface and you'll see there *are* problems everywhere."

The dining room at Rhinelander Pavillion was small and pretty, with soft lighting and pale blue table linen and one long, spectacular view of the city. Patrick took a table by the window and ordered a carafe of white wine. He tasted the wine and then turned to his notebook, checking it page by page, looking at the door every few minutes.

Patrick had been waiting fifteen minutes when he saw Ann O'Hara standing hesitantly at the entrance. He waved and then stood up as she came to the table.

"I'm not dressed for this place," Ann said, fingering the collar of her blouse.

"Nonsense. It's only a hospital dining room and you'd look fine anywhere," he said, surprised at the warmth in his voice. "Some wine or would you like something else?"

"Wine, thank you."

He filled her glass. "Did you finish everything?"

"I've never been so thoroughly examined in my life. I hope it does some good."

"To Buddy's better grades," Patrick said, lifting his glass.

"Yes," she nodded, sipping the wine.

"Tell me about Buddy. Why is he angry all the time?"

Ann looked uncomfortable for a moment. She sat up very straight in her chair and looked directly at Patrick. "I know my son, Dr. Dain. I know he's no prize sometimes. But underneath that hard shell he's a different person. He's sensitive. He can be kind, and good."

"I've seen some of that. His concern for you, for example. It's the hard shell I want to know about."

Ann looked down at the table, her hands playing with the stem of her glass. "He wasn't always like that. As a child—no, what I mean to say is that when his father left us, he started building defenses. Those defenses have built and built through the years. Anger is one of them."

"It says in Buddy's records that his father is deceased."

"He died four years ago but he left us long before that. He went out one day and never came back. Buddy loved him very much, maybe too much, I don't know. He never understood, never got over it. He became suspicious, angry. There was never a phone call, never a card or anything from his father. For months he waited for the mailman every morning. He jumped when the phone rang. One day I guess he realized he was never going to hear from his father and he became a different child."

"I'm sorry," Patrick said. "Did you ever try to find Mr. O'Hara?"

Ann looked sharply at Patrick. "I went to the police. Not because I wanted him back, but because he had an obligation to the children. They listed him as a missing person and then told me how many married men disappear every year. The officer told me he'd thought about disappearing himself. It was nothing to him. a big joke! A statistic! So we were on our own. Like thousands of other people, but Buddy never accepted that."

"I really am sorry, Mrs. O'Hara. I hope you understand it's not my intention to pry, or to open old wounds."

"You're the first person who's taken enough interest in Buddy to ask about him. I'm grateful. I get angry but it's because I know that all these years later Buddy is still hurting and I can't help him."

"Does he talk about it?"

"Never. He hasn't mentioned his father's name in years. If anyone else does, he leaves the room. I know what you're saying—it would help him to talk about it. He won't, I've tried."

Patrick stared thoughtfully at Ann O'Hara. He'd felt

her compassion, her sense of helplessness, yet these were accompanied by a high, fiery spirit, a spirit which would not be dimmed, and he found himself wondering why any man would leave a woman like that.

"What did you do?" he asked.

"Life goes on, Doctor. I went to work and the children went to school."

"And Buddy decided he had to be the best in whatever he did?"

Ann nodded, her blond hair falling softly about her shoulders. "He was, too. He studied all the time. After a while it came naturally to him. He was always at the top of his class. He was skipped twice."

"Forgive me, but he's an arrogant young man."

"Another defense," Ann said firmly.

"Possibly. The day I met him I thought I detected some insecurities."

"Oh, yes. About everything, even girls. He dates, but as soon as it starts to get serious he breaks it off. Like he's afraid he's going to do to someone what his father did to us. His need to be the best is part of that, too. His father never amounted to much, it wasn't in his nature. Buddy is scared of failure. He's confused, Dr. Dain, he doesn't mean half the things he says or does. I *hope* you'll remember that," Ann said urgently.

"He's young, he has time."

"No, the years go very quickly," she shook her head. "It's important that he be understood now, helped now."

"I intend to try. He's very stubborn."

"He comes from a stubborn family," Ann smiled and her blue eyes lit up.

"I see that," Patrick smiled back. "And a proud one. Unfortunately, in Buddy the pride often turns into contempt. Especially for our Larrimer Wing patients. It's a sticky situation."

Ann was silent. She looked off, considering something and then slowly returned her gaze to Patrick.

"Dr. Dain," she began, "I had a high school education—at a time when high schools really taught something. I also took a few college courses at night. But when I began looking for work, I couldn't really do anything. I had some learning but no training. I took what jobs I could get and was grateful for them. For several years the jobs were housework. I was a cleaning woman, a maid, in private homes. Wealthy homes. I'm not ashamed of it, I never was. But Buddy was. He asked me never to tell anybody and I agreed. I'm telling you because it might help you to understand why he's the way he is. If you have the time?"

"Of course," Patrick said. "Please."

"Buddy hated it. He told his friends I was a secretary. Right or wrong, I went along with it. It came to a head on my last job. My employer was Mrs. Miles Crowder, the Crowder Spice family. She was a kind woman," Ann paused, taking a deep breath.

Patrick made no comment though he knew Eve Crowder; she had been a friend of Catherine's and she was in no way a kind woman, he thought to himself.

"She was particular," Ann continued. "The hours were long, but she was thoughtful. When there was a party or a dinner there was always a lot of food left over. She had her cook make up packages for me. I accepted them. I didn't think it was charity. The food would have been thrown out anyway, and we needed it. Mrs. Crowder understood that."

Patrick nodded, his expression unchanged, though he was irritated. He remembered Eve Crowder, remembered the condescending little stories she told about her servants, referring to them as her "waifs."

"Buddy was furious. He thought it was insulting, demeaning. He hated her. And then he started hating all the people like her. People with money. I was taking typing and steno courses at night and I finally got my job with the phone company, but Buddy's never forgotten those days."

"Young people are often very foolish," Patrick said. "But you have answered my question. His tender male ego was involved."

"He ate the food, by the way," Ann said with a mischievous smile.

Patrick liked her smile. It was bright and natural, nothing like the practiced expressions of the women he'd known.

"Well," he said, "I have a good idea of Buddy's problems now. If he can keep his temper—and I can keep mine—" he smiled, "we may make some progress."

"Thank you for listening. For being interested. No one ever was before."

"Buddy has extraordinary medical potential, Mrs. O'Hara. I'm going to keep the pressure up. He may not like it, but he'll be given every opportunity." Patrick sat back, sipping his wine. "Tell me about your daughter."

"She's the opposite of Buddy. She's a happy person."

"And you? Are you happy in your work?"

"I know everyone hates the phone company," she said, her hand reaching to her throat, "but it saved my life. All our lives. Buddy and I were arguing all the time before I got this job. It couldn't have gone on that way."

Ann looked away, looking questioningly at a woman who'd been staring at her for the past few minutes. Patrick followed her glance and then waved. The woman said something to her companion and then left her table, walking in their direction. Patrick stood up.

"Hello, Julie," he said, "I didn't see you come in. Julie Carlson, Mrs. O'Hara."

Ann smiled and Julie nodded, quickly taking in Ann's cheap clothing, her unevenly cut hair, the thin, dime-store lipstick she wore.

"How do you do, Mrs. O'Hara?" she said. "Are you any relation to Buddy O'Hara?"

"I'm his mother. Do you know Buddy?"

"Everybody knows Buddy," Julie replied smoothly, looking at Patrick. "I was hoping you'd let me know about that meeting."

"I'm sorry, Julie. My schedule—why don't we have lunch next week? I'll tell you my plan."

"I'd like that." Julie glanced back at her table. "I'm with a member of the board, I ought to get back. Call me?"

"I will."

"Mrs. O'Hara," Julie nodded again, gliding away.

Patrick sat down, glancing out the large window at the slowly darkening sky. "Shall we have something to eat, it's getting to be that time."

"Oh, no, I couldn't, Dr. Dain," Ann said, her hand going quickly to her throat. "It's very nice of you but I couldn't."

"Please, can't I convince you? The food's not bad," he smiled.

She shook her head and he saw she was uncomfortable. "All right. Stubborn, you're as bad as your son," he laughed. "I'll see you to the lobby then."

Ann rose and Patrick put some bills on the table. He took Ann's arm as they left the dining room.

Julie Carlson watched them leave, her dark eyebrows arched slightly, her mouth a thin line. She was annoyed, for she'd seen the close attention Patrick had paid to the O'Hara woman. Hanging on every word, she thought contemptuously, smiling all the time. She couldn't understand what a man like that would find so interesting in such a shabby, plain, woman. Whatever it was she didn't like it.

"Is something wrong, Julie?" her companion asked.

"What? Oh, it's nothing, nothing at all. Nothing I can't handle," she said sweetly, her beautiful hazel eyes hard and cold as stone.

12

"Good morning," Patrick said brightly, striding into the outer office, one hand hidden behind his back.

Grace looked up. "Good morning," she said, looking closely at him. "You're pretty happy for a Monday morning."

He brought his hand forward, holding out a bouquet of flowers wrapped in filmy green paper.

"For me? Really? Thank you, Patrick." She tore the paper away, smiling broadly. "They're beautiful," she said, gazing at the bright yellow roses. "What did I do to deserve them? Should my husband be jealous?" she laughed.

"Always. At the very least he should be vigilant."

"I'll tell him you said so. Serve him right for taking me for granted. Patrick, you made my day, maybe my whole week."

"Good." He perched at the edge of her desk, looking down at a small stack of messages. "Mine?" he asked.

"Afraid so," she replied, handing him the slips of paper. "Do you want me to start calling them?"

"After rounds. Is David in yet?"

"He's in your office."

Patrick walked to his door. "Could you bring in some coffee?"

"For a dozen long-stemmed roses I could bring in

eggs Benedict."

"Coffee will do," Patrick waved, going into his office. "What do you do, sleep here?" he asked David.

David continued to write on a long white pad. "The early bird catches the worm."

Patrick hung up his coat and jacket. "I will have to remember that," he said, walking around to the back of his desk. "May I have my desk back?"

David made a last notation and tore off the top sheet, handing it to Patrick. He stood up. "All yours."

"What is this?" Patrick asked, settling himself in his chair.

"It's a list of the members of the board. By order of influence. Stuart wanted you to have it. Don't ask me why, perhaps he's planning a tea."

Patrick shoved the list in his desk drawer, slamming it shut. He heard a knock at the door and glanced up. "Come in."

Grace entered, carrying a carafe of coffee and two cups on a small tray. "Patrick brought me roses," she said to David.

"Did he?"

"*Some* people around here could learn from that example. That's a hint."

"Very subtle, too," David said. "Anything else?"

Grace went to the door. "You have a meeting with orthopedics in ten minutes."

"Thanks." He turned back to Patrick. "Roses? You're in a good mood today."

"It was a good weekend. I had a nice letter from Tony, I got a lot of work done, and I got a lot of sleep. Who can ask for anything more?"

"I told you Rhinelander Pavillion would agree with you."

Patrick signed some waiting correspondence. He read over a memo and initialed it, pushing it toward David.

"There's the clarifying memo you wanted. You'll be getting a copy."

Patrick took up his cup, taking several quick sips of coffee.

"This is fine," David said.

Patrick drained his cup and stood up, going to the closet. He took a fresh white jacket from its hanger, slipped it over his blue-striped shirt.

"I'm going to have a look at the wards," he said, going to the door. "What time is the pediatrics conference?"

"Four o'clock."

"Okay," Patrick said, walking into the outer office. "Good morning, Dr. Potter."

"Good morning, sir," Henry Potter jumped to his feet.

"All ready?"

"Yes, sir," he said, following Patrick into the corridor.

"Let's take the stairs," Patrick said, leading Henry to a steel door at the side of the corridor. They walked up the stairs slowly, Patrick glancing at the young man. "Tell me about the wards."

"They're not much to look at, sir. The rest of the hospital's been remodeled several times, but the wards are old. They're used by our clinic patients. They're almost always full. The food is good, sir," he said, smiling nervously at Patrick. "Central kitchen. Same food as the semi-privates get. The bad part is—do you want to hear the bad part, sir?"

"Yes, I do."

'It's not very well staffed, Dr. Dain. Not enough nurses, sir, and not enough floor doctors for the occupancy rate."

"Why is that?" Patrick asked as they reached the top of the landing.

"Why?"

"Why, sir?"

"It's a management decision, Dr. Dain. Nobody's said so, but I don't think management cares much about the wards," he explained, his face flushing a deep pink. "That's only my opinion, sir."

Patrick pulled the heavy door open and they walked into a pale green corridor.

'We start rounds at ward 1A, sir," Henry said, walking toward a group of doctors and students gathered around a rolling chart holder.

"Good morning, ladies and gentlemen," Patrick said.

He nodded at the resident in charge and then glanced at the others, staring at each young face, stopping for a moment when he came to Buddy O'Hara. Patrick had seen him briefly on Saturday; he'd tried to reassure him, though he guessed it had done little good.

"Anytime you're ready," he said to the resident.

The young people had been looking at Patrick—sizing him up, wondering why he'd come in with Henry Potter—but now they turned their attention to the resident. He rolled the metal holder down the corridor and they followed, Patrick and Henry at a slight distance. They entered the first ward and Patrick stopped, looking around.

It was a large, long, high-ceilinged room. It was sunny but that, Patrick thought, was the only pleasant thing he could say about it. The walls were a pale watery color, not quite blue, not quite green, smudged with fingerprints and scuff marks. There were small, jagged cracks in the plaster of the ceiling and along one wall. The linoleum floor, through freshly washed, had many dark splotches which were beyond cleaning.

There were six beds in the ward, three on each side

of the room. There were plain gray metal cabinets at the side of each bed; at the end of each bed was a pole with a small television set attached at a clumsy angle. The formica bed trays were chipped, and the bed linen was gray with age.

"They are all like this?" Patrick asked.

"Yes, sir."

The group moved to the first bed. The resident took a chart from the rack and flipped it open. "Okay, this is the acidosis," he said, "admitted last night." He nodded at an intern. "Go ahead."

Patrick watched as the intern looked at the chart and then leaned over the patient. "Close the curtain," he said.

"I beg your pardon, Dr. Dain?"

"You are going to examine the patient, are you not? Close the curtain."

The young people exchanged glances, though both Buddy and Henry looked at Patrick.

"Sorry," the intern mumbled, "Trying to save time."

'We're in no hurry," Patrick said coolly.

The young man drew the curtain and bent to the examination, asking questions of the patient as he went along.

"All right," he said after several minutes, "you're better, but we're going to continue the medication and do a couple of tests."

The woman in the bed nodded, pulling her hospital gown back in place. The intern looked at Patrick.

"Undiagnosed diabetic, presenting in acidosis. Blood sugar 350 per 100, hematocrit and BUN elevated."

Patrick looked at a student, looking at his name tag. "Treatment, Mr. Marley?"

"Insulin, replacement of fluids and electrolytes, treatment of shock and precipitating cause."

"Explain the insulin."

"100 units, I.M. stat, then 50 units q.h. until sugar is less than 4 plus."

"Symptoms, Mr. O'Hara," Patrick ordered. He saw Buddy tense and then draw a deep breath. "Go ahead, please."

Buddy described half a dozen symptoms. He spoke haltingly, his eyes averted, his hands tightly grasping the bed railing.

While Buddy spoke, Henry took a step forward and bent over the patient. "How do you feel, Mrs. Barone?" he asked softly.

She smiled gratefully. "Still the pain, but better. Doctor, I will be well?"

"You will be well," he said, patting her hand. "The pain will start to go away, ma'am."

"How long I am being here?"

"Two weeks or so. The time will go quickly, don't worry. You'll rest and you'll feel much better. Better than you've felt in a long time, Mrs. Barone."

Patrick was impressed with Henry's manner. The gentleness and concern were real, and he'd seen how his few words had relaxed the woman. He was annoyed to see the other students and interns shrugging, rolling their eyes at the exchange, impatient to move on to the next bed.

"I want a CBC," the resident instructed a student, "right after rounds. Blood sugar and serums."

The student edged over to Henry. "Do that for me, Potsy? I've got at least an hour in the library."

"You will do it yourself," Patrick said. "Period."

They continued on rounds, Patrick growing more and more disturbed as he saw clear patterns emerging. It was a well-trained group, but at the same time it was a group almost oblivious to the patients themselves, their needs, their fears.

In some instances the examinations had been merely perfunctory, and one or two had been careless. They'd questioned the patients but they'd often asked the wrong questions and the patient histories, he saw, were sloppily done, some incomplete.

Other things disturbed him. The resident in charge was responsible for too many patients to be able to give the students much help. The students, in turn, had formed questionable work habits. One of the students was allowed to dominate, while another paid little attention to what was going on, and Buddy O'Hara tried hard to be ignored. Almost all of them, Patrick noted, had tried to throw their scut work at Henry Potter and he'd acquiesced without a word of protest.

They came out of the last ward and Patrick gathered them in a circle. "I want to see all of you in the doctor's lounge. Dr. Rogers," he said to the resident, "you are excused. The rest of you follow me."

They crowded into the doctor's lounge, Patrick at one end of the room, the students and interns at the other. There was a sudden clatter at the coffee machine and Patrick looked up.

"Never mind the coffee," he said, "This isn't a party."

The young people were quiet then, their eyes on Patrick. He stared back at them for a moment and then spoke.

"I wasn't pleased by what I saw this morning. Indifference. Rudeness. You had better learn—right now—to show some respect for your patients. *All* your patients." Patrick looked from face to face.

"They are entitled to be called by their names, not the names of their illnesses. They are entitled to all the privacy we can give them. They are entitled to be *asked*, not told, how they feel. They are entitled to ask questions and have those questions answered. And surely, ladies and gentlemen, you can find time for a friendly word or two once in a while."

The young people looked away in embarrassment, staring at the floor or the wall, at imaginary spots on their sleeves.

"Your patients are entitled to respect. Anyone who forgets that isn't going to be around here too long. Is that clear?" Patrick demanded. "Furthermore, you had all better learn to take and write a decent history. Those records are the only things we have to work from. Don't try to save time at the expense of a patient. It's a stupid habit, even a dangerous one. Ask the questions you were trained to ask. Search out the clues you were trained to search out, no shortcuts.

"Lastly—for now—" Patrick smiled slightly, "you are each to do your own assigned work. When a senior man assigns work to student X, it is not to be passed on to student Y or Doctor Z. We have our reasons." Patrick looked at his watch and took a few steps across the room. "I'll be seeing the other interns and students in due time, but you might get the word around—no more slacking. No more carelessness. No shortcuts. Now, you have two minutes to grumble and complain before you go back to work. Dr. Potter, Mr. O'Hara, come with me, please," Patrick said, walking out the door.

Henry and Buddy looked at each other and then followed Patrick out.

"Yes, sir?" Henry asked.

"Come with me," he directed, walking rapidly down the corridor.

He stopped at the desk, taking the resident aside. "Dr. Rogers, I want a few minutes with Potter and O'Hara. Will you excuse them for a while?"

"Sure, Dr. Dain."

"Thank you. And Dr. Rogers, I think you know that

interns—and especially students—are impressionable. When they see you merely go through the motions with a patient, they do the same thing. It's a habit I want to break."

"Doctor, this is my fortieth hour of duty and it was hell last night in the E.R. I'm tired and I've got patients coming out of my ears. What am I supposed to do?"

"Your job. Dr. Rogers. You're not the only resident who's ever worked forty hours, or twice forty hours."

Dr. Rogers exhaled a great breath. "Well, you're right," he said tiredly. "You know, nobody around here's ever given a damn about wards. Sometimes I feel like I could phone it in and nobody would care. You're right, sometimes I just go through the motions. I guess I've been waiting for somebody to tell me to shape up. To *notice*."

"All right," Patrick smiled. "But I don't want to have to tell you a second time."

Patrick walked away, motioning Buddy and Henry to the staircase.

"Well, do you think the troops got the message?" Patrick asked as they walked downstairs.

Henry looked at Buddy, waiting for him to reply.

"Well?" Patrick asked again.

"Dr. Dain, sir," Henry began, "were you asking me?"

"Yes. Both of you."

"Well, sir," Henry said, "I think you . . . that is, I mean you . . . they . . . " he stammered, blushing.

Patrick stopped and looked at him. "Just tell me what you think, Dr. Potter."

"Yes, sir. I think it's . . . about time someone told them those—things. They look at those people, sir, but they don't see them. It's what I would have told them, if I could."

Patrick continued down the stairs. "Why couldn't you?"

"I'm not . . . much of a talker, sir."

"Mr. O'Hara?" Patrick asked.

"Potsy's right. He's no talker."

Patrick glanced at Buddy and then opened the door to the corridor. They returned to the office in silence. Patrick asked Grace to hold his calls and ushered the young men inside.

"Sit down, please," he said, going to his desk.

They sat down, looking wonderingly at each other before looking back at Patrick.

"Is something wrong, sir?" Henry asked.

"Yes. Individually you are both problems, if in different ways. Together you may be a solution. Let me explain," Patrick said, smiling. "Dr. Potter, you are quiet and shy. Mr. O'Hara you are anything but. Dr. Potter's student grades were near the top of his class, Mr. O'Hara is failing," he said, looking at each of them.

"Mr. O'Hara is now thinking 'so what?' " Patrick laughed. "Well, I remember that one year I went to a camp. The loudmouths were put with the shrinking violets, the strong swimmers with the weak swimmers. Deliberately. It was hoped that each would pick up some of the characteristics of the other, some of the ability. It worked quite well."

"*Jesus*," Buddy howled. "This is no damn kids' camp."

Patrick ignored him, continuing, "I have drawn up several pairings of interns and students. One of them is Potter-O'Hara."

"Are you *kidding?*" Buddy protested. "Potsy and *me?*"

Henry Potter had been listening intently and now he smiled. He liked the idea very much for he'd envied Buddy's confidence, his nerve. He looked at him, hoping he would agree.

"Mr. O'Hara," Patrick said, "when I spoke about respect, I meant for everybody. You are a second year student and Dr. Potter is *Dr*. Potter. You will call him that, or Henry, or Hank, or anything he wants, but you will *not* call him Potsy. That is a child's name, it's not suitable, and I don't want to hear it again. Now," he said, addressing them both, "Dr. Potter will be in charge, but I want you to work together. You'll be assigned to the same shifts and services and, in addition, I expect you to spend some of your break time together, reviewing cases and classwork. Particularly the classwork of this term as Mr. O'Hara has makeup exams coming up." Patrick paused. "I believe this arrangement will help you both. Comments? Dr. Potter?"

"I'm all for it, Dr. Dain," Henry said excitedly. "I still have most of my med school texts, we can review the work together. If it's all right with Buddy, I mean, sir," he added.

"Mr. O'Hara?" Patrick asked.

"I think it's a dumb idea, okay?"

"No, it's not okay. You have makeup exams which you must pass and pass with respectable grades. You have new work and new exams to prepare for at the same time. All that considered, I'd suggest you give it a try."

"Do I have a choice?"

"None."

Buddy threw up his hands and Patrick suppressed a smile. "I'm glad that's settled," he said.

"Stupidest thing I ever heard of," Buddy grumbled.

Patrick stared at him. "Mr. O'Hara, my patience is not unlimited. You would do well to observe Dr. Potter, to practice some of his restraint. *Abeunt studia in mores*. Practices zealously pursued pass into habits."

"Yeah," Buddy scowled. "Sure."

"I'm serious about this, make no mistake."

"Yes, sir," Henry said.

"You may go now. Dr. Rogers will be informed."

The young men stood and walked quickly across the room. Buddy paused at the door.

"Anything new on those tests?" he asked.

"Not yet," Patrick said. "I repeat, I don't see any reason for concern."

Buddy turned and walked wordlessly through the door. He hurried through the outer office into the corridor, Henry following. Buddy looked at him and then looked quickly away. After a moment he looked at him again.

"Look, it was nothing against you personally. I thought it was a dumb idea, that's all."

"I understand."

"That Dain guy really gets under my skin."

"Why, Buddy?"

"He thinks he knows it all. All that stuff about respect for the ward patients, did you hear that? All that stuff about helping us."

Henry did not reply, for he saw nothing wrong with what Patrick Dain had said or done.

Buddy shook his head impatiently. "Guys like that, they always think they know it all," he said, hurrying down the corridor. "Listen, what do you want me to call you?"

"I don't mind Potsy," Henry said quietly. "I'm used to it."

Buddy stopped and looked at him. "That's what Dain was talking about . . . you should be more— assertive, stop taking all the guff around here. Like your name. It's *your* name, you got a right to be called what you want to be called. How about it? Hank, do you like Hank?"

"Henry would be all right," he answered.

"Okay," Buddy said, resuming his pace, "then it's

Henry. When people call you Potsy, ignore 'em. Tell them your name is Henry, that's all. If they don't like it, screw 'em. That's what Dain meant, you have to learn to speak up. In this world, Henry, you got to speak up for yourself, nobody's going to do it for you. Don't forget that."

Buddy smiled slightly. He'd heard those words before, from his father—though when his father had spoken them he'd spoken in anger, in near despair at having produced a son so unlike himself.

They stepped into the elevator and Buddy looked at Henry.

"Don't worry," he said, "I'm going to show you how. As long as we're in this together, you might as well learn something."

13

"It's admirable the way you've taken charge around here," Julie Carlson said to Patrick.

She sat on a couch in his office, the folds of her mauve wool skirt gathered prettily about her. Patrick sat in a chair opposite her, their drinks on a small table between them.

"Thank you, but it's much too early for praise. I'm still getting my bearings."

Julie went on speaking, smiling at him, tilting her head, occasionally raising her graceful hands in the air. Patrick watched her, nodding now and then though he felt a growing impatience. It had been a long day and he was tired; more than that, he was expecting the results of Ann O'Hara's tests and he was anxious about them, barely able to concentrate on Julie.

It was odd, he thought to himself; earlier in the day he'd looked forward to seeing her, but now he wished she would leave. He enjoyed looking at her for she was beautiful, but he found no enjoyment in Julie herself. He found her empty, nothing but empty space behind the beautiful facade. And she talked too much, he thought, moved around too much; it was tiring.

Ann O'Hara came into his thoughts. Julie was reminiscent of many women he'd known, but there was something different, something fresh about Ann O'Hara. He found himself thinking that he'd like to know her better. Given the choice, he knew he'd rather be sitting with her now.

"Don't you agree, Patrick?" Julie asked.

There was an edge in her voice, for she'd seen his distraction. He'd been attentive, charming, when she'd first entered his office, but after the first ten minutes he'd seemed to forget about her, off in some world of his own.

Patrick looked at her, embarrassed. "I'm sorry, Julie. I'm not usually this rude. I'm waiting for some tests to come back, I was thinking about them."

"I understand. Nothing serious, I hope."

"I don't think so. But our lab isn't exactly the fastest lab in the east."

She smiled. "We have our disadvantages but we have our advantages as well."

"I hear Larrimer Wing gets test results right away."

"We couldn't very well keep people like that waiting, could we? I don't think it's so bad. Maybe for things like the clinic, but that's all."

He didn't like the careless way she'd tossed off the last few words and he looked at her closely. "You don't approve of the clinic?"

Julie realized from his expression that she'd made a mistake. She opened her eyes very wide. "Oh, no, I didn't mean that. I meant that in a busy week the lab will give priority to in-patients over out-patients. I don't know *anything* about medical matters, Patrick. Isn't that the way it's supposed to be?"

"Well," he said shortly, "it really isn't your problem. Here's something that is your problem, though — our volunteers take a book cart around the semi-private floors, is that right?"

"Yes."

"But not the wards. Why?"

"The wards? Well, I," she shook her head, flustered, "I never thought about it."

"People read books in wards, too. I'd like the volunteers to cover the wards from now on. All right?"

"Yes . . . of course. I'll take care of it."

"Good," Patrick smiled. "May I freshen your drink?"

Julie nodded and Patrick took her glass to the cabinet at the side of the room. He removed the sherry bottle, stopping as the door opened and Grace came in.

"I thought you'd gone home. Anything wrong?" Patrick asked.

"I knew you wanted those tests, so I went up to the lab and gave them a goose. Pardon me," she said to Julie. "And here they are," she held out a folder.

He took it eagerly. "Grace, you're wonderful."

"*I* think so."

Patrick went to his desk and sat down. He opened the folder and began reading, absorbed in the findings to the exclusion of all else. Julie stared at him. She felt the completeness of the exclusion and she stiffened with anger, her eyes dark and cold.

Grace watched Julie. She enjoyed her discomfort. "How you doing?" she asked pleasantly.

"Very well, thank you," Julie replied, looking away.

"You look a little tense to me. Would you like an aspirin?"

"No," Julie glared at her, "I would not like an aspirin."

"Just trying to be helpful."

Julie said nothing. Grace strolled over to a chair and sat down.

"I'm sure you needn't wait," Julie said.

"I don't mind," Grace smiled. " But don't let me interrupt you. The bottle's out, pour yourself a drink."

The women stared silently at each other for a while and then looked at Patrick. They were surprised to see the sharp look of relief on his face.

"It's good news?" Grace asked.

"Yes, it is," Patrick smiled.

"I'm really glad," Grace said. "Do you want me to find Buddy O'Hara?"

"Would you, Grace? I'd appreciate it. Here, use my phone," he said, taking up the folder and walking a few steps away.

He glanced again at the first page and smiled broadly. After a moment he turned around, remembering Julie.

"I'm so sorry, Julie. I've done it again. Please forgive me."

"Of course," she said with a tight smile. "I'm happy for your good news. Shall we have a drink and celebrate?"

"I'd love to, but I'm afraid I have to speak with O'Hara. It's his mother, you see."

Slowly, Julie made the connection. O'Hara's mother—the woman with whom she'd seen Patrick a few days before—the woman to whom he'd paid such elaborate attention. Julie was stunned. How could Patrick show such interest in a woman like that, she wondered furiously; how could he even consider it?

She'd taken a good look at Mrs. O'Hara. She'd found her ordinary, drab, without style. A picture of Mrs. O'Hara came into her mind. She was pretty, Julie conceded, but she was pretty in such a *plain* way, and those clothes, she thought to herself, those *dreadful, cheap* clothes.

Julie couldn't believe it, wouldn't believe it. She looked at Patrick and saw him again buried in the reports, almost savoring each word, each percentage. It was more than the usual interest of a doctor in his patient, she was sure: how *much* more remained to be seen. Julie sat rigidly, quickly collecting her thoughts. After a while she rose and quietly left the office, closing the door behind her.

For now, she said to herself, she would let Patrick feel guilty for his rudeness. She would let him come to her with apologies. She would act hurt but she would give in. She would forgive him.

"Later on," she muttered aloud, "when he's least expecting it, I'll fix him. Fix him good!"

Grace hung up the telephone and looked at Patrick. "He's on his way down."

"Thanks."

He closed the folder and returned to his desk. He sat down and then glanced quickly at the couch.

"I forgot all about Julie. Where is she?"

"She left."

"I don't blame her," he shook his head. "No one could have been ruder than I was tonight. I owe her an apology."

"Don't make too much of it. This is a hospital, patients come first. Julie's been here long enough to know that."

"She's tried so hard to be helpful, to be friendly. I haven't been very responsive. She's really put herself out."

"I doubt that," Grace said.

"What do you mean?"

"Julie's a very practical girl. She doesn't do anything without a reason."

"Well?" Buddy O'Hara stood in the doorway.

"Come in," Patrick said.

Buddy crossed the room rapidly, the anxiety clear in his eyes. "What did you find?"

"A small problem. Nothing we can't handle. Sit down and catch your breath."

Patrick looked at Grace. "Thank you for staying."

"Any time. Night, Patrick, Buddy," she said, leaving the office.

Patrick slid Ann O'Hara's folder across the desk. "You may read it."

"Everything's okay?"

"There's the slight low pressure I told you about. There's also a nasty anemia. A deficiency anemia. We can treat that."

"That's it?"

"That's it. We'll continue to see your mother in clinic for a while. I'm going to put her on iron and protein supplements, but she's going to have to pay strict attention to her diet. She must eat and eat the proper foods. I want you to encourage her in that. I'm not suggesting you make a pest of yourself, mind you, but keep after her. High proteins, low carbohydrates, vitamins, you know how it goes. Stop by the dietician's office. I've spoken to her. She has a booklet of recipes for you. High protein, high iron, low cost. See it's used."

Buddy wiped his damp forehead. "You're sure that's all it is? It couldn't be—"

"I'm sure. Your mother is run down. Badly run down. She needs a proper diet and rest. Not bed rest, but rest nevertheless. She must take care of herself."

"She had a vacation from the phone company this summer. So she went and worked full time at the dress shop. She's never taken a vacation," Buddy waved his big hand at Patrick. "Sunday's the only day she doesn't work, that's her vacation. There's no money for a vacation. It all goes on me and Jill," he said and Patrick was surprised to see the blush spread over his face.

"Education is expensive, Mr. O'Hara. Your mother is in a double bind—because she works, has an income over some arbitrary level—she's not eligible for as many loans as some people are. I've checked your records. Disqualifications aside, she—and you—are still carrying substantial debt. It's natural for her to be concerned, to work even harder. It's natural for you to be concerned, perhaps to feel guilty. But hanging your head and beating your breast makes no sense at all."

Buddy's head shot up and Patrick saw a brief, appreciative flicker in the young man's eyes.

"Start being realistic," he continued. "You and your sister are not betting horses, you're preparing for careers. It's expensive, damned expensive, but in a couple of years you'll be able to help. To ease the burden. *Then*, not now. That's the way she wants it. She is quite clear on the subject. Stop thinking about your guilt and start thinking about what is best for her."

"I don't know what you mean."

"You know very well. I'm not so sure there isn't a connection between your guilt and your failing grades. I think you feel so guilty you literally can't see straight. Well, you defeat your own purpose, and your mother's, that way. Your job now—your only job—is to succeed at your studies."

Buddy took the folder from the desk. He opened it and read slowly, carefully.

"Hemoglobin *8* per 100?"

"I said it was a nasty anemia. But that's *all* it is. You have no further excuse, Mr. O'Hara. From this moment on I want to see vast improvement. You work hard with Dr. Potter and be the student you ought to be."

"Did you tell her the results?"

"I will phone her when we're finished here."

Buddy stood up. "I'll get back to work."

"Your work is the *only* thing I want you to worry about. Is that clear?"

"Clear."

Buddy took a few steps toward the door and then looked back at Patrick. He opened his mouth to speak but said nothing, instead staring down at the floor.

"You're welcome, Mr. O'Hara," Patrick smiled.

"Okay," Buddy said, going quickly from the office.

Patrick smiled after him. Breaking through to Buddy O'Hara was no easy task, he thought, but he was making progress; the young man had almost smiled, almost said thank you.

Patrick looked down at Ann O'Hara's folder and then reached for the telephone, dialing carefully.

"Mrs. O'Hara? This is Patrick Dain."

Ann O'Hara hung up the telephone and then sat staring off into space. Her mind was on Patrick Dain, much as it had been since she'd met him days before. Time and time again she'd tried to chase him from her thoughts and each time she'd failed, her thoughts drawn irresistibly back to him. She'd see his dark blue eyes, or she'd hear his deep, quiet voice, or she'd remember the smile lighting his handsome face.

Ann had been distracted, lightheaded, all the week. She, who never made mistakes at work, had made many careless errors, and several times her co-workers had found her sitting motionless at her desk, smiling at nothing in particular. She'd burned bright red at such moments but she'd offered no explanation, for she had none to give. Ann refused to believe she was interested in Patrick Dain; the very idea made her feel shame, for what right, she scolded herself, had she to be interested in a man like that?

"What is it, Ann?" Mae asked, coming into the living room.

Ann looked up, startled, for she'd forgotten Mae was there. "Nothing, Mae. Good news. I'm a little anemic but otherwise I get a clean bill of health."

"Oh, I'm glad, Ann. Was that Buddy calling?" she asked, sitting on the couch.

"It was Dr. Dain. I have to go back to the clinic for a while, and take some medicine, but that's all."

Ann left her chair and went to the couch, curling her legs under her.

"He's been so nice about everything."

"What's he like, Ann? You never told me."

"He's nice . . . kind. About my age."

"What's he look like? Is he handsome? I remember the picture of his wife—they called her the Belle of New York."

"You told me. He's handsome, yes," Ann smiled.

Mae stared at her. "A certain doctor made a big impression on a certain Mrs. O'Hara, looks like."

"What? Mae, don't be silly."

"Are you sure it's me being silly, Ann?"

"What do you mean by that?"

"You haven't been yourself, Ann. Not since you saw that big muckymuck, you haven't. I know the signs, Ann, a woman doesn't forget the signs," Mae said, her small eyes troubled. "I'm the one was always telling you to find a man. Find a man before it's too late. You're the one was never interested, even though you had your chances."

"Mae," Ann shook her head.

"Vinnie, he would've done anything for you, Ann. And he had a nice little business in the bargain. The TV repair, remember?"

Ann nodded, staring at the floor, her lips pressed tightly together.

"And there was Gary from your office. He was crazy about you. And a couple of others who you didn't even give a chance. It was always, 'No, Mae, Vinnie's not for me, no, Mae, Gary's not for me, no, Mae, I don't have time, no, Mae, I'm doing fine on my own.'"

"That was a long time ago. Why bring it up now?"

"It wasn't so long. I bet you could still have Vinnie if you wanted."

"I don't."

"Better him than mooning over some big muckymuck you can't have. You heard Buddy talking about him—so rich, such an important family. He's who he is and you're who you are, Ann. Ann O'Hara, and before that an O'Reily. Only a generation away from the peat bogs, both our families. You think that matches with a Dain?"

"Of course not."

Ann spoke impatiently though she recalled that she hadn't once thought of Patrick Dain's wealth or importance in the time they'd been together. She'd felt more comfortable with him than she'd ever felt with Vinnie or Gary, or the few other men she'd dated in the last ten years.

"You were always a girl who knew her place," Mae continued, "don't go forgetting it now."

"Mae, don't talk like that. You're jumping to conclusions."

"Am I? I know you, Ann, you can't fool me so easy."

"I guess I can't," Ann said, a sad, half-smile on her face. "I don't know what's gotten into me but I can't get him out of my mind. I've tried and I can't."

"You have to, or have your heart broke all over again."

"It's nothing like that. I'll never get past the daydream stage. He's not breaking down my door. Even if he were," she said slowly, "I know O'Haras and Dains don't mix."

"You're past pigtails and short skirts, Ann. You're a grown woman. What's the use of a daydream to a grown woman? It hurts to moon about something you can't have and nobody knows that better than me. I'm surprised at you, Ann. You the practical one and all."

"It's harmless, Mae. Don't worry."

"I have to worry. You're closer to me than a sister. And all the heartache you had. Now I see you going wrong, I have to say so. It's the loneliness, you're alone too much, Ann."

"I don't have time to be lonely," Ann smiled.

"You don't have time to be mooning about the doctor, neither. Call up Vinnie. Pretend your TV's broken. Break the ice that way. You'll see, he'll ask you out and once you start going out again, you'll forget all about muckymuck Dain."

"I enjoy the time I have to myself," Ann said truthfully. "I wish I had more of it. I don't want to go out with Vinnie or anybody else. Mae, I liked Dr. Dain and I'll like seeing him when I go back to the clinic. But when I finish with the clinic that's it. I'll have no reason to see him after that. I'll forget all about him."

"Sometimes these things don't go away so easy. Take my word," Mae said stubbornly. "Ann, what would Buddy think?"

"Buddy?" Ann's eyes opened very wide. "Why should he think anything at all?"

"He'll notice the way you're acting. I did. Maybe he'll put two and two together like I did."

"Buddy's hardly ever here and when he is he worries about my health, not my . . . moods. Mae, don't you say a word to Buddy. If he thought . . . Mae, he'd go through the roof. Why are we talking about this?" Ann sighed. "It's only daydreaming, it'll go away."

"I wish I was as sure as you. It's the daydreams that break a woman's heart," Mae said, staring straight ahead. "Don't I know that?"

14

"Come in, Stuart," Patrick said, rising.

"Good morning, Patrick. I know how busy you are, I won't take too much of your valuable time."

"Surgical schedules," Patrick tapped the pile of yellow sheets on his desk. "The paperwork never ends. What may I do for you?"

Stuart sat across from Patrick, his hand fluttering nervously in his lap. "You have been with us two weeks—doing a wonderful job, wonderful, may I say—and I am interested in knowing your impressions."

Patrick said nothing for a moment, staring thoughtfully at Stuart. "Do you want an honest answer?"

Stuart blinked rapidly, clasping his eyes together. "Honest, yes, of course."

"Well, the services, *per se,* are in good shape," he began slowly. "The surgical floors are fine. The semi-private floors are not too bad."

"But?"

"I have some serious reservations. We have Larrimer Wing, which is a luxury operation. A luxury operation at the expense of the wards and—sometimes—the other services."

"Go on," Stuart said, his eyes narrowing.

"The clinic and the E.R. are substandard operations. I find that very hard to justify."

Stuart had grown very still. He sat very straight, his hands resting quietly on the arms of his chair, his eyes fast on Patrick.

"You are mistaken in your facts," he said. "Larrimer pays its way and turns a profit. On the other hand, the clinic and the wards cost us dearly. As for the E.R.," he said, brushing a speck of lint from his carefully creased trousers, "it is only busy on weekends."

Patrick leaned forward. "Stuart, we know numbers can be made to say anything one wants them to say. The fact is, enormous capital sums are spent on Larrimer and nothing is spent on the wards. The fact is, the ongoing costs of Larrimer—profits or no—eliminate any possibility of upgrading the wards. And please don't be so quick to write off the E.R. I heard about the patient who died because an ancient piece of equipment failed."

"We were not sued."

"That is hardly the point. I spent a part of Saturday night there and what I saw was frightening. We had a *tiny* staff, admissions coming in bang, bang, bang. I had to pull staff from Larrimer. They had plenty to spare."

"A scheduling quirk," Stuart said. "That is Dr. Murdock's department."

"David does the best with what he has. And unfortunately he has to follow the directives about Larrimer."

"I didn't realize you were a . . . radical, Dr. Dain."

"I am no radical. I'm a doctor and I don't like the idea of one group of patients suffering because of another group of patients. The motto of Rhinelander Pavillion is *A Maximus Ad Minima*. From the greatest to the least. Do we live up to our motto?"

"Larrimer Wing is a showplace. We are all very proud of it."

"We are not in the showplace business. We are in the hospital business."

Patrick was interrupted by the intercom and he turned impatiently. "Yes, Grace?"

"Dr. Waverly. He says it's important."

"I'll take it."

Stuart Claven stood up. "I don't wish to keep you from important business. This has been a very interesting conversation. I will think about what you said."

"You asked for my impressions, Stuart. I know they weren't the impressions you wanted to hear, but they are true ones."

"We will have an opportunity to talk about this another time, I am sure," he said, his eyes chilly. "Keep up the wonderful work," he added.

Patrick waited until he left and then took up the telephone. "Yes, Dr. Waverly? . . . Who? . . . I see . . . no, wait there for me, I'm coming up."

Patrick hung up the telephone and left his desk, straightening his tie as he went to the door.

"Do you know where David is?"

"Larrimer, I think," Grace said. "I think Miss Parrish is checking out today."

"I won't be too long," Patrick said, walking into the corridor.

"Hold it, please," he called, running to catch the elevator. He greeted several doctors and then faced forward, staring at the lighted floor numbers until he reached Larrimer Wing.

Dr. Waverly was there to meet Patrick as he stepped off the elevator. "Here it is! Here it is!" the young man said excitedly, waving a piece of paper in Patrick's face. "A check for a thousand dollars from J.J.

Caldwel, just like I told you."

Patrick took the check and looked at it, frowning. "Where's the note?"

"Here," Dr. Waverly handed it to him. "It's just like I said. For the inconvenience his men caused me."

Patrick returned the note. "Dollar diplomacy. Who have you told about this?"

"Nobody. Only you. He just called me into the solarium and gave it to me. Can I keep it, Dr. Dain?"

"I don't like the idea. I'm going to speak to Mr. Caldwel before I decide. Don't say anything about this. Do you understand?"

"Yes, Dr. Dain. But he won't miss it. A thousand bucks is cab fare to him."

Patrick stared at him for a moment. "That's not the point," he said finally, striding away. "Wait for me."

Patrick went to the big gray door of the solarium. He walked inside, stopping when one of John Caldwel's guards stepped in front of him.

"Oh, it's you," the guard said.

"It is. I would like to see Mr. Caldwel."

The guard nodded, gesturing toward the far end of the room. Patrick saw John Caldwel seated in a chair, a guard at each side. He walked across the room, watching as the two guards stiffened and then bent to their charge. He waited until one of the guards waved him over.

"Good morning, Mr. Caldwel."

"Call me John. I prefer it."

"John, then. May I speak with you privately?"

John Caldwel moved his hand and the two men stepped back.

"Thank you," Patrick said. "John, it's about the check to Dr. Waverly. I'd like you to reconsider."

"Why? Hospital policy?" he asked. He looked rested, though his voice was still a flat, tired monotone.

"There's no hospital policy on this, none I know of. But I don't think it's a good idea. I'd like you to reconsider."

John Caldwel stared past Patrick to the skyline beyond. "I am a man who pays his debts. When I owe an apology I pay that, too. Write a check. Why not? It's what people expect J.J. Caldwel, crazy as a bedbug. They don't say crazy, they say eccentric. Same thing."

"Is that your last word?"

"Yes, I won't take back what I've already given. Handle it any way you want. Leave me out of it."

Patrick sat down, looking closely at John Caldwel. "You don't make my job easy," he smiled. "How are you feeling?"

"I feel well. The attack wasn't much. I leave in two days. For Saudi Arabia. I don't want to go. I have no choice. Whole empires crumble if I don't get on my plane," he smiled very slightly. "Or so I'm told." He looked at Patrick. "I've liked being here. I always like it here. I'm not bothered too much. I sleep well. There's usually someone I know. If I want conversation. This time it was Gail."

"Gail?"

"Gail Parrish. Smart. Smart as they come. I have never used her myself. One of my presidents used her for three months. He brought her on my yacht a few times. Smart. Smart as they come."

Patrick looked curiously at him. He was surprised because Gail hadn't mentioned knowing John Caldwel. "She worked for you?"

"For one of my presidents. He spoke highly of her."

"She's lovely. I imagine she's a good model."

John Caldwel stared at Patrick. "Model?" He stared at him another moment and then laughed loudly. "Gail Parrish is no more a model than I am. She is a whore. A high-priced one. A high class one. You have to be referred by another client. But a whore all the same." He smiled at Patrick's astonishment, enjoying it, a lively twinkle coming into his eyes. "That's a clumsy thing to put on a hospital questionnaire. But I didn't know she was calling herself a model. Last I knew—by way of occupation—she just put it around that her father had money."

"You're mistaken."

"I'm never mistaken."

Patrick was too startled to speak. He sat where he was, collecting his thoughts.

"Didn't you see her body?" John Caldwel asked. "Her body's too ripe for the model business. Didn't you see that?"

Patrick stood up hastily. "We should not be discussing this."

"Why not?" he laughed loudly again. "She does. We talked a long time. No pretense about it. She loves her work." He gazed at Patrick. "Don't confuse her with some fifty dollar hustler. She spends time with important men. They treat her well. She has enough cash and jewelry stashed away for a sweet old age. A hefty stock portfolio, too. Thanks to insider information."

John Caldwel was quiet for a moment, the mirth leaving his eyes. "I am not a happy man. Not in my money. Not in my work. Not in anything. When I meet a person who is happy I pay attention. I remember. It interests me. Gail Parrish is one of those people."

Patrick took a step away. "Yes, well, we shouldn't be talking about—"

"Wait a minute. I want to tell you something. There's no secret to these things. After a man pays out millions in divorce settlements he finds wisdom. He finds a Gail. He buys what he wants. No strings attached. If there's a wife at home she's busy spending his money. Showing it off. Playing great lady. A man is lucky if he sees his wife fifteen minutes a month. Or wants to."

"John, I don't think—"

"I know. Two marriages," he continued. "One a secretary. The other an actress. Same thing with each one. After I married them it didn't take them a week to find *culture*. Business was too crass. Money was too crass. This while spending it with both hands. I was too crass. This while making damned sure everyone knew they were married to me. Never home. Draped in mud or oil or adhesive tape when they were. Girls like Gail can do well. If they're as smart as Gail they can do very well."

"*Please*, John," Patrick said. "that's enough. Miss Parrish is a patient here."

"Best laugh I've had in months. A model."

"About your check . . ."

"You handle it any way you want. Leave me out of it. I'm too damned tired."

Patrick looked at him. "Can I do anything for you before I leave?"

"You gave me a good laugh. That's more than I expected." He stared at Patrick. "Thank you for asking," he said and then waved his guards back.

Patrick walked away. He stopped at the door and looked back, then continued into the corridor.

"Dr. Dain?" Dr. Waverly hurried over. "Well?"

"Why did you call me about the check? Why didn't you put it in your pocket and forget about it, no one the wiser?"

"I don't know. Procedure, I guess."

"I think you called me because you felt uncomfortable accepting it. You wanted me to decide for you. Well, I would prefer you return the check, but it is up to you."

Dr. Waverly looked at the check. "It did make me

uncomfortable . . . but if it's up to me, I'll keep it. A thousand bucks'll salve a lot of conscience."

"Very well. But you are not to tell anyone. Do I have your word?"

"Yes, Dr. Dain."

"If this gets out they'll be standing in line to get into arguments with Mr. Caldwel's guards. And you will be responsible. Do you understand?"

"Yes, sir. I won't say anything."

Patrick nodded. "That's all," he said, walking over to the nurse's station.

"Where is Dr. Murdock?" he asked.

"He's in with Miss Parrish. Do you want me to call him?"

"No," Patrick hesitated before speaking. "Do you know—has Mr. Caldwel had any visits from the other patients?"

"Oh, his guards are very strict. He doesn't see anybody, really."

"Thank you," Patrick said, walking away.

"Except—"

"Yes?" Patrick turned quickly.

"He and Miss Parrish play backgammon sometimes. In the solarium or in her suite."

"I see. Thank you."

Patrick walked away, thinking about his encounter with John Caldwell. *She is a whore*. The words had stunned him. He'd never been so surprised and he wondered if David knew the truth.

Patrick turned into another corridor and went to the door of Gail's suite. He knocked and went inside. He crossed the sitting room and then hesitated as Gail poked her head out of the other room.

"Hi. Come in," she said brightly.

She was dressed in a gold wool dress, a jade-colored silk sash around her narrow waist, gold and jade clips sparkling at her ears. Patrick's eyes were drawn to her full, exquisitely rounded body.

"I had to listen to fifteen minutes of the most boring lecture ever," Gail laughed. "The price for getting out of this place."

"Getting out isn't the problem," David said. "*Staying* out is the problem."

"Like prison," she smiled, turning back to an open suitcase on the bed.

"I hope you paid attention," Patrick said. "We don't encourage return business here," he smiled slightly.

"Don't worry. I've had my fill of Rhinelander Pavillion, darling place." She closed one case and turned to another, smaller one.

"David," Patrick said, "may I see you for a moment? If Miss Parrish will excuse us."

"It's Gail, remember?" she asked, looking around.

Her eyes met Patrick's. She stared at him briefly and then slowly looked away, the smile leaving her face.

"If Gail will excuse us," he corrected.

"She will," she said quietly.

David and Patrick walked into the sitting room. "What's up?"

"Caldwel gave a thousand dollar check to Dr. Waverly. Amends for that little shoving match I told you about. I talked to Caldwel; he wouldn't take it back."

"Caldwel ought to have his head examined. I mean that literally."

"Well, Waverly's keeping the check. I'd appreciate it if you had a word with him before you leave. I don't want it getting around. I don't want anyone getting ideas. And I don't trust Waverly to keep his mouth shut."

"I'll talk to him. I'll be damn glad when Caldwel gets out of here."

"Yes, but I wish he were leaving in better shape. He's depressed."

David smiled. "He tells everyone he's unhappy. He probably believes it. But I saw him when he was preparing to leave the last time. He was surrounded by lawyers and aides and secretaries. They were all concentrating on a new business proposal. A coup, more likely. And he was loving every minute of it, practically twitching with anticipation. He smelled blood and he was going in for the kill. Depressed!" David laughed. "Hah! Where's he going now?"

"Saudi Arabia."

"With his resources," David nodded, "and theirs, they could start their own planet. Or take over this one."

"That's probably occurred to him." Patrick went to the door. "I'm going back to work. See you later."

David returned to Gail. "Do you have all your diets and medicines?" he asked.

"Right here," she said, tapping a small suitcase.

"I can't talk you into a few more days of rest?"

"Not a chance."

David looked at the luggage, the gold wool coat folded on top.

"That's it, then. A nurse will be in soon to help you with everything."

Gail closed the closet door and looked at David. "Did you tell him?"

"Patrick? I haven't had the chance."

He stared at her for a moment and then went to her. He took her in his arms and held her close.

"Love you," he said.

She buried her head on his shoulder. "I love you. Will I see you tonight?"

"You couldn't keep me away."

"When are you going to tell Patrick about us?"

David took her face in his hands and looked into her eyes. "As soon as we have a chance to talk. Why are you so concerned about him?"

"I know how close you are. I want him to like me."

"He does." David laughed. "He thought I was trying to get him into a romance with you. Little does he know."

Gail held him to her, saying nothing, though her eyes were dark, troubled. David knew so little of the truth about her; Patrick, she was certain, now knew it all. She'd seen the look in Patrick's eyes and she knew he'd learned the truth. She'd seen that look before, in the eyes of other men. There was no mistaking that look; the look of someone who had been surprised and then sorry and, at the last, appalled.

15

The first night of November was cool and still. Patrick stood at the window of his library, looking out at the dark sky, at the great circle of moon hanging over the park.

Hollis set a gleaming silver tray and coffee service on a table near the fireplace. "Will there be anything else, sir?"

"No, thank you, Hollis. We have everything we need."

"Very good, sir. Goodnight. Goodnight, Dr. Murdock."

"Goodnight," David said as Hollis quietly left the room.

David poured coffee into two pale blue china cups. "Get it while it's hot."

"Coming," Patrick said.

He crossed the wide room and sat down in the wing chair opposite David. He took up his cup, sipping the coffee slowly.

"How does it feel to have a whole night off?" David asked. "You've been working like a demon."

"It feels good. We started at the crack of dawn today. My fourth year observing in surgery."

"You're doing a good job with them. With all of them."

"I hope. It's hard to tell sometimes. It takes an *awful* amount of concentration to deal with all those different personalities. All those clashing egos."

"Is that what you were thinking about at dinner? You faded out on me once or twice," David smiled.

Patrick stared into the fire, watching the rosy flames wave and leap, changing colors as they changed shapes.

"I was thinking about a patient. Mrs. O'Hara."

"How is she doing?"

"Very well. She's gained a few pounds, she's getting some color back."

"I haven't had a complaint about Buddy in two weeks. That's an official record."

"He doesn't have to worry about his mother anymore, that helps. And Dr. Potter is doing a good job. But the makeup exams are pending. He's not out of the woods yet."

Patrick reached for the coffee pot and refilled his cup. He took a sip of coffee and then reached again to the tray. He opened a decanter and poured brandy into two crystal snifters. He carried his drink to the fireplace, gazing down into the flames.

"I switched her to Lola," he said softly.

"Who?"

"Mrs. O'Hara."

"Oh? Well, I knew you were trying to handle too much. Your schedule is too heavy by far."

"It isn't that." Patrick bent down. He moved a poker about, stirring up the flames, "I asked her to dinner."

David looked at him. "Good. It's time you started going out. And Lola's a wonderful woman."

"Not Lola. Mrs. O'Hara," he said, poking around the ashes.

"What did you say? Patrick, I can barely hear you."

"I asked Mrs. O'Hara to dinner."

David said nothing for a while, staring at the back of Patrick's head. "You did? Old I'm-not-in-the-market-leave-me-alone-Dain?" David laughed.

Patrick put the poker down and took a drink of brandy. He swiveled around, looking up at David.

"I don't know how it happened. I didn't plan it, the words just came out. I was as surprised as she was. More."

"Don't be so apologetic," David smiled. "I think it's great. Any woman who can get you out of this mausoleum gets my vote. What is she like?"

"David, didn't you hear what I said? I asked Mrs. O'Hara to dinner!"

"So? What's wrong with that?"

Patrick stood up. He returned to his chair, looking at David. "Everything's wrong with it. I hardly know the woman. I've seen her a grand total of three times. I'm too busy. I'm too preoccupied. I don't want to do it."

"Nobody twisted your arm."

"I don't know what came over me. The words just came out," he stared into his drink.

"It's only a dinner date. A simple thing. You met her, liked her, wanted to know her better. I'm delighted. There's more to life than Rhinelander and this library."

"I'm not ready."

"When will you be ready? A month from now? A year? There's no calendar to these things, Patrick. When they happen, that's the time. You have a case of jitters. You haven't had a date in a long time. You're nervous about it." David smiled, "It will come back to you, like riding a bicycle."

"Thanks a lot."

"Anytime."

Patrick rubbed absently at the place where his wedding band had been. "I liked her from the very beginning," he said quietly. "I felt good. She comes into my thoughts and I feel good. That bothers me."

"It shouldn't. You're entitled to some happiness. It's your turn. I know you're reluctant to even risk getting involved, but there are times when one must take risks."

Patrick looked curiously at David. "That's odd, coming from you."

"When does this momentous dinner take place?"

"I don't know. My schedule . . . and she works almost all the time. I don't know."

"I'll cover at the hospital for you anytime. You're not going to use your schedule as an excuse."

"Well, I don't know. I have mixed emotions."

David looked away, staring straight ahead. After a long moment he looked back at Patrick.

"I have some mixed emotions of my own."

"Oh?"

"I've been seeing somebody. For six months now. It's serious. Not yet fatal," he smiled briefly. "but serious."

"Congratulations," Patrick smiled broadly. "Why all the mystery?"

"I wanted you to meet her before I said anything."

"Tell me when and where and I'll be there."

"You already were," David said slowly. "It's Gail. Gail Parrish."

Patrick's eyebrows shot up. "Gail Parrish?"

He sat back in his chair and took a quick sip of brandy, his mind reeling. He thought back a month to John Caldwel and his flat, blunt, words: *She is a whore.* The phrase echoed in his mind and Patrick had to force himself to stay still. He wondered what David knew, if he knew anything at all.

He felt a sudden, sharp worry. "Well," he said and said nothing more.

"Is that all?"

"I'm surprised . . . you certainly are good at secrets. I had no idea. None."

"We met at a party at the Venables'. We went out a few times. Almost before I knew it, it was serious."

"How serious is serious?"

David glanced away. "I've thought about marriage. We haven't actually discussed it, but Gail knows the thought is there. There are—adjustments. Certain adjustments. Emotional adjustments."

Patrick heard the uneasiness in David's voice. "Is there a problem?" he asked.

"My ego is the problem."

"What does that mean?"

"Gail . . . isn't a model."

David hurried the words and Patrick stared at him; could he *know* the truth and still speak of marriage, he wondered.

"Gail's been the mistress of a very wealthy man. Paid mistress," David took a breath, studying Patrick's expression. "He's supported her—quite splendidly, too—for a long time. That's how she's lived since she came to New York."

The look on Patrick's face was unchanged though he was deeply angry. Gail Parrish had deliberately deceived David, he thought, giving the kindest possible interpretation to the way she earned her money.

"Please say something, Patrick."

"It happens. How do you feel about it? Only a few weeks ago you told me you like a neat, orderly life, no complications. Well, this is not uncomplicated."

David sipped his brandy. "I didn't know, at first. By the time Gail told me the truth . . . Patrick, when I found out I didn't see her for two weeks. I called her every nasty name I could think of, I insulted her a thousand times in my mind. But I went back."

"That says a lot."

"When I'm with her, nothing else matters. When I'm away from her I tell myself it's an impossible situation. How can I forget the way she's lived? When I'm with her, I do forget. Almost. The trouble is we've reached the stage where it's time to take a step one way or another. Decision time. We were on the verge when Gail got sick." David nodded. "Yes, I saw the connection. Now I don't know what to do."

"Whatever you do, do it slowly. Gail needs time to recuperate. Beyond that you need time to be certain of your feelings. If I were you I would think about it long and hard."

"You liked her before I told you about her."

"Gail brings certain cumbersome problems. You are a tidy man. Everything in its orderly, tidy place. And that's as true," Patrick smiled, "of your emotions as it is of your desk."

"I know."

"Do you?"

"There are times when it's very hard for me to deal with her past. I would like to erase it. Pretend it never happened."

"Have you . . . discussed it?" Patrick asked.

"As little as possible. Enough to know she's not apologetic about it. That was hard for me to accept. It still is."

"You would prefer she felt guilt?"

"I would prefer she knew right from wrong."

"As you see it."

"As anyone sees it. It's not a thing to be proud of."

"Is she proud of it?"

"She's not sorry about it."

Patrick was quiet. He refilled their glasses and then stared into the fire. When he looked back at David his eyes were troubled.

"There are fundamental differences between you. You ought to be discussing them with Gail."

"I can't. I can say these things to you, but when I'm with her it's a different story. There's no past, there's no future, there's only the moment. When I'm with her all's right with the world, I'm king of the world, it's wonderful. It's when I'm *not* with her that I start thinking and then it's hell," David said and Patrick saw the weariness in his eyes. "I don't know where we go from here and it's tearing me apart. It's a relief to finally be able to talk about it."

"What about Gail? How does she feel?"

"She's been patient with me. Watching me struggle with my little moral dilemmas."

"They're not so little," Patrick said, more sharply than he'd intended.

"I knew how you'd feel. I don't blame you."

"David," Patrick shook his head. "It's how *you* feel. That's the real problem. You disapprove, that's clear. What can you live with? Can you live with one half of you loving a woman and the other half disapproving? Is she going to have to be *patient* half the time?"

"It's not easy."

"You're juggling head and heart as if they are separate from each other. They're not, they work together. Your head and your heart must reach approximately the same conclusion or it's no good. I tried it the other way. And had only pain to show for it. Everybody's pain."

David stood up. He walked over to a window and stared outside.

"This is a different situation," he said.

"Not so different, David, think about it."

"What should I do?" he asked after a long silence.

"I know what you shouldn't do, and that is set up time limits. Neat little squares all signed and dated.

Take all the time you need to think things through." Patrick ran his hand through his hair. "Give Gail all the time she needs to think things through."

David walked back to his chair and sat down. "I hate leaving things up in the air. You know that. I'm lost without those neat little squares."

Patrick smiled. "I'll point you in the right direction every once in a while. You can do the same for me."

"Women! It's always complicated. I'd rather take on OPEC."

Patrick looked at David. "Some men wouldn't be that bothered by Gail's—background. Have you thought about that?"

"I'm not *some* men."

"I don't know what to tell you, except to go slowly. It's easy to be wise about someone else's problems. One's own problems, that's the trick."

"One's *woman* problems, that's the real trick. Between us we're eighty years old and we're still stumbling and bumbling around, wondering that to do."

Patrick fell silent, thinking about Ann O'Hara, thinking about her plain, honest life. He thought then about Gail Parrish—about her life, anything but plain, anything but honest.

"You're drifting off again," David said.

"I was thinking that a lot of complications begin with *simple* dinner dates."

"Speaking of dinner dates, I don't suppose you'd . . . will you have dinner with Gail and me one night?"

"Of course, David, if you're going to be ashamed of her, you're finished before you start. We're adults, we didn't fall out of a Disney movie."

"I think different things at different times. I can't get it out of my mind that she's almost a . . . there's a name for it."

Yes, Patrick thought worriedly, and there was no "almost" about it.

"Do you remember Josh Whitfield?" Patrick asked. "He married a girl whose—background—was similar to Gail's and I was best man at the wedding."

"Josh Whitfield is a joke all over town and you know it."

"David, do you want me to argue against Gail? Is that what you want?"

"I don't know what I want. I'm counting on you to help me find out. It will help if I can talk about it as I go along."

"That goes without saying. But if you will accept some advice, talk to Gail, too."

David looked at Patrick for a moment and then looked away. He glanced at the clock on the mantel and then stood up.

"It's getting late. I should be on my way."

Patrick rose. They walked out of the library into the hall.

"I told you about the staff meeting Monday, didn't I?" David asked.

"I cleared the time."

"Stuart will be there."

"He hasn't come near me since I told him what I thought about Larrimer," Patrick grinned.

"I wish I'd been there."

They reached the center hall and Patrick went to the closet, helping David on with his coat.

"I really feel better, now that the truth is out," David said.

Patrick looked away to a vast jumble of cartons and furniture and packing crates—the last of Catherine's belongings from her bedroom and sitting room, all carefully boxed and labeled by Hollis and Delia.

"Goodwill picks up tomorrow morning," he said,

gesturing at the array. "Are you sure there's nothing you want? A few things belonged to Murdock ancestors."

"I don't want anything of hers," David said. "I'm glad to see it go. You didn't leave anything, did you?"

"I shipped the Dain family pieces back to Mother. This is what's left. Hollis didn't want any of it, neither did Delia."

David stared at the assembled possessions for a moment. "Good riddance," he said. He looked at Patrick. "Thank you for dinner. Thank you for listening."

Patrick opened the door and David stepped into the vestibule. He rang for the elevator.

"Goodnight," Patrick said, closing the door.

He walked away and then stopped. He retraced his steps, gazing down at the sealed boxes. He kicked gently at one of them and then, his face closed, harsh, reared back and kicked it hard. He kicked it one more time and then walked swiftly away.

16

Patrick came awake quickly. He sat up and lunged for the light switch. His hands beat frantically at the air, for the laughter surrounded him, coming closer and closer. For one terrifying moment he thought he would be crushed by it and he scrambled out of bed, falling, righting himself quickly.

He held one hand in front of his face as if to deflect a blow, while his eyes darted around the room. He saw nothing unusual though the laughter grew louder and louder, moving him back, step by painful step, into a corner. He felt the laughter upon him, no longer mocking, but enraged, maniacal, a sound of such horror he thought his heart would stop.

Patrick crouched in the corner, his face a deathly white, glossy with perspiration. He tried to escape underneath the laughter but it pursued him. He moved to the left and then the right but each time the crazed sound followed, pinning him to the wall. He turned his back to it, his hands covering his ears as the laughter screamed in his head. His legs wobbled uncertainly beneath him and with one desperate burst of strength he turned and pushed himself through the sound and across the room, knocking over a chair and a small table as he went.

Patrick staggered on until he reached the door and then, as his trembling fingers groped for the doorknob, the laughter swooped down on him, beating at him mercilessly, relentlessly. With one hand clinging to the side of the door, he forced his other hand on, his fingers creeping closer, closer to the doorknob. With one agonized thrust his hand plunged forward and found the knob, grasping it tightly. He turned it once, weakly. And then the laughter stopped.

Patrick listened for a moment, listening to the silence, and then fell against the door, his eyes tightly shut. His chest heaving, he struggled to take a deep breath and then another and another. He turned slowly and made his way back to the bed, walking in short, shaky steps.

He fell on the bed, fighting to get control of his breathing. There was a sudden loud knocking at the door and he jumped. He looked at the door, his heart pounding. He tried to speak but had no voice.

"Sir? Dr. Dain, sir? It's me, Hollis. Are you all right in there?"

Patrick took another deep breath. He cleared his throat once, twice, three times before he was able to speak.

"Come in, Hollis." he called in a faint voice.

The door swung open and Hollis rushed into the room. He looked at Patrick.

"Sir . . . what is it, Dr. Dain?" he asked, seeing Patrick's ashen face, his pajamas soaked through with perspiration.

He stared at him another moment and then hurried to the night table. He poured a brandy and took it to Patrick.

"Please, sir, it will do you good."

Patrick took a sip and then drank the brandy down in one gulp.

"I'll get you another," Hollis said anxiously.

"No, thank you. I'm . . . all right," Patrick said as he felt the warmth of the liquor spread through him.

He clasped his hands together, trying to quiet them. Hollis watched him and then rushed away, returning with a large brown towel.

"Thank you," Patrick said, wiping at his face, his head, the back of his neck.

"What happened, sir?"

Patrick looked up. "Why did you come up here?" he asked urgently. "Did you hear something, Hollis? What did you hear?"

"Well, sir, I can't rightly say. Something woke me up, I don't know what. I thought it was the wind. This time of year, sir, I thought it might be a storm. I went round checking the windows, but everything was closed tight."

"But what did you *hear*?" Patrick prodded.

"I wish I could say, sir, but I don't know. The sound seemed to get louder, it seemed to be coming from up here. I started up the stairs to check the windows and I heard things crashing to the floor. Those, I imagine, sir," Hollis said, nodding at the overturned table and chair. "Was there an intruder, sir?" he asked, moving toward the pokers at the side of the fireplace.

"I don't know . . . I don't think so," Patrick said tiredly.

He wanted to question Hollis further about what he'd heard but he stopped himself. How, he wondered, could he ask more questions without revealing the horror of the last few minutes? And if he did, would Hollis believe him, or would Hollis think him mad?

"Did you check the safe, sir?"

Patrick glanced at the painting which covered the wall safe. "The safe hasn't been disturbed."

"Perhaps I should have a look around," Hollis said.

He took up a poker and crossed the room to the door of Patrick's sitting room. He opened the door cautiously and reached for the light switch. He peered around and then shook his head.

"Nothing, sir," he called, turning out the light and closing the door. "I'll have a look at madam's rooms."

He walked to the other end of the room, the poker held high before him. He opened the door, disappearing inside.

Patrick flung the towel aside and reached across to a cigaret box on his night table. He lit a cigaret and inhaled deeply, his eyes on the door to Catherine's suite.

"Tight as a drum, sir," Hollis said, returning.

"Thank you, Hollis. You're very brave," Patrick managed a wan smile.

"I can't pretend as my knees aren't knocking together, sir."

"Have some brandy. Help yourself."

"Thank you, sir. I don't mind if I do," Hollis said, pouring a large drink. He swallowed it quickly and then looked around him. "Your windows are open as usual, sir, but there doesn't seem to be much wind now. Do you think it was some kind of freak storm, sir?"

"I don't know."

"Did you see anyone, sir?"

"No."

"Did you hear anyone?"

"I . . . don't know."

"Perhaps we should call the police, eh, sir?"

"No," Patrick said quickly. "Whatever it was, it's gone now."

"But how, sir? If there was someone here—"

"As you say," Patrick interrupted, "a freak storm. It's over now."

Patrick spoke as calmly as he could, for Hollis was uneasily shifting the poker from hand to hand, looking around nervously.

"If you say so, sir."

"Yes, let's . . . forget it."

They were silent for a while, each with his own thoughts, when the sudden ringing of the telephone caused them both to jump.

"Don't answer it!" Patrick ordered.

He stared at the telephone, a new terror coming over him, for in that moment he was certain that if he lifted the receiver he would hear Catherine's voice at the other end.

Hollis saw the color drain from Patrick's face. He took a step toward the telephone and then stopped, looking in confusion from Patrick to the telephone and back again. They remained as they were for several moments, both frozen in position, their eyes locked on the telephone. Hollis felt his hands grow damp and when the poker slipped from his grasp he cried out in fright at the sudden noise.

Patrick looked quickly at Hollis, jarred by the real fear etched on his face. "I'm . . . I'm sorry, Hollis," he said, straining hard with every word, "go ahead, answer it."

Hollis glanced uncertainly at Patrick and then went to the phone. He lifted the receiver warily, looking at it before speaking.

"Dain residence," he said. "Yes . . . oh, yes, sir . . . right away, sir." He covered the mouthpiece and looked at Patrick. "It's Dr. Murdock, sir. An emergency at the hospital."

"I'll take it . . . yes, David?"

Patrick listened and then spoke briefly. He hung up and looked at Hollis.

"There's been an explosion at a club on Sixth Avenue. I have to hurry."

He stood up, stumbling a little, for his legs were still weak.

"Begging your pardon, sir, but do you think you should?"

"I'm fine now, Hollis. Really. I apologize for all the—disturbance. I don't know what happened. The wind, I'm sure. It's all over now. We must forget about it."

"Couldn't you rest a while, sir? Before you go?"

"No time for that. I'll have a quick shower. And I'd appreciate some coffee."

"Right away, Dr. Dain."

"Please don't worry," Patrick said as he disappeared into the bathroom.

Patrick peeled off his wet bedclothes and threw them into the hamper, stepping quickly into the shower. He turned on the taps and stood under the rushing water, letting the water revive him, trying to blot out the last half hour from his mind. He soaped himself, rubbing vigorously at his chest and arms until he felt his strength returning. He let the water splash over him again and then moved closer to the shower head, adjusting the nozzle until the water came out in a prickly spray, sharp needles of water waking the tired muscles of his back and neck.

After another full minute Patrick stepped out of the shower. He wrapped himself in a huge towel plucked from a heated rack.

"Coffee, sir," Hollis called to him.

"In a minute."

Hollis walked out of the dressing room, walking over to the windows. He rattled the window frame, frowning as he did so, for it was solid; there were no spaces, no holes, he thought to himself, to catch the wind and cause such odd sounds.

Patrick walked into the bedroom. He picked up a mug of steaming coffee and took a long sip. "It's good, thank you."

Hollis turned. "Your things are all laid out, sir. In your dressing room, Dr. Dain."

Patrick drank more coffee and then rushed away, returning moments later in flannel slacks, blue shirt and a heather-colored pullover sweater. He took another gulp of coffee, checked his watch, and went to the door.

"You're still—a little pale, sir," Hollis said, handing Patrick his bag.

"I'm fine." He looked at Hollis. "Are you fine? I know it was a terrible night."

"Don't worry about me, Dr. Dain. I'll be back to sleep in no time at all."

"Good. Goodnight, Hollis," Patrick said, rushing from the room.

"Goodnight, Dr. Dain."

Hollis followed slowly, watching as Patrick ran down the stairs. He heard the click of the closet door and then the louder sound of the front door closing. Hollis returned to the bedroom. He straightened Patrick's bed and took the used glasses and mug to a tray near the door. He went into the bathroom and cleared away the crumpled towels, taking fresh ones from a cupboard, arranging them neatly on their racks. He walked through to the dressing room, picking up Patrick's robe, returning it to its hook on the bathroom door. He turned off the lights and went back to the bedroom, gazing around for a moment before he left.

Hollis walked slowly down the stairs, pausing in the center hall. He looked around. He didn't see anything unusual; he hadn't really expected to, for whatever it was, he thought, could not be seen. He turned in the direction of his rooms, taking his time for he knew there'd be little, if any, sleep for him this night. Hollis sighed, his eyes puzzled, troubled. He didn't like what was going on in this house, he thought. He didn't like it at all.

* * *

Patrick threw his coat and bag on a chair behind the nurse's station. He draped his stethoscope around his neck, stuffing a small flashlight, notebook and pen into his pocket as he hurried past the examination cubicles of the Emergency Room.

He reached the Emergency Ward entrance, shocked by what he saw. The first wave of ambulances had arrived, discharging stretcher after stretcher of the wounded. The corridors echoed with the cries and moans and shrieks of the victims. Others, those able to walk, wandered around in dazed shock, their silent stares in eerie contrast to the noise all around. Attendants, orderlies, nurses, students and doctors ran back and forth in chaos, shouting orders above the din, rushing with I.V. bottles and blankets and oxygen masks, transferring bleeding, weeping patients from stretchers to hospital gurneys.

The blood was everywhere. It was on the victims, on those who attended them, on spattered walls, on pieces of clothing hastily ripped away and thrown to the floor. One doctor's crisp white jacket was bloodied from neck to waist and yet another doctor had grotesque bloody fingerprints running the length of his arm.

Patrick pushed his way through the confusion of people and noise closer to the E.W. He looked to the other end of the corridor. There, at the street entrance, yet more ambulances were careening in; beyond them was the glare of television lights as reporters and technicians spilled out of press cars. Patrick looked around desperately for there was so much to do he hardly knew where to begin, and the situation was nearly out of control.

"Patrick," David took his arm. "Thank God!"

"Where do you want me?"

"Here. You're on triage with me. We're all set up inside the E.W. but we have to organize out here. All the operating rooms but one are open. I'm waiting for Roth to open that one."

"What's the procedure?"

"Move all surgical cases to the O.R. floors. They'll have to wait, but pre-op has more room than we have. There isn't one extra inch of space here."

"Beds?"

"Ten beds open in the E.W., twelve in I.C.U. . . . Boyer!" David shouted at an orderly, "Where the hell are those cots? Get a move on!" He turned back to Patrick. "We've been told to expect fifty, maybe more, as our share. We're setting up cots for the overflow. Calls have gone out for blood, meanwhile we pray. Lola's been in touch with the burn centers. We transfer the serious burns out . . . Jackson!" he shouted, "I told you to clear a path. How do you expect us to move patients inside with that crowd? Do it!"

"David, Patrick," a short, balding man, out of breath, squeezed through the crowd to them. "What the hell's going on?"

"An explosion, a bomb, I don't know. You took your sweet time, Roth," David said angrily. "Stop off to inspect your real estate?"

"I—"

"Never mind," David snapped. "Get scrubbed and stand by. It's going to be hot and heavy tonight."

"Is my team here?"

"Scrubbed and waiting for you, genius. Go."

"Okay," David said to Patrick. "Let's . . ." he broke off, staring at a man staggering toward them.

The man's hair and face and hands were smeared with blood. His shirt front had been ripped away and the flesh of his chest hung down in bloody, jagged strips. Staring vacantly, his mouth agape, his hands worked at his chest, trying to put the pieces of torn flesh back in place.

"My God," Patrick said.

He hurried to the man, about to grab him when the man fell against him. He held him tightly, looking around.

"Waverly!" he shouted at the nearest doctor, "get this man on a gurney, stat."

David rushed over and with Patrick on the other side they half-walked, half-carried the man to the side of the corridor.

"You'll be all right," Patrick said to him. "We'll take care of you," he said, watching him intently for any sign of recognition.

Dr. Waverly, shouting for people to make room, pushed a gurney alongside and the three doctors lifted the man onto it.

"Get an I.V. on him. Type and cross." Patrick flashed his light in the man's eyes and then stepped back. "Stat," he said, hurrying away.

"David, I'll take the other side."

Patrick made his way across the corridor, sickened by what he saw around him. The victims lay moaning on their gurneys, some of them unrecognizable for the blood streaming down their faces. Others of them had shards of glass protruding from their flesh, while still others had pieces of broken bone jutting out from beneath the skin of mangled arms and legs. He saw one woman whose hand had been blown away, and a young man, no more than eighteen, whose arm had been severed at the elbow. One man had his nose smashed flat against his face and another, on the bed behind, was spitting out broken, bloody teeth. The acrid stench of burned flesh was everywhere.

"Dear God," Patrick murmured to himself, "help these people."

Patrick reached a long row of new arrivals and stopped. Buddy O'Hara and Henry Potter, silent, grim, worked over them.

"Dr. Dain," Henry said, "can we move them to O.R. yet?"

"Move them along. The elevators are waiting."

Patrick moved on, going from stretcher to stretcher, checking vital signs and reflexes, barking out orders to the hovering nurses. Nurses and students ran back and forth, attending the orderlies; orderlies slipped in and out, transferring patients to other floors, returning to move out the next group. At the end of fifty minutes the whole of the back corridor had been cleared, Patrick, Henry and Buddy wheeling the remaining cases to the E. W. entrance.

David slammed out of the E.W. doors. "I have two beds. What do you have there?"

"Concussion," Patrick said, tapping the metal bar of one gurney. "That one has a partially collapsed lung, and that one has multiple fractures."

David exhaled a breath. "O'Hara, we'll take the concussion and the lung in there," he said as Buddy and Henry moved them inside.

David looked at Patrick. "We have only one orthopedic man down here. He's tied up and so is everybody else. Take him over to the side, there'll be a wait."

Patrick took the gurney to the side of the corridor, rolling it flush against the wall. He bent over the man. "I'm sorry, there's going to be a delay. How's the pain? Did the shot help?"

"Tell you the truth, I'm still so stunned . . . I don't feel anything."

Patrick patted his shoulder. "Just as well. The mind helping the body. If you start to feel pain," he said, walking away, "yell and we'll get you something."

Patrick gazed at the other waiting patients; they'd all had preliminary treatment and were waiting to be moved on. Some, with only minor injury, would be released.

"Patrick," David called to him.

Patrick hurried to the E.W. door. "Where do you want me?"

"Inside. We're short-handed as hell. I don't know what we're going to do," he said anxiously. "What *are* we going to do?"

"We'll handle it," Patrick said quietly, looking at David. He saw the worry in his eyes, the uncertainty. "We'll handle it," he said again.

They were one step inside when the screeching of sirens stopped them.

"Christ!" David said as they saw additional ambulances pulling in.

"I'll take care of it," Patrick said. "How do we stand?"

David threw up his hands. "We're in trouble."

"What about the other hospitals?"

"City has room, I asked Lenox Hill to stand by."

"Right," Patrick said, running down the corridor.

He rushed through the doors, past two policemen standing guard, to the first of the ambulances. He was momentarily blinded by the glare of television lights flashing on, surrounded by a group of cameramen and reporters, shouting questions and directions as microphones were thrust in his face and cameras whirred.

"There's no statement now . . . there'll be a statement later. Please let me through, we have wounded . . ."

The group fell away and Patrick ran to the first ambulance.

"These are the last we got out, they're hurt pretty bad," the attendant said.

Patrick jumped into the back of the ambulance,

213

quickly checking the man on the stretcher. There was profuse bleeding from a gaping head wound; his pulse was faint, his breathing shallow and he was unconscious.

"Get him inside," Patrick instructed, scrambling out, hurrying on to the next.

"You got room for us?" the attendant asked.

"Maybe," Patrick said, entering the back of the ambulance.

Six people sat huddled together, coughing, gasping, their eyes red and streaming. He went from victim to victim, checking each one, carefully adjusting oxygen masks.

"Do you have enough oxygen?" he asked the attendant.

"Plenty."

"There's nothing serious here. Take them to City."

Patrick climbed into the last ambulance. He looked down at the woman, then rushed his stethoscope to her chest. He took a deep breath, rubbing at his tired eyes.

"She's dead, right?" the attendant asked. "I told 'em she was dead, but they loaded her on anyways. She's dead, right?"

"Yes," Patrick climbed out of the ambulance. "Are there any more coming?"

"You and Roosevelt got the last. More'n two hundred we handled tonight. You believe that?"

"I believe that," Patrick said, walking away.

He turned toward the E.W. entrance, deliberating for a quick moment as he saw a policeman trying to move the crowd back. He saw an open space at the edge of the crowd and he ran toward it, his head down, his arms extended, ready to throw a block. He ran in great, loping strides, making it through the door before he was noticed.

Patrick rushed into the E.W. The ward was at

capacity; there was hardly room to walk for all the doctors, nurses, and equipment jamming the narrow spaces between beds. The noise was impossible. Doctors' shouted orders flew through the air, some lost in the shouts and cries of patients or the rumblings of equipment which stood at almost every bed.

Patrick made his way to David. "We have to do something about a statement," he said, bending to adjust a piece of equipment. "There's a big press crowd outside."

"Julie's getting something ready," David said, stitching a wound on a unconscious woman. "That's not the only crowd we have to worry about. The victims' relatives are starting to come in. We're holding them in the E.R. waiting room." David glanced quickly about the room. "It's going to be a long wait. For some of them."

At eight o'clock in the morning a nurse raised the shades to daylight and David and Patrick gathered the exhausted doctors and students together. Most of the staff was sent off for a couple of hours of sleep before returning to their services; the students were sent to their quarters, morning classes cancelled.

They stood back then, surveying the ward. It was quiet now, the patients sleeping or hazy with drugs, most of the heavier equipment removed. David and Patrick looked at each other; they were haggard, their clothing caked with dried blood. They could hardly believe it was all over. They left the incoming morning shift to tend the ward and walked into the corridor.

"I never thought we'd make it. Never." David said as they rode upstairs.

"I wondered myself."

"No. You didn't. You're good in a crisis. The staff went to you when they had a problem, needed help. Not to me."

"You had your hands full," Patrick said, though he'd sensed David's nervousness all throughout the ordeal and he suspected the staff had sensed it too.

They walked to their offices in silence. Grace nodded at them as they came in. She stood behind her desk, simultaneously talking on the telephone and scribbling notes on a long yellow pad. She concluded her conversation and hung up, looking hard at David and Patrick. She'd never seen them looking so terrible; she was especially surprised by David, who was uncharacteristically dishevelled, his face very pale and drawn.

"There's juice and coffee waiting," she said hastily, nodding to a small tray.

"Coffee, I need coffee," David said, pouring the hot, dark liquid into a mug.

Patrick poured a glass of juice and drank it down. "What's the status?" he asked Grace.

"All elective surgery has been cancelled for today. Lola's closing the clinic for today. Patrick, Buddy had his makeup exam scheduled for today. I took the liberty of giving your permission to postpone for two days."

He nodded, pouring coffee for himself. "How do we stand on staff? Are all the floors covered?"

"The morning shift is in—all the guys we couldn't reach last night, they're here. Fresh as daisies. department heads are covering where it's thin. The only place we're *really* short is Larrimer. We had to pull staff to compens . . . " she broke off as Stuart Claven walked into the office.

"Good morning, doctors, Grace," he said impatiently.

"Stuart," David looked at him. "Are you here to congratulate us on a job well done?"

"Of course, of course, excellent work. Everybody is

to be commended. I have been in touch with my friends at the newspapers to insure we get our full credit."

"Our full credit," David said dully, looking at Patrick.

"But I am here on more pressing business," Stuart said. "I have just been to Larrimer Wing. To apologize personally for all the noise last night. All those sirens. Ordinarily we don't allow—but I expect it couldn't be helped, we must be understanding. As I was saying, I have just been to Larrimer Wing. There is only a skeleton staff up there. Where is the staff?"

"I had to move them to other services," David said.

"Moved?" Stuart's eyes narrowed. "You moved the staff from *Larrimer Wing?* Hospital directives clearly—"

"Everybody we could find worked long and hard last night. Under the worst possible circumstances. This creates some scheduling problems. We must give them a few hours rest, a shower, a change of clothes. At the same time the services must be covered. Therefore, until further notice, we're filling in with Larrimer people."

"Out of the question. I leave the scheduling of services to you, but Larrimer must be covered."

David slammed his cup to the tray and walked over to Stuart. "I'll tell you what's out of the question," he glared at him. "A patient dying for lack of care. *That's* out of the question. We have some *very sick* people here, Stuart. *Very sick.* We have to see them through. We can't do that with mirrors. Or with your damned hospital directives."

Stuart glared back at David. "If there is any problem—any problem whatsoever—in Larrimer Wing, I will hold you personally responsible. Is that understood?"

"It is," David turned away. "Now please go."

"Stuart, *please* GO."

"I am holding you responsible," Stuart said coldly, stalking out of the office.

David took his coffee and walked into his office. He sat down behind his desk and looked at Patrick. "He's holding me responsible."

"That wasn't like you. That outburst."

"I'm tired. I've never been so tired. And I had one good scare. This hospital in an emergency—not enough staff, equipment so old it creaks. It's a miracle we didn't lose more than we did."

"I'm sure they were short all over the city. There's no way to prepare for an emergency like this."

"Yes, but we raise a lot of money. It could go into equipment, into things we need. Instead it goes to Larrimer. I should have done something about it. I should have."

"It's not too late."

David looked up slowly. "What?"

"You're right, the emergency services are disgraceful. It's not too late to do something about them. And Stuart."

"Topple the Claven regime?"

"Why not?"

David looked at Patrick. After a while he smiled. "Yes. Why not?"

17

Patrick let himself into his apartment. He hung up his coat and started across the center hall when Hollis appeared.

"I was listening for you, sir, there's . . . why, Dr. Dain, what happened to you, sir?" Hollis asked, staring at Patrick's stained clothing.

Patrick glanced down at his sweater. "It was a very bloody night."

"The explosion. It's been all over the radio this morning. Terrible thing, sir. Terrible."

"Yes. I was going up for a shower and some sleep. Did you want something, Hollis?"

"I almost forgot what I came to tell you. There's a lady waiting to see you, sir. A Miss Parrish. I suggested she come back another time but she insisted on waiting. You look so tired, sir, shall I send her away?"

"Miss Parrish?"

"Yes, sir."

"Are you certain that's the name?"

"Yes, sir. Heard it clear as a bell, I did. Shall I send her away, sir?"

"No. No, don't do that," Patrick said slowly. "I'll change and be right down. Where is she?"

"The living room, sir."

Patrick went to the stairway. "Please tell her I won't

be long. And perhaps we could have a pot of coffee—and one of cocoa."

"Very good, sir."

Hollis crossed the hall, going to the living room doors. He knocked softly and then went inside.

"Dr. Dain will be with you shortly, madam."

"Thank you," Gail said, putting out a cigaret, quickly lighting another.

"I hope you will excuse the noise, madam, the women are cleaning."

"Yes," she said, looking off to the sliding doors, "it's a big place, isn't it?"

"It is that. It takes a lot of cleaning." Hollis deftly removed the brimming ashtray and put a clean one in its place. "May I get you anything, madam?"

"What? Oh, no, no thank you. What's your name?"

"Hollis, madam."

"Thank you, Hollis, I don't need anything," she said as he nodded and left the room.

Gail had been hugging her dark mink jacket close about her. Now she slipped it off and took a deep breath, trying to relax. She was nervous; she wondered if she'd done the right thing in coming here. She took a silver compact from her purse, looking into the mirror, brushing her hair back with her fingers. She put the compact away and took up her cigaret, taking short, steady puffs until she was wrapped in a cloud of gray smoke. After a few moments she stubbed the cigaret out and immediately lit another. By the time Patrick strode into the room her ashtray was again full.

"Good morning, Gail," Patrick said. "How are you? Nothing wrong, I hope?"

"It's rude of me to come over like this. Without calling," she said, fidgeting on the yellow couch. "I'm sorry."

"Not at all," Patrick said and then was quiet as

Hollis put a silver service on a low, square table.

"Thank you, Hollis," Patrick said. "Do you think you could ask them to postpone the vacuuming for a bit?"

"Straight away, sir," Hollis said, hurrying from the room.

Patrick sat down, looking at Gail. "I'm sorry I wasn't here when you arrived. There was an emergency at the hospital. Perhaps you heard?"

"Heard? No, no, I didn't. Something bad?"

"Very bad."

"I didn't hear the news this morning, I didn't see a paper . . . I had other things on my mind."

Patrick poured a cup of cocoa for Gail and coffee for himself. He stared at her for a moment and then looked at the full ashtray.

"That," he said, "is one of the worst things to do for an ulcer."

"I know. I'm—jumpy."

"I can see that. Why don't you stop fretting and tell me why you're here."

"It's . . . this is a lovely room," she said finally, looking around at the simple, elegant furniture, at the pale yellows and greens and whites of the room.

"Thank you." Patrick sipped his coffee, his eyes studying her.

There were slight shadows beneath her eyes, but otherwise she looked as fresh and pretty as ever. She wore no makeup save for a light covering of poppy-colored lipstick. Her dress was a dark brown, high-necked wool and her rich brown leather boots extended to her knees. Patrick sensed she'd dressed carefully, even conservatively, for this visit; he wondered what it was all about.

"I wish you'd say something."

Patrick shrugged. "I know you're here for a reason. I

don't know what it is, but I know it isn't the design of my living room. What's on your mind, Gail? Aren't you feeling well?"

"I feel okay, it's not that. This isn't a medical call."

"Then what is it? Tell me, I won't bite."

"This is difficult for me," she looked away.

"If it's that difficult perhaps it should wait. You're supposed to avoid stress. Your ulcer needs rest. I would hate to see you back at Rhinelander Pavillion."

"No, I have to talk about it. There are—things—I have to know. Please."

"Go ahead, if it will help," Patrick said, watching her closely.

"It's . . . really about David. David and me. David said he told you about us."

"That's right."

"And about other things."

"Now I understand what this is all about." Patrick leaned forward, "Gail, I think we ought to stop playing games. David told me about your background. As he knows it to tell," he added slowly. "David and I are close friends, we go back many years. It's natural he'd talk to me."

"As he knows it to tell," she echoed. "You mean you know better?"

"I know mistress is the wrong word. I know there is more than a semantic difference."

"Did you tell David? *Did* you?"

"No."

"Why not?"

"For many reasons."

"You're still considering it?"

"I'm still considering David, his feelings. Are you?"

"Why else would I be here?"

"You're here to find out if I spilled the beans. Or intend to. Which is different from considering David's feelings."

"I knew you'd found out. I saw it in your eyes the day I was leaving the hospital. It was John Caldwel, wasn't it?"

"That doesn't matter. David matters. Why didn't you tell him the truth?"

"I never thought it would get this far. It was casual in the beginning. Just fun. And he isn't the type you tell those things to. He ran around a lot, but he's a straight arrow if ever there was one. I knew that."

"Then why tell him anything?"

"When things started getting serious I thought I should say something. Before he heard it from someone else."

"There's the rub," Patrick said. "He's quite likely to hear the truth. I did. How will he feel then? What will it do to him? Your mistress fiction won't be much good then."

Gail lit a cigaret. "I thought he could handle mistress better than call girl," she stared at Patrick. "I got into—my line of work—by accident and I stayed in because I liked it. I didn't plan it. Anymore than I planned on meeting David. Or loving him. Mistress, call girl, what's the difference?"

"Mistress implies a degree of affection. I think that's what David's hanging onto. Your business is a straight cash transaction. There's not a hell of a lot to hang onto there. Not for David."

Gail sat back. "I know how David thinks. If I told him I'd been forced into my life of sin," she smiled, "by poverty, or by brutal parents, or something like that, it would be okay. But to do it by choice, that's another matter."

"Don't sneer at David's values. And don't be so sure it would be okay."

"You talk about values. Marriage is a value and what is it but a straight cash transaction? Legal sexual extortion? Hubby can come to bed all right, but he better not forget about the mink stole or the refrigerator-freezer, or the trip to Miami Beach."

Patrick stared at Gail. He'd been taken aback by her tone; he was shocked by her attitude.

"I wholeheartedly disagree," he said coolly. "What's more, David would disagree. Gail, we sometimes tell ourselves little stories to get us through the night, and maybe that's yours. But David will never buy it."

"Little stories, hell!"

Gail stood up and walked around the room. She stopped at a small table inlaid with mosaic tiles in a pattern of wild violets.

"I like what I do, no apologies." She bent to examine the table, running her finger over it. "I told you about my Aunt Lucy, the spinster lady who fainted a lot. What I didn't tell you was that she was the town tramp. An amateur—she didn't take money or gifts—but the town tramp nevertheless.

"Any man who came along found a home in her bed. The salesmen who came through town, the farmers who came in a few times a year for supplies. Drifters, even the goddamned census-taker. They were her *beaux*—to use her phrase—and she loved it."

Patrick stared down at the floor. This was a different Gail, he thought; not the friendly, open woman he'd met at the hospital, but a cynical, *hard* woman. He was sure David would not know this woman, sure that he had never seen this side of her, much as he was sure that this side was the real side.

Gail walked away from the table, picking up a small crystal vase. "She was the family disgrace. Mom pretended not to know anything about it, but you could see the confusion, the shame in her eyes. Dad harumphed a lot and talked vaguely about Lucy's 'problem.'"

Gail put the vase down and leaned against the mantel. "As if it was a problem," she said slowly. "It may have been a problem to the town, to my family, but it was no problem to Aunt Lucy. She was a timid woman ordinarily, but you should have seen her when she had a new beau. She glowed. She was—joyous. She had all the confidence in the world. I understood that. She loved the excitement of new men, of new adventures, of never knowing what to expect. And she loved sex," Gail looked at Patrick. "So do I."

"Do you love taking money for it?"

"That's power and I love power. What moves the world along, Patrick? Money, sex, power. I have it all."

Patrick poured a fresh cup of coffee. He drank it slowly, saying nothing for a long time. When he looked back at Gail his face was impassive but his eyes were very dark.

"Just where does David fit into all of this?"

"I love David. You *must* believe that."

"You *love* a lot of things. You use that word very loosely. Don't tell me about what you love. Tell me about what you understand. If David were here now, hearing this, he'd be destroyed. If he knew this is how you really feel, he'd be destroyed. Do you understand that? Do you understand David? I do. I understand him as well as I understand myself, perhaps better. David is not the man for all of this."

"Now who's sneering?"

"Call it anything you like, but my concern in this is David. I don't think you know him at all. He's a precise man, emotionally and in every other way. Things are good or bad, black or white, honest or dishonest, right or wrong. And character is all. Did he tell you anything about his marriage?"

Gail returned to the couch and sat down, gathering her coat about her. "He told me about his divorce."

"I wonder. I wonder if he really told you about his divorce, about the truth of it. He and Abby had a child, a daughter, did you know that?"

"He said she died a long time ago."

"They had a big summer place on Cape Cod. Abby and Ellen stayed there all summer, David got up as often as he could. One Thursday as he was preparing to leave for the Cape he got a call. There'd been an accident. Something about Ellen. She was six at the time.

"We hired a plane," Patrick continued. "We got there just as they were taking Ellen's body from the water. There'd been a swimming accident."

Patrick glanced away for a moment, remembering that tragic day with a terrible clarity.

"Ellen swam before she walked. She was an excellent swimmer for her age. And that day she'd been with other children, with her governess watching from water's edge, and with Abby watching only ten feet away. We never did find out exactly what happened. As close as we could make out, she was caught by a wave and swept away." Patrick took a deep breath. "I remember Abby saying over and over again, 'one minute she was there and then she was gone.' Over and over again. There were some rocky bluffs around there. It was concluded Ellen was swept along, hit her head and went under."

"It's an awful thing, but what does that have to do with me?" Gail asked.

"As soon as Ellen disappeared," Patrick went on, "Abby and the others went after her. The others gave up but Abby stayed in the water for hours. They couldn't get her out. She only came out when Ellen's body was found.

"The tragedy very nearly destroyed them both. It certainly destroyed their marriage. David knew it wasn't Abby's fault. He knew the tragedy couldn't have been prevented. He knew Abby did everything she could. He *knew* that. And he loved Abby very much. Very much. But somehow he couldn't stop blaming her for what happened. He couldn't help himself. In his world of right or wrong, good or bad, black or white, there wasn't room for distinctions. He tried. My God, how he tried. But it was no good. He couldn't get it out of his mind—his heart—that Abby was somehow responsible. In his black or white world *somebody* had to be responsible. Unfortunately it had to be Abby.

"Abby understood. With all her own pain, her own loss, she still understood. She finally suggested the divorce and she made everything as easy as she could. Because she understood David. She understood it had to be that way. Do you see what I mean?"

"I don't see what it has to do with me."

Patrick wiped at his tired eyes. "It has everything to do with you. David will never be able to live with the truth about you. No matter how hard he may try. He's not a man who can forget. He couldn't for Abby, and she was blameless. He won't for you, and you're not blameless. Aside from the fact of the matter, there is the deceit, deliberate deceit. David is not the man for that. For any of it."

"He loves me."

"He loved Abby."

"That was then, this is now."

"David hasn't changed," Patrick said tersely. "Gail, do you want to chance tearing David apart? Is that what you call love?"

"What do you know about it? We have something special. There's never been a man like David in my life and I'll chance anything to keep him," she said, her face set in cold determination.

Patrick looked at her for a long moment. He sighed. "I was married to a woman who had no scruples, no morals to speak of. But worse than that she had no kindness in her. There was a cold hard stone where the kindness should have been. She would do anything to get — or keep — what she wanted. She, too, would *chance* anything."

Angry red color streaked Gail's cheeks. "How dare you?"

"How dare I?" Patrick sighed again. "You talk proudly about your seamy business . . . you lie to David . . . you disregard his feelings . . . you try to con me into some grimy acquiescence . . . and you ask how I dare? You're nervy, I give you that."

"It's a business, like any other," Gail said loudly. "No more, no less. It's my honesty that shocks you."

"Your honesty. Let's examine that wonderful honesty. It's a business, yes, and I don't doubt that it has its place, but let's see it for what it is. You are bright, pretty, swathed in fur and jewels and designer dresses . . . and no different from the teenage pathetics on Times Square, hustling in mini-skirts and monkey fur jackets."

Gail jumped up, glaring at Patrick. "I won't be insulted this way."

Patrick stood, glaring back at her. "There is no way to insult a woman who takes money to open her legs."

Gail slapped him, hard. "Damn you. Damn you."

Patrick stepped away, rubbing his face. "Perhaps I deserved that. But it's sex-for-hire and that's not a gift a bride gives to her groom on their wedding day."

Gail swung around, color draining from her face. "Bride," she repeated softly. "Then I was right. Is David talking about marriage? Is that it?"

Patrick helped her into a chair. "Any pain?"

"A little," she said, "a little spasm here," she said, patting her abdomen.

"Do you have your pills?"

"Not with me."

"I'll get you something. Stay put," he said, rushing out of the room.

Patrick went to the hall closet. He opened the door and grabbed his bag.

"Dr. Dain, I was coming to get you. Master Tony is calling, sir."

Patrick looked at his watch. "Oh? I'll take it out here. Would you take some water to Miss Parrish? Not too cold," he said. "And give her these," he added, handing a small packet to Hollis.

Patrick went to the telephone. He picked up the receiver eagerly, smiling as he talked to his son. After a few moments the smile left his face. Disappointment was clear in his eyes when he hung up the phone.

"Tony won't be home for Thanksgiving," he said, returning to Hollis.

"I'm sorry, sir."

'Skiing with some of his schoolmates. In Vermont." Patrick said, going back into the living room.

"How do you feel?" he asked.

"I took the pills. They work right away. Thank you," she sat back. "It was a medical call after all."

Patrick sat down. "Gail, you're sick and I'm tired. We shouldn't continue this conversation."

"This is the important part. I . . .I never wanted to marry David. I had an idea that's what he had in mind, that's when I got sick. I don't want to lose him, but I never wanted to marry him."

Patrick looked at her in surprise. "What did you want?"

"For us to go on as we are. It's perfect the way it is. I don't want to marry him, I don't want to marry anybody. I like my life the way it is. I like my freedom. I love David, but living his life would drive me crazy. It wouldn't last a month and I can't lose him. I can't."

Gail took a sip of water. "Even if there are other men, I'll still love David."

"*What?*"

"Oh, don't look that way," Gail said. "I may need other men, one man's never satisfied me for long. But that has nothing to do with the way I feel about David."

"You can't be serious. Why don't we just throw David into the path of an oncoming train and have it over with?"

"What he doesn't know won't hurt him. And he *won't know.* You have my word."

"Forgive me if that doesn't fill me with confidence."

He stared at her. She was like Catherine, he thought, cold-bloodedly going after what she wanted, unwilling to count the cost.

"It has nothing to do with David. *No* man has ever satisfied me for long."

"I don't want to hear this. No more," Patrick said, standing.

"I didn't think you were as stuffy as David," she said, looking him up and down. "I was wrong. Well, I wanted to know where I stand."

"And do you?"

"I know I'm going to keep David off the subject of marriage. And you'll help."

"Count on it. But count on this too: David is not one to leave things undecided. A time and place for everything. There is a dating stage and then there is a serious stage and then there is marriage. He has a logical mind. What I'm saying is that while you're lining up bed partners, he's designing an ivy-covered cottage."

"I can handle David. Now that I know what he's thinking."

"Maybe. But you can't handle me. And when the

time is right I'll get through to him about you."

"You've made up your mind?"

"I have."

"So. We're enemies."

"Bitter."

Gail stood up. "I'm a formidable enemy."

"I don't doubt it."

"But then you have right on your side," she laughed. "Is that it? Tell me, why did a righteous man like you stay so long with an unscrupulous, immoral woman? The answer to that is also the answer to why David will stay with me."

"You're wrong. I was fully prepared to start divorce proceedings years ago. I was fully prepared to give Catherine half of everything I had, which is a considerable sum. But Catherine was fully prepared to fight it by dragging our son through a messy, public custody action. I could not allow that. She knew it. That's how she hung on. That's the kind of woman she was. I think that's the kind of woman you are." Patrick opened the door. "Get out."

Gail gathered up her coat and purse. "She won."

Patrick stared at her. "Did she?"

He took her elbow and propelled her through the door. "Hollis!" he called.

"Yes, sir," Hollis hurried out of the dining room.

"Please show Miss Parrish out."

Patrick walked to the staircase as Hollis came forward and helped Gail on with her coat. He opened the door and held it for her. "Shall I ring for the elevator, madam?"

"No, thank you, Hollis," she said, walking into the vestibule. "Goodbye."

"Good day, madam."

Hollis closed the door. He hurried to the stairs. "Dr. Dain, sir?"

Patrick, near the top of the landing, stopped and looked down. "Yes, Hollis?"

"Do you want anything, sir? Breakfast? Coffee?"

"All I want is sleep. I could sleep for a year." He continued up the stairs. "I don't want to be disturbed."

"Very good, sir."

Patrick continued on to his rooms. He entered his bedroom and walked slowly to the bed. He flopped down, staring at the ceiling. His head spun with the events of the preceding hours. They had been, he thought, among the worst hours of his life.

He thought about Tony's call. Now, he thought, he wouldn't see Tony until December — more time with his son lost, irrecoverable. He pictured Tony, tall and dark, gliding surely down the slopes, and for a moment he thought about flying to Vermont for a day, an afternoon, an hour. But that would be the last thing Tony would want, he thought, and quickly dismissed the thought.

Patrick closed his eyes but he was almost too tired to sleep; he had seen too much, heard too much, in the past hours and his mind was in turmoil. Pictures of the Emergency Ward flashed into his mind, pictures of blood and pain, and he tossed restlessly.

He remembered the eerie, enraged laughter coming at him, chasing him into a corner. He buried his head in the pillows and Gail's words floated back to him in uneven snatches — "other men, but David will never" . . . "that has nothing to do" . . . "can handle David" . . . "will never know" . . . "a business like any."

Patrick turned over on his side. He pounded the pillows and again closed his eyes. He saw Gail, her face suddenly hard; he saw David, worried, upset, his clothing bloody; he saw Tony swooping down a snowy slope. Finally he saw Ann O'Hara, her steady blue eyes, her smile, first shy and then mischievous. He would call her, he thought to himself; he would call her today. And then he slept.

18

"We could take the crosstown bus," Buddy said, looking at Henry Potter.

"Why don't we take a cab? I'll pay."

Buddy grinned. "Okay. An intern can afford it better than I can. Hey, Henry, you just disagreed with me again."

"What? Yes, I guess I did. How many does that make?"

"I can stop keeping count, now that you're learning to speak your mind. I'm doing a pretty good job with you, if I do say so myself. Did you notice on rounds today how the students waited for you to give them instructions?"

Henry looked down at the sidewalk. "It was the first time. I felt like—"

"Okay, okay, don't go humble on me. I'll have to start the lessons all over again."

"You're right."

"You're getting there, Henry."

The two young men turned, walking toward Madison Avenue. They saw Lola Shay coming their way and they stopped.

"Hello, Dr. Shay. Can we help you with your packages, ma'am?" Henry asked.

"I can manage, thanks," Lola said, shifting two Bonwits' shopping bags around. "Are you two going off duty now?"

"Yes, ma'am. We have the night off."

Lola looked closely at Henry Potter. He'd been changing subtly but surely in the past few weeks and she was as surprised as she was pleased. She'd hadn't had much confidence in Patrick's pairing of these very different young men, but now she had to admit it was working; she'd seen Henry's assurance growing day by day.

If he was not yet fully at ease with his peers, he was closer to it than he'd ever been. He was different at rounds as well, taking his first tentative steps to his rightful place in the hospital order. She heard fewer jokes about him now, she thought, and once she'd even heard him speak sharply to an erring student. It was amazing, she thought. Why, he even looked different!

"You can't figure it out, can you?" Buddy crowed. "It's the haircut. I made Henry get a good haircut. And some new ties. Pretty sharp, hah?"

"Sharp," Lola agreed. "And you, Mr. O'Hara, I understand you passed your lab makeups."

"*Sailed through,*" Buddy said exuberantly. "The champ is back."

"I don't know whether to be glad for you or worried for us," Lola laughed, shaking her head.

Buddy glanced at Henry. "Henry, here, helped a lot. What's the champ without his trainer, right?"

Lola laughed again. "If you say so, Mr. O'Hara." She looked from Buddy to Henry and back again. "Amazing," she said, for she realized with a start that these two were actually becoming friends. These two, who'd gone it alone for so long, had found a friend in each other. "Amazing," she said again. "But I don't have the night off and I have to get back to work."

"Can we take your packages inside, Dr. Shay?"

Henry asked.

"I can manage. Have fun," Lola said, walking up the street.

Buddy and Henry walked to Madison Avenue and hailed a taxi. Henry gave his address to the driver and they settled back for the ride.

"Henry, are you interested in her?"

"In Dr. Shay?" Henry asked, surprised. "I like her. She was very nice to me. She was nice to me when nobody else was."

Buddy pantomined a long, sad face and Henry smiled slightly.

"I like her, but the answer to your question is no. I'm not interested in her. Not the way you mean."

"That's good, because she's kind of old for you, and the girl you met the other day sounds more promising."

"I don't know about that. She's a dancer, wants to be a dancer. Show business types . . ." he left the sentence unfinished.

"Like you know so much about show business types," Buddy hooted.

"A little," Henry said softly. "Buddy, I appreciate your coming over to help me pack up."

"Sure, but I still don't see why you have to move out of your apartment."

"My parents' apartment."

"Okay, your parents' apartment. Just because they're coming to town. Don't you get along?"

"We get along. You'll understand when we get there," he stared out the window. "I'm not taking too much, so it won't take too long to pack. It's the books I'll need."

The cab came to a stop. "This is it," the driver said.

Henry paid him and they got out. Buddy stared at the tall, sleek apartment building.

"You live *here?*" he asked.

The doors opened at twenty-five and they walked into a long, carpeted corridor.

"It's over here," Henry said, fumbling for his keys.

A long, low whistle escaped Buddy's lips as they entered the apartment. "Hey, man, you're rich! You must be loaded!"

"My parents."

"How come you never told me?"

Henry stared down at the black and white tiles of the foyer. "It's their money . . . it has nothing to do with me."

Buddy walked into the living room and gazed around. "Wow!" he said, looking at the white linen couches, the glass and chrome tables, the shining parquet floors decorated here and there with area rugs in stark greens and blues and reds. He looked at the many plants massed by a large, glass-doored terrace. "Man," he said softly, "this is living. What a place. What do they do, rob banks for a living?"

Henry gestured to a gleaming baby grand piano banked with photographs in silver frames. "Have a look."

Buddy crossed the room and peered at the photographs. "These are all pictures of movie stars," he said, confused. "Mostly Melanie Lawrence and Don Potter," he added, taking a closer look. "Potter," his head snapped up. "Potter, *your* name is Potter. Is he a relative?"

"My father."

Buddy stared at Henry in disbelief. "C'mon," he said after a while.

"No joke. He's my father."

Buddy looked back at the photographs. He picked up a two-shot of Don Potter and Melanie Lawrence. "And your mother is *Melanie Lawrence?*"

"Yes."

Buddy sat down. He looked again at the photograph, shaking his head. There was Don Potter, dark and handsome, flashing his famous smile—and there was Melanie Lawrence, her perfect, elegant face tilted toward her husband; together one of the most beautiful couples he'd ever seen.

"I inherited my father's height and coloring," Henry mumbled. "The rest of me looks like my grandfather. The family ugly, until I came along."

"It's . . . not that," Buddy said lamely.

He was embarrassed, for he knew Henry had read his thoughts. He felt badly, for he wondered how many times before he'd had to read similar thoughts.

"Hell, I'm not going to lie," Buddy said finally. "So you're no movie star. So what?"

Henry smiled. "Thank you. Most people do lie. To make me feel better, but it only makes me feel worse.

"Me, I'd like to be Robert Redford, but I settle for what I got," he laughed. "Ever watch girls watching Redford? Their eyes get all glazed over, their mouths get dumb little half-smiles. Jesus, they hardly *breathe*. But I settle for what I got, and you'll settle for what you got. And with the right haircut and a few more pounds, it's more than you think."

"What I don't understand is why you didn't let on? Remember last week in the lounge? We were all watching TV. *The Girl Next Door*, your father's biggest movie. I've seen it a hundred times on TV. My Aunt Mae, she knows it by heart. You didn't say a word."

Henry shrugged. "You can imagine what they would have said. Buddy, I don't want you to tell anyone. I'm just starting to—fit in. This would ruin it."

"It's up to you. But if I had famous parents—"

"We keep our lives separate," Henry said quickly. "It's always been that way."

"Are they kicking you out of here?"

Henry sat down. "They never say anything directly. But it's more comfortable this way. First of all, I'm twenty-six years old. That's a clue to Mother's real age. She's an actress, she cheats on her age. Then," he said quietly, "there is the way I look."

"C'mon, Henry, that's not fair."

"Maybe I can settle but they can't. They were always this . . . golden couple. In real life, too, not only in the movies. I don't exactly fit into their—image. So when they come to town they rent me a suite at the Plaza.

"They don't come often but when they do there are a lot of parties. And interviews. This way they're free to do what they want and so am I. It works out well."

"It sounds like a rotten deal to me."

"It isn't. When I get my residency I'll get my own place. This is fine for now. Anyway, I'm used to it. I went away to school when I was seven. I've never seen much of them."

A quick anger came into Buddy's eyes. "They sent a seven-year-old away?"

Henry looked at Buddy. He smiled slightly. "They didn't send me to Siberia. It was a very nice military school in Virginia. There were a lot of other kids my age in the same boat—once we got used to it, it wasn't so bad." He shrugged. "Some people aren't meant to be parents. Some people shouldn't have children. I understand that. Now."

"No, that's wrong," Buddy said quickly, intently. "Once you have a kid you have to do everything you can for him. You can't walk away."

Henry looked thoughtfully at Buddy. "It doesn't always work that way."

"You *make* it work that way! If it's your kid you *make* it work that way."

"You're not talking about me, about my parents, are you?"

"Yeah . . . who else?"

Henry looked down. "You," he said softly.

"Me? No, I'm talking about you, your parents had no right to get rid of you that way."

"I'm sorry . . . I didn't mean to . . . I'm sorry, Buddy." Henry said. "My parents were involved with their careers and with each other. They did the best they could. They gave me everything I wanted—and things I hadn't even thought of. They're not really that rich, but they always lived as if they were. I had everything."

Buddy got up and went to the terrace. He was quiet, staring at the sky, but his hands were clenched in tight fists.

"Everything but love," he said angrily. "Walking away like that! How can you do that to your own kid!"

Henry went to the terrace and looked at Buddy. He was distressed by what he saw. Buddy's face was white with rage, the vein in his temple throbbing furiously. His lips were pressed tightly together, his eyes blue fire.

"Buddy, I'm so sorry . . . please, let's forget it . . . I didn't mean . . ."

Buddy walked away, flinging himself on a couch. "It's not your fault. What you said before . . . it's true. I started thinking about your folks and that got me thinking about my old man. The bastard of all time. A bastard's bastard."

"I'm sorry, Buddy."

"Stop apologizing. You have nothing to apologize for." He looked at Henry. "My old man left us a long time ago. Took a walk and left two little kids behind. The bastard left us with nothing. He even took his insurance policy. Cashed it in and bye bye kiddies. He didn't even bother to say goodbye. The bastard."

Henry's brown eyes were very sad as he looked at Buddy. "I wish I could—say something. I wish I knew—what to say."

"Nothing to say. You know," Buddy said slowly, "the worst thing was I thought he loved us. I mean he really put on a great act, like we were everything to him. Then he's gone. I could never get over that a parent wouldn't love his kid. How could that be?"

"What if he loved you but . . . couldn't help himself? If he had to do what he did?"

"Baloney. You love somebody, then you love them. They're the most important thing. There are no two ways," Buddy stared at Henry. "I never talked about the old man before. This is the first time."

"Maybe you should get it out of your system, Buddy."

"We loved him and he took a walk. How do you get that out of your system? You mean to tell me you accept that your parents didn't want you? It doesn't hurt? Bad?"

Henry looked away, his finger tracing small circles on the glass tabletop. "I don't think about it much anymore."

"Sure you do. It's why you have that inferiority complex. It's why you were like a scared mouse."

Henry smiled. "No. I was like a scared mouse because I *was* a scared mouse. I gave up on my parents a long time ago. My home was the military school. We were all misfits there, so we belonged. And every move we made was planned for us. We had discipline but no independence. When I left military school for the real world I got scared. I didn't belong anywhere and I had to do my own planning. I was scared."

"Because you didn't know your own value," Buddy said. "Henry, that's something you're supposed to feel from the day you're born—your own value. It's something your parents are supposed to show you."

"Parents can give you values, but not your own

value. That's something everybody has to decide for themselves. It's not that I didn't know my own value. It's that I didn't have courage. That's where you came in. You've shown me things, Buddy. Maybe without knowing it."

"I could have been passive, like you," Buddy said. "But instead I got angry. I used the anger, made it work for me."

"And you had your mother," Henry offered quietly.

"Ma . . . she's the best. She did everything for me. Soon I'll be able to do everything for her. I'll look after her interests like she did mine. If it hadn't been for Ma . . . man, the old man might have really messed me up."

"Buddy, I've heard people, even old people, still blaming their parents for their own actions. That's wrong, I think. There comes a time when we have to grow up and take responsibility for ourselves."

"What are you saying? You think I'm making *excuses*?"

"Sometimes," Henry said gently, "it's not our parents who mess us up. Sometimes we mess ourselves up. I think," Henry took a deep breath, "I think you still love your father. That's what you're angry about."

"He died. We heard about it."

"His memory then."

Buddy let out a great whoop of laughter. "Love him? His memory? I *hate* him. I *hate* everything I remember about him. Everything. He'd come home from work, you know, *when* he worked, and he'd tell us jokes . . . or he'd get us around the record player and we'd all sing these old Irish songs . . . or he'd tell us . . . old . . . Irish . . ." Buddy's voice broke off as sudden remembrances of those times flooded his mind.

He saw his family gathered around the kitchen table, around his father's chair in the living room; he saw his father bent over his and his sister's beds as they said their prayers; he saw him reading poetry to them, telling stories, making them up as he went along.

Buddy blinked rapidly as he felt the moisture in his eyes. Henry stood up. "I think I'll put some coffee on," he said, quietly leaving the room.

Buddy nodded and turned away, covering his face with his hands. He felt the tears come and he didn't try to stop them. They were slow, sad tears, old tears he should have cried a long time before and he felt somehow better for them. Yet more memories ran through his mind and he examined each one, seeing each one as clearly and perfectly as he might a recent event. The last memory was of the last morning he'd seen his father. A rainy morning, his father cursing the rain. His father hugging them as he always did, going jauntily out the door, a long wool scarf flying behind him.

There were more tears—hot tears at first, harsh, and then suddenly soft, caressing, until they were gone. After a few minutes Buddy took a tissue from his pocket and wiped his eyes. Henry came back into the room.

"You have good timing," Buddy said, looking up.

"Dr. Shay says it's one of my best things."

"We had some good times . . . my father and all of us."

"So did we," Henry smiled. "I went home to Bel Air during the holidays. It wasn't always perfect, but I was always glad I'd been there. I'd rather have had those times than not."

"The same for me. But . . . he *shouldn't* have left. He shouldn't."

Buddy smiled. "You have a sensible way of seeing things."

"You can't live your life on that."

"I've been an observer all my life. I see some things other people don't see."

"Yeah? Well, I see something you don't."

"What?" Henry asked.

"Those," Buddy said, pointing at the photographs. "My date's a student, but yours wants to be in show business. You want to go through all that stuff about your parents again? You want to have her hanging on you wanting an introduction to them?"

"I hadn't thought about it. No, I don't."

"We'll take them down for tonight. If she asks, tell her your father's a . . . dentist, or a lawyer, something like that. The point is, she likes you for what you are or the hell with her. No distractions. Understand, Henry?"

"I'm learning."

Buddy threw a bunch of crumpled tissues into an ashtray. "See, Henry, with women, they have to take you on your own terms or it's no go. There are plenty out there for a guy like you. Plenty, I guarantee it."

Henry smiled, taking the pictures from the piano. "They haven't been breaking down my door."

"That was for the old Henry. This is a new deal."

Henry turned around. "Thanks . . . I mean for everything."

Buddy stared at the floor. He was quiet for a moment and then he looked at Henry. "I guess it's mutual . . . for everything."

19

"There," Ann O'Hara said, making a last adjustment on a broad lace collar. "How does that look?" she asked, peering into the mirror in her tiny bedroom.

"It's the perfect touch. You look wonderful, Ann," Mae said. "Such a glow on you."

Ann turned to Mae. "I wasn't sure I could get away with this dress, it's so old," she said, fingering the plain black wool. "The collar makes such a difference. Thank you, Mae."

"It's yours as much as mine. Been in the O'Hara family for a hundred years, fine Irish lace. You could say it's our family heirloom."

"I'll be very careful with it. I promise." She looked at Mae. "You look so worried. Why?"

"It's you I'm worried about, Ann. I knew there was trouble coming and now it's here sure."

Ann sat next to Mae on the bed. "Where, what trouble?"

"Dr. Dain, that's the trouble I'm talking about. Ann, a sensible woman like you, what are you doing going out with a man like that? We're not his kind of people, you'll only get your poor heart broke."

Ann took Mae's plump hand. "It's only dinner. And he's a *nice* man, you'll see. You'll like him. I do."

"That's plain to see. Your eyes all glowing, and that

color in your cheeks didn't come from any makeup bottle. You look like a young girl again."

"Is that so bad?"

"It is when it's Dr. Dain that's causing it. He who he is and you who you are. It wasn't so long ago you were cleaning house for people like him."

"He knows that. It doesn't seem to bother him."

"But where can it lead to? Nowhere. People like that don't take people like us serious."

"Mae, it doesn't have to lead anywhere. It doesn't have to be serious. That's not what this is about, please believe me."

"How can I, looking at you? You're floating up there on cloud nine now. But when you fall off, what then, Ann? What then? Look at yourself, glowing like a young girl."

Ann glanced away. It was true, she thought to herself, she looked better than she had in years and it was more than vitamin pills or iron capsules. It was a radiance that came from deep within her whenever she thought of Patrick Dain. She'd been almost giddy the last few days, giddy with anticipation of tonight, and she knew Mae was right; she must not take this seriously, for he would not.

"He's coming *here*, Ann? I thought you were meeting him."

"He insisted."

"You should've . . . well, I'll hide in here."

"You'll do no such thing," Ann said, steering Mae from the small room. "Let's answer the bell before he thinks there's no one home."

Ann pressed the buzzer and then opened the door. She went into the hall and leaned over the stairway railing.

"It's up here," she called. "I'm sorry about the climb."

"Be right there," Patrick called back.

"Ann," Mae pleaded, "I can't meet him. Let me go back in the bedroom—or the kitchen."

"I want you to meet him. I want him to meet you. You're my best friend, aren't you?" she asked, giving Mae a quick hug.

"I look a wreck, Ann."

"You look fine." Ann turned back to the railing. "It's one more flight."

"Right there."

Ann met him at the top of the stairs. "I'm sorry . . . such a long climb. I could have met you downstairs."

"Not at all," Patrick said.

"Come inside."

Patrick walked into the apartment. Mae stood near the door, nervously patting her hair, and he smiled at her.

"Good evening," he said.

"Hello," Mae whispered.

"Mae," Ann said, "this is Dr. Dain. My sister-in-law—my friend—Mae O'Hara."

"A pleasure," Patrick smiled.

"Hello, Dr. Dain."

Mae offered her hand briefly and then stared up at him. He certainly was handsome, she thought; Ann was right about that.

"Please," Patrick said, "may we be Patrick and Mae and Ann?" he asked.

"Would you like a drink?" Ann asked. "We have some wine. It's not very good," she added quickly, "but after the long climb maybe . . . please, would you like to sit down?"

Patrick smiled at Ann. She looked beautiful, he thought, her eyes sparkling, becoming pink color in her cheeks, her blond hair shining, framed in an exquisite old lace collar.

"We're all feeling a bit ill at ease," he smiled. "Let's not." He sat down. "I'd love a little wine. But first," he handed Ann a small bunch of violets. "I understand bringing flowers is considered chauvinistic. I hope you don't mind."

"They're beautiful. Thank you," Ann said, looking down at the delicate flowers.

"I know just the place," Mae said suddenly. She took the flowers from Ann's hand. "I'll get the wine, too," she said, scurrying from the room.

Ann smiled after her. "She's—nervous."

"Aren't we all?" Patrick laughed. "I haven't had a dinner date in quite a while. It feels a little strange."

Ann felt reassured by his words. She had the feeling he would always find the right thing to say and she was relieved, for she'd been worried about an evening of conversation with a man she hardly knew.

Patrick gazed around the room. "It's comfortable, warm," he commented after a while. "I envy you that. My place is cold, not at all comfortable. Too big."

"We don't have that problem here," Ann smiled. "As you can see," she said, sitting down.

Mae came back into the room carrying three glasses of wine on a plastic tray. She put the tray on the scarred coffee table and then looked at Ann, shaking her head in Patrick's direction.

"What?" Ann looked up at Mae but she only continued shaking her head.

"What is it, Mae?" Ann frowned.

"His coat. The doctor's coat, Ann."

Ann looked at Patrick. "Oh! I'm sorry, I forgot to ask if I could take your coat. We don't get many visitors around here; I'm out of practice."

"I'm comfortable. Please, Mae, sit down and be comfortable too."

Mae took a glass of wine and sat down on the couch. Ann and Patrick took up their glasses.

"Let's drink to Buddy," Patrick suggested.

"To Buddy," Mae said, drinking down half the wine in one gulp.

Ann and Patrick chatted about Buddy for several minutes. Mae was silent, fidgeting on the couch, though her eyes were fast on Patrick.

Mae liked his manner. He was polite but easy about everything; it was, she marveled, as if he always spent his nights sitting in a shabby apartment in an old tenement building. He was an easy man to be around, she conceded, though as far as she was concerned, he was not the man for Ann to be around.

Patrick tried several times to draw Mae into the conversation. Each time she replied in hushed monosyllables, her eyes fixed on him. She watched him, listened to him, studied him. Mae recalled the newspaper stories she'd read, the stories of Catherine Dain's death. She felt a kind of shock, for he didn't seem like the kind of man to do harm to anyone.

Patrick returned his glass to the tray. "I think we ought to be making our way," he said to Ann. "Mae, why don't you join us? I can easily change the reservation. Please come."

"Yes, Mae," Ann smiled, "that's a wonderful idea."

"I couldn't, Dr. Dain," Mae said shyly. "Thank you for the invitation . . . thank you, Doctor, but I couldn't."

"Another time then." Patrick stood up. "But only if you'll call me Patrick."

"Patrick," Mae said and then covered her mouth with her hand, surprised at herself.

"Good. Ann, where's your coat?"

"Right there. One good thing about this apartment is that we never have to go very far to get anything."

Ann opened the closet door and took her coat from the hanger. Patrick took her coat and held it for her. It was a gray wool, worn about the collar and elbows, but if Patrick noticed, he gave no sign.

"Mae—" Ann began.

"Don't you worry about me, Ann. I'll clear up here and go right home."

"I brought the car," Patrick said. "It's such a bad night. We'll drop you off."

"I couldn't. The reservations and all."

"We'll drop you off," Patrick said, helping Mae into her coat.

"Wait, I almost forgot," Mae said.

She hurried away, quickly returning with Ann's small, black suede purse. The violets were carefully pinned to the purse, pinned over the shiny spots where the suede had worn away.

They left the apartment then, Patrick leading the way down the stairs. He took Ann and Mae's arms as they reached the street.

"There it is," he said.

"Dear God!" Mae said.

She stared open-mouthed at the curbside. Parked there was a sleek black Mercedes, a man in uniform holding the car door open.

"This is Hollis."

"How do you do, ladies, this way please," Hollis said, helping them into the car.

"If you will give Hollis your address," Patrick said when they were settled inside.

"We're subway and bus people," Ann said to Patrick. "This is a little more than we're used to," she smiled in the darkness.

Mae grabbed Ann's arm. "I wish I'd known," she said. "I'd've called Mrs. Foley to look out the window at me arriving in style."

Patrick pressed a button for an overhead light and then moved a panel at the side of the car.

"You may call from here," he said as Ann and Mae gaped at the telephone. He spoke briefly to the mobile operator and then gave the phone to Mae. "If you will give her Mrs. Foley's number."

Mae spoke uncertainly into the receiver, all the while taking quick glances at Patrick.

"Hello, hello? Is that you?" they heard her say. "Well, Edna Foley, I dare you to beat what I'm going to tell you now . . ."

Patrick tilted his head toward Ann. "She's enjoying herself."

"So am I. This is something out of the movies," Ann replied, watching Mae.

The car glided to a stop before a crumbling old building similar to Ann's. Hollis hurried out to open the door. Patrick helped the women out.

Mae looked up, waving at the woman framed in an open window.

"That takes care of Mrs. Edna Foley!" Mae said triumphantly.

"Have a nice evening," Ann smiled, kissing Mae's cheek.

"It was a pleasure, Mae," Patrick said. "Remember, dinner one night soon," he added and then impulsively bent and kissed her hand.

"Thank you, I had a real good time," Mae said. "Take good care of our Ann."

"I will," Patrick said, helping Ann back into the car.

Hollis walked Mae to the door of her building, waiting until she was safely inside. He returned to the car and they drove off.

"That was very nice," Ann said, "what you did for Mae. She'll never forget it. Good things never happen to her."

"Perhaps it's her turn. Ann, I have a bone to pick with you. You've solved the problem of what to call me by calling me nothing at all. My name is Patrick. Say it."

"I—will."

"Say it. Now."

"Patrick."

"That's better."

They said little on the way to the restaurant. Ann savored every detail of the young evening, looking hard at everything as if to memorize it. Patrick, watching, understanding, did not interrupt.

"Shall I wait, Dr. Dain?" Hollis asked as they got out of the car.

Patrick glanced at his watch. "If you'd come back about ten."

"Very good, Dr. Dain. Madam," Hollis nodded, returning to the car.

They entered the restaurant and Patrick checked their coats. He took Ann's arm and steered her ahead.

"Good evening, Dr. Dain. Your table is ready, sir."

"Thank you, Ricardo," Patrick said as they crossed the pretty room to a corner banquette.

Patrick ordered a bottle of wine and then was silent as Ann looked around. It was a quiet room with snowy white linen, candlelight and small bunches of fresh flowers on each table. The upholstered banquettes were deep and comfortable and Ann sat back.

"It's beautiful," she said. "I've never been in a real restaurant before."

"I'm glad you like it."

Patrick tasted the wine and nodded at the steward. "Excellent," he said.

Ann sipped the deep ruby wine. "And I gave you Gallo," she laughed. "And you drank it."

"And enjoyed it."

"You're too polite."

"Never mind me. Tell me about you."

They talked easily through three courses. Ann had never tasted such food before, and in such a beautiful setting, with such a handsome man at her side, she was having the time of her life. She'd found it easy to talk to Patrick and she thought she must have smiled and laughed more this evening than she had in all of the ten years before. She wished she could save the evening, preserve it whole in some kind of vast book.

"Why so pensive?" Patrick asked as their coffee was put before them. "What are you thinking about?"

"This evening. I've had a wonderful time. I'm . . . Cinderella tonight. Can you understand that?"

"I think so. Ann . . . forgive the personal question, but why didn't you remarry?"

"I don't know. The first years after Brendan left I was just too busy to think about it. As the years went by it didn't seem that important. I met a few nice men. I suppose I could have gotten them to the altar. But they weren't right. I married Brendan for love—obviously not for common sense." She smiled. "If I ever married again it would be for the same reason. But in the back of my mind I have an idea that love comes along only once. I'm sorry," she said quickly, "I know you're a recent widower. I didn't mean to—"

"How do you know? Did Buddy tell you?"

"Mae. She reads a lot of newspapers."

"Ah, yes, the newspapers," he smiled slightly. "Is Mae your only family, aside from the children?"

"Just about. I have a brother living in Ohio, but we never see him. We exchange Christmas cards, that's all. Another brother died when he was six. The rest of Brendan's family is in Ireland, a whole branch of the family I've never met. Mae never married, so there are no nieces, no nephews."

"Has it been lonely for you?"

"Well, for a long time I had Buddy and Jill clattering around the apartment. Now, they're gone. Buddy's still here, but he's gone, really." Ann sipped her coffee. "I work, I have things to do, and Mae's over a lot. Mae's the one who's really lonely. I've never minded being by myself."

Patrick stared thoughtfully at Ann. He remembered Catherine, how she'd hated, *refused*, to be alone. "I don't *care* how sick your precious patient is," he remembered her shouting during one of their arguments. "I *won't* be alone. I *won't*. She's old. She's going to die anyway, and you promised to take me to Elizabeth's party. If you don't take me, I know someone who will. Jock is *dying* to take me out. He's *dying* to get into my pants if you want to know the truth. I'll call him. If you go to that stupid hospital, I'll call him. All right, you asked for it. I'm calling him and tonight's going to be his lucky night. Don't wait up for me."

"Patrick? Are you okay?" Ann asked.

"Forgive me. An unpleasant memory. I can't imagine why. This evening has been one of the nicest of my life," he smiled at her.

"I'm probably boring you to death. It's so nice to talk to someone. I talk too much."

"You are *not* boring me. And I heard every word you said. Please go on."

"I was just saying that it's mostly around the holidays I feel sad. This year especially. Jill won't be able to come home. Buddy has to work on Thanksgiving."

"I wish I could do something about that, but I can't. Thanksgiving is a slow day at the hospital and we cover with students, interns and junior residents. I appreciate how you feel. My son will be away too."

"You have a son?"

"He's sixteen. He's at school at St. Botholphs in Massachusetts. He's going skiing in Vermont over the holiday. You're right, holidays can sting a little. What will you do?"

"Mae will come over. We'll have a small turkey. Nice but not very festive."

Patrick stared at Ann and then smiled. "I have an idea. A truly magnificent idea."

"What?" Ann asked, caught up in the excitement in his eyes.

"Well, I also happen to have a truly magnificent place in the country. Lots of woods and snow and fireplaces. I think we deserted parents should band together. You and I—and Mae—should have an old-fashioned Thanksgiving in the country. How about it?"

Ann was quiet for a long moment. She wanted to enjoy his words, his invitation, for as long as she could before having to decline.

"I'd love it, really. But I couldn't."

"Why not? Even you must have the day off from all your jobs."

"That's not it."

"Hollis can drive you and Mae to Connecticut early Thanksgiving morning. It's only a couple of hours away, but what a difference those hours make. It's a great big place, Ann, but it's a wonderful place. Alice, the caretaker's wife, is a wonderful cook. She'll put out a feast, wait and see. Even if you can deny yourself, you can't deny Mae," he smiled. "I can imagine the look on her face when she sees it all."

"Patrick, Mae doesn't think this is right. She didn't think I should go out with you tonight. She'd be very upset if I mentioned Thanksgiving. And she has a point."

"What point?"

"You've been . . . wonderful to us. All of us. And

I've never had a more wonderful time. But we . . . we're from two different worlds. I have no business being here with a man like you. Mae's right about that. I couldn't get myself to say no to tonight, but I can't take it any further."

"Is that all it is? How foolish. How foolish of Mae and how foolish of you. I like your company and I think you like mine. I like Mae. When she stops being afraid of me, I think she'll like me. I have a wonderful place in the country which I know you both will like. Why not put all those things together and have a nice holiday?"

"We don't . . . belong," Ann shook her blond head.

"I tell you what," Patrick said crisply, "we'll leave it up to Mae. You propose it to her the way I've proposed it to you. Add that you want to go. Then see what she says."

"She'll say no."

"Maybe not. If for no other reason than Mrs. Edna Foley," he laughed. "Bless her heart."

Ann smiled, though her fingers toyed nervously with a book of matches. She wanted very much to go, but if she did, she wondered, would she be opening a door to something more than she could handle? If she went, she'd never be able to get Patrick Dain out of her mind for there would be too much to remember. She could not take that chance, she decided; she must not.

"Thank you," Ann said softly. "It's kind of you but we . . . can't. Thank you anyway."

"We have agreed to leave it up to Mae."

"No," Ann said firmly. "I . . . Patrick, I don't want to get in over my head."

"Neither do I. Don't make this complicated."

Ann was flustered. She wondered if there had been a rebuke in his answer. She looked at him, his eyes gentle, a little amused, and decided no rebuke had been intended.

"We—don't even have the right clothes."

"Slacks, a warm sweater. Or you can change there. My sister Betsy keeps some things there. She's about your size. Alice will come up with something for Mae. No more arguments. We will leave it up to Mae. Yes?"

"What would I tell Buddy?"

"The truth. There's nothing to hide. He doesn't dislike me as much as he wishes he did," Patrick smiled. "We've had our arguments. A great big, fat one just the other day as a matter of fact. But that's helping him learn and he knows it."

"He's very protective."

"As well he should be. He's been the man of the family for a long time. But you're still the parent and he the child."

Ann sipped the last of her coffee. She put the cup down and stared at Patrick. "He doesn't trust people like you. I told you about that."

"People like me. What does that mean?"

"Your kind of money. There's so much of it. Your kind of family. They've accomplished so much. They have *towns* named after them." She was embarrassed, her voice no more than a whisper.

"It sounds as if he looked me up in a book!"

"He did." Ann smiled despite herself, a twinkle coming into her eyes.

Patrick laughed. "That boy will go far. But Ann, whatever his feelings for a particular group of people, he must learn to deal with them. His prejudices shouldn't stop you from doing what you wish to do."

"I don't know how to handle it. I've never kept anything from Buddy. Never."

"Don't begin now. Secrets are dangerous things. The truth has a way of getting out and then people feel deceived. How did you feel when you learned Buddy lied about his grades?"

"Terrible. But I realized he was trying to save my feelings."

"Buddy may not be so generous. Tell him the truth."

Patrick motioned to the waiter. He ordered fresh coffee, brandy and the check.

"Tell him the truth," Patrick said again.

Patrick signed the check and waved the waiter away. He poured coffee for Ann and then sipped his brandy.

"Try some," he smiled. "Like my family, it is old and distinguished. With just a touch of robber baron for piquancy."

Ann laughed and her eyes lit up. The tension was gone for now and she looked young, all aglow.

"Did I tell you how pretty you look tonight?" Patrick asked.

"Oh, I—I shouldn't even be in the same room with some of these women," she said, looking away.

"That's a beautiful collar. Irish lace?"

Ann's hand went to the collar. "It's not mine," she said quickly. "It belongs to Mae. Sort of a family heirloom. It's very old."

Patrick frowned. "I've given you two compliments and you deflected both."

"I'm not used to compliments, I guess."

"A situation which needs correcting," Patrick said, lifting his glass.

20

Gail Parrish came out of the bathroom into her bedroom. She wore a fleecy, gold-colored robe and her hair, freshly washed, shone in the morning sunlight.

David, lying in bed, opened his eyes and smiled at her. "Good morning."

"Good morning. How do you feel?"

"Sensational. No one has ever felt as sensational as I do," he stretched his arms high above his head, 'at this moment."

"That's what I like to hear."

"Come, sit here," David patted the bed.

Gail sat down. David pulled her close, kissing her, his fingers in her hair. He held her close. "Ivory soap and baby powder," he said, stroking her cheek.

"My beauty secrets."

"It is possible," he said, kissing her about the face and neck, "that in the entire history of the world," he kissed her lips lightly, "there has never been a night like last night. What do you think?"

"I agree. Nothing will top last night . . . except tonight," Gail smiled, stroking his hair.

David opened her robe, his hand going to her breasts. "Why wait until tonight?" he asked, burying his head in the deep cleft of her breasts.

Gail kissed him, a long, soft kiss. She sat up then,

buttoning her robe.

"Then you'll have something to look forward to."

"No."

"Yes."

"Never put off to tonight what you can do right now," he smiled.

"No. Besides it's Thanksgiving and I'm going to cook you a proper Thanksgiving breakfast. I've been practicing all week."

"Who needs food?"

"We do. Sausage and pancakes, the works."

David propped himself up on one elbow. "You're mean," he said, his finger tracing the outline of her mouth.

"Cooking you a big breakfast is mean? Slaving over a hot stove is mean? Do you know how many eggs I wasted this week trying to get that damn recipe right?"

"All right," David laughed, "I know when I'm beat." He sat up, drawing the covers around him. "But no sausage for you. It's not on the diet."

"Yes, sausage for me. Because it's Thanksgiving and I'm entitled to a day off. And because I'm the cook and what I say goes. Cooks outrank doctors on holidays."

"*One* sausage."

"As many as I want," Gail tossed her head. "So there." She slapped at the covers. "Take your shower while I assemble my pots and pans." She stood up. "I brought the paper in. It's over there."

"You've thought of everything."

"Not yet. I'm saving a few things for tonight."

David threw a pillow at her and she laughed, running from the room. He leaned back against the cushioned headboard, his mind on the night before. A perfect night, he thought, an absolutely perfect night.

They'd had dinner at a tiny restaurant in Little Italy. They'd gone dancing afterwards, at a club sixty floors above the city, the majesty of the cityscape all around them. They'd come back to brandy and vintage Sinatra records, the lights turned low. Later they'd walked hand in hand to the bedroom. David smiled.

"Perfect," he said in the direction of the kitchen. "Perfect."

He got out of bed and put on a blue silk robe. He paused, looking out the window at a quiet Park Avenue. After a few moments he turned toward the bathroom.

Gail heard the door close. She finished setting the table and then sat down, lighting a cigaret. She didn't have much time, she thought. Ever since she'd had her talk with Patrick she'd realized she'd have to plan her moves carefully. Patrick wouldn't ruin the holidays for David, she was certain, but after Christmas, after the first of the year, he might feel free to sit David down and tell him the truth. She had from now to New Year's, she thought, to see to it that whatever truths David heard wouldn't, couldn't, matter to him.

Gail stamped out the cigaret and lit another. She was determined to hold on to David. He was the only stability she had in her life, the only stability she'd had for many years. Many men had wanted her but only David had loved her; she would not let that go. She was getting older, she thought to herself; she would need the security of David's love and she would have it at all costs.

"Ready or not, here I come," David called out.

David, scrubbed and combed and dressed, walked out of the bedroom, the newspaper folded under his arm. He hesitated in front of a closed, locked, door. It was the second bedroom and it was always locked. It was, he knew, the bedroom Gail had used with the man whose mistress she'd been. He hated the room as much as he wondered about it. She'd refused to show it to him and that had been the occasion of one of their rare arguments. The room had not been mentioned since, but still he wondered.

He looked uneasy when he entered the kitchen. Gail smiled at him. "Good morning again."

"Morning," he said, sitting down.

"What's the matter?" she asked, bending to kiss the top of his head.

David looked up, staring into her eyes. He smiled then, his discomfort fading as it always did when he looked at her.

"Where is the banquet you promised?"

"Coming up." Gail removed a pitcher of orange juice from the refrigerator. "Fresh squeezed, I'll have you know."

"So far I'm not impressed. I have fresh orange juice every morning."

"Yes, but you have your man to do it for you. I did this all by myself."

"Should the medal be gold or will silver do?"

"You'll be singing a different tune when you taste the pancakes."

"I certainly hope so," he smiled.

He looked around at the disarray of the kitchen and wished they'd gone out to breakfast as he'd planned. He looked at the wall clock, checking it against his watch.

"I think I'll call Patrick. I want to wish him a happy Thanksgiving. Do you mind?"

"Why don't you call from the living room, where you can be comfortable?"

"No," he said quickly, realizing all over again how much he hated her apartment when she wasn't at his side. "I'll call from here," he said, going to the phone.

"This way you can wish him a happy holiday, too."

"Okay," Gail said, though talking to Patrick was the last thing she wanted to do.

"It's funny," David said, dialing the number, "Patrick didn't say anything about joining him for the holiday. I expected he would."

"Oh?"

"He always has before. We've spent most holidays together."

David waited, drumming his fingers on the counter top. "Happy Thanksgiving, country boy," he said as Patrick answered the phone.

"No," Patrick was saying, "I drove the Audi up last night. Hollis is ferrying the ladies. They should be here any time now. I asked Grace and her husband, too—at the last minute. They're coming."

"Coward," David laughed.

"Perhaps. So far everything feels right, but that remains to be seen. Say, I have fresh snow and a roaring fire. Are you jealous?"

"A little. Patrick, I'll put Gail on, she wants to say hello."

"There's a small crisis brewing in the kitchen. I ought to get in there. Wish her a happy day for me, will you?"

"All right. Enjoy. Throw a snowball for me."

"I will," Patrick smiled. "David, happy Thanksgiving."

"And to you. I hope everything is perfect."

"Thanks, and thanks for calling. See you Sunday."

Patrick hung up and walked away from the phone.

He went to one of the big picture windows and stared outside, watching the light snow swirl gracefully about. There was a deep, peaceful silence all around, only the crackling of the fire and the sound of holiday music playing in the kitchen to disturb his thoughts.

He thought about David and Gail and then decided that was a problem for another time, another place—sometime after the holidays when he and David were alone. For now he would enjoy this time and this place. He'd had a good night's sleep and a hearty breakfast and a long walk in the woods and soon he'd be with people he liked. He thought about Tony, missing him, and about David, sorry he was not there, but nothing, he decided, was going to hurt too much today for he was in too good a mood.

Patrick sat down on the pillowed window seat. He gazed around the room and smiled, for the room looked wonderful. It was a large, high-beamed room, filled with comfortable, roomy couches and chairs in warm colors, and fine old tables and chests which had been in his family for generations. The furnishings bore the mark of age and use but over all was the mark of happy memories and associations, for each piece had a history of its own, a continuity.

Alice had put bowls of holly all about and a great bowl of eggnog sat on a gleaming sideboard, a pungent fruitcake at its side. There were bowls of fruit and nuts, and at the end of the sideboard, a tray of wines and liquors.

"Hello, Willie, hi, boy," Patrick laughed as a small black and tan terrier bounded toward him. "Come here," Patrick smiled, bending close. "Did you enjoy our walk, boy? Did you have a good time?" he asked, petting him, ruffling his coat, as the dog stood on his hind legs, his little tail wagging, licking Patrick's face.

"Willie? Willie, where are you now?" Alice Parsons came into the room. She wiped her hands on her apron and shook her head. "I knew he'd be running in here. I'm sorry, Doctor, but he does love to play. Loves it better than food, I think sometimes."

"Please let him stay," Patrick said, looking up.

"Okay with me. Willie, you mind your manners now," she said and then laughed.

She was a short, plump woman with merry eyes and short, curly hair which was always a little askew.

"As if he listens to a word I say. Specially when you're here, Doctor. You're his favorite."

"Well, he's my favorite," Patrick scratched the dog behind his ears. "How's everything going, Alice?"

"Dinner'll be on the table at two. On the dot . . ." She looked toward a window. "I hear a car now, Doctor."

"I'll go," Patrick said, hurrying into the hall, Willie at his heels.

Patrick slipped into a heavy jacket and went outside. He waved at a blue Chevrolet coming up the driveway.

Grace rolled down the car window. "Happy Thanksgiving. Do we leave this here or what?"

"The garage is around the turn there."

"I'll wait here," Grace said to her husband as she got out of the car. "Well, who's this?" she asked, bending down to the excitedly barking dog.

"Meet Willie," Patrick said.

"Hi, Willie. I'm Grace," she patted his head. "How are you, Willie?" Grace stood up. "Can we go inside? The car heater wasn't working right, I'm frozen."

"Of course," Patrick said as they walked to the house.

"We passed a *gorgeous* black Mercedes a few minutes ago. Chauffeur and all. Yours?"

"I hope so," Patrick said, hanging Grace's coat in the closet.

Grace went to the door and looked out. "This way, honey," she called as a tall man with sandy-colored hair approached the door.

He carried two suitcases and Patrick rushed to help him.

"We're here for two days and she packs everything but the shower curtain," he said.

"Here, let me take one of those," Patrick said.

"Thanks, I'm used to it. You should see what she packs for two weeks."

"Never mind that," Grace smiled. "Dr. Patrick Dain, Detective Sergeant Rudy Evins."

"How do you do, Doctor," Rudy said.

"Let's make it Rudy and Patrick. Nice to meet you. Do you know I love your wife?" Patrick smiled.

"Somebody has to," Rudy said and Grace poked him playfully.

"Your rooms are ready. Would you like to get settled upstairs?" Patrick asked. "Top of the stairs, first door on the left. Are you sure I can't help with the luggage?"

"No, thanks," Rudy said. "We won't be long."

They went to the stairs and Patrick turned back to the door. Willie began to follow Rudy and Grace and then changed his mind, dashing out the door to catch up with Patrick.

Patrick smiled as the Mercedes pulled up in front of the house. He opened the door before Hollis was halfway around the car.

"Hello, Happy Thanksgiving. Happy Thanksgiving, Mae."

"Hello, Patrick," Ann said.

She stared around her at the large house, the expansive grounds, the carefully manicured bushes and trees, the terraced gardens waiting for spring.

"You said you had a place in the country. This is—an estate," Ann said nervously.

"It's roomy," Patrick agreed.

"Happy Thanksgiving to you, Doct . . . Patrick," Mae said. "It was a real nice ride."

"I'm glad," he said, turning to Hollis. "Happy Thanksgiving, Hollis. Any problems?"

"Thank you, sir. No, sir, not a one. I'll park the car and be right in."

"No hurry," Patrick said. "Why don't you find Paul? I saw him setting up the chessboard, I know you're both anxious to get at it. There's plenty of eggnog and whisky and anything you want. Have a good time."

"Why, thank you, sir. If you're sure."

"Absolutely. Go on," Patrick said, walking over to the women.

Mae was balancing several flat boxes in her arms. Ann was bent over, playing with the dog.

"Meet Willie," Patrick said, leading them into the house.

He closed the front door and then took their things, depositing them in the closet.

"Would you like to freshen up?" he asked. "Your rooms are ready, first door on the right at the top of the stairs. There are some warm clothes in the closet, and Alice laid out some things for you, Mae," Patrick said, glancing at the flimsy slacks and blouses they wore. "If you like," he added.

"Thank you . . . thank you, Patrick," Ann said. She took the boxes from Mae. "These are for you. Mae's special pies."

"How nice. Thank you."

Ann took Mae's arm. "We'll look later," she said as Mae craned her neck for a look at the living room.

Patrick put the boxes on the sideboard. "Take your time," he said as they walked up the stairs. "Come on, Willie, let's see to the fire."

Patrick put more wood on the fire. He stepped back, watching the flames. The aroma of the sweet-burning wood filled the room and he inhaled deeply, patting Willie all the while.

"Do you need anything, Doctor?" Alice asked, carrying in a bucket of ice and a tray of crackers and dip.

"Not a thing. We'll help ourselves."

"Dinner at two. On the dot. I hope they brought their appetites with them, there's enough food to feed the Chinese army."

"On the dot," Patrick nodded. "Oh, Alice, one of our guests brought some pies. There on the sideboard. I hope you don't mind."

"The more the merrier. What we don't eat, Willie will."

She took the boxes and walked out of the room, chuckling happily to herself.

Patrick heard Ann's voice and he went to the doorway. He looked at Ann; she looked elegant in his sister's tawny, well-cut wools, her blond hair spilling onto the shoulders of a caramel-colored sweater.

"Come in," he said, "be comfortable. Everybody warm enough? Grace, Rudy, we have lots of extra sweaters around."

"We're fine," Grace said, "and we introduced ourselves, so we can get to the serious business, the drinks."

"Right this way," Patrick smiled. "Name it. I'll be bartender."

Drinks in hand, they made themselves comfortable on the couch and chairs around the fireplace. They toasted the day and then looked around.

"Incredible!" Grace said.

"It is," Ann agreed.

"All the rooms and all," Mae said, taking it all in, hardly believing it, for she had never seen such a place, not even in a magazine. "How do you keep it up?"

"Alice and Paul Parsons—and their oldest son—have a house on the property. And we have a cleaning service and a gardening service and a pool service."

"The only way to fly," Grace said.

"Don't go getting ideas," Rudy said lightly, slipping his arm around his wife.

"Spoilsport. Ann, how is Buddy?" Grace asked. "Toiling away in the vineyards of Rhinelander today?"

"Oh, do you know Buddy?"

"Sure. I remember a time . . ."

Ann and Grace fell into conversation. Mae joined in now and then, though she continued to look around, taking in every detail of the room, of Patrick: Patrick, Willie snoozing in his lap; chatted easily with Rudy; talking about their work; about Grace; about sports.

After a second round of drinks the conversation flowed smoothly. It was Grace, Patrick noted gratefully, who steered the conversation to include everybody. The initial tension of strangers coming together for the first time disappeared in the conviviality of the day.

At two o'clock sharp they sat down to an enormous meal. The table groaned with turkey and dressing and homemade cranberry sauce. There was a fat glazed ham and stringbeans and creamed onions and cinnamon-whipped sweet potatoes and Alice's special pickled beets. There were loaves of bread fresh from the oven and tubs of butter from a farm a few miles away.

Alice came into the dining room a little after three.

"Everything all right in here? Everybody have enough?"

There was a chorus of approval and Alice smiled. "I like people who enjoy their food. I'll give you a half hour to rest your stomachs and then I'll be serving coffee and pies. Got a big choice today, hope you left room."

They offered to help Alice clear up but she shook her head.

"Could I help, just me?" Mae asked. "I'd like to. Ask Ann, here, I'm happiest when I'm in the kitchen."

Alice nodded. "Okay, long as you know your way around a kitchen."

"I'm Mae, Alice," she said, jumping out of her chair.

"Shall we go into the living room?" Patrick asked. "If we can move—that is," he added, standing up. "Alice, what about Willie's dinner?"

"He's eating now, in the kitchen. He'll be running back to you when he's finished. There's no keeping him away," she said, handing Mae a tray.

"When does Alice eat?" Ann asked as they walked back to the living room.

"She and her family and Hollis ate when we did. There's a staff dining room in another wing of the house. They ate the same food, too." Patrick smiled. "Or did you think I'd have them eat gruel and stale bread?"

In the living room, they settled themselves around the fire, too full of food to say very much. "Who's for brandy?" Patrick asked.

Rudy held up his hand and Patrick poured two drinks. He took a glass to Rudy and then sat down.

"Later on," Patrick said, "anyone who's game should take a walk in the woods. There's a stream at the edge of the woods. It's beautiful."

"Can you fish the stream in summer?" Rudy asked.

"There's a pond at the other end of the property. Well-stocked. You'll have to come up again and try your luck."

Grace laughed. "He always talks about going fishing, but he never goes. Three years ago I bought him a rod and reel and all that stuff and it's still sitting in the closet. The closest he's going to get to fishing is shooting his gun into the Hudson River."

"We must get together this summer," Patrick said.

"There's the pond for fishing and the woods for hiking. There's the pool. And a grass court for tennis."

"It's like a resort," Grace said.

"Not a bad place to spend a vacation. You're welcome to it. Keep it in mind."

"Thanks, we will," Rudy said.

Patrick turned to say something to Ann and Rudy stared at him. After ten years on the force he prided himself on knowing something about people, what they were like deep down.

"You're right," he said to Grace, "he's a nice guy."

"The Evins seal of approval," she smiled at him. "Would I work for a jerk? Ann," she said, "did you ever notice that—to a man—no observation is valid until a man makes it?"

Ann smiled. "Yes, of course. Some of the men I work with . . ."

"Tell me about your work," Grace prodded. "I always wanted to know what makes Ma Bell tick."

They chatted for the next half hour, the four of them talking back and forth, agreeing, disagreeing, but laughing and enjoying themselves.

Mae stood at the doorway. "Alice says do you want coffee and pie here or in the dining room?"

"Here," they said in unison and Mae walked off.

"She's loving every minute," Ann said to Patrick.

"And you?"

"I'm loving every minute. Someone is going to pinch me and I'm going to wake up from a wonderful dream."

Patrick reached over and pinched her. "Anything happen? Did you wake up?"

"No," Ann looked away. "But it's still a dream."

Patrick gazed at Ann for a moment. "Firelight becomes you. It puts little golden lights in your hair."

Ann's hand went to her hair. "I . . . thank you."

They all turned as Alice and Mae rolled two carts across the room. One cart held a large coffee pot, cups and plates; the other was laden with pies.

"Apple, mince, custard, raisin, and chocolate. Pick your calories."

21

"Here's my recipe for the coconut custard," Mae said, "but the raisin pie is kind of a family secret. Do you mind, Alice?"

The two women sat at a big oak table in the kitchen, a steaming pot of coffee before them. The kitchen was warm and quiet, still fragrant from the morning's cooking.

"No, I know how that is. Got a secret or two myself. I'll say this though, your pies are the best I ever tasted. You got a real gift for baking."

"Do you mean that?"

"I'm not one for flattery. I say what's on my mind."

Alice sipped her coffee, glad to relax now that all the dishes were done and put away. She looked to a window, to a narrow road beyond. Her house was at the end of that road and Paul and Hollis would be inside, playing chess. Her son and daughter-in-law would be out hauling the old sled, taking wood from the shed to the house. The doctor and his guests had gone for a walk.

"Mae, why aren't you with the doctor and his party?" Alice asked suddenly. "You're a guest, after all."

"I like it in here. Do you mind, Alice, am I keeping you?"

"I like the company. Don't get much of it. But don't

you want to be with your friends?"

"They're not really my friends. Ann, she's my sister-in-law, my friend, too, but I don't know the others. To tell you the truth, we don't even belong here, me and Ann. We're just poor people, working people. In all my life I never thought I'd be in a house like this. Now I'm here . . . it's nice and all, and Patrick, Dr. Dain, is a nice man. But we're not in his class."

"Class! You'd have to go a long way before you found somebody who cared less about those things than the doctor."

"But he's so rich and all."

"He is. But he's regular, no airs about him. He's always treated us as good as family. He's a good man and I was glad to see him having a good time today. He's been lonely."

"I read about it. When his wife died."

"Since long before that. The doctor loves this house like anything. Partly because there's none of her here. His missus never came here. She came once, about twelve years ago. Didn't stay long, but I got her measure. She left and never came back. Nobody's loss, I say and I'd say it to the doctor's face."

Mae thought about that. There were many photographs around the house—photographs of a young boy, others of Patrick with the boy, photographs of many other people, but there were none of the beautiful woman she'd seen in the newspaper. Mae wondered if she dare ask Alice about the woman's death when she heard a door slam and a dog bark.

"That'll be them," Alice said. She stood up. "In return for the pie recipe, I'll show you how to make the best hot chocolate in all Connecticut."

"Maybe I should see if Ann's all right."

"Course she's all right. She's with the doctor, isn't she?" Alice laughed. "How you take on."

"I'll just see," Mae said.

She walked the long corridor, pausing when she saw Ann, her face rosy with cold, her eyes shining, her blond hair windblown and glistening with bits of fresh snow.

"Oh, Mae," Ann said happily, "you should have come. It was wonderful. We had a snowball fight. Can you imagine?" she laughed, handing her borrowed coat to Patrick.

"Ann and Grace won," Patrick said, putting their coats in the closet. "I always knew women were treacherous in battle. Come sit with us," he said, "I'm going to put some chestnuts on to roast."

"No . . . Alice is making hot chocolate. I'll help her," Mae said, turning back toward the kitchen.

"Why has she exiled herself to the kitchen?" Patrick asked as they entered the living room.

"She likes kitchens, she's always wanted a big one of her own. And I think she's more comfortable with Alice than with . . ."

"Me," Patrick finished the sentence for her. "Why? I thought we were all getting along quite well."

"It's not that. I think she feels—easier—with Alice."

Patrick sat on the floor in front of the fireplace. He took his handkerchief from his pocket and wiped Willie's head and paws, wet from the snow.

"Okay, Willie," he smiled, "stay by the fire and get warm."

Patrick took up a small knife, making slits in the chestnuts.

"Did you have much trouble convincing her to come?" he asked.

"She was set against it. I think she gave in because she saw how much I wanted it."

"And Buddy? What did he have to say?"

Ann was silent. She looked away, staring out a window.

"What did Buddy say?"

"I didn't tell him."

Patrick put the chestnuts and the knife aside. He looked at her. "I'm beginning to worry about you, I really am."

"I couldn't. He wouldn't understand."

"*I* don't understand. Ann, look at me," he said and she turned to him. "I want to see you again. Do you want to see me again?"

"Yes," she said in a small voice.

"Well, I will not sneak around behind Buddy's back. What is it he wouldn't understand? What awful thing are we doing? What do we have to hide?"

"It's not that."

"Then what is it? This is important, Ann. I like you and I want to see you again. It's been a long time since I thought that about anyone. It has probably been a long time since you thought that about anyone. What's so wrong about it?"

Ann went to a window. She looked outside, watching Grace and Rudy in the snow, flapping their arms and legs to make angels.

"Well?" Patrick asked.

"You of all people should know how—volatile—he is. When he gets upset his work, his studies suffer. We've seen that. I can't take the chance. What he does now affects his future. I can't upset him."

"Not good enough. Why would he be upset? What in the world is so upsetting about this? You're allowed to go out with men, are you not?"

"Men from my own world. I've heard him talk about you. What you have. What you are. He has a 'them' and 'us' attitude. He and Mae and I are the 'us.' You're the 'them.' And 'us' doesn't go out with a 'them.'"

Patrick smiled. "Right now you're at the hub of his world. A couple of years from now, when Buddy is involved with his own life, his career, it wouldn't matter if you went out with a dozen 'thems,' a hundred. Or is Buddy suspicious of any man who comes around, any man who might?"

"You don't understand. He thinks rich people *use* poor people. Use them and throw them away."

"Buddy must learn to make distinctions. If you won't talk to him, I will."

"No," Ann looked at Patrick. "What will you say?"

"I can't tell him that his mother's deceived him. But I can tell him that I enjoyed meeting you at the hospital. That I wanted to take you to dinner."

"You make it sound so simple."

"I'm not afraid of Buddy. You are. And don't shake your head at me. Buddy must grow up and so must you."

Patrick took the bowl of chestnuts back in his lap, looking down as he slit the shells.

"I'll speak to him as soon as I get a chance," he said. "Best to clear the air. Especially as he is one of my students."

Patrick slipped the chestnuts into a pan, which he put on a rack in the fireplace. He reached out to Willie then, stroking him gently. The dog opened his eyes, peering for a moment at Patrick before going peacefully back to sleep.

"Is he yours?" Ann asked.

"I wish he was. I wish I had a dog. I used to, I had some great dogs. I got interested in medicine because of a dog. Really," he nodded. "When I was about twelve my dog was hit by a car. We rushed him to the vet but all during the ride there Dad kept warning me not to expect miracles. Well, we got there and the vet worked and worked—saved my dog's life. Less than two weeks later he was scampering around as if nothing ever happened."

Patrick smiled, remembering. "I went back to the vet and asked him if it was a miracle. He said in a way it was . . . that medicine was a kind of miracle . . . to be able to take a sick creature and make him well was a kind of miracle. I started hanging around the vet's office after that. I became his unofficial, unsolicited, unpaid, helper. And decided, of course, to be a vet. Later on I decided to work on people rather than animals, but it all started there."

"And the dog?" Ann asked.

"Lived to a ripe old age. My last dog was a sheepdog. Great big shaggy fellow, all white except for one black ear. He was getting on by the time I married," Patrick said quietly, "needed a lot of care, attention. He died a few months after the wedding . . . then when my son was six we got him a puppy, a cute little thing. But he ran away."

Patrick shook the chestnut pan, staring into the fire. He was quiet for a long moment before glancing up at Ann.

"That's not true," he said, turning back to the fire. "I found out sometime later that my wife took the pup to Central Park and left him there. The sheepdog . . . she'd emptied some sleeping capsules into his food."

"Oh," Ann gasped.

"She didn't hate dogs, it was nothing like that. She couldn't tolerate anything that took attention away from her. Anything which took attention away from her had to be—disposed of." Patrick looked at Ann. "I don't know why I'm telling you this."

Ann watched as Patrick reached to pet Willie. She was shocked at this glimpse into the woman Patrick had married. What kind of woman could she have been, she wondered, horrified; what kind of years could they have been?

"I'm so sorry," was all she managed to say.

"Cruelty. It comes easily to some."

They were quiet then, the fire snapping and popping, the aroma of roasting chestnuts filling the room. They were both startled when the front door banged open and laughter echoed in the hall.

"We're back," Grace called out. "It's great out there."

Grace and Rudy put their coats and boots in the closet and walked into the living room.

"Chestnuts, too!" Grace said as they sat next to Ann on the couch.

"It's hard to believe all this is only a couple of hours out of the city," Rudy said. "How much land do you have?"

"Almost two hundred acres. Most of it woods and animals. Sometimes late at night, we see raccoons foraging in the cans outside the kitchen door. They take the food and run to the stream to wash it off before eating it. Very tidy. Very charming, And in spring and summer the woods are full of birds. It's almost primeval."

"I bet you've had some offers," Rudy said.

"Land developers are advised to keep their distance," Patrick replied. "We've resisted them for three generations; I expect we'll go on resisting."

Mae rolled a cart into the room. "Alice's hot chocolate," she said.

They gathered around the cart, taking cups of the dark, rich liquid. Patrick turned the chestnuts into a bowl and put it on the floor near the couch.

"Alice says there'll be sandwiches at eight o'clock."

"Oh, no," Grace groaned, "more food. I'll be a blimp by the time I get back to New York."

"Alice says she'll set them on the table and you help yourselves." Mae took her cup over to Ann and sat down. "When do we have to leave, Ann?" she asked.

Ann looked at Patrick. "We can't get back too late. We work tomorrow."

"What time do you want to be back?"

"No later than midnight."

"No problem. I'll call Hollis and ask him to be ready about ten," Patrick said, going to a telephone. He spoke briefly and returned. "All set," he said.

The twilight deepened into darkness and inside they had hot chocolate and chestnuts and relaxed conversation. Their laughter rang through the house, interspersed with easy, companionable silences. The men stoked the fire from time to time while the women talked about the coming holidays, about the Christmas shopping to be done, about Christmas trees, about Mae's gingerbread.

At seven o'clock Patrick turned on the outside lights and they gazed in awe at the snowy grounds, the graceful shadows cast by the first moonlight. At eight o'clock they returned to the dining room, to trays of thick ham and turkey sandwiches on homemade bread, to trays of condiments and thin-sliced cucumbers and homemade pickles.

There was more coffee and brandy and talk and then—too soon—it was almost ten. Grace and Rudy drifted off to an enclosed veranda at the back of the house. Mae went upstairs and Ann turned to Patrick.

"I'd better get changed."

"You may wear the clothes back if you wish."

"I'll change," she shook her head. "This has been . . . I said it before, it's been like a dream, like a movie. I loved every minute. Thank you, Patrick."

"Thank *you*, because you helped make it one of the nicest days of my life. I don't mind at all if that sounds corny," he smiled, "because it's true."

He bent over and kissed her cheek. He hesitated for a moment and then drew away. "Thank you."

Ann hurried up the stairs. He watched her go and then went to the closet, getting their coats. Grace and Rudy joined him in the hall.

"It's too bad they're not staying," Grace said.

"Perhaps another time. How about you, did you have a nice day?"

"Terrific," Rudy said. "It really felt like Thanksgiving. You're a great host."

Patrick turned. "Have everything?" he asked as Ann and Mae came down the stairs.

They nodded. There were thanks and goodbyes and more thanks. Willie, barking loudly, ran down the hall from the kitchen, catching up with them as they walked outside. Ann bent to pet him, planting a big kiss on his head.

"Goodbye, Willie," she said. "Patrick," she looked at him, "thank you. Thank you, thank you, thank you."

He smiled. "I'll call you," he said quietly as Hollis helped her into the car.

"Good night, Mae. Thank you for the pies. They were the hit of the day."

Mae smiled shyly. "Thank you for saying it. I really . . . this was the best time I ever had. I'm grateful to you, Patrick. For the day, and all."

"My pleasure. See you again, Mae," he said as she got into the car.

Hollis closed the door and went around to the front seat. Patrick followed him, poking his head in the window.

"I'll thank you properly when I get back to the city, but I want you to know I appreciate everything you did for today. It was splendid, Hollis, thank you."

"Not at all, sir. Had a lovely time myself, I did. Oh, here comes Alice."

Alice ran to the car, thrusting three large boxes at Hollis. "One for each of you. Some turkey and ham and a few other things. Nobody likes to cook the day after Thanksgiving."

They thanked her and Hollis turned the key in the ignition. Patrick picked Willie up, cradling him against his shoulder as the car drove off.

"Say goodbye, Willie," Patrick said, staring after the car.

The car turned into the driveway and after a few minutes disappeared beyond the trees onto the road. They waited another minute and then returned to the house.

"Well," Grace said, "the Christmas season is officially begun."

"Yes, Christmas," Patrick said, feeling a sudden loneliness. "Santa Claus and silver bells."

Grace studied him for a moment. "You okay?" she asked.

"Tip top. How about a movie?"

"Great. What's on?" Rudy asked.

"That's up to us," Patrick said. "I have a screening room here. And a fair collection of films. How about some Hitchcock?"

"Great," Rudy said, Grace nodding agreement.

"Step this way," Patrick smiled, "the show's about to begin."

"Everything all right?" Patrick asked as Grace came into the living room.

"Fine. Rudy's in bed watching television. He says he wants to hear the football scores but he really wants to hear if there were any murders or robberies in the city today. My husband the cop. Well," she shrugged. "Patrick, we didn't know what to bring to the man who has everything . . . I hope you like this," she said, handing him a small package.

"Thank you," he said, tearing the wrapping away.

"Grace, it's exquisite," he said, looking at a beautiful square wood box, the top intricately carved. "Where ever did you find it?"

"Rudy made it." Grace sat down and stretched out her legs. "I wish you could see some of the things he's made. That's what he was planning to do when I first met him—carpentry, woodworking. But his father's a cop, and his father's father was a cop, plus uncles and cousins . . . so he became a cop. Now it's in his blood."

"And this is his hobby?" Patrick asked, looking again at the box.

"We turned an extra room into a workshop for him. He uses it when he has the time, which isn't often enough to suit me."

"Well, I'll treasure it. It's wonderful," Patrick said.

He went to a small table and put the box down, moving it around until he was satisfied.

"There, how does that look?"

"Good, it looks good."

Patrick returned to his chair. "I like Rudy," he said, "you chose well."

Grace smiled. "I don't think he did badly either."

"That goes without saying."

"Thank you, sir."

"You wish he had some other job, don't you?"

"Show me any cop's wife who doesn't have that wish. Of course I do. But you take a person as is. Start tinkering around and before you know it you have a shaky marriage. He's plainclothes, so I don't have to worry about the maniacs in the street, but his work is still dangerous. He's had to use his gun . . . he's been shot at himself. I'm hoping he'll do his twenty and get out in one piece."

"Meanwhile?"

"My work keeps me sane. Hard as that may be to

believe, knowing that madhouse," Grace laughed. "Rudy works crazy hours and I work crazy hours, but the time we have together is very important. We have a good marriage, Patrick . . . the kind I wish you had. The kind I wish David had."

"Ah, do I hear a mother hen or a matchmaker speaking?" he smiled at her.

"A little of both. I know David's seeing a patient. A Larrimer Wing patient. Did he tell you about it?"

"A little."

"I even have an idea which patient it is. And I also have an idea it's not all peaches and cream. *Mucho* trouble there. You though, there may be hope for you."

Patrick grinned. "What hope do you see for me, Sherlock?"

"Ann."

The grin faded from Patrick's face. He was surprised. He looked at Grace and then looked quickly away. "What about Ann?"

"Look, Patrick, you know me. I talk first and think later. Ann's a terrific woman. Level-headed. Kind. Not too bad in the looks department either."

"So?"

"So get with it. Opportunity's knocking. I know it's none of my business but you're a good guy and I always root for the good guys. Plus I've had a lot of scotch," Grace laughed. "Loosens the tongue, don't you know." Grace leaned forward. "You like her and she likes you, I saw that. But I talked to her and she's scared. She doesn't know what to do about you, about all this," she said, waving her arms around. "Don't let her get away."

Patrick stood up. He walked around the room and then stopped, looking at the box Rudy made.

"Ann is scared?" he asked.

"Don't worry, we weren't gossiping. Ann didn't say all that much, but she didn't have to. I was scared myself once, I remember how it was. See, I was engaged to a carpenter but all of a sudden I was marrying a cop. I didn't want to marry a cop. I didn't think I could handle it. I didn't want to take the chance of getting hurt emotionally. What did I know about that kind of life? What if I couldn't fit into it?"

"You're way ahead of yourself, Grace," Patrick said quietly. "You're talking about marriage. I hardly know Ann."

"You may not get the chance to know her better. She's scared, she may call it quits before it goes any farther."

"What do you suggest?" Patrick smiled slightly.

"Don't let her. Call her as soon as you get back to the city and keep calling her. Make a date and make it definite. Don't lose any time. She's overwhelmed by all this. Let's face it, Patrick, who wouldn't be?"

Patrick laughed. "You, for one."

"I'm only a guest here, Ann was your date. If I'd been the date of the lord of the manor I'd be damned overwhelmed."

"Ann wasn't exactly my date. I like her, her company. She is, as you say, a nice woman. And I would like to see her again. But as for anything serious, there's nothing like that in my mind."

"I think you're fibbing. I can see your nose getting bigger."

Patrick laughed again, returning to the couch. "Grace, the last thing I want is a serious involvement. Friendship, yes, companionship, yes. A nice evening now and then with a nice woman, of course. Anything beyond that is out of the question."

"Men are so stupid."

"The old men-are-so-stupid argument doesn't apply

here," he smiled. "You misinterpret my intentions."

"*You* misinterpret your intentions. Men are so stupid because something has to be staring them in the face before they see it. David's the same way. Rudy's the same way."

"Poor Grace," Patrick chuckled, "surrounded by clucks."

"Not clucks . . . wonderments."

Patrick reached behind to the table. He poured a brandy. "Want one?" he asked.

"No, thanks. One more and I'll *really* hate myself in the morning."

Patrick drank the brandy down in one swallow, quickly pouring another. He'd been shaken by Grace's words, deeply shaken, for she'd supposed a seriousness which hadn't occurred to him. Or had it, he wondered nervously. Had it occurred to him somewhere deep in the back of his mind, and had he refused to admit it—even as he'd made dates with Ann, even as he planned another date with her?

"Did I give you something to think about?" Grace asked.

"Perhaps."

"Good. Then I've done my job," she smiled. "And having done it, I will say good night. And where do you keep the aspirin?"

"You'll find some in your bathroom, next to the bicarb."

"Thanks," Grace said, rising.

She walked across the room, stopping at the door.

"Patrick, I know I spoke out of turn. I'm not too far gone to notice. But I wasn't trying to be a busybody. I like you, that's all."

Patrick went over to Grace. He kissed the top of her head. "I know and I appreciate it. Sleep well."

"We will. Good night," she said, going to the stairs.

"Good night."

Patrick went back into the living room. He walked to a window. He stood very still, staring out at the snow. Grace had indeed given him something to think about. He didn't want to mislead Ann; he didn't want to mislead himself. It had seemed so simple before but now he felt the complications closing in and he wondered if Ann hadn't seen them from the beginning. He stood at the window for a very long time.

22

"Copies to each department head, if you will, Grace," David said, handing her several sheets of paper.

Grace stood in front of Patrick's desk. She made a notation on her pad and looked up.

"Right, is that all? What about the mid-term reports?"

"Tomorrow is time enough," Patrick said, stretching his arms. "Remind me after morning rounds."

"Okay. That's it?" she asked, looking from Patrick to David.

They nodded and she turned to the door. "Patrick, can I get Ann on the phone for you?"

Patrick shook his head. "You have been asking me that question three times a day, every day, for a week. Is your needle stuck?" he smiled.

"Just being my usual efficient self. I'm the brains of this operation, you know."

"Not to mention the modesty of this operation," David said.

"Grace," Patrick said, "you will be pleased to know I called Ann today. You may stop being so—efficient."

"Really?"

"Really."

"Good boy," Grace said, leaving the office.

David closed his pen and looked at Patrick. "What's this about Ann?"

"I had my doubts, but I called her anyway."

"What doubts?"

"Ann doesn't want to get in over her head. *I* certainly don't. It's a time to be careful, David. I don't want an involvement."

David laughed. "Perish the thought."

"I'm serious. I don't want an involvement and I don't want to fall into one by accident."

"You intend to spend the rest of your life in splendid isolation?"

"I'm not talking about the rest of my life. I'm talking about here and now. Here and now I don't want an involvement."

"You can't plan a thing like that."

"I can stop something before it starts."

"Is that why you called Ann and made another date?"

"David, *please*. I have a lot on my mind."

"What?"

"Ann, Tony, the holidays . . . I'm giving the Christmas party for the students and interns, by the way. I sent out the notices this morning." Patrick glanced at David. "And you. You haven't exactly been a barrel of laughs. You almost took my head off this afternoon."

"I had a blowup with Stuart. Our third one since the big emergency. I took a long look at the wards and then came downstairs loaded for bear. The bear I happened to run into was Stuart."

"Well, something has to be done. My students and interns are shaping up, but when they work the wards they see how hopeless it is. They know the hospital doesn't give a damn. They're let down. That's dangerous."

"I know. Meanwhile Stuart is thinking he has two revolutionaries on his hands: Us. And *that's* dangerous. We have to face facts, Patrick. He's holding all the cards."

"We agreed," Patrick smiled, "an overthrow of the government was in order. Are you backing down?"

"No. But I like my job. I don't want to lose it."

"The idea is to get Stuart out, not you."

"You know about the best laid plans."

"David, the teaching accreditation keeps Rhinelander Pavillion afloat. That's important, don't forget it. Without that . . ." Patrick shrugged.

David stared at Patrick. "You're not thinking what I think you're thinking?"

"I'll threaten anything. If it comes to that. Meanwhile it's our hole card."

"I can see some interesting times coming." David looked at his watch. "Are you free for dinner?"

"Aren't you seeing Gail?"

"She cancelled. She has someone visiting from out of town. How about it?"

"I'm free, but I'm exhausted. You're welcome to come home with me and take pot luck. Or why don't you call Lola? I saw her upstairs only an hour ago. She's probably still here."

"Maybe I will," David said. "I've been feeling guilty about her anyway. We used to see each other all the time and now . . . and then she invited me to her Thanksgiving open-house, but Gail didn't want to go."

"Why not?"

"Who knows."

"Call Lola," Patrick said.

"I guess."

The intercom buzzed and Patrick answered it. "Yes, Grace?"

"Julie Carlson is here to see you."

"Ask her to come in," he said, though with little enthusiasm.

"And I'm going home now. Okay?"

"Okay, Grace. Goodnight."

"Hello, Julie," David stood up. "Hello and goodbye," he said, going to the door.

Patrick looked at Julie. "Please sit down. Would you care for a drink?"

"I wanted to give you the Larrimer schedules."

"Thank you," Patrick said, taking them from her. "Won't you sit a moment?"

"No, thank you."

"A drink?"

"No, thank you."

"Is something wrong?" Patrick asked, puzzled by her cool tone.

"No," Julie turned away.

"Wait a minute, Julie. Are you angry with me?"

"No. Goodnight, Patrick."

"Julie . . . if I've offended you in some way . . . it wasn't intentional."

Julie turned around slowly and looked at him. "Do you mean that?"

"Of course."

"It's—well, Patrick," Julie said, demurely lowering her head, "I've tried to be friendly. I've tried to be of help to you. But you've made it quite clear you don't want my friendship or my help."

"I'm sorry you think that. I didn't mean to give you that impression. I appreciate all your many offers of help. And friendship. But I've been so busy. I know that's a poor excuse, but it's the only one I have. Please accept it, with my apologies."

Julie tilted her head up. "I was so afraid you didn't like me. I felt awful about it."

"You musn't be so sensitive, Julie."

"I like to think of everybody at Rhinelander as one big family. It's hard when you think someone doesn't like you."

She looked so wounded, so vulnerable, Patrick thought. "How may I make it up to you?" he asked.

"Well," Julie said, clasping her hands together happily, "let's make it up over dinner tomorrow night. I'm not a bad cook and I'd love you to come to dinner. I'd feel *so* much better."

Patrick hesitated, frowning. "Please don't take this the wrong way, but I'm busy tomorrow night. I really wish I could say another night, but my nights are . . . uncertain. Why don't we have lunch next week? How's that? Friends again?"

"Friends," Julie smiled sweetly, though the anger simmered within her.

David poked his head into Patrick's office. "Did I leave my notes in there?" he asked.

Patrick glanced down at his desk. "Yes, here they are." He moved some papers around. "And you forgot to initial the conference report . . . wait, I'll bring them in."

He gathered up the papers. "Excuse me, Julie," he said, "I won't be long."

Patrick went into David's office. Julie hurried to Patrick's desk. She reached for his appointment book, quickly flipping through the pages. She stopped when she came to a notation: Ann O'. She saw that notation twice more before slamming the book shut.

Ann O', she thought hard. Ann O'Hara! That stupid man was really seeing that dull woman! Hot tears, tears of anger, welled in her eyes and she forced them back.

Julie managed a smile as Patrick came back into the office. "I'll look forward to that lunch," she said, going to the door. "Don't forget now."

"I won't."

Julie rushed through the outer office into the corridor. She plunged through the door to the stairs just as the tears began streaming down her face. She pounded at the stairway railing, enraged; she had never been so angry. How dare he, she thought furiously, pounding away at the railing. How dare he pass over her for that drab! How dare he ruin all her carefully made plans, she demanded, for now she knew her plans would come to nothing.

Friends! That fool had offered to be friends, as if that was what she'd wanted. What, she wondered, enraged all over again, was he offering Ann O'Hara while he offered her only friendship? Julie pounded at the railing so fiercely that blood spurted from the side of her hand. She took a deep breath and sat down on a step.

She took a dainty linen handkerchief from her pocket and wiped at her hand, using the other side of the handkerchief to wipe her eyes. After a few minutes the tears stopped and she felt herself calming. Her eyes grew cold and mean.

She would have to think about this very carefully, she told herself; she would have to plan carefully. She would not have Patrick, but she would have revenge, she thought, and suddenly the word seemed very sweet indeed. She would have her revenge on Patrick Dain and Ann O'Hara and she would enjoy their pain. It would not be easy, she knew, but she would think of something. Yes, she thought, rising from the step, she would think of something. Julie returned to the corridor, the tiniest flicker of a smile about her mouth.

Gail Parrish opened the door to her apartment. She reached for the light switch and soft, low light cast the living room in rosy shadows.

"Hang up your coat and make yourself a drink," she

said. "I'll be right with you."

Gail walked down the hall to the second bedroom. She unlocked the door and went inside, tossing her coat and purse in a closet. She went to another closet and unlocked the door, removing a square metal box. She unlocked it and rifled through the index cards until she came to the one she wanted: Melton, Mike A.

Gail glanced at the card, smiling. Yes, she remembered, Mike Melton was the one who liked red. She walked into the closet and adjusted the dials on a small lighting panel. Red he would have, she smiled again. She went to a wardrobe and opened the door, peering down a row of robes and negligees until she found the red satin she wanted. She bent to a shoe rack, selecting a pair of red satin mules. She took the clothing and laid it carefully on the bed.

Gail looked back at the card, feeling a tingle of anticipation as she read her notes on Mike Melton. She returned the card to the box and locked it away, undressing hurriedly, changing into the red gown and shoes.

She went to a triple mirror and studied herself. The satin clung to her naked body, the tops of her lush breasts exploding out of the low neckline. She checked the two thin straps and the zipper at the side of the gown and then went to her dressing table.

Gail rouged her lips red. She dusted some color on her cheeks and in the cleft between her breasts. She ran a comb through her hair and then dabbed perfume about her neck and shoulders and arms. Gail stood up, twirling around, smiling at her images in the mirror. She went to the door, flipping a small switch. Warm red light illuminated the room and she closed the door behind her.

"Find everything you need?" Gail asked, walking into the living room.

Mike Melton gazed at her and then patted the couch. "Not yet."

Gail sat next to him. "You like?" she smiled.

"I like. You remembered . . . the red dress."

"I couldn't forget a man like you, Mike."

He reached over and put his hand in her gown. "As ripe as ever," he said, squeezing her breast. "Like sweet melon."

"How about another drink?" she asked.

"How about we get to the main course?"

Gail laughed heartily. "Follow me," she said. "I will show you the way. And a lot more."

They entered the bedroom and Mike Melton looked around. There was a king size bed, and on the ceiling above it, small mirrored panels, their surfaces reflecting the red light. There was a portable bar at one side of the bed, and video tape equipment at the other side. The bed was covered with satin sheets and double size satin pillows.

"Paradise," he said.

Gail helped him undress, carefully folding his clothing on padded hangers. He went to the bed and lay down. Gail flipped another switch and the soft rhythms of Latin music filled the room.

She stood in front of the bed, swaying to the music, her arms high above her head. She dropped one strap and then the other, moving her body slowly, expertly. She touched the zipper at the side of her gown and the top slipped away, sliding slowly, slowly down until her breasts were naked. She jerked her body once, twice, until the gown was about her hips.

"Let me do the rest," Mike said.

Gail went to the side of the bed and he pulled the gown away, running his hands over her. She knelt on the bed and then lowered herself slowly.

Hours passed. Gail, waking from a short sleep,

glanced at the clock. It was almost six in the morning; David, she thought to herself, would be getting up soon, getting ready to go to the hospital. He would call her at ten, as usual. They would talk about his evening, and hers. She frowned, trying to remember who her visitors were supposed to have been. Yes, she recalled, her cousin and his wife from Indiana. "Much too boring to bother about," she'd told David, "no need for both of us to be bored." She remembered it all now.

Gail thought about David. He was so solid, she thought; she needed that. She would see him tonight and she would see his love for her shining in his eyes. She'd never seen that look in any other man; she would not, she thought, ever be without it again.

She thought about her evening with Mike Melton. She lied to David, she'd taken a big chance, but there was no harm done. David would be none the wiser and meanwhile she felt *good*. Her whole body felt alive, brand new, every fiber and muscle refreshed.

Mike Melton stirred beside her. "Are you awake?"

"I'm awake. It's almost six. Do you want anything?"

"Coffee. I have a plane at eight. Back to Chicago I go." He looked over at her. "You're really something. You know how to treat a man."

"You're some man."

He leaned back against the pillows. "Lorraine — that's my wife — she just lays there, staring at the ceiling . . . as if she's planning a menu. Doesn't move. I don't think she'd move in an earthquake. It never used to be that way. It's like making love to wallpaper."

"What a waste."

"To top it all off, she's turning into one of those religious fanatics. Joined one of those lunatic groups. They work themselves into frenzies, shouting and yelling like crazy people. You could teach them something about frenzy," he grinned. "We've been going to the same church for twenty-two years and all of a sudden it's not good enough for her. We have our own *pew* and everything." He shook his head. "Well, never mind. What are you doing the week after New Year's?"

"Why?" Gail looked at him.

"I'm going to Germany. Caldwel business but there'll be free time. I've had a damn good traveling companion for the past two months, but she has a better offer. Why don't you come with me? And don't think I'm saying you're second best. You're *the* best. But you know how it is; she was convenient. What do you say? I know some places in Germany—we'll have a ball."

Gail was excited at the prospect. She hadn't been away for almost a year and a week with Mike would be just right—long enough, but not too long. She was tempted, sorely tempted. But how would she explain it to David? What could she tell him? What could she tell him that Patrick wouldn't suspect?

"Could I think about it for a day or two, Mike?"

"I can't wait any longer than that. You understand, I want to line up some quality. I'd hate to be stuck in Germany with something I could get on any street corner. It takes time. You understand."

"Sure. I'll think about it."

"I'll understand either way, but I hope you can make it. There'll be a nice bonus in it for you."

"You're always very generous, Mike."

"I give as good as I get. I'll be leaving January third. I'm stuck in Illinois on the second. Lorraine and I are having an engagement party for our daughter. Big party, all the family, all the friends."

"I'll see what I can do." Gail looked at him, hesitating before she spoke. "The thing is, I've been seeing someone."

"He'll understand if you got a better offer. It's only a

week or so, anyway."

"No, it's not like that. He's not like that."

Gail explained briefly about David. Mike listened, saying nothing.

"That makes it complicated," Gail finished.

"I think you're wasting your time," Mike said. "That's not for you. Not yet, anyway. You have a lot of good years left."

"It's emotional security. I want that. Like a hedge against old age."

"You're not the marrying kind; you're kidding yourself."

"I don't want to marry him. I just want him around."

"You don't need him. Take my word. You like to live, you know how to live. Enjoy it while you can." Mike stretched. "I'll take that coffee now."

Gail slipped out of bed, buttoning her robe. "I'll run your bath."

"I'd like that. Nice and hot."

"Won't take a minute," Gail said, going to the door.

Mike watched the sway of her body under the thin robe. He wanted that body with him in Germany, he thought.

"Gail, let me have a last look to take with me," he smiled.

Gail opened the robe, holding it away from her body. After a moment she took it off, throwing it to him. He sat up and pulled her to the bed, running his hands roughly over her body. He saw the hunger in her eyes, and the abandon, and he smiled.

"Does your bathtub still fit two?" he asked.

"Easily," she said, moving under his hands.

"What are we waiting for?" he laughed.

It was a coarse, ugly laugh and Gail had heard it a hundred times before from a hundred different men.

She took satisfaction in the sound; she felt the power of her body rising and pleasure flooded her senses.

"Oil or bubbles?" she asked, opening the door to the bath.

"Both. I'll catch a later flight."

23

"Your reports are in fine order, as always, Julie," Stuart Claven said. "If everyone did their work as well as you we would have no problems, would we?" he smiled. "But we cannot expect miracles, can we?"

"Are you having problems?" Julie asked sympathetically.

"You have no idea how many problems. But when one has a job such as mine it is to be expected. All of this," he glanced around his large, stately office, "carries great responsibility. Each day I hope I will be up to the task."

"You are, Stuart. No one works harder, or does a better job than you," Julie said, for feeding his ego was part of the game and she played it well.

Julie neither liked nor disliked Stuart Claven, but he had been useful to her in the past and she was certain she'd found a way for him to be useful to her again.

"We're very lucky to have you," she said.

Stuart's hands fluttered about the papers on his desk. "You are too kind. You flatter me."

"No, I mean it."

"So much work, so many details," he looked down at his desk, "it isn't easy to keep up."

"I'd hoped the coming of Dr. Dain would—ease your burden."

"Dr. Dain? He is doing a fine job on the student-intern program, fine. I give him full credit for that."

A flicker of interest appeared in Julie's eyes. She knew Stuart well; she knew how his mind worked and the restraint in his voice told her he wasn't altogether happy with Patrick. She hoped that was true, for that was the opening she needed.

"Is there something you're not saying, Stuart?"

He stared at her, considering. "I know you are a friend. May I speak frankly?"

"Please."

"It is comforting to be able to talk to someone of similar mind. There are so few who understand," he waved his hands in the air. "Our Dr. Dain has expressed—shall we say—doubts about Larrimer Wing. He has, in fact, spoken against it. Several times."

"Really?"

"Yes, indeed. I don't like these philosophic differences among members of my staff. It leads to—disharmony. Dr. Dain has not been with us very long, but already he has stirred up Dr. Murdock. Dr. Murdock, too, has recently spoken against Larrimer Wing."

"I heard about that. The hospital grapevine."

"You see how distressing it has become. All the more because it is so unexpected. Dr. Dain, a man of his breeding, of his class—he, above all, should understand the importance of Larrimer Wing. It is a showplace! A showplace, nothing less! When I think how hard we all worked to make it what it is. I hardly saw Mrs. Claven during the renovations, that is how hard I worked."

"You can handle David."

"Alone, certainly. With Dr. Dain involved . . . it is very worrying, his influence is strong. It is worrying to have all we worked for threatened."

"Threatened? How?"

"Dr. Dain is an important man. His family is known and respected. His own reputation is highly regarded. I have observed him," Stuart looked intently at Julie. "He is smart. He is a true Dain, he understands power."

"But I don't see—"

"There is a meeting of the full board in April. I cannot prevent Dr. Dain from addressing the board if he wishes. If he wishes to address the subject of Larrimer Wing," Stuart spread his hands apart, "problems could arise."

"Larrimer Wing runs in the black," Julie prodded, for she knew she was on to something.

Stuart saw the interest in her eyes. He had chosen well when he hired her, he thought, for he sensed she was ready to be his ally. Whatever her reasons, she was ready to align herself against Patrick Dain and that was help not to be taken lightly, he thought.

"Projected costs for Larrimer Wing in next year's budget are quite high. Substantially higher than this year. That cannot be helped. But it leaves little for the rest of the hospital. If Dr. Dain should make an issue of this . . . throw his weight behind a moral issue, so to speak. You see what I mean."

"He could make trouble."

"Why should we throw our money away on the poor?" Stuart asked angrily. "It's a losing proposition. I, myself, came from a very poor family, but I made something of myself and did it without help from anyone." Stuart shook his head. "Only a few years ago we put television sets in the wards. What more are we supposed to do? Should we turn Rhinelander Pavillion over to the ward people, or to the Blue Cross people in the semi-privates? We have our full share of that and there are also other hospitals for that. Larrimer Wing is something special; we must fight to keep it."

"Of course we must," Julie agreed vehemently.

There was truth in Julie's agreement, for now with Patrick out of the picture, Larrimer Wing was the door to the life she wanted. She would not let them tamper with Larrimer, she thought.

"Dr. Murdock and Dr. Dain may present problems. Especially Dr. Dain. His credentials are impeccable. His reputation also."

Julie was silent for a moment, thinking. "What if," she asked slowly, "Dr. Dain's reputation was called into question?"

"I have investigated his background very carefully. There is no blemish on it."

"What if there were an—ethical—blemish?"

"I have looked, there is no such thing. If you refer to his wife's—"

"No," Julie said quickly, "I don't. If I could show . . . let's say ethical misconduct . . . a lack of prudence, on Dr. Dain's part, would that help your case?"

Stuart smiled. "I see you share my devotion to Larrimer Wing."

"I find Larrimer Wing useful."

"When one weakens a man's reputation, one weakens his position."

"I'm not certain, *yet*," Julie said. "But I may be able to help."

"That is most encouraging. Any assistance you may require is yours for the asking."

Julie gathered her papers together and stood up. "I'll let you know."

"I am very glad we had this little talk. Perhaps hope is not lost."

"Not by a long shot," Julie said firmly. She turned to the door. "I'll let you know."

She left Stuart's office, nodding at his secretary as she walked through his outer office to the corridor. She headed toward the elevators, deep in thought.

"Excuse me," Buddy O'Hara said, bumping into Julie as he got off the elevator.

"Why, Buddy," Julie smiled brightly. "How are you?"

"Me? I'm okay. Why?"

"I haven't seen any bad reports on you lately."

"Yeah, I know," he said, trying to step out of her way.

"How is your mother? I met her one day, when she was visiting the clinic."

"She's fine. Why?" he asked, frowning at Julie's sudden interest. She'd never said more than hello to him before, and that with disdain. "Why?" he repeated.

"I like to know all our patients are getting on well."

"She's getting on fine. Listen, excuse me, but I have an appointment. With Dr. Dain."

She smiled again. "I'm glad you're getting along so well."

"It's okay. Look, I have to get going."

"Sure," Julie said, stepping out of his way. "I hope one of these days we'll have time for a real talk."

"Yeah."

Buddy walked up the corridor, deeply puzzled. He didn't like Julie Carlson; he'd never liked her and she'd made it clear the feeling was mutual.

Buddy reached the office and walked inside. "I'm on time," he said to Grace.

"So I see," she smiled. "But Dr. Dain's running a little late. It shouldn't be long. Want some coffee?"

Buddy shook his head. "I only have to see him for a minute."

"It's all right. He wanted to see you anyway."

"Yeah? Am I in hot water again?"

"I don't think so," Grace laughed. "I haven't heard the yelling and crashing I usually hear when you're in hot water. Guilty conscience?"

"No! It's just . . . well, you never know with him," Buddy said, though he said it not with rancor but with a kind of fond tolerance.

Grace noticed his tone and she looked at him closely. He was still brash, still cocky, but he'd come a long way from the deep, solitary anger of a few months ago. He seemed more relaxed now, more at ease with himself and the people around him.

"You like Dr. Dain, don't you?" she smiled.

Her question caught him by surprise. He hesitated before replying. "He's . . . not as bad as I thought he'd be, put it that way."

"Coming from you that's high praise."

"Well, he doesn't lord it over everyone, like I thought he would. And he knows medicine, he doesn't fool around. He's helped me, I admit it. And he's helped my . . . he's helped, that's all."

"Don't be so defensive. I'm a fan of his myself."

"I didn't say I was a fan," Buddy said quickly. "I like the way he handles things, that's all. Like he cares."

"He does. Is that so hard to believe?"

Buddy shrugged. Yes, it was hard to believe, he thought, yet he was beginning to believe it. He knew Patrick Dain, unlike his predecessors, made rounds in a different part of the hospital every morning without fail. He knew Patrick Dain held frequent student conferences, and that was also unlike his predecessors. He knew Patrick Dain was the first one at any emergency, often coming in on Saturday nights to lend a hand in the E.W. or the wards, and that was certainly unlike his predecessors.

Buddy turned as Patrick's door opened and a student walked out.

"Hi, Buddy."

"Hi, Janie. Good mood or bad?" Buddy nodded at Patrick's door.

"He's always in a good mood. You could take a lesson from him," she smiled, going to Grace's desk.

"You can go in, Buddy," Grace said, opening her appointment book.

Buddy entered Patrick's office, closed the door, and crossed the room and sat down, anxiously tapping the arms of the chair.

Patrick closed a folder and looked up. "Good morning, Dr. O'Hara."

"Morning. Grace said you wanted to see me about something."

"I did. We're starting a new seminar series next month and I would like you to consider enrolling. I know your schedule is tight, but I think it will be worth it. It's the theories and techniques of general practice, or family medicine, if you will. I know this is the age of the specialists, but family practice is coming back. And for good reason."

"I plan on specialization. That's where the money is. The real money. Minimum hours, maximum money. I figured cardiology."

"Half the student population of this hospital figures cardiology."

"What's wrong with that? Heart attacks in this country are epidemic . . . a guy can make himself a bundle working only half a week."

"What's wrong with that—for you," Patrick said, "is that underneath the dollar signs dancing in your heart, you have a true interest in medicine. A true talent. There are a great many fine cardiologists, but very few fine family physicians. You'd be useful as a cardiologist; I'm not saying you wouldn't. But you'd be a hundred times, a thousand times more useful in general practice."

"That means handling everybody, everything."

"Yes. Naturally there is consultation with specialists from time to time, but general practice treats the whole patient. It can be immensely rewarding. In terms of what medicine is all about. And there's a good living to be made, too. An excellent living, if not an extraordinary one."

"It's the extraordinary part that's always interested me."

"I don't think so, Mr. O'Hara." Patrick smiled. "I think that's something you tell yourself, nothing more."

"You can read my mind now?" Buddy half smiled, half scowled.

"I don't have to read your mind. I've watched you on rounds. Your medical interest is wide, far too wide to be happy in a specialty. Don't misunderstand me, I don't knock any branch of medicine. But you, Mr. O'Hara, would be bored to tears working in one narrow area. And that's all you get in a specialty. One narrow area of a patient. You treat that one area and then move him on to the next specialist. In general practice you are in the middle of everything. The challenges are enormous. New every day. Most important of all, you have the opportunity for interaction between doctor and patient—the way it's supposed to be and seldom is. That is something a specialist cannot have."

"No, but he can have a million bucks instead. No thanks."

"This is not something I would have suggested a few months ago. A few months ago," Patrick stared at Buddy, "you seemed incapable of interaction with other people. The Lone Ranger. But that's changed. Opening yourself up to Dr. Potter allowed you to open yourself up to other people as well. *Ab uno disce omnes.* From one, learn to know all. It's what you've needed for a long time. That one, simple, little nudge."

"You think you're pretty smart," Buddy laughed.

"I think you will always be too big for your britches. But that aside, I think you need challenge, you need to use *all* your talent, and you will enjoy being all things to all people. In short, a family practitioner."

"You didn't have a family practice."

"Internal medicine. Close, but hardly the same thing. That's why I'm here and why I like it here. I have a little of everything—from pediatrics through geriatrics. In any case, Mr. O'Hara, I want you to get the information sheets from Grace and read them carefully. Think about it carefully. It's only a series of seminars; it doesn't commit you to anything. I believe you will find it valuable."

"You can't force me."

Patrick sighed. "You will get the information sheets from Grace. You will read them carefully. You will think about it carefully. You will report back to me with your conclusions. Conclusions other than money and sunny days on golf courses. Is that clear?"

Buddy stared at Patrick, his jaw jutting forward. "Because you say so."

"Because I say so."

"You never give me any choice."

"I give you the choice of making something of yourself or not. There is no more important choice. And I give you the best advice—*nosce te ipsum.* Know thyself. Now, you wanted to see me about something?"

Buddy sat straighter in his chair. "It was sort of a favor."

"Shoot."

"I got the notice about your Christmas party."

"Yes?"

"Is that at your house? I mean the address on Fifth Avenue?"

"Yes, what about it?"

"Well, I'm coming, and I already asked a date . . . but I wanted to know was it okay if I brought an extra person?" Buddy asked, squirming around in his chair.

"Certainly. Ask Grace to add the name to the list. There'll be a little something under the tree for everyone; I don't want to run short."

"No, you don't have to . . . it's . . . I want Ma to come," Buddy said, looking away, coloring slightly. "She's never been . . . I mean I want her to walk through the front door of one of those places. Like a guest. Good as anybody."

Patrick saw how difficult it had been for Buddy to make his request, how much more difficult the last words had been.

"You're too sensitive about some things," he said quietly. "I know how hard your mother has had to work. That's something to be proud of."

"You don't know," Buddy shook his blond head. "It was demeaning."

"I know she did domestic work. In private homes—perhaps in a place like mine."

Buddy gaped at Patrick. "She *told* you?"

"Why not? Mr. O'Hara, if someone had worked that hard for me, I would be proud. You should be proud. She's a fine woman. She doesn't demean herself. Why do you demean her?"

"She was a *maid*. A maid for some rich bitch who wasn't fit to wipe Ma's shoes. How do you think that makes me feel?"

"You are a snob."

"A snob? Me? You're crazy, I was always the poorest kid on the block."

"You take it upon yourself to judge people by their jobs. You take it upon yourself to judge people by the money they have or don't have. Your mother said you had a 'them' and 'us' attitude and she was right. And that is being a snob."

"Ma seems to have said a lot. Are you her doctor or her psychiatrist?" Buddy snapped. "Why did she do all this talking?"

Patrick smiled. "We had a long talk the first day she came to the clinic. We had a drink and a long talk."

"She didn't tell me."

"She was probably afraid to."

"Why?"

"Having a drink with the enemy? What would you have said?"

"She could have told me," Buddy pouted.

"Your mother and I have had several nice conversations. I enjoy talking with her; we have much in common. As a matter of fact, we're dining together tonight. Did she have a chance to mention it?"

Buddy's mouth fell open. He stared at Patrick. "You and Ma having dinner? What for?"

"As I said, we've had several nice conversations. We have common interests and problems."

"You and *Ma?* What could you have in common with Ma?"

"I wish," Patrick laughed, "you would stop thinking of your mother as the Poor Little Match Girl. She's an intelligent, capable woman . . . a good deal more charming than her querulous son."

Buddy was silent, thinking about this turn of events. He wasn't entirely sure what to make of it, for he realized he'd never before stepped back and looked at his mother as a person. She was only Ma to him, loving, hard-working, stubborn about some things, lenient about most others. He supposed she was pretty, or had been once, but he'd never have thought to use the word charming.

He tried to picture his mother and Patrick Dain together at a restaurant and a sudden resentment stirred him as he thought of her old, shabby clothes, the contrast between those and Patrick Dain's custom-made suits and shirts. The resentment quickly gave way to a feeling of excitement. He was excited for his mother, for at last she would have a night out—and with no less a man than Patrick Dain. She would go to a good place, she would be treated like a somebody, he thought, the way she deserved to be treated. But why, he wondered, would Patrick Dain take the trouble?

"If this is your good deed of the week, Ma doesn't need it," Buddy said suspiciously.

"My good deed of the week, Mr. O'Hara, is deciding not to strangle you. That is my good deed every week."

"You have nothing in common. What do you have in common?"

"For one thing, we both have sons who can be extremely trying."

"Very funny."

"We both have sons who are not always easy to handle. We both work very hard and we understand the pressure of work. We've both gone through difficult times. We have more in common than you think. If that is not enough, your mother is a great fan of mystery stories. So am I," Patrick concluded.

That was not all there was to it, Patrick thought, but he could not explain the warm, happy feelings he had when he was around Ann. He could not explain his pleasure at the sound of her laugh, or the twinkle that sometimes came into her eyes. He could not explain how touched he was by her gentleness, how invigorated by her spirit. Nor did he think he should explain, for he, himself, didn't know where all these feelings would take them.

"Ma's never been to a—real—restaurant," Buddy said slowly.

"Then it's time."

"She doesn't have any good clothes."

"I didn't invite her dress," Patrick sighed, "I invited her. She can wear burlap for all I care."

Buddy looked at Patrick. He frowned. "I want her to have a good time."

Patrick hid a smile behind his hand. "So do I."

"I mean it should be a nice place, but it shouldn't be too fancy because—"

"Trust me. I have been choosing restaurants for a good many years. Are you finished, or does this go on forever?"

"Yeah . . . I guess."

"You will get the seminar information from Grace. Don't forget."

Buddy stood up. "Don't expect me to—"

"*Mr. O'Hara!*"

"Okay, I'll get it. Don't expect miracles is all I'm trying to say."

"We'll discuss that another time," Patrick said, turning back to the papers on his desk.

Buddy went to the door. He opened it a crack and then stopped, looking back at Patrick. He opened his mouth to speak but no words came. He stood there, his hand on the knob, groping for the right words.

Patrick looked up. He saw Buddy, his confusion. He smiled. "It's only dinner, Mr. O'Hara. We're not calling on the president."

Buddy stared at Patrick another moment and finally a small smile curled the corners of his mouth. "Yeah. Okay," he said, going out the door.

Patrick sat back, staring thoughtfully at the door. He'd been wary about his date with Ann but now, the more he thought about it, the more he looked forward to seeing her. It had been that way from the beginning, he realized; there was an initial uneasiness and then an anticipation that was unlike any he had known before. Once he was with her the time would go all too quickly and he, who had often wished time away, would want to hold on to every minute, every second.

Patrick rose and went to the door. He walked into the outer office just as Buddy was leaving.

"Did he take the seminar information?" Patrick asked.

"Yes," Grace nodded. "He practically grabbed it out of my hand. You must have done some selling job."

"I was selling him something he wanted to buy," Patrick smiled. "And he knew it."

"I've really seen changes in him."

"I have too. He's growing up, *slowly* but surely. Ann worries about him so much, I'm glad I can give her some reassurance."

Patrick looked at a pile of messages on Grace's desk. "Are those for me?"

"Dr. Karsh would like a meeting about the surgical services."

"Try to fit him in tomorrow."

"Okay. And the Interns' Committee is having its regular meeting next week. They'd like you to attend."

"Fine. Put it in my book."

"And Janie Powers, the student?" Grace went on. "Do you want her to have her tutoring with Randolphs or Rothman?"

"Try and set it up with Rothman. He's much better for lab work."

"Okay. Now, last but not least, the gifts for the Christmas party. How much do you want to spend?"

"Let's spend a lot of money," Patrick grinned. "Let's have some fun."

Grace smiled up at Patrick, studying him. "I love

seeing you so happy. Rhinelander Pavillion is the best thing that ever happened to you."

"There were only two possibilities. It could have been the best or the worst. So far . . ." Patrick held up his hand, crossing his fingers as he returned to his office.

24

It had been snowing for several hours. The first tentative, lacy flakes had given way to great chunky cutouts, tossed about in the breeze until the city was under a cover of white.

Patrick stood at his bedroom window watching the snow swirl through Central Park, watching the odd silvery light that always came with snow. He'd watched many such snowfalls from this window and he remembered the glee with which he and Tony would haul their sleds across the park. He could see children and parents playing in the whitened park now, but he and Tony would not be among them this day.

Tony had arrived home the afternoon before, laden with suitcases and canvas bags stuffed full and Christmas packages. He'd arrived in a good mood and indeed, he and Patrick had enjoyed a long, talky dinner, bringing each other up to date, laughing happily and often. But, as had happened before, after a few hours Tony grew restive and very quiet, retreating early to his rooms.

Patrick regretted scheduling his Christmas open-house so close to Tony's homecoming. He should have put it off a few days, he thought, for the extra days might have given them the time they needed to ease the strangeness between them. To ease it or make it worse, he added ruefully, turning from the window.

He looked at his watch, knowing he should be downstairs yet reluctant to face the hours ahead. He had much on his mind and so little time to sort out his thoughts. There was Tony, Patrick thought—and how desperate he was to repair his relationship with him. There was the hospital with all its problems. There was David, for Gail Parrish still had to be dealt with. And there was Ann.

Patrick smiled slightly, remembering their dinner the week before. They'd had a wonderful evening, talking and talking, learning about each other, Patrick mesmerized all the while by Ann's steady blue eyes, the new light in them, the new glow which shone about her. They'd walked hand in hand down Fifth Avenue, gazing into the Tiffany windows, into the Bonwit windows dressed for Christmas. They'd walked to Rockefeller Center, staring quietly at the magnificent Christmas tree. He'd taken her home and held her in his arms. It had been only a brief moment but that moment told him all he needed to know.

Patrick was startled out of his thoughts by a knock at the door. "Yes, come in."

"I'm sorry to trouble you, sir, but the guests are beginning to arrive," Hollis said.

"I'll be down shortly. Make them comfortable."

"There's another thing, sir."

"Yes?"

"Well, Dr. Dain, it's about the carpets, sir."

"The carpets? What about them?"

"The snow, sir. All those wet shoes. Shall we take up the Aubussons, sir?"

Patrick smiled. "It's a party, Hollis. Everything should look its best. Why don't you put some mats by the door, let people wipe their boots?"

"I've done that, sir. But young people . . . you know, sir."

"Hollis, it's about time there was some laughter, some disorder around here. If it costs us stained carpets, it's cheap at twice the price."

"If you say so, sir," Hollis nodded. "We'll make the best of it, eh, sir?"

"That's the spirit," Patrick said, walking into the hallway with Hollis. "I'll be down soon. Relax, Hollis, everything will be fine."

"Yes, sir. As you say."

"Have you seen Tony?"

"I believe Master Tony is in his bedroom, sir," Hollis said, starting down the stairway.

Patrick walked down the hall to Tony's rooms. He knocked at the door but got no reply. He knocked again and then opened the door. Tony's bedroom was a jumble of clothes and books and record albums, of suitcases open, only partially unpacked.

"Tony?" Patrick called.

He peered into the sitting room and then left, closing the door quietly. He was about to go to the stairs when another door noisily banged shut. He turned to see Tony coming from Catherine's rooms.

"Why, Tony, what were you doing in there?"

Anthony Murdock Dain, tall, slender, dark-haired, looked angrily at his father. "It didn't take you long, did it?"

"What?" Patrick frowned.

"It didn't take you long to empty Mother's rooms. All her things. You couldn't wait."

Patrick walked over to Tony. He put his hand on the boy's shoulder but he shrugged it away.

"Tony, what was there to wait for?" he asked quietly. "Those things were sitting around gathering dust. Making unnecessary work for Delia and the women. I sent some family pieces to your grandmother, and the rest to charity. Wouldn't you prefer your mother's things were put to some good use?"

"You should have waited!"

"Sooner or later—either way—it would have hurt you just as much," Patrick said, gazing into his son's light blue eyes.

"I wasn't thinking about myself."

"Yes. You were. *Things* are not important, Tony. Our memories of the people we lose don't depend on things. Surely you understand that."

"Mother would have wanted you to keep it as it was."

"I couldn't do that."

"You could never do anything Mother wanted."

"That's neither fair nor true."

Tony stared down at the floor. "At least her portrait's still downstairs. Mother always said her soul was in that portrait."

"I remember . . . Tony, would you like me to drive you to the cemetery one day while you're here?"

Tony looked up, staring at his father. "Would you do that?"

"Of course."

"I don't know if I want to go, but thanks for asking, Dad. I'm . . .I'm sorry for what I said. I was—surprised."

"I know. Let's forget it."

Tony offered a small smile. "Hey, is there a party here or not?"

"There is." Patrick put his hands on Tony's shoulders. "Are you all right?"

"Sure, Dad."

"Good. Let's go."

They walked down the stairs. Hollis, standing in the center hall looked up at them and smiled, for they looked so alike. They were of similar build and coloring, the same casual assurance in their walks. Today, with both of them dressed in turtleneck sweaters, gray

317

slacks and navy blue blazers, the similarity was the more striking. Master Tony was as handsome as his father, Hollis thought, and soon he would be as tall.

"Good afternoon, Master Tony," he beamed. "There's plenty of food and . . . drink," he added, glancing at Patrick.

"I take a beer now and then, Dad," Tony said.

Patrick nodded, smiling as Tony walked off to the drawing room.

"Well," Patrick said, turning to Hollis. "Let's have a look."

Patrick gazed around the center hall. A graceful eighteen-foot Christmas tree stood in the recess of the stairway, its branches bedecked with glittering ornaments and hundreds of tiny angel lights. Underneath the tree were dozens of packages wrapped in gold and red and green papers, each with great fluffy bows. The stairway banister was trimmed with greenery, and off in a corner a pianist tuned up for the Christmas carols he would play through the day and evening. Off to the side of the drawing room was an attended bar and a little ways away was another attended bar, that one for wine and beer.

"Very nice, Hollis. Very, very nice."

"Thank you, sir. Would you like to see the dining room?"

They walked to the dining room. Patrick peeked inside, smiling at the handsome array. The table was arranged for a buffet with trays of roast beef and smoked ham and Scotch salmon. There were tureens of curried chicken and large iced bowls of shrimp and crabmeat. There were mushrooms stuffed with eggplant and two enormous green salads. Gleaming silver flatware was stacked neatly next to stacks of china plates and rows of carefully folded linen napkins.

"Bravo," Patrick laughed. "You've done it again."

"Thank you, sir. May I get you a drink?"

"I'll help myself," Patrick said as they walked back to the drawing room. He glanced inside. "Not too many people here yet," he said. "Now, you understand, Hollis, they'll be coming and going all day. As they get off their hospital shifts. Let's be sure we don't run short on anything."

"Oh, I do understand, sir. We've plenty of everything."

"Good," Patrick looked at his watch. "Two o'clock. It's going to be a long day. I don't want you to overdo. I hired a lot of help; let them share the work. And help yourself to anything you want. I want you to have a good time."

"Thank you, sir. I expect to enjoy myself, I do. I'm a man that likes parties. And, sir, if I may say so, it's very good having Master Tony back home."

"Yes. I hope it works out," Patrick said slowly.

"Now, sir—" Hollis turned at the sound of the door bell. "I'll see to it, sir," he said, hurrying to the door.

Hollis opened the door and Lola Shay, her arms full of packages, struggled inside.

"Hello, Dr. Shay. Merry Christmas," Hollis said, taking the packages from her. He put them on a side table, helping her off with her coat.

"Thank you, Hollis. And Merry Christmas to you."

Patrick came forward. He kissed Lola's cheek. "Merry Christmas, ho, ho, ho, and all that."

"The same to you," Lola laughed. "I'm always the first one at parties. So gauche. Am I first today?"

"Some senior staff beat you to it."

"Hurray," Lola said, handing her gloves and scarf to Hollis.

Hollis put them with her coat on a long metal rack and then gave her packages back to her.

"Thank you. Patrick, point me to the tree."

He took her arm, guiding her across the hall. "Are you filling in for Santa this year?" he asked, glancing at the many packages.

Lola bent down, arranging the packages around the tree. "You know how I am about Christmas. Anyway, it's not so much. Some things for you and Tony and Hollis. Something for Henry Potter, and a couple of students who've worked my service." She stood up, looking around. "It all looks wonderful. You have such a flair."

"Hollis has the flair."

"And a piano! Do we get to carol later?"

"Absolutely."

Lola looked at the tree. "There's something for David, too. He's coming, isn't he?"

"I expect him a little later."

"With the lady of his dreams?" Lola asked, looking at Patrick.

"What do you know about that?"

"Not much. David and I had dinner last week. First time in a long time," she said as they walked to the bar. "He didn't come right out and say so, but I gather our boy is smitten." Lola ordered a drink and looked back at Patrick. "Right or wrong?"

"Right, I'm sorry to say."

"Thank you," Lola took her drink. "Interesting you say that, because for someone in love he seemed pretty unhappy. No, maybe that's the wrong word. He seemed—subdued."

"There are complications."

Lola sipped her drink. "Is that all you're going to tell me?"

Patrick stared at Lola. "You're in love with David, aren't you?"

Lola took another sip of her drink. "We're pals."

Patrick smiled. "Lola, you fight for your patients,

for your service, for Henry Potter. You fight for everything and everyone but yourself."

"Are you suggesting I use my feminine wiles?" she laughed, batting her eyelashes.

"I suggest nothing of the sort. But David can be obtuse sometimes. I'd bet he doesn't know how you feel."

"And if he did? *I'd* bet his lady love has him on a string. Short, tight, and on her finger."

"Strings break."

"How cryptic we are today. Are you trying to tell me something?"

"Fight for yourself, Lola. And don't count yourself out. Not yet."

Lola was silent, staring straight ahead. "The bottom line is I want David to be happy. Even it that includes me out."

"The bottom line is, don't include yourself out," Patrick hugged her. "Shall we join the others?"

People came and went throughout the day, their voices rising in laughter and relaxed holiday conversation. They mingled easily, drifting between the drawing room, living room and dining room, stopping often at the bar or the white-gloved waiters passing trays of champagne. The pianist played the familiar music of Christmas, now and then changing tempo with Rodgers and Hart or Cole Porter. Patrick circulated among the guests, pleased with the party, even more pleased to see Tony enjoying himself.

By five o'clock most of the senior staff had departed, replaced by a boisterous group of students and interns and their dates, carefree and exuberant on this day. The rhythms of the music quickened to match the rhythms of the party and room after room echoed with high spirits.

Hollis was seated in a chair by the front door, a

brandy and soda on a table nearby. His foot tapped along with the music and he thought it had been a long time since there had been such happiness in this house, even a longer time since Dr. Dain had looked so happy and relaxed. He was watching Patrick laughing with a group of young men as the bell rang. He rose to answer it.

"Good evening, Dr. Murdock. And it's Miss Parrish, isn't it? Merry Christmas," he said, stepping back as they entered. "Oh, and it's Mrs. O'Hara, too. Merry Christmas one and all."

They returned holiday greetings to him while they slipped out of coats and mufflers and boots, carefully balancing Christmas packages all the while. So busy were they that no one noticed the odd look which passed across David's face.

"There now," Hollis said as the last of the coats was hung on the rack. "The party is going great guns, if I may say so."

David took a small envelope from his pocket and handed it to Hollis. "Merry Christmas. And not," he held up his hand, "another word about it. Ladies," he smiled slightly, "let's see about this great party."

Ann glanced at David. She'd run into David and Gail in the lobby. They'd introduced themselves, riding upstairs together. David had been smiling, chatting excitedly. Now, she thought to herself, he seemed distracted, upset about something.

"Ready, Ann?" he asked.

"I don't know," she said, looking around.

Ann gazed wide-eyed at the magnificent sweep of the center hall, of the graceful staircase. She stared at the extravagant Christmas decorations, the great regal tree with its endless presents underneath. She looked up and caught her breath, entranced by a Waterford chandelier, sparkling and glittering with golden light.

"It's beautiful," she whispered.

"To compliment two beautiful ladies," David said, looking from Ann to Gail.

His glance lingered on Gail. A small frown wrinkled his brow and then he turned back to Ann.

"Shall we? Here," he offered his arm, "hold on."

They walked to the tree. Gail, resplendent in a copper-colored satin dress, high-necked, backless, led the way. Ann, in her old black dress with Mae's lace collar, followed with David. They put their packages under the tree and then turned toward the drawing room.

Ann stopped at the threshold of the room. "I'm *scared*," she laughed.

David looked at her. He'd met her only minutes before but he'd liked her immediately. There was a forthrightness about her, he thought, and a fine spirit. Even now, though she was nervous, her head was high, her posture straight and sure.

"Walking in is always the worst moment," he assured her. "Take a deep breath, hang on, and you'll be fine. I swear it," he smiled.

Ann, David, and Gail entered the room together. David stopped the waiter and then, champagne glasses in hand, they made their way across the room, smiling and nodding until they spotted Patrick.

Patrick was off in a corner, deep in a conversation with Grace. As Grace saw the three approaching she pointed in their direction and Patrick turned. He saw David and Gail only dimly, for all his attention was focused on Ann. He didn't notice her old dress, or the nervous way she clasped and unclasped her fingers; he noticed only her smile, her lovely face flushed with bright color, the special light which seemed to be hers alone. He wanted to rush to her, to hold her close, the way he had the last time they'd been together.

"Merry Christmas," she said softly, staring into his eyes.

"Merry Christmas."

He held out his hand, kissing her lightly on the cheek. They stared at each other until David cleared his throat.

"It's not that I mind being ignored," he smiled.

Patrick smiled. "Sorry," he smiled back. "It's about time you got here." He looked at Gail. "Hello, Gail."

"Hello. I love your place. All dressed up for Christmas."

" 'Tis the season. There's plenty of everything, help yourself."

"Patrick," Ann said, "is Buddy here?"

"Yes," he looked around. "I saw him a minute ago. He must be in one of the other rooms. I'll take you."

"No, I'll find him."

"Hurry back."

Grace looked at Gail and then introduced herself. The two women began talking and Patrick turned to David.

"Lola's been asking for you. She's in this crowd somewhere."

"Later. Patrick, may I speak to you alone?"

They excused themselves and walked a few steps away.

"What's up?" Patrick asked.

"A curious thing just happened."

"Oh? What?"

"When we arrived . . . Hollis greeted Gail by name. She returned the greeting. By name."

"I don't see what—"

"How does he know her, Patrick?" David asked. "How does she know him?"

"I suppose I might have mentioned her name to Hollis," Patrick said, hastily gathering his thoughts.

"And Gail? How does she know Hollis?"

"I suppose you mentioned his name to her."

"You suppose wrong."

"David, this is a silly conversation. What are you suggesting?"

"I don't know. But I want an answer."

"Did you ask Gail?"

"I am asking you. I'm not in the habit of questioning other people's servants, but I will. If I have to."

"You're making too much of this. However," he added quickly, seeing David's impatience, "I'll question Hollis myself. But later, when the party isn't so busy. All right? Will that make you happy? I'm sure there's a simple answer. They probably shop at the same market or something."

"You will speak with him later?"

"Yes. Now would you mind loosening up and enjoying my party? It's only three days to Christmas, David. Let's see some spirit."

David said nothing. After a moment his expression softened and he smiled. "Okay. By the way, I like her. Your Ann."

"Don't be so quick with the possessive pronouns."

"One look is worth a thousand words. I saw how you looked at each other."

"You're doing a lot of deducing tonight," Patrick smiled. "Did someone give you a junior G-man kit or have you been watching Charlie Chan movies again?"

"When I'm right, I'm right," David said, sipping his champagne. "How's it going? Oh, I see Julie's having a good time. All the men clustered around her as usual," David said, looking at Julie.

She sat on a small sofa, surrounded by a dozen men. Her black hair was piled atop her head. Her dress was a ruby red.

"It's funny about her," Patrick said. "She spent an

awful lot of time talking to Tony. And then an awful lot of time talking to Buddy O'Hara. I saw him trying to get away from her several times, but each time she followed him. Very persistent. She must have got talked out finally because then, abruptly, she turned around and walked away."

"Kids aren't usually her style. But who knows, she's an odd duck. I never could figure her out . . . She's beautiful though, look at her."

"Too beautiful. Like Catherine."

David's lips parted in surprise. Catherine! That's who Julie had reminded him of all this time. The same overwhelming beauty. The same cunning, he realized with a start. Sleek, silky cunning, he thought, and that was what had disturbed him all along.

"You say she singled out Tony and Buddy?" he asked.

"Indeed she did."

"I wonder why?"

"Well, it doesn't matter. Buddy obviously wasn't having any of it. Tony's half in love with her, but he has a date tonight and he'll get over it. Fast."

David smiled. "A special girl?"

"You know Tony's friend, Kip Warren? Well, Kip's sister Georgiana. All dewy young eyes and precocious figure. In fifteen years she'll look like a pouter pigeon, but right now I can only hope Tony remembers he is a gentleman."

"So it begins," David laughed.

"The worries certainly begin. Do you remember when you were sixteen? Or almost seventeen, as Tony puts it."

"I remember."

"The worries begin."

They turned back toward the party, rejoining Grace and Gail.

"Miss us?" David asked.

"Terribly," Gail laughed. "Didn't we?"

"Terribly," Grace agreed.

"David," Patrick said, "there's Lola. Why don't you take Gail over and introduce her."

"Yes, you'll like her, Gail," David said, leading her away.

Patrick stared after them, deep lines creasing his forehead.

"Problems?" Grace asked.

"Could be."

"Can I help?"

"I wish."

Patrick saw Tony cutting through the crowd. He stopped to talk with David and then gestured at Patrick to meet him in the hall.

"Excuse me," Patrick said to Grace. "I think Tony's leaving."

Patrick squeezed past the guests, edging into the hall. He saw Tony at the closet door, Hollis helping him into his coat.

"All ready?" Patrick asked.

Tony nodded. "I hope there's no trouble getting a cab."

"Do you have enough money?"

"I cashed a check," Tony patted his pocket. "It was a nice party, Dad. I'm sorry to run out on you like this."

"You were a big help. Have fun," Patrick said, walking him to the door. "Say hello to the Warrens for me."

"I will. Night, Dad."

"Good night."

Patrick waited until the elevator came and then closed the door.

"He's growing up, eh, sir?" Hollis smiled. "A proper host he was today."

"How about you, Hollis? Enjoying yourself?"

"Yes, sir. That I am."

"I think we might start doing something about the gifts. Would you call everyone to come to the tree, please?"

Hollis scurried off and Patrick went to the tree, smiling down at the beribboned boxes. The first wave of guests surged into the hall and Patrick stepped back.

"Students should look here," he said, pointing to an area to the left of the tree. "Interns, there," he said, pointing to the right. "Everyone else is on their own."

"Need some help?" Grace asked.

"It's under control, thanks to you," Patrick said, putting his arm around her shoulder. "I appreciate it," he added, for Grace had made the lists and attended to the delivery of the gifts and then carefully tagged each one. "Isn't Rudy coming? There's a package for him there somewhere."

"He's working."

Patrick and Grace stood back, smiling as paper and ribbon flew through the air, and the young people laughed and nudged each other, and the pianist played *The Twelve Days of Christmas*.

"I think they like them," Patrick said. "What do you think?"

"Why shouldn't they? At the last Christmas party they got ties or scarves. This time . . ."

This time the students received sleek Mark Cross notebooks and silver pens. The interns received gold Cross pens, and all of their dates received silver Tiffany keyrings. There were other, more personal gifts for some of the guests, but those, Patrick knew would not be opened now.

The students and interns and their dates began moving away from the tree, each of them stopping to thank Patrick.

"You have no further excuse for lost notes. No more

scribbling on tiny scraps of paper," he smiled over and over again.

They drifted away slowly, forming a great circle around the piano, singing along with the music. Buddy O'Hara was the last to come up to him.

"We didn't expect anything like this. With our initials, too. We . . . appreciate it. Elaine, my date, she can never find her keys. She'll find 'em now."

"I'm glad. Are you having a good time?"

"Yeah."

"Do you mean to tell me that Buddy O'Hara cannot find *one* thing to complain about?" Patrick smiled.

"No complaints. But there was one thing—"

"Aha!"

"No, not a complaint. I was wondering though . . . I mean this is some place. You have it all. You have everything . . . I mean, why do you work so hard? I wouldn't."

"Don't be too sure."

"I wouldn't give up medicine, but I wouldn't break my back either."

"Don't be too sure."

"There you go again. Talking like you know me better than I know myself."

"At least as well, Mr. O'Hara," Patrick laughed. "At least as well," he said, walking back to the drawing room with Grace.

"He always has to get in the last word," Buddy grumbled through a smile. He watched Patrick go over to his mother, bringing her a drink. "He's been nice to Ma, though."

"We talked for a while," Henry said. "I liked her."

"Did I tell you he took her to dinner?"

"About a hundred times."

"A guy like that," Buddy shook his head. "You know what I mean? He said they have things in common.

Imagine that?" he addressed Henry's date. "He's got like fifty million bucks! And he's lonely!"

"Maybe he just likes her," she offered.

"I guess he can let his hair down with Ma. It's not like when he's on a date. I guess it's good," Buddy said thoughtfully. "I mean I guess it's good people their age have someone to talk to about their problems."

Henry looked at Buddy. He thought to say something and then changed his mind.

"They don't look so old to me," Henry's date said, but Henry quickly steered her away.

25

Ann O'Hara came to the end of the hall and tapped lightly on the door.

"Come in," Patrick called.

Ann entered the library and looked slowly around. "Patrick, it's wonderful," she said. "There must be thousands of books. And this room is so—cozy."

"Unlike the others."

"I didn't mean—"

"Of course you did, and I couldn't agree more. I intend to move when Tony is settled at Yale. Come, sit down," he took her to a chair near the fireplace. "How's the party doing?"

"The kids are dancing. In between, they eat," she smiled.

"And you?"

"I feel like I'm leading a double life. Sometimes an ordinary secretary, sometimes a jet-setter. I'm very grateful, Patrick."

"Now you sound like Buddy. He stopped me at the hospital to thank me for taking you to dinner." He smiled. "As if I am doing you a favor. Given time, he'll see how it really is."

Ann stared at Patrick. "How is it?"

"Are you fishing for compliments?" he laughed.

Ann turned away, looking down at her hands. Her

heart pounded rapidly and her mouth felt dry, but she'd come to the party to talk to Patrick and this, she thought, might be her only chance.

Patrick took her hand. "I'm so sorry, I didn't mean to upset you."

"Oh, Patrick. I don't want to spoil all this. I hate the idea of spoiling it." She looked into his eyes. "But I've been playing a dangerous game and it's time . . . to . . ."

"Ann, what is it? What dangerous game?" he asked worriedly.

"You. This," she said, glancing around. "Us. Each time you asked me out I went, knowing I shouldn't. Patrick, I've always tried to teach Buddy not to kid himself, to be realistic. But I'm the one who's kidded herself, and realistic is the last thing I've been. I'm getting in too deep. I'm in way over my head. It . . . has to stop."

Patrick's fingers caressed her soft blond hair. He smiled. "Has Mae been talking to you again?"

"It's not just Mae. It's me. I'm not the same. I—daydream—all the time now. I can't concentrate at the office. There's a big basket of sewing sitting at home. Undone because I can't keep my mind on it. Yesterday I made a pot of coffee, except I forgot to put the coffee in," she threw up her hands. "And I'd hate to tell you about the stew."

Patrick laughed and Ann looked sharply at him.

"I'm not kidding. My life is upside down."

"Ann, I told you once this needn't be complicated. I was wrong. It gets more complicated every day, for both of us. And I'm glad," he said, tipping her chin to him. "Being with you makes me happier than I've ever been. I know you feel the same way. And we're not going to destroy it because we're frightened. Ann, I'm falling in love with you."

"No!" she said, rising quickly from her chair.

Patrick followed her, putting his hands on her slim shoulders. "And you with me."

Ann shook her head, averting her eyes. "Don't you see it's impossible? I don't take these things casually. When I'm involved I'm involved. And that's impossible."

"Why?"

"Why? Look around you. Look how you live. You saw how I live. How I've always lived. You're rich, you're important. I'm Ann O'Hara, one generation away from the peat bogs. I don't belong. I knew that the moment you walked into the clinic office. It was like God walked in," she said, smiling despite herself.

"I have been called many things before but never God."

"You know what I mean."

"I know I've been unhappy for many years. I know I never expected to be happy again. I know I met you and everything changed. Ann, the more I know you, the more I want to know you. The more I'm with you, the more I want to be with you. Can you honestly tell me you don't feel the same way?"

"I'm trying to be sensible. You're not helping."

"It's not sensible to walk away from what we have. I didn't want this, you know. I wasn't going to call you again. But I called and we saw each other again and we knew. We can't deny it any longer."

"It's a mistake."

"Why? Because of the peat bogs?" he smiled. "My great-great grandfather built a great fortune, but I would hate to look too closely at how he did it. They say he was a man of character, of principle. Perhaps he was about some things, but great fortunes are seldom built on principle. The bulk of our fortune was made before child labor laws, before alien work laws.

Remember that when you think about my family."

"However it was made, you have the fortune."

Patrick pulled Ann back to the chair and sat her down.

"We certainly do," he said. "I would tell you precisely how much it is if I knew. I don't. We have attorneys and financial managers to figure it out. My portion is many millions. Sixty million, perhaps more," he said flatly and Ann cringed. "There will be more one day and Tony has his own trusts. Would you like me better if I were poor?"

"If you were poor we'd be the same. Patrick, I used to clean houses like this. I used to serve at parties like this. Don't you see, it's all upside down."

"Ann, money is a practical matter—the absence of pressure. There's nothing mystical about it. Given a choice I'd rather be rich, but enjoying it is an altogether different thing. I'm enjoying it now because I see the things I take for granted through your eyes. There is pleasure where there was little pleasure before."

"I'm not a charity case," Ann said, a fiery little light in here eyes.

"No. No, you are not," Patrick smiled. "You are a joy. My joy." He bent, taking her hand. "There is a poem. It begins, *When I am not with you I am alone.*"

Ann stared up into his eyes. She should fight this, she thought; should she walk out of the room and never see him again? She looked at his face, his beautiful, handsome face, and his words echoed in her mind. She felt a kind of bliss, a bliss so wide and deep she thought she would burst with it. She put her other hand on his.

"I'm so scared."

"Ann, no one is given many chances at happiness. The chances we're given are ours to take or throw away. Let's see where our chance takes us."

Ann was silent for a long time. When she looked back at him she was smiling. "Yes, I'll try."

Patrick pulled her to her feet and held her in his arms. "Thank you," he said.

He took her hand and led her to the desk.

"There are some things for you and Mae under the tree. But I have another package for you and this one you'll open here," he smiled, opening a desk drawer.

He removed a long, slim box and gave it to her. "I've anticipated all your arguments, but I insist you have it."

Ann unwrapped the package and gazed at a velvet jeweler's box. She opened it slowly, cautiously, peeking inside before she pushed the cover back. She gasped, her eyes wide and round as a child's as she looked upon a double strand of pearls clasped with a brilliant sapphire.

"God!"

"Are you talking to me?" Patrick laughed.

"Patrick," her mouth fell open. "I . . . can't."

"There is no such word. Not around here. It's a no-strings-attached-Merry Christmas-I think-you-are-wonderful present. I want you to have it. It's like you in a way," he said, taking the necklace from the box. "Delicate, glowing, the sapphire for strength. And to match the color of your eyes. Here," he said, slipping it about her neck. He closed the clasp and led her to mirror. "Look."

Her fingers brushed the pearls carefully, gently, as if she were afraid she would hurt them. "I can't . . . How would I . . . what would people . . . ?"

"People see what they expect to see. They'll think it's costume jewelry. Do you like it?"

"It's beautiful. I've never had . . . I . . . Patrick, I'd be afraid to wear it. What if I lost it? What if I were robbed?"

"Do you like it? Does it make you happy?"

"I love it . . . I don't know what to say."

He reached to kiss her but as he did so the library door opened and Julie Carlson walked into the room.

"Oh, I'm sorry. Excuse me, Patrick, Mrs. O'Hara. I wanted to see the family portraits. Somebody told me they were very interesting."

"Upstairs," Patrick said.

He stared curiously at Julie for it seemed to him she was always popping up in unlikely places, usually when he least expected her.

"Hollis will be glad to show you," he said.

"Of course, thank you," Julie said.

She looked quickly around, her eyes settling on the desk, on the discarded wrapping paper, the open jewel box. She looked at Ann, at the necklace she wore.

"Thank you," Julie said again, smiling sweetly at them as she left.

"That's the woman I met at the hospital that first day," Ann said.

Patrick stared at the door. "She pops up on street corners, in corridors, everywhere. I returned to my office late one night last week and there she was. Sometimes I wonder if she's twins. Well," he looked back at Ann, "I suppose we ought to be getting back to the party."

Ann unclasped the necklace and took it back to the box. She arranged the pearls reverently on the satin and closed the case.

"I'll put these in my purse. And hold on to my purse for dear life," she laughed.

They walked to the door. "I won't see you until after Christmas," Patrick said. "Mother and Dad are coming up from Washington. We always spend the holiday with my aunt in Westchester. I would invite you, but I need to concentrate on Tony for a while."

"I have some catching up to do with Buddy. He's off Christmas Eve and we're going to have a little family dinner."

"Buddy's going to be all right, Ann. That tough shell of his is beginning to show a crack or two."

"I'm not going to tell him about the pearls."

"Tell everyone or no one. I only want you to be happy."

Patrick opened the door. Ann turned to him. "Do you believe in fate?" she asked.

"We used to argue about predestination in school," Patrick smiled. "We never did come to a conclusion. I don't know if we were fated to meet," he said slowly. "But having met," he kissed her lightly, "we were fated to fall in love. Because it's so right. If it was part of a plan . . . then it's a wonderful plan."

They returned to the party. Ann joined Grace and Lola in the living room. Patrick stopped at the bar.

"Hangovers, gentlemen, hangovers," he grinned, going into the drawing room.

He stopped to talk with each of the remaining guests, seeing departing ones to the door. By midevening most of the visitors had gone, save for a small group of new arrivals just coming off duty. They formed a mini-party of their own, taking drinks and plates of food into the center hall, sitting in a circle by the tree, opening packages and singing songs, trading jokes back and forth.

Patrick watched them for a moment and then returned to the drawing room, joining David on the couch.

"Where's Gail?" he asked.

"She went home. I told her there was a hospital problem we had to discuss. She looked for you to say goodbye."

"I took Ann to a cab."

"Good party."

"I thought so," Patrick said.

"So much for small talk. Did you speak to Hollis?"

Patrick shook his head. "You're like a dog with a bone."

This was the moment, Patrick thought; he could lie or he could tell David the truth, all of it.

"Let's go into the library," he said.

They walked in silence to the library. Patrick poured two brandies.

"Unless you'd prefer something else?" he asked.

"This is fine," David said, taking the glass. "Well?"

"David, why didn't you ask Gail about it?"

"You must have that figured out by now. I didn't ask her because I thought she might lie."

"Why?"

"I don't entirely—trust—her. She's broken a few dates lately . . . cousins from out of town. I'm not sure I believe that."

"I see." Patrick sipped his brandy. "Isn't trust a part—"

"Lectures are *not* what I want," David interrupted. "I said I don't entirely trust her. It could be I'm overreacting. Or it could be I'm right. What's your opinion?" he asked, watching Patrick carefully.

Patrick sat down. He ran his hand through his hair, staring off into space.

"Well, David," he said slowly, quietly, "there is more to Gail than she's told you. She and Hollis knew each other because she was here. Once, to speak with me."

"I thought as much," David drank his brandy. "She described a table she'd seen. She wanted one like it. The way she described it—it's the tile table in your living room. Made to Catherine's design, one of a kind. I remembered because I remember the argument when Catherine decided she didn't like it." David stared at

Patrick. "Why did she come to talk to you? What hasn't she told me?"

"Do you want the truth? Think about it," Patrick urged gently, "because the truth isn't so pleasant. Perhaps you're better—"

"I want the truth. Now. I am slow about some things, but not so slow I haven't noticed that something, somehow, somewhere, is wrong. Let's have it."

Patrick rose from his chair. He took the brandy decanter and put it on the floor between them.

"I have to start with John Caldwel," Patrick began.

He spoke slowly, deliberately, for twenty minutes. His voice was low and sad, sadder, it seemed, with each new word he spoke. David's expression didn't change; he sat stiffly, one hand tightly grasping his glass, the other grasping the arm of his chair. He'd grown pale and an awful tiredness seemed to settle about him. His eyes did not move from Patrick's face.

Patrick came to the end of his story. He stared down at the floor, shaking his head back and forth, his arms hanging limply in front of him.

"I'm sorry, David."

There was a deep, dark silence in the room. Patrick waited several minutes and then looked at David.

"Are you all right? Or is that a stupid question?"

"You intended to let me go along my merry way? Knowing what you knew? If Hollis hadn't—"

"No," Patrick said quickly. "I was going to tell you, of course. But I didn't want to tell you before the holidays. Merry Christmas, and here's a kick in the stomach for you," Patrick said unhappily. "There was going to be a pain whenever I told you, I thought it could wait until a less . . . emotional time of year."

"How kind. I sat in this very room, in this very chair, telling you about my great love. All the time I was talking about a slut. All the time you knew it."

David threw his glass at the fireplace. It smashed against the firescreen, shattering on the floor. David rubbed his eyes. He sat back, his shoulders sagging.

"I apologize. It wasn't a shock, yet it *was* a shock. I'm sorry. I shouldn't blame the messenger of bad news for the bad news."

Patrick got a fresh glass and poured another drink, handing it to David.

"I don't think there's any — malice — in Gail," Patrick said. "She doesn't see anything wrong in what she does, or she's rationalized it away. She was trying to protect you."

David gulped his drink. "You know, starting around Thanksgiving I felt something was wrong. It's hard to explain but I felt it. And I began to realize I didn't trust her. And if I didn't trust her, what did we have? I kept telling myself it would be all right. I didn't really believe that. The bedroom is a powerful weapon," David said wearily. "And that's where we spent most of our time. I began to wonder about that, too. Whenever we disagreed — whenever anything was even slightly off-key — we'd wind up in the bedroom. Presto, everything was resolved."

David's face was a terrible dead white and Patrick looked worriedly at him. "Are you all right?"

"The knife sticking out of my heart didn't come with the suit . . . I loved her, dammit. I still do. *Odi et amo*. I hate and I love . . . I'm telling this to you," David laughed dully, " — an expert on the subject."

"Yes," Patrick said quietly. "That's why I knew you had to be told. After a while it would have been horror. Catherine and I had four perfect years, the rest were horror. The rate of exchange is . . . too steep. You saw it, you saw how it was."

"Did Gail think she could get away with it? Did she

340

think she'd be able to keep me in the dark forever? Or did she plan to keep me locked in her bedroom forever?"

"Anger is good, for now. It will help, for now. But in the long run it will hurt you. You've never been a bitter man."

"I've never had quite so much reason."

"I'm not so sure Gail can help it. I had the impression she was without a moral center—without a capacity to feel regret, or sorrow."

"It's not only Gail I'm bitter about. It's me. Way, way, deep down, I think I suspected something like this. I didn't have the courage to face it. My courage atrophied somewhere along the line, like an unused muscle," David said, going to a window.

"In her own way, she loves you," Patrick said. "Whatever else there is to say about her, there is that to say as well."

"I'm probably the only man who's never treated her like a commodity. That's probably what her *love* is all about . . . she needs one man in her life who doesn't treat her like a commodity."

Patrick crossed the room, and sat at the edge of his desk.

"You sell yourself short," he said.

"No, *she* sold me short. And for that I will never forgive her. Because that touches everything I am as a man, as a human being."

Patrick said nothing, for he agreed. Gail knew David, she knew his values, the things which were important to him; she had betrayed each of these and in doing so had cut very deeply.

"What now?" he asked.

David turned around. "I have a few things to say to Gail. I will say them."

"David, why don't you stay here tonight? You can be

alone, but if you want to talk I'll be right down the hall."

David smiled slightly. "Don't worry, I'm not going to Gail's tonight. I'll give it a day or two; then I will say what I have to say. Thanks for the offer, but I'd rather go home. I'll phone you, if I want to talk."

"Do you promise?"

"Scout's honor." David looked at his watch. "I think it's time we bring this evening to a close."

They walked to the door, walking quietly into the hall.

"I'm sorry," Patrick said. "If there's anything, anything at all."

"I know. I appreciate it. I know this wasn't easy for you either."

They reached the center hall, now quiet, empty, strewn with the debris of the party.

"If a good party can be measured by its garbage," Patrick said, looking around. He turned and saw David hurrying toward the coat rack. He followed, helping him on with his coat.

"David, are you all right? You're sure you want to go home?"

"Yes and yes." David clasped Patrick's shoulder. "When the chips are down . . . thanks," he said, fumbling at the doorknob.

Patrick opened the door and David walked into the foyer.

"Don't wait," David said. "I'm okay."

"See you tomorrow."

"Tomorrow. Good night."

"Good night, David," Patrick said.

He hesitated and then closed the door. He leaned against it, feeling a heavy sadness. He'd seen the tears gathering in David's eyes and he knew the night would be long.

* * *

Patrick, in his bathrobe, his hair tousled, his eyes groggy from too little sleep, paced around the center hall. He glanced back and forth between his watch and the front door, stopping every few moments for a sip of coffee.

He glanced around at the messy remnants of the party, at the crumpled gift wrappings, the dirty plates and glasses and ashtrays he'd told Hollis could wait until morning. Morning, he thought, looking at his watch; it was well past five in the morning, *where* could Tony have been all this time?

There was the sound of a key in the door and he whirled around.

"Dad," Tony stopped, startled, "what are you doing in the hall?"

"Waiting for you. In this damn house the only place to wait is the hall."

Tony hastily hung up his coat and walked to the stairs. "Waiting for me?"

"Tony, obviously I don't monitor your comings and goings when you're at school. I didn't plan to do so here. I didn't think it would be necessary. Until Tom Warren called."

"Oh," Tony said, sitting on a step.

"That's a fine answer. Mr. Warren was very upset, and Mrs. Warren was beside herself."

"Mrs. Warren is a lush."

"Tony!"

"I'm sorry, Dad," he said quickly. "I meant that she's always beside herself. Kip says—"

"Never mind what Kip says. What do you say about keeping Georgiana out to five o'clock in the morning? She's a child, Tony. The only reason the Warrens allowed her out was because she was going with you and Kip."

"She'll be fifteen next month."

"That old? Is she very gray?"

"Don't do that, Dad."

Patrick looked carefully at Tony. "You don't look like you've been drinking. Neither you nor Kip has a car, you couldn't have been driving around. The movies are closed. Where were you until five in the morning? I must know, Tony. Georgiana is very young."

"It won't happen again," Tony said, glancing away. "Couldn't we let it go this once?"

"No."

"I didn't think so," he sighed.

"I'm waiting."

"Well . . . she, Georgiana, wasn't exactly my date. This is a little complicated."

Patrick sat down next to Tony. "I'll do my best to follow you."

"Well, Georgiana's been seeing this fellow. He's a freshman at Brown. Her parents would never allow it—the fellow, I mean. So Kip and I left with Georgiana. She met her date on the corner and we went on to pick up our dates. Georgiana was supposed to be back on the corner at one o'clock—we had permission to stay out until one. Kip and I took our dates home and were on the corner at one exactly. Georgiana wasn't. We waited and waited and waited."

Patrick shook his head. "You knew of this arrangement in advance?"

"Yes, sir. Georgiana nagged Kip and then he nagged me. I finally said okay. I told her it was crazy . . . it's my fault," Tony said quietly. "I should have refused."

"You waited on a street corner for four hours?"

"Off and on. A police car stopped once. They wanted to know what we were doing there. We made some dumb excuse and they told us to go home. So whenever we saw a police car coming we had to hide.

We couldn't wait in Kip's lobby because he was afraid the doorman would tell Mr. Warren. He's a big tipper."

Patrick passed a hand over his face. "And then?"

"Georgiana showed up a few minutes before five. Kip chewed her out and we went upstairs. Mrs. Warren chewed Kip out. Mr. Warren chewed us all out. It was a mess, Dad, the biggest mess I ever saw."

"And now?"

"It won't happen again."

"Not good enough. You've all been dishonest, but worse, you've been reckless with Georgiana's safety. She's very young, Tony. This could be a serious situation. In my day," Patrick said, looking at Tony, "when a college fellow dated a fourteen year old, there was only one reason."

"In my day, too."

"You've got yourself involved in this now. You can't let it go as it is. Tom Warren must be told the truth, preferably by Georgiana. If not, then by Kip. If not, then I will have to talk with him myself. Is that clear?"

"Dad, Georgiana will *never* tell him. He'd lock her in her room for a hundred years," Tony argued earnestly.

"Is that clear?"

Tony twisted around on the step. "I'll talk to Kip . . . I *warned* him this might happen . . . skulking around like James Bond—except we were more like Inspector Clouseau. This is going to cost Kip the car he was expecting for graduation."

"There is a more important point to this," Patrick said.

"It was wrong and I shouldn't have gone along, I know that. By two o'clock I was beside myself, too. I was worried something might have happened to her."

Patrick stood up. "All right, that's enough for tonight. Tomorrow I expect you to get it straightened out."

They walked up the stairs into the hall. Tony turned toward his rooms and then stopped. "I guess this is a dumb time to ask . . . but I promised."

"What?"

"Might as well get it over with," Tony shrugged. "Georgiana asked me to ask you if you'd give her a prescription for . . . uh . . the pill."

"I take it you mean *the* pill, and the answer is no. Because I don't prescribe anything without an examination. However, *after* the matter of tonight is settled, I'll give her the name of a reputable doctor to see." Patrick stared thoughtfully at Tony. "The pill is only one kind of responsibility, you know," he said slowly. "There is such a thing as emotional responsibility. It requires maturity. Some adults are without it; many young people are without it."

Tony smiled slightly. "We had this conversation before."

"Did it take? It's hard to know, these days."

Tony went to his door. "The guys do a lot of talking at school. It's *mostly* talking, if you ask me. But there are still girls who do and girls who don't, just like in the old days. The only difference is it's harder to tell them apart. Goodnight, Dad."

"Call me at the hospital tomorrow and let me know what Kip decides."

Tony exhaled a deep breath. "To jump out the window, probably. And take me with him."

"Stay away from high places," Patrick smiled. "And out of tight spots."

26

David stood in the hallway outside Gail's door. He'd been there for several minutes, several times raising his hand to ring, each time pulling back. Now, composing himself, he reached out and rang the bell.

"David. Merry Christmas, darling," Gail smiled, opening the door.

"Merry Christmas."

David walked inside, sidestepping her kiss as he walked to the living room. He took off his coat and scarf and laid them on a chair.

"Pretty tree," he said, glancing at the large fir propped against a wall.

"I'd thought we'd have a traditional Christmas Eve and trim it together."

David sat down, looking at her. "Are you traditional, Gail?"

There was an edge in his voice, an odd look in his eyes and Gail stared at him.

"About some things. What's the matter, David? Still having problems at the hospital? Is that it?"

"This is for you," David said, holding out a long, thin box.

Gail took the package. "Thank you. I thought we'd open our presents tomorrow."

"It's not exactly a Christmas present," David said

slowly. "Go on, open it."

Gail looked at David, curious about the flat, tired tone in his voice. She looked quickly at the package, ripping the silver paper away. She opened the velvet box, staring at a broad diamond bracelet, squinting at the brilliant light emitted by the many stones. The stones were perfect, perfectly cut and polished and set, yet the bracelet was ugly; despite the perfection of the stones, despite their obvious cost, the bracelet was ugly, vulgar. Gail had never seen anything so vulgar and she took a breath, sinking into a chair.

She looked at David, looking into his eyes. "David," she shook her head back and forth.

"It took quite a while to find exactly the right thing," he said. "I had to go from jeweler to jeweler."

She saw it then, the look of revulsion, of anger, the look of pain behind it all.

"So," she said softly, "Patrick had a little talk with David."

"Silly of him to worry about a friend."

"You're not twelve years old. You could have managed on your own."

David laughed, a brief, harsh sound in the silent room. "You really have no idea who I am, what I am. And you don't care."

"I love you. What difference does the rest of it make?"

"You don't love me. You love the way I made you feel. I made you feel like you were something other than what you are. Who else comes around here with big cow eyes and romantic notions? I probably remind you of the high school kid who took you for sodas and talked about getting married. Who talked about living in a little white house with green shutters and flowers in the yard," David said angrily. "Who looked at you with respect and admiration and awe, because love was such a wonderful thing. Love! Love by association. I gave you something the men who hire you don't — a pretty picture of yourself. There it was, all reflected in my eyes. Well, what do you see in my eyes now?"

Gail looked away, her face flushed, her eyes very bright.

"I did all right before you came along."

"Then why did you need me? Why bother? Because from the first I treated you as a woman to be cherished. Not bought. And how long has it been since *that* happened? So you made me the town clown. The first to care and the last to know." He put his head in his hands. "Gail, the lies, the terrible lies . . . why didn't you shoot me? It would have been easier," he said, his voice breaking.

"It doesn't have to matter," Gail said quickly. "It's in the past . . . let the future take care of itself. David, we *have* something together. Don't think only of what you give me, think about what I give you."

David looked up. "And everybody else."

He stood up, going to her chair, pulling her up roughly.

"Let's see what you have to offer. Let's take a look at the famous locked room," he said, pulling her into the hall.

"No," Gail struggled in his grip. "No!"

He grabbed her by the shoulders and held her near the locked door. "Open it!"

"No!"

"Open it or I swear I'll knock it down. Open it. Now! This minute," he ordered, shaking her.

"All *right*, damn you!"

Gail staggered to a desk. She opened a drawer and removed a key.

"Enjoy it," she said, turning the key in the door.

"Oh, no. We're going to enjoy it together. You'll be

my tour guide in Eden."

He pushed her into the room and turned on the lights. He looked at the vast bed, the built-in amenities at each side, at the mirrored panels in the ceiling, at a small screen and projector, at the video tape machine.

"Yes, you have a lot to offer," he said, going to a closet.

He pulled the door open, gazing in dismay at the rows of negligees in every color and style. He went to the other closet. The door was locked.

"Open it!"

Gail unlocked the door. "Are you disgusted or just jealous?" she demanded.

David pushed her out of the way and walked inside. He saw the shelves of film, each in neatly labeled metal cans. He glanced at the titles, his face growing pale. He looked at the lighting panel, the music panel, the bottles of liquor stocked at the bottom of the closet. He looked at another shelf. There were several clear plastic containers of various drugs, and next to them, tiny coke spoons and sniffers and papers for rolling joints.

David walked out of the closet. His face was a dead white and his hands trembled. He reached for the top of a chair and held on.

"This is what you offer me," he whispered, almost unable to speak. "Dirty movies, drugs, booze, and satin nightgowns."

He sat down hastily for he felt his legs would fail. "My God, my God."

Gail sat on the bed. "It's a business. A *business*. Like your business. You use special equipment in your business, so do I. People have to pay you to stay healthy, to stay *alive*. For Christ's sake, is this so much worse?"

David put his hands to his head, rubbing his temples. "You really don't see anything wrong in this?" he asked quietly.

"It's a business. There's no morality in business. *Any* business."

"I see," he said, though he didn't.

He'd accused her of not knowing him, while all this time he hadn't known her at all.

"I see," he said again, for he didn't know what else to say.

"David, I can make you happy. There are men who'd give anything, *anything*, to live this way all the time. What's more important than sex?"

David stood up. "I have to go."

Gail rushed to him, blocking his way. She pulled the zipper of her robe and the robe parted. She moved her shoulders back and then side to side and the robe fell away.

"This is what I offer," she said.

David slapped her so hard the impression of his fingers was clear on her face. She staggered back and then lurched forward, grabbing him. She hit at him, hitting at his arms, his shoulders, his head.

"Stop it," he tried to push her away, "stop it or I'll . . ."

He pulled away from her grasp and stumbled out of the room. He grabbed his coat and hurried from the apartment. He heard the sound of things crashing to the floor, and then other sounds, louder sounds, as things were thrown against the wall.

David went to the elevator. He stood there a long time, stooped over, gasping for breath, his stomach churning, sick.

"My God," he said over and over and over again, all the way home.

"I won't keep you long, Dr. Potter," Patrick said. "I

know we're all anxious to get on with Christmas Eve."

"I don't mind, sir," Henry said, sitting very straight. "I have the night off."

"First of all, I want to congratulate you. You've found yourself in these past months. You're not the same Henry Potter I met back in September. You should be proud of the changes you've made in yourself. I know it wasn't easy."

"Buddy helped me, sir. He gave me confidence."

"Yes, well, I want to congratulate you on that score as well. You've done a fine job with Mr. O'Hara. I had my doubts about his future here. You changed that. He can still be difficult, and often is," Patrick smiled, "but he's improved."

"It's really your doing, sir, getting us together."

"Dr. Shay had a lot to do with it. At her request I reviewed your records. There was no question about your talent—but sometimes doctors need more than talent. They need strength, some force inside them which keeps them from being deterred. You found that. A doctor also needs confidence, because it inspires confidence in others. I've noticed on rounds that the students look to you for help, for guidance, as they should. I've noticed the other interns treating you as a full partner, as their peer, as they should."

"Thank you, Dr. Dain."

"The point of all this is that I need your assistance now."

"Really, sir?" Henry smiled.

"It is something of a special project. Something of a secret project. There are others I might have asked, but I chose you. This is an important responsibility."

Henry stared eagerly at Patrick. He was elated, his heart beating rapidly. He knew he'd made progress, that the students and his fellow doctors looked at him differently, but to have Patrick Dain ask for his help gave him a deep sense of pride.

"I want you to prepare a report for me," Patrick said. "A comprehensive report on the clinic and ward services. Objectivity, Dr. Potter, keep that in mind. I want to read the good things, where they exist, and the bad things. What we do well, what we do badly, what we fail to do at all. It needn't come out even. I want to know exactly what our failures are." Patrick leaned back, clasping his hands together. "Go into equipment, staffing, emergency preparedness. Go into everything—if the bed linen is torn and old, I want to know even that. Do you understand?"

"Yes, sir. From A to Z, sir."

"In as few words as possible, being factual at all times. I cannot, now, tell you the purpose of the report. I can tell you it is extremely important and must be kept in confidence. Dr. Shay is aware of the project; she will open her files to you. You may tell Mr. O'Hara *if* he will keep mum. No one else. Few people know—or care—more about those services than you do. Your report is in the best interests of those services."

"I'm very good at reports, sir," Henry said anxiously, surprised at his boldness.

"You have until the middle of March. Don't worry about typing it. When you're finished, give it to Grace. I know your schedule is already tight but—"

"I can handle it, sir."

"Good."

"I'll start right away," Henry said, standing. "Dr. Dain, the way everything's turned out . . . up until a few months ago I thought I'd wind up buried away in a lab somewhere. If I continued my training at all. Now, this is a whole . . . new . . ." Henry waved his hand in the air.

"Make good use of it."

"I will, Dr. Dain. I will, sir."

Henry turned toward the door. He reached the door and stopped, looking at Patrick. He hurried back across the room.

"Merry Christmas, sir," he said, shaking Patrick's hand, "and *thank* you, sir."

"You're quite welcome," Patrick said, taking his hand from Henry's enthusiastic grasp. "Go along now, enjoy yourself."

"Yes, sir," Henry said, returning to the door. "Thank you, Dr. Dain."

Patrick smiled, moving some papers to the side of his desk, putting others into his briefcase. He continued to sort the papers, deciding which to leave and which to take with him. After a few minutes he snapped the briefcase shut. He rolled down his sleeves and buttoned the cuffs, reaching to the back of his chair for his jacket.

"Patrick," David said, walking into the office.

"I was just getting ready to leave. All the reports have been assigned. The wheels are in motion . . ." Patrick stopped, looking at David's haggard, drawn face.

"What in the world—" he rushed to him, sitting him on a couch. "David, what is it?" he asked in alarm.

"I was home, I couldn't stay there," David said. "I saw Gail tonight."

Patrick went to the bar and poured a drink, taking it to David.

"I don't think I could keep it down," David said.

"Was it very bad?"

"Awful."

David's eyes were vacant, his hair slightly disheveled. His hands trembled.

"Patrick, I need a favor."

"Anything."

"I need to get away for a few days. I want to know if you can take over for me, and if I can use your Connecticut place?"

"Of course."

"I have some meetings. You'll have to take them."

"Forget about the meetings, forget about everything. I'll take over everything. I'll phone Alice and tell her you're coming . . . David, you can't be up there all alone."

"It's what I want. I want to be alone. I want to get out of the city."

"When do you want to leave?"

"Now. Right this minute. I didn't bother to pack. I'll use what you have up there."

"How will you get there?" Patrick asked. "You're in no condition to drive and I . . . Mother and Dad are in, they're waiting at home with Tony. We're supposed to have dinner. I'll call them, they can do without me," he started toward his desk.

"Don't do that. I can drive."

"Can William drive you there?"

"I gave him the week off."

"Hollis is going to Jersey tonight. I can't. . . . Let me see if I can hire a car and driver on this short notice."

Patrick hurried to the telephone. He was turning the pages of a directory when the phone rang.

"Yes?" he answered impatiently. "Yes, Dr. Karsh . . . and to you too . . . yes, examples if they help make a point . . . what I really want in the report is where the surgical section shines and where it fails and why. You know what I need, facts, facts, facts . . . right . . . thanks, goodbye."

Patrick glanced at the directory. He dialed several numbers and on the fourth call found a service to provide a car and driver.

"A car will be here shortly."

"You don't have to wait."

Patrick sat down. "Do you want to talk about it?"

"What is there to say? I forced myself into the room she uses for her . . . clients," David said, almost choking on the word. "I couldn't believe it. And Gail, she sees *nothing wrong* in what she does. I ran out of there." David shook his head. "All this time she's been doing . . . *that*, and telling me she loves me. It's unbelievable."

"Are you sure you want to be alone, David? I don't think it's a good idea."

"I want to be alone. I can walk in the woods, putter around. It's what I want."

"Why don't you wait until morning? I can drive up with you."

"I want to go tonight. I'm so tired . . . I haven't slept in a couple of nights." He took a sip of his drink. "I dreaded seeing Gail again, but it had to be done. I suppose I was hoping she'd say it was all a terrible mistake. But the moment I got there I saw how it was going to be."

"Don't think about it. You look ready to collapse."

"There was a moment, leaving her apartment, when I thought I was going to die. Just fall down and die. I didn't, though. I'm the walking wounded but I *am* walking." David sat back, staring up at the ceiling. "I've been a fool. Fools deserve what they get. I deserved to die . . . cause of death, terminal stupidity."

"That's melodramatic."

"I'm being the injured party. I'm entitled. It's what they're wearing with pain this year."

Patrick went to the bar. He poured a drink and sipped it slowly.

"I'm having second thoughts about letting you go off alone. Should I?"

David sat up. "I let you do things your own way,

after Catherine. Return the favor."

"I wish you'd stay with us in the city."

"I need to get away. I need solitude. You, above all, should understand that."

"Yes," Patrick said softly. "I understand."

"I'll be all right. Just please let me do this my own way."

Patrick stared at David. After a while he took a ring of keys from his pocket. He slipped two keys from the ring and gave them to David.

"I'll be phoning," Patrick said. "I expect you to answer the calls."

"Yes."

"Alice will keep you well fed, and the house has everything you might want. I gave you the key to the garage, too, but if you decide to tool around the place, use the snowmobile or the four-wheel drive."

"Do you want to sew tags in my underwear?" David sighed.

Patrick smiled. "I can't convince you to stay with us in the city?"

"No." He looked at his watch. "Let's go downstairs."

He stood up slowly, hesitating until he got his balance.

"The old legs are a little rubbery."

Patrick gathered up his coat and briefcase. They walked into the outer office.

"I'm leaving you to cope with our project alone," David said. "I'm sorry."

"Don't worry about it. It's in motion. When the board convenes we'll be ready."

They walked into the corridor, turning toward the elevators. Patrick looked quickly to his right for he was sure he'd seen a flash of Julie Carlson as she darted into the stairway.

"What's the matter?" David asked.

Patrick frowned. "I'm not sure. I could have sworn I saw Julie."

"Where?" David looked around.

"She ran into the stairway, as if she didn't want to be seen."

They reached the end of the corridor and Patrick rang for the elevator.

"What is she doing here at this hour?" Patrick asked. "Most of the offices closed two hours ago. And what is she doing around my office? She always seems to be—popping up. I found her in my office several times. At odd hours, hours when she'd have no business being there. She always has some kind of report or memo with her, but nothing that couldn't wait until morning. It's strange."

"I think," David said as they stepped into the elevator, "she had some ideas about you when you first came. Romantic ideas."

"She tried a dozen times to maneuver me into dinner," Patrick nodded. "But what does that have to do with her hanging around my office? Some mornings I noticed my appointment book wasn't where I left it. What do you make of that?"

"You're asking the wrong man, at the wrong time, about women. Who in hell ever knows what they're thinking? She could be Stuart's new spy, for all I know."

They walked into the lobby and Patrick looked at David. He was shaken anew by David's pallor, by the deep fatigue etched in his face.

"David, I'll drive up with you. I'll call Tony, he can be host tonight. I can drive to Westchester in the morning."

He stared at David, waiting for his reaction. He realized then that David hadn't heard a word he'd said.

"David? Are you with me?"

358

"What? Sorry, I was thinking about . . . that room. She has drugs, you know. Amphetamines, cocaine, pot, amyl nitrate, demarol. She had vials of male hormones for injection . . ."

"*David*, I'm going to drive up with you. I'll join the family in the morning."

"No. No such thing. I'll call when I get there."

Patrick looked hard at David. He was pale and dazed. His hands still trembled.

"I'm going with you. Period."

"No."

Patrick pushed David along to the car. The driver came up to them. He looked at David.

"Are you okay, sir?"

"Better times are coming," David said vacantly. "*Fata viam invenient.*"

"What'd he say?" the driver asked.

Patrick pushed David into the car, getting in after him.

"He said the fates will find a way."

27

In early January a savage storm paralyzed the city under almost fifteen inches of snow. Through most of that month, and much of February, the city was buffeted weekly by new storms, some bringing several inches of snow and ice, others bringing heavy, drenching rains.

The unusually severe weather strained Rhinelander Pavillion to its limits and, some thought, beyond, as pneumonia and cardiac and accident admissions filled nearly every bed. There were several deaths, at least one of which, the staff was convinced, was unnecessary.

Patrick, abandoning his office for the wards, the Emergency Rooms, often worked round the clock. David too worked long, cruel hours, both he and Patrick agonizing over the frequent breakdown in services and equipment.

Neither man had much free time. David spent what little time he had sitting alone in his office, drinking coffee and thinking. He was subdued, still pale, and Patrick was certain he'd not yet come to terms with the blow he'd suffered.

Patrick spent most of what time he had on the telephone. He'd had to give up writing to Tony, phoning him instead. He'd spent much time on the phone with Ann, too. They'd managed a few brief dinners together and one leisurely evening of dinner and theater, but most evenings the telephone had to suffice. The calls were quick but frequent, as many as half a dozen in one night as Patrick remembered something else he wanted to tell her, or ask her, or as he simply wanted to hear her voice.

Sometimes Patrick sat quietly in his office. He thought about the past, and the past few months, about the future. And about Ann, for it was clear to them both now that with each day they were more deeply in love.

He thought, too, about Julie Carlson. She spoke little to him now, and coolly at that, though he saw her often, usually in the vicinity of his office or Stuart's. Several times he'd glimpsed Julie and Stuart in the dining room and once he'd seen them sitting serenely together in the cafeteria as all around them doctors and nurses scrambled to hurry down a sandwich.

It troubled him and he didn't know why. He sensed some threat in their liaison, though he was hard put to describe what threat it might be. He'd confided his apprehension to David, expecting to be laughed out of it; he was all the more troubled when David admitted his own apprehension, adding that Julie would be a dangerous enemy, if enemy she was.

Julie noticed their wariness, their confusion; she enjoyed it hugely. Patrick had destroyed her plans; he had, she believed, humiliated her. He would pay. Ann O'Hara would pay.

It had taken time and patience; patience to learn Buddy O'Hara's nature, the nature of his relationship with his mother; time to assemble the dates of Patrick's meetings with Ann, time to cajole the reluctant jeweler into revealing the purchase price of the pearl and sapphire necklace. This information, Julie thought, given a certain interpretation, flung in the right faces, would take care of Patrick.

And then there was David. David, she knew, was showing new strength. He was threatening Larrimer Wing and in so doing, her future. He would pay. She'd learned all she needed to know about Gail Parrish and David's connection with her. That information, flung at the board, would take care of David.

Julie sat back in her chair, savoring the triumphs to come. With Patrick and David out of the way, with Stuart Claven in her debt, her way would be clear. She wanted a seat on the board; she wanted it as a mark of achievement, of pedigree, and she would get it; Stuart could not deny her.

There was a knock at the door and Julie glanced at the clock on her desk. "Come in."

"You wanted to see me?" Buddy O'Hara frowned.

"Yes, sit down, Buddy."

"I don't have much time. What's this about?"

"Please, sit down."

Buddy, shaking his head, went to a chair and sat. "Okay, let's get to it, huh?"

Julie dipped her head, staring at the desk top. "I'm trying to find the right way to say this."

"Say what? I don't know what this is all about, but I don't have much time. I've got no time for games."

"This isn't a game," Julie looked at him. "It's quite serious."

"*What's* quite serious?"

Julie took a little breath. "Well, Buddy, I want you to know I'm going to do everything I can to keep your mother's name out of the board meeting. I may not be successful. Things have a way of getting out."

"What the hell are you talking about?"

"My interest in this is the integrity of the hospital's teaching program. It can't be compromised. You can understand that, I'm sure," Julie went on quietly. "I, personally, give no credence to the talk, but you know hospitals. Gossip mills."

Buddy stared at her in confusion. "What the *hell* are you talking about? What talk? What gossip? If you're saying something about my mother, you better go ahead and make your point," he said, his color rising.

Julie folded her hands, leaning forward. "Are you saying you don't know?"

"Look, lady, no games!" Buddy said angrily. "You got something to say, say it."

"I thought you knew," Julie looked away. "The talk is all over the hospital . . . " she said, timing her pause. "Buddy, I won't keep you any longer, you may go."

"Not until I know what this is all about. You started it, finish it!"

"No, I couldn't be the one to . . . tell you."

Buddy stood up. "Start talking," he demanded, leaning over her desk. "I mean it!"

"I suppose you would have heard it sooner or later. I suppose it's best we get it over with. But remember, I didn't want to tell you. You insisted."

"Get to the point."

"All right, Buddy. Try to be calm. There's been some talk, a lot of talk, really. As you know, you were about to be dropped from the student program. It was assured. But you were not dropped. You have, in fact, been touted as the best student in the program. Now I know you accomplished this on your own. Your teachers know that. Any—responsible—person knows that. Unfortunately, some people are not very responsible. And unfortunately your rise began at the same time as . . . " Julie looked away.

"As . . . as what?" Buddy asked, sitting down at the edge of the chair, a thin film of perspiration beading his forehead.

"As your mother's . . . relationship . . . with Dr. Dain."

"My mother's *what?*"

"Her relationship, her . . . affair," Julie hit the word hard. "I'm sorry, but there it is."

Buddy's mouth dropped open. He stared at her. "Are you *crazy?*" Buddy shouted. "I'm not going to listen to this."

He jumped up, hurrying to the door. He stopped, turning slowly around. "You're crazy," he said.

"Ordinarily, it wouldn't matter," Julie said calmly, "but as Dr. Dain is in charge of your career here . . . as he is your mother's doctor as well . . . let's say it has raised a question or two. *I* am not saying he has been unethical, but other people are not so sure. You see how it looks. You are beholden to him. She is beholden to him. The ethical line is a fine one, no?"

Buddy felt himself shaking inside, with rage, with disbelief.

"How dare you say that about *my mother?* You don't know anything about it. It's nothing like that! They had dinner a couple of times. Big deal! Maybe they're friends. Big deal!" He came forward and grasped the edge of her desk. "And if I hear any more of that garbage out of your mouth, I'll shut your mouth for you. *Personally.* You got that?"

"Buddy, I wish it were that simple. There is talk. There is even talk of introducing a motion at the board meeting. Asking Dr. Dain to desist in this . . . relationship, for the integrity of the program. They have proof."

"I don't believe you."

"Your mother spent Thanksgiving weekend with Dr. Dain at his Connecticut estate. They have gone out many times since. Dr. Dain gave your mother a pearl and sapphire necklace worth many, many, thousands of dollars. Is that the gift of . . . *friendship?*"

Buddy's jaw tightened, his face a bright red. "You're a liar."

"I'm not. Ask her. Ask Dr. Dain."

Buddy felt as if his head would explode. He couldn't believe it, but he wondered what reason Julie would have to lie. She'd never liked him, but that wasn't enough of a reason. And she'd been so specific—Thanksgiving, a pearl and sapphire necklace.

"You're lying," Buddy said, rushing blindly to the door.

"Your mother is beholden to him. You are beholden to him. You see how it looks."

"Ma doesn't need Patrick Dain. And Patrick Dain doesn't need Ma," Buddy shouted. "I don't know why you're lying, but you're lying."

"Patrick Dain is a busy man," Julie said crisply. "A woman who is . . . available at his whim . . ." she let the thought sink in. "And you and your mother owe him *so* much. Or so the talk goes."

Buddy smashed his fist into the wall. *Using* her, he thought with an anger that was white-hot, using her like all the rich sons of bitches had used her before. At their whim, their pleasure. To serve them.

"If it goes on the reputation of the program will be damaged. One student talks to another, then somebody says something at a party and it goes outside the hospital. Spreads like wildfire. It's sure to be discussed at the board meeting. That's three weeks off, if they broke it off before that . . . but I guess that's unrealistic," she sighed.

"Where'd you hear all this?" Buddy asked, wiping at his forehead.

"You know how hospitals are. I called you here to ask you to keep yourself available the day of the board meeting. We may need you to speak for yourself. For the program," Julie said smoothly, smiling to herself.

There had been no gossip, she knew, and there would be none until she prompted it—beginning the day of the board meeting, continuing until she drove Patrick Dain from Rhinelander Pavillion.

"Buddy, won't you sit down. Perhaps some coffee?"

Buddy straightened his shoulders, fighting for control. "I don't want your chair, I don't want your coffee . . . and I don't want to hear any more garbage out of you. If I hear any more garbage from you, I'll kill you. You got that? You got that?" he shouted, flinging himself from her office, slamming the door behind him.

A wide smile crossed Julie's beautiful face. "Bingo," she laughed.

Buddy stumbled into the corridor. Henry Potter closed his book and rushed over to him.

"Are you sick?" he asked, taking Buddy's arm for he seemed about to fall.

"Yeah. I'm sick. I'm—going home. Get somebody to cover for me."

"Can I help? Are you in pain?"

"It . . . must be one of those bugs. It hit me suddenly," Buddy said, wiping the perspiration from his face. "I've got to get home. Right now, Henry. Get somebody to cover," he said, lurching down the corridor.

He hurried into the staircase, sitting heavily on a step. He couldn't believe the things Julie said, couldn't believe them of his mother or of Patrick Dain.

Buddy thought about Patrick Dain. He'd come to like him; he'd come to respect him—he couldn't remember respecting any man more. Buddy recalled his early doubts, recalling how they'd been swept away by Patrick Dain's consideration, his help, his knowledge. He'd been stern but he'd been fair and quick to smile; more, he'd offered what Buddy had taken to be genuine kindness, even friendship. He couldn't believe he was the kind of man who would use a woman so cheaply; he couldn't believe his mother would allow it. But Julie had sounded so *sure*.

Buddy got to his feet and started down the stairs, picking up speed as he went, for he was anxious to see his mother. He rushed through the lobby into the street, running to the corner to hail a taxi. He gave the driver the address and then sat anxiously at the edge of the seat, silently urging the traffic in front of them to move. He replayed Julie's words in his mind all the way home, rage and disbelief seesawing back and forth.

The taxi pulled up to Buddy's building and he pushed several bills at the driver, rushing out without waiting for change. He barreled inside, taking the stairs two at a time, his heart pounding. He raced down the hall and jammed his key in the door.

"Ma?" he called. "Ma?"

Mae came out of Ann's bedroom. "Hello, Buddy. I wasn't expecting you tonight . . . where's your coat, Buddy? Running around in that flimsy hospital jacket, you'll catch your death."

"Where's Ma?"

"She's gone out. I can make you some—"

"Out where?"

"To dinner. With Dr. Dain," Mae said, staring at him. "You don't look good, Buddy, are you sick? Would you like some soup, I have a pot of soup on the—"

"When did she go out?"

"A while ago. She'll be back soon," Mae said slowly. She walked over to Buddy, stretching out her hand. "Bend down, let me feel your forehead. There's a lot of flu—"

Buddy pushed her hand away. "Leave me alone.

What are you doing here anyway?"

"What's got into you, Buddy?" Mae asked, taking a step back. "Carrying on so?"

"I asked you what you're doing here?" His voice was loud and harsh, his eyes angry. "Well?"

"I'm helping your Ma make a dress. She asked me would I get it started while she was out. We're going to work on it later."

Buddy threw himself into a chair. "She didn't tell me she was going out."

Mae sat down on the couch. She looked at Buddy, at the tension in his face, in his eyes, at his hair damp with perspiration. She had never seen him so upset and she twisted her hands nervously.

"What's wrong, Buddy? Did something bad happen? Tell me."

"How often has Ma seen Dain?"

"Oh, I don't know, she . . ." Mae stopped, her eyes opening wide.

So that was it, she thought, something about Patrick Dain and Ann; and hadn't she warned Ann that something like this was sure to happen?

"I don't keep tabs on your Ma. It's not my place. Not yours neither, if you want to know what I think."

"I don't."

Buddy stood up, pacing impatiently. His broad bulk seemed even larger in anger, too large for the small room; he seemed about to break through the walls, to demolish everything in his path. Mae watched him helplessly, her fears mounting.

"Buddy, I'll get you some coffee," she said, rising.

"Leave me alone, damnit," he turned on her, and the look on his face drove her back to the couch.

They said nothing more to each other. Mae huddled on the couch, rubbing her hands together, watching Buddy. Buddy paced back and forth, avoiding her glance.

* * *

Patrick followed Ann into the small, dirty vestibule. He took her shoulders and turned her gently to him, kissing her.

"I had a wonderful time. Did you have a wonderful time?"

Ann looked at him. Her eyes danced with bright lights; her face was radiant. "I always have a wonderful time with you. You're just looking for compliments," she smiled.

"You're right."

He took her in his arms, holding her close. He stepped back then and they held each other lightly, gazing at each other.

"I could look at you forever," he said.

Ann kissed his cheek and then turned away, opening the door to the stairs. "I'd better be going up, Mae's waiting."

"In a minute."

"Mae's waiting."

"She's a resourceful lady, she'll find something to do. I'm serious," he said, tilting her chin to him, "I want to make some plans."

"What plans?" she laughed.

"I'm going to tear myself away from the hospital Saturday night and we're going to have a special evening." He smiled at her. "The time has come, the walrus said, to talk of many things."

Ann stared at him. She felt suddenly giddy and weak; she felt a happiness so great it took her breath away. Ann loved Patrick; she wanted nothing more than to spend the rest of her life with him, yet she'd dared not let herself think about the future. Now, looking into his eyes, she sensed they were on the verge of that future.

"Many things?" she asked.

"I refuse to talk about it in this little cell, but come Saturday . . . You get all dressed up and I'll get all dressed up and we'll go to a beautiful place and talk about our beautiful future."

"Patrick," Ann said softly.

"I'll give you a clue. It involves something square and shiny, from Tiffany's." He kissed her lightly. "We'll save the rest for Saturday. I want it to be perfect. I want it to be something we will always remember."

Ann's eyes were misty. She wanted to laugh and she wanted to cry, for it was incredible that this was happening to her. Even now she feared it was a dream.

"I don't—"

Patrick brushed her lips with his finger. "Don't say anything. Anything but that you love me."

"I do. I do love you, Patrick," she threw her arms around him.

"And I love you. So very much. Now," he took her face in his hands, "was it worth the extra minute?"

"Minute? Oh, Patrick, I forgot about Mae, about everything but us."

"Keep it that way," he smiled. He held the door open. "I'll see you upstairs."

"No, I'd like a moment by myself. This is—"

"If you say this is so sudden, I will punch you in the nose."

Ann laughed. It was the laugh of a young girl—carefree, happy, her whole life before her.

"Saturday," she said.

"Saturday." He kissed her again, holding her tight. "I'll call you tomorrow."

"Good night," Ann said, starting up the stairs.

"I love you," Patrick said, watching her go.

Ann walked up the stairs slowly, recalling Patrick's every word, recalling the love, the fire, in his touch. She stood outside her door for several minutes, smiling, remembering. She was smiling when she entered the apartment.

She slipped out of her old raincoat, reaching for the closet door when she stopped and looked around. The smile disappeared from her face, the laughter died in her throat as she saw Mae's stricken expression, and Buddy, his face white with anger.

"What . . . ?" she looked from Mae to Buddy. "What's happened?" she asked.

For one brief moment they all seemed frozen in time; Mae and Buddy motionless, staring at Ann; Ann, standing rigidly near the door, her mouth open, her eyes unblinking.

Buddy broke the mood, striding angrily over to Ann. He stared at her and her hand flew to her throat, to the pearl and sapphire necklace she'd worn for Patrick. She'd enjoyed wearing it, for to them it was more than a necklace; it was a symbol, given in love, accepted in love.

Now, Buddy's large hand loomed close, ripping the necklace away. The delicate pearls scattered everywhere and Ann heard Mae scream.

"It's true," Buddy walked slowly away. "It's true."

"*Buddy,*" Ann followed him. "What's true? Why did you do that?"

He whirled around. "Did you spend Thanksgiving with Dain?" he demanded.

Ann stiffened. "Yes," she said, her mind reeling, "but—"

"*Jesus*, Ma," Buddy said and the pain in his voice made Ann feel faint.

"Buddy, please, listen to me. We—"

"It's all over the hospital," Buddy fell onto the couch. "Everybody knows. I couldn't believe it. I couldn't believe it, Ma."

"What? *What* is all over the hospital?" Ann asked desperately.

371

"You and Dain," he said dully. "You and that bastard."

Ann was very pale. She clung to a chair with all her strength.

"I don't know what you heard, but we've done nothing wrong. He's the nicest—"

Buddy jumped up, his arms flailing the air. "Nice! Oh, he's nice. He's nice enough to give you the pleasure of his company. Nice enough to give you expensive presents. Nice enough to be a pal, a real friend to your son. All you have to do in return is screw him whenever he damn well pleases!"

The torrent of words hit Ann with the force of a physical blow. She staggered back and then quickly sat down, hugging her arms together for she was shaking.

"Buddy," she said in a ragged voice, "I—"

"Well, it's no secret anymore. They're going to discuss it at a *goddamned board meeting*. Your name's going to be rolled in the mud along with his." Buddy brought his fist down on the table, sending an ivy plant crashing to the floor. "How do you like it? How do you like being the hospital's dirty joke?" he thundered.

Ann sagged against the chair. She looked very small, very fragile. Mae, her eyes wet with tears, went to Buddy, pulling on his arm.

"Look what you're doing to your Ma," she pleaded. "*Stop* it, *stop it*," she beat her small fists on him. "It's not like that. It's not what—"

Buddy pushed her away, sending her sprawling on the couch.

"Buddy!" Ann screamed. "That's enough! You've made . . . your point."

"That's all you got to say?"

"I could say it's not true. Would you believe me?"

"Did you spend Thanksgiving with Dain?"

"Yes, but—"

"Did he give you that necklace?"

"Yes, but—"

"Out of the kindness of his heart? No strings attached?"

"*Yes.*"

"Sure," Buddy sneered, "a regular Santa Claus. Look, I don't care what happens to Dain, but I'm not going to let you be anybody's dirty joke. And I'm not going to have people laughing behind my back. Tell the bastard to get lost. There's time before the board meeting; you don't have to have your name rolled in the mud. You probably did it for me, but I don't need him. I can make it on my own."

Ann pressed her lips tightly together. She felt a great anger rise inside her for Buddy's arrogance was as incredible as it was inexcusable. To believe that Patrick had used her—to believe she had allowed herself to be used—for the sake of Buddy's career . . . when they were all calmer she would have to take Buddy in hand, she thought.

"Is that all?" she asked.

Buddy saw the hurt in her eyes, the disappointment behind the hurt.

"I'm . . . sorry I had to . . . be the one," he mumbled.

"So am I."

"Ma, all we have is each other. We got to stick together. You see how it is," he said.

"I see how it is," Ann said, sitting as still as a statue.

"*Tell* him," Mae said. "Tell him the truth, Ann."

"I know the truth!" Buddy shouted. "The bastard used us, like we've always been used. The old man started it, using us and then walking out . . . and then all the bastards Ma worked for, using her to clean up their mess," tears started in Buddy's eyes, "sending her home with their leftover food, like that's all we *de-*

served," he said passionately, the tears slipping down his cheeks. "I'm tired of us being used. I'm tired of leftovers nobody else wants. We're better than that," he said, slamming across the room.

He pulled a sweater from the closet and stomped to the door.

"Can't you see we're better than that?" Why can't anybody see that but me?" he asked, the anguish in his voice deep and terrible. "We're not dirt. We're *not dirt,*" he shrieked, slamming out of the apartment.

Mae clasped her hands to her mouth, hurrying to Ann. She bent down, taking Ann's hand.

"Why didn't you tell him the truth? Aw, Ann, why didn't you tell him the way it was? He's not a bad boy, he'd've understood."

Ann stared straight ahead. "Patrick and I were going to go out Saturday. He was going to ask me to marry him and I was going to say yes."

"See, Ann," Mae said anxiously, "if Buddy'd of known that. Why didn't you tell him? If he'd of understood how . . ." Mae's eyes blinked rapidly. "To marry him?" she asked in surprise. "Ann, did you say to *marry him?*"

Ann nodded and suddenly she felt the impact of the past hour settle on her. She remembered the sweetness of those moments with Patrick; she remembered his words, his touch, the look in his eyes, the happiness as vast as the sky. And then came the pain, sharp and searing, as she remembered the ugliness in Buddy's voice, in his mind. She felt a numbing weariness, as if every emotion she had had been spent on this evening—this happiest evening of her life so quickly become the saddest evening of her life.

"Ann," Mae shook her arm, "why didn't you tell Buddy? If he'd of known you was getting married . . . Ann?"

"Buddy had no right to say such things."

"He was upset."

"No, Patrick was right, Buddy has to grow up. But he's not going to do it at Patrick's expense."

"What do you mean?"

Ann looked quickly at Mae. "Buddy must not know what I told you. Do you understand, Mae? Promise me!"

"But why? You have to make it up with him. And if he knows the truth . . . you had a shock, Ann, you're not making sense."

"I'm making sense. There'll be no marriage and Buddy must not know the subject came up. Mae, do you think you could get me a little wine?"

Mae scurried away to the kitchen. Ann remained in her chair, staring vacantly at the floor.

"Here, Ann," Mae said, handing her a large glass of wine, keeping a glass for herself.

Ann took a few measured sips and then looked at Mae. "I'll make it up with Buddy in due time. There are a lot of things I have to say to him. He has a lot of growing up to do."

"What about Patrick, Ann?"

"You heard what Buddy said. The board meeting, a scandal. Patrick's had enough scandal in his life. Enough trouble. I can't let it happen to him."

Ann drank more wine, forcing it down, hoping it would quiet the storm inside her. "I always thought this was a dream, that I would have to wake up. I was right. It was the best dream I ever had, but I'm awake now."

"I don't understand. What are you saying, Ann?"

"I'm not going to see Patrick again. It's over. That's the right thing for all of us."

It took Mae a while to understand Ann's words. When she did she emitted a small cry of distress.

"You can't do that. You can't do that," she said excitedly. "I was against it at first, I know, but I was wrong. Like you're wrong now. Patrick's a good man, Buddy will—"

"It's not just Buddy. It's Patrick. I know what he went through with his wife, with her death. He told me that going to work at Rhinelander saved his sanity. If there's a scandal, even a small one, I don't know what will happen. I won't risk it."

"Ann, think! What scandal could there be? You've done nothing wrong."

"There was a scandal over his wife's death; you told me so yourself. He did nothing wrong and there was a scandal. They could make this sound nasty, I guess they already have. You heard Buddy."

Ann put her glass down. She was so exhausted—mind and body—that the effort of holding the glass seemed too much. She sighed.

"Nasty for him, nasty for Buddy. Nobody wins."

"There's other hospitals," Mae said.

"No. You can't live your whole life under a cloud. It's too complicated, Mae. And I'm too tired."

"You're forgetting Patrick. He has a say in this."

"No matter what Buddy thinks, Patrick respects me. If I'm firm," she took a deep breath, "he'll accept it. He'll have to. It hasn't gone so far that . . . maybe in time, a year . . . or so . . ."

"Aw, Ann, you do these things right away or you don't do them. Nobody waits around forever."

"Then . . . I guess . . . we won't do them," Ann said, looking away.

"It's the curse. The curse of the O'Hara's, it's on you now," Mae said, tears in her eyes.

"There's no such thing as a curse. There is . . . bad luck."

Ann saw one of the pearls lying near the couch. She

rose unsteadily and went to pick it up.

"Will you help me gather these, Mae? I'd like to . . . save . . ."

And then the tears came, great, sorrowful tears rushing down her cheeks as her shoulders shook with her sobs. Mae put her arms around Ann, her own face wet with tears.

"Oh, Mae," Ann cried. "Oh, Mae," she repeated again and again, holding on to her hand for dear life.

28

Patrick was dreaming about Ann, a pretty dream. He didn't want to awaken; he wanted to stay in the dream, to stay with Ann, but something was forcing him farther and farther away. He opened his eyes slowly and then jumped up, putting his hands over his ears. The laughter was an insane circle around him, high, broad and impenetrable.

"No, *please*, God," he implored, for the laughter had not come in some time and he'd thought it gone forever.

There was only the light of a fading moon in the room and he reached to the lamp. He pulled back as the crazed sound came closer, howling and shouting him away. It was a fierce, savage sound, a murderous sound, the worst he had ever heard; it was so loud he thought the walls must be shaking with it.

Patrick moved to the right of the bed and then to the left but there was no escaping the wall of fury. It was everywhere—around him, atop him, beneath him—and drawing closer with every breath he took. Suddenly Patrick sat very still, stunned, for in that split second he was sure it had come to kill him. He felt the icy beads of perspiration on his body, the irregular beating of his heart. He opened his mouth to scream but no sound came.

"Dr. Dain! Dr. Dain, sir!" Hollis pounded on the door.

The door flew open and Hollis snapped the lights on. He stared in disbelief, a baseball bat hanging forgotten from his hand. His eyes were fixed on the bed, staring at the deranged sound; he didn't move.

"Sir," his voice shook, "are you all right, sir?"

"Do . . . you . . . *hear* it?"

"About to bring down the house, it is, sir," Hollis said, his eyes as round as saucers.

Patrick, shivering, put his hands to his eyes. "My God."

He took his hands away, looking around desperately. He felt it coming nearer; it was only a breath away and he grabbed a pillow, hitting out at the sound, waving the pillow crazily in the air. The laughter rose and fell, veering away then.

For one moment it seemed headed in Hollis' direction. Hollis fell back, raising the bat, but then the sound was gone, the room silent.

Neither man moved; neither man spoke for a long while. They stared mutely at each other, as if struck dumb. Patrick lifted the edge of the sheet and wiped his face. Slowly, cautiously, he got out of bed. He poured two drinks and waved Hollis over. Hollis dropped the bat on the floor, walking uncertainly to Patrick.

Patrick drank the brandy quickly. "I thought I was having hallucinations," he said, pouring another drink.

Hollis sat down. He swallowed his drink in one gulp and Patrick refilled his glass.

"We have a ghost, sir."

Patrick stared at him. "What did you say?"

"We have a ghost, sir."

Patrick sat on the bed. "That's not possible, Hollis.

There's no such thing."

"Begging your pardon, sir, but there is. All kinds. Some you see, some you hear, all kinds. We know all about ghosts in England, sir. Part of our heritage, you might say. Why, there are some people," Hollis said, beginning to warm to his subject, "who think no self-respecting house is without one."

"Hollis—"

"My grandmum, she was in service, sir. In a big house in Surrey and they had *two* ghosts. A man and a woman. Always appeared together. You never saw one without the other. My grandmum thought it was the third Earl of Locerby and his Lady, but of course we never knew for sure."

Patrick smiled slightly. "Hollis, those are romantic—stories. That's all."

"Yes, sir, there's romance in some of them. I know of one, very sad it was, sir. Seems this young lass was sitting by the fire one night, sewing she was, waiting for her young lad to come home. Sparks from the fire caught in her hair and she was burnt to death. It was a long, long time ago, sir, but every year, on the anniversary of her death, she comes back and sits by the fire. Waiting for her lad, they say. Essie is her name, sir. She's famous in those parts. You can set you calendar by Essie, sir."

"Hollis . . . you don't believe that?"

"Most ghosts are gentle sorts, sir. There are some as have a bit of the dickens in them, but all in fun, if you see what I mean. Now, our ghost, she's a bad one."

"*She?*"

"It was a woman, sir. I heard it clear."

Patrick rose, going to the window. He knew now that he wasn't going mad, that the sound was real; but *what* was it? He gazed at the trees in the park. There was no wind, not even a breeze; he could not use that for explanation. He shook his head. *What* was it?

"Can't blame it on the weather, sir," Hollis said, watching him. "That's what I said the other time but I had my doubts, even then."

"Hollis," Patrick turned around. "You really *believe* it is a ghost?"

"I do, sir."

Patrick sagged a little, leaning against the sill. "There has to be a more—reasonable—explanation. There has to be."

"Reasonable, sir?"

"Scientific."

"Science doesn't know it all. You see, sir, a ghost is only a spirit of the deceased. Some strong emotion brings it back. Lets it cross right over from the other side. Poor Essie, she came back for love."

Patrick frowned at Hollis. "How about hate?" he asked.

"Yes, sir, there are ghosts as come back for revenge, for hate. A powerful hate, sir."

Patrick looked carefully at Hollis. "You have an idea who our—ghost—is, haven't you?" he asked, afraid to hear the answer.

"It was Madam, sir. I'd swear to it."

Patrick went to the bed and sat down quickly, for he felt the quaking in his legs. "Perhaps we're both mad," he said.

"Only thing, sir . . . with Madam's things gone, it make it harder."

"What? What do you mean?"

"Well, sir, my grandmum always said there had to be some tie to the deceased, some item that had special meaning. She said it helped the connection. In England, sir, it's sometimes the houses themselves as brings them back. Or with Essie, it's her sewing scissors. Her lad was a cutler, sir. Made the scissors himself, he did, as a present. Engraved her name on them. They were found after the fire and all the owners of the house since then kept the scissors on the mantel for her. Or with the third Earl of—"

"Hollis, this conversation is making me nervous."

"Not at all, sir. It's all in knowing how to deal with your ghost."

Despite everything, Patrick laughed. "Perhaps there's a book on the subject."

"Now, our ghost, she's a bad one. Evil she is, sir."

Evil, Patrick thought, that's what he'd heard each time; it was the sound of evil. Could it be so strong as to resist even death, he asked himself, shocked at the thought?

"Now with evil ghosts," Hollis went on, unperturbed, "one must be very firm. No loopholes, as it were, sir."

"There is nothing of Mrs. Dain's here," Patrick said dully. "You saw to the packing up yourself. Perhaps it's the apartment," he said and then put his hands out. "Listen to me! Good God, I'm losing my mind."

"I don't think it's the apartment, sir, though you never know. It's something with a powerful association. *Powerful,* sir."

"All right, all right. Let's think about this for a minute," Patrick said, breathing hard. "Let's say—for the sake of argument—there is such a thing as . . . The item, the possession, would have to have special meaning. Special enough to have touched her very soul. There's nothing here . . . that . . ."

The color drained from Patrick's face; his hands trembled violently. He remembered standing in the hall with Tony. He remembered Tony's words: "Mother always said her soul was in that portrait."

"Hollis . . . Hollis, the portrait!"

Hollis stared at Patrick for a moment and then

nodded his head up and down. "The very thing, sir. Madam always said—"

Patrick tried to stand but fell back on the bed. His legs, his entire body shook so badly he could not keep his balance. He reached for his drink and tossed it down, holding the glass with both hands.

"More, sir?"

"No, give . . . give me a minute. You're very calm about . . . all this."

"Oh, it was a terrible shock, sir. Terrible. But now we've got it figured out we'll make short work of it. You see, sir, in England—"

"Yes, yes, I know. Part of your heritage." Patrick fumbled for a cigaret, lighting it on the third try, inhaling deeply. "We have to do something about the portrait."

"We'll chuck it right out, sir."

"No, we have to . . . finish it."

"Then we should burn it, sir."

Patrick rose gingerly, bracing himself against the night table until he was certain he could stand. He took a few halting steps and then nodded to Hollis. "Let's go."

"Are you sure you're up to it, sir? I can take care of it."

"No, I have to. It's mad, it's damned *insanity* . . . but I don't care."

They walked to the door, Patrick pulling nervously on his cigaret. Hollis opened the door and they went into the hall. They descended the stairs in silence, Hollis hurrying ahead of Patrick to unlock the drawing room door.

Patrick entered the drawing room. He stared up at the portrait. He stared at the beautiful gray eyes, the smile that was invitation and challenge, promise and mystery. He stared at the perfect porcelain complexion, the soft golden hair.

He turned his head away, every muscle in his face clenched tight, in pain as much as in anger. He watched as Hollis got a fire started.

"Will the portrait . . . fit?"

"Oh, yes, Dr. Dain. I'll just get a ladder."

Patrick tossed his cigaret into the fire. "Never mind the ladder," he said, pulling two chairs to the mantel.

"The good chairs, sir."

"Never mind," Patrick said, stepping up on one of the chairs.

His hands reached out to the portrait and a terrible dizziness came upon him. He stood very still, waiting for his head to clear.

"Help me with this, will you, Hollis?"

Hollis stood on the other chair and together they removed the portrait from the wall. They lowered it to the floor and stepped off the chairs. Patrick bent down, staring again at the portrait. He ran his fingers over the face and then stood up, looking at the fire.

"Let's get it over with," he said, his face grim.

They pushed the chairs aside and lifted the portrait, moving it to the flames. Patrick hesitated and Hollis looked at him.

"Yes, all right," Patrick said, and they lowered the portrait into the fire.

They stepped back, backing away to a sofa, sitting down side by side.

"You don't want to watch this, sir," Hollis said, but Patrick silenced him with a wave of his hand.

They watched as the flames began eating at the bottom of the portrait, small curls of fire at first and then great leaping ribbons of fire crackling and spitting. The flames neared Catherine's face; Patrick held his breath, his fingers digging into the palms of his hands.

The flames raced, their reds and golds joining together until the portrait was a solid sheet of fire. A piercing, terrible scream shattered the silence of the room. Hollis jumped at the sound, staring in shock at the fireplace. Patrick buried his head in his hands.

"Dear God, dear God," he murmured.

The scream rose to a deafening pitch, shattering a small crystal vase. The scream dropped sharply then, to a low moan; and then it was gone. A slight, icy, breeze ruffled through the room. It hovered for a moment and then it, too, disappeared.

Patrick and Hollis, their faces white, stony, did not move. Almost fifteen minutes passed—minutes which seemed like years, like centuries—before either man stirred.

Patrick put a shaking hand on Hollis' shoulder. "Is it . . . over?"

"I . . . think so," Hollis gasped.

"My God."

"You were right, sir," Hollis looked down at the floor. "It was the portrait. She'll rest now."

Patrick looked at the fire. It was tame now, licking gently at the splintery remains of the frame. He eased himself back on the sofa, staring into space.

"I . . . ah, don't think we ought to . . . mention this."

"No, sir. Not a thing we'd want to get around. And Delia and the women might be scared."

"*I* have never been so scared in my life. Was that . . ." Patrick broke off, shaking his head, rubbing at his eyes.

"The spirit, sir, going back. Where it belongs."

Patrick glanced quickly at Hollis. It wasn't possible, he thought. It wasn't possible and yet it had happened.

"Best to forget it, sir," Hollis offered.

The color was slowly returning to his face, his

breathing returning to normal.

"Country people know about these things, sir. They know there are some things man isn't meant to understand, for all we go to the moon and send rockets to Mars. Country people . . . well, sir, look at country medicine—there's been many an illness cured by old-fashioned potions. No scientific reasons, sir, but there it is."

Hollis stood up. "I'll be cleaning out the fireplace now. Would you like a toddy before you go back to bed, Dr. Dain?"

"Back to bed?" Patrick shook his head. "I wouldn't be able to sleep after . . ." He stretched his arms out, startled to see bloody traces where his nails had dug into his palms. "I'll put some coffee on." He looked at Hollis. "I'm sorry. About all this."

"Not your doing, sir. Not your doing at all. We take what comes and make short work of it, eh, sir?"

The morning passed for Patrick in a blur of fatigue and preoccupation. He'd made rounds, kept all his scheduled appointments and chaired a meeting, though his mind often slipped away to the extraordinary night before. His recollections had a dream-like quality to them, as if what had happened had happened in another time and space, happened to him but to a different him.

By early afternoon the deep tiredness seemed to lift. He felt his energies returning, his mind clearing; indeed, he felt something like relief, for however it had happened, it *had* happened, the terrors of the night banished forever. He'd returned to his office and attacked a great pile of paperwork, gliding through it.

It was mid-afternoon when Patrick hung up the telephone and looked at David. "Odd," he said.

"What?"

"Ann. She was in a hurry, but she cancelled our date. She said she was sending me a note, and to please understand."

"Understand what?"

"I don't know. You heard my end of the conversation. I barely got two words in."

"Do you want to call her back? We have a couple of minutes before the meeting."

Patrick looked at the telephone. "I'll call her later, when we both have more time. Let's go."

They walked to the outer office. Patrick stopped at Grace's desk, about to say something when the door crashed open.

"Mr. O'Hara, I'm glad you're here. Is your mother—"

Buddy's fist slammed into Patrick's jaw, throwing him into the shelves of books behind Grace's desk.

"*That's* for my mother," Buddy said, advancing on Patrick again.

Grace jumped from her chair and David rushed forward, both of them restraining Buddy. Patrick stared at him in astonishment.

"Let him go," Patrick said, massaging his jaw.

"Not until—"

"*Let him go.*"

David and Grace looked at each other and then released him. Buddy's fist flew up at Patrick, missing. Patrick grabbed his arm and twisted it behind his back. He grabbed his other arm and pushed him into the office, pushing him down on the couch.

"Move and you will regret it," Patrick stared down at him.

Buddy glared at Patrick, his mouth a thin, angry line.

"Explain yourself," Patrick ordered.

"You're the one who should explain," Buddy said

irately. "Patrick Grayson Dain, big shot! You think you can get away with anything. Well, you got another think coming."

"I don't know what you're talking about."

"Then you're the only one who doesn't! It's all over the hospital. It'll be all over the board meeting . . . You really had me fooled. I really thought you were something special. You're nothing special. You're a bastard, like all the other bastards. You don't care who gets hurt."

Patrick looked at David. David shrugged his shoulders, frowning.

"I still don't know what you're talking about," Patrick said.

"I'm talking about Ma. About what's been going on. You don't care that her name is going to be dragged through the board meeting for everybody to laugh at. You don't care that the whole hospital is laughing already."

Buddy rose from the couch; Patrick pushed him back down.

"Tough guy," Buddy sneered. "Big shot. Who the hell do you think you are? You think your name gives you a right to—"

Patrick grasped Buddy's shoulders, shaking him. "What are you talking about? Who's laughing? You knew I was seeing your mother. I told you I was seeing her. If you had something to say—"

"Oh, sure," Buddy said, twisting out of Patrick's grasp. "You're a smart bastard, I'll give you that. You and Ma have things in common, you and Ma have nice talks—*that's* what you told me. That's a long way from the affair everybody's talking about, from Thanksgiving weekend in the country, from pearl and sapphire necklaces. Bought and paid for, is that how it goes, Dain? You'll help the O'Hara kid as long as

Ma . . . as long as Ma . . ."

There was a cold fury in Patrick's eyes. He reached out. Dare to raise your hands to me or anyone else, and you are out."

"Buddy," Grace began, her hand at her mouth.

"Hold it," Patrick said and she fell silent. "You have heard this—gossip?" he demanded.

"I heard it all. When I got tipped off about the board meeting."

"And you believed it?"

"I asked Ma about Thanksgiving. I saw the necklace. I can add two and two as good as anybody."

"And come up with five," Patrick said in disgust, turning away. "Who was kind enough to—tip you off?"

"None of your damn business. I'd like them to bury you, Dain. But you're who you are, so you'll probably get a polite tsk tsk and Ma'll be the heavy. Well, I put a stop to that,"

"Did you?" Patrick wheeled around.

"*Yeah.*"

"I see. You took some cheap talk and *threw* it at your mother. Did it make you feel good, Mr. O'Hara? Did it make your *mother* feel good? Is that what you call *love*, Mr. O'Hara?"

"It's what I call protecting—"

"It's what *I* call bullying."

Patrick took a few hurried steps away, for he feared he would hit Buddy.

"Stand up. *Stand up!*" he thundered and Buddy got to his feet.

"You are a child, Mr. O'Hara. And not a very bright one. I don't know if anything will repair the damage you've done. But then that isn't your problem, is it? Your problem is hot air. Six feet of hot air and not one inch of sense. There is quite a lot I would like to say to you, but I will settle for this: *For the time being*, you are a student here. *For the time being*, we have to work together. Any further insult—any at all—and you are out. Dare to raise your hands to me or anyone else, you are out."

Patrick took a breath. His eyes were cold as he looked back at Buddy. "I needn't add that you will find it impossible to get into any medical program *anywhere* again. *Afghanistan* won't be far enough away. And while you are considering, consider this: people who spread ugly gossip usually have motives of their own, ugly motives. And they seek out fools. With the cooperation of fools, Mr. O'Hara," Patrick said evenly, staring at him, "any ugliness is possible. Now get out of here."

Buddy didn't move. He looked at Patrick, confused. He'd been stung by Patrick's words for they'd held none of the defense he'd expected, but a deep disappointment, a sadness, finally contempt. He wondered uneasily if he could have been wrong. But he'd seen the necklace, he thought to himself; he'd seen it and it spoke for itself.

Patrick sat down at his desk. "I said get out. I meant it."

Buddy looked at David and then at Grace. They turned away from him. After another moment he left the office, closing the door quietly behind him.

"Why didn't you—"

"Grace," Patrick interrupted her, "what's the current gossip?"

"None about you. I always know who's saying what about whom and there's nothing."

"The truth."

"There . . . was a little gossip. Months ago. But not about Ann, about . . . Catherine. It lasted a week or so and then stopped. I know everything on the grapevine now and you're not on it."

"He mentioned the board meeting," Patrick looked at David. "Somebody's planning to attack me before I can attack. A power play. Whose?"

"Stuart's," David said.

Grace brought a cold cloth to Patrick. "Julie Carlson's," she said.

"What?" David asked.

"Stuart will launch the attack but it will be Julie's ammunition," Grace said.

Patrick and David looked at each other. "Julie," they said in unison.

"Something strange has been going on," Grace said. "I keep duplicate appointment books for you," she said, looking from David to Patrick. "When I leave for the day, I put the books in two different drawers. There have been some mornings when I found the books in the wrong drawers. I thought it was the cleaning woman. It was Julie, keeping tabs."

"But why?" Patrick asked.

"She had her sights set on you, Patrick. That didn't work out. Larrimer is her ace in the hole. She wants a rich guy; Larrimer gives her access. You two are threatening that."

"She saw the necklace," Patrick mused. "She barged into the library when I was with Ann. Said she was looking for the gallery."

"I bet," Grace said.

Patrick looked at David. They nodded and Patrick rose, walking quickly around the side of the desk.

"Where are you going?" Grace asked.

"To pay a call on Julie."

"You do and you're tipping your hand," Grace said. "So far the gossip is only in Julie's mind. Start something now and the gossip becomes a reality. That's what she wants. More ammunition for the board."

"Grace is right," David said. "We can't say anything

yet. We have to act as if nothing's happened . . . and find some way to speak first at the board meeting."

"That won't be a problem."

"Then that's what we have to do," David said. "*We* attack first and that leaves them with nothing. It also leaves Ann out of it . . . Patrick, Ann's call."

"Now I understand it," Patrick stared at David. "O'Hara hit her broadside with that nonsense. And last night of all nights," he shook his head. "She was so happy. I could kill him," Patrick kicked the side of his desk. "How could he do that to her?"

"You can fix it," Grace said.

"I could straighten out O'Hara fast enough—with the truth."

"I'm not sure that solves the problem," Patrick said slowly. "Ann could have told him the truth. Why didn't she? O'Hara has a way of creating guilt, putting it where it doesn't belong. The hurt . . ." Patrick stopped, thinking about the pain Ann must be feeling.

Grace went to answer the telephone. She spoke briefly and replaced the receiver.

"The meeting. You're late."

"Patrick," David said, "I'll take it. Why don't you call Ann?"

"She's at work. How can we talk? I'll talk to her tonight . . . I'd just as soon go to the meeting. If I think about this too much I'll be tempted to wring Julie's neck."

They left the office. Grace returned to her desk.

"Do you want calls there?"

"No," David said.

"Unless it's Ann," Patrick said quickly.

They walked into the corridor.

"I can't believe this is happening," Patrick said.

David rang for the elevator. "I can. Julie is—"

The elevator doors opened and Julie stepped out.

Patrick stiffened, trying to compose himself.

"Hello, Julie," David said.

"I looked for you at the meeting. They told me you were still here," she smiled.

"We're late," Patrick said. "If you'll excuse us."

"I'm afraid there's been some—bad news. Would you come with me?"

"What bad news?" David asked.

"I can't discuss it here. Please come with me. It's important."

David and Patrick glanced at each other and then followed Julie to her office. She led them inside and closed the door. She went to her desk and picked up the afternoon newspaper, giving it to David.

David looked at the headline and then looked again. He shut his eyes tightly and then opened the paper to the story. A small cry escaped his lips. Patrick took the paper from him.

He read the headline: Park Avenue Call Girl, Industrialist, Slain on Caldwel Yacht.

He turned to the story: Mrs. Lorraine Melton, of Chicago, is being held by French police in connection with the shooting death of her husband, Michael Melton, President of Caldwel Industrial Division, and his companion, Park Avenue call girl Gail Parrish. The shooting took place in Cannes, aboard the yacht of J. J. Caldwel. Caldwel, the billionaire industrialist, was reported to be flying to France from Greece where he . . .

Patrick read the story twice, unwilling to believe it. He sat down.

"David, I'm so sorry. David," Patrick looked up, looking around the room.

"Where is David?" he asked and then sighed, as the outer door clicked closed.

"I suppose he wants to be alone," Julie said.

393

Patrick glanced back at the paper and then stood up. "I'd better find him."

"Patrick, I would like permission to remove her records. We wouldn't like it to get out that Miss Parrish was a Larrimer patient. We wouldn't want to give people the wrong impression of the . . . clientele at Larrimer Wing."

"*What?*"

"I want to remove her records. I don't—"

"I heard you. I couldn't believe I heard you correctly. A woman is dead, and your only concern is the reputation of Larrimer Wing."

"I don't want to sound crass, but life goes on. And a woman like that . . . takes her chances."

"I see," Patrick said, going to the door. "Well, you don't have my permission. You don't have David's permission. And let me remind you that tampering with medical records is a serious offense."

"I'm trying to protect Larrimer Wing!"

Patrick looked at Julie. He wanted nothing more than to tell her what he thought of her, but he knew he could not, not yet.

"You'll get no cooperation from me," he said finally.

Julie's smile faded away. Her face hardened, all pretenses gone.

"Nasty bruise you have there. Been fighting? Not with a student, I hope," she said defiantly. "The board takes a dim view of such things."

Patrick touched the sore spot at the side of his chin.

"The proverbial door."

He hurried out then, hurrying to find David.

29

Patrick poured a cup of coffee and carried it to the window. He sipped the coffee and stared idly outside. It was a pretty day, soft and pink, a gentle breath of spring. Long lines of cars snaked their way down Fifth Avenue and the sidewalks were busy with shoppers and strollers taking advantage of the fine weather. In the park a young girl with long blond hair tossed a frisbee high in the air; a sleek black dog bounded after it, leaping up, snatching it triumphantly from the air.

Patrick turned away. There was too much happiness out there, he thought, and he was in no mood for it. He sat down at his desk, drinking more of the coffee, hoping it would give him the energy he would need. He looked drawn, and the dark color about his eyes told of the sleeplessness of recent nights. He couldn't recall a time when he'd felt so dispirited, so helpless. It had been two terrible weeks and he felt an immobilizing fatigue in every part of his body, his mind.

He hadn't seen or spoken to David since the day they'd read of Gail's death. David had gone home and locked the doors. His answering service took all his calls and his butler was under instructions to let no one in. Patrick left dozens of messages with the service, their urgency increasing with each call he made. They had all been to no avail for David had returned no calls.

Visits to his apartment brought only William's voice at the other side of the locked door, relaying David's instructions to go away.

It had been no better with Ann. He'd received her short, simply written note and although its tone had been direct, almost formal, he'd read the pain in every line and the pain became his own. She didn't answer the phone at home, and when he'd reached her at her office she'd mumbled a few polite words and hung up. Visits to her apartment brought only silence, a silence so loud he thought he would scream with it. He'd waited for her to come out of her office after work, but she'd begun to cry—she'd begged him to leave and he'd seen no other choice.

Patrick had barely eaten in the last weeks, managing on coffee and half-hearted bites of the sandwiches Grace pushed in front of him. He was at the hospital night and day, handling as many of David's duties as he could, delegating some of the administrative work to Grace.

He'd worked relentlessly on the reports to be presented to the board. He spent hours on the telephone, checking facts, many more hours working with a calculator, checking his figures against the reports; he worked until his eyes refused to read another word, another number. The reports had become a cause for him; he was determined to present them, to make his case, and in so doing rid Rhinelander Pavillion of Stuart Claven and Julie Carlson.

Patrick looked up as he heard Grace's voice raised in the outer office. The door opened and Buddy O'Hara walked in, Grace following.

"He insisted," she said. She looked at Patrick and then at Buddy. "You two look worse than any patient here," she shook her head. "Buddy, you make any more trouble around here and I'll come after you myself."

"I'm not here for that," he said quietly. "Can . . . can I talk to you?" he asked Patrick.

Patrick looked at him. He was pale; he looked shaken.

"Is it hospital business?"

"It's important," Buddy said. "*Please*."

Patrick nodded at a chair and Buddy sat down.

"It's all right, Grace." Patrick said. She hesitated and then closed the door behind her. "Yes?" Patrick asked.

"I don't know how . . . to say this. I made . . ." Buddy took a deep breath. He looked as if he were about to fall off his chair and Patrick pushed a pitcher of water to the front of the desk. "Thanks," Buddy said, pouring a glass of water, drinking it quickly. "I made a . . . bad mistake."

"With a patient?" Patrick asked, rising. "Where? How bad?"

"No, no, not a patient," he said and Patrick sat down. "Not a patient."

"Mr. O'Hara," Patrick said wearily, "I am in no mood for games. I'd as soon shoot you as look at you. If you have something to say, say it. If you don't, please leave."

"I made a mistake . . . about . . . listen, I was in Julie's office. I went there to ask her . . . I got to her office. I was about to knock and I heard her talking to some guy. She was talking about how it was all set. For the board meeting this afternoon. She was laughing," Buddy said, perspiration starting on his brow. "She was telling him how she got the ball rolling, how I took the bait. I . . . I was set up. To get you. I heard her and I heard him. He said the best part was they'd get you out without even a word of scandal to hurt the hospital. I was wrong. I was set up."

Patrick sat back, folding his hands on the desk.

"Why are you telling me this?"

"*Why?* Didn't you hear me? They're going to try to get you. With lies. With stuff they made up . . . or changed around, or something."

"Thank you for the information. You may go."

Buddy stared blankly at Patrick. "I don't understand. I—"

"No. No, you *don't* understand," Patrick said, quick anger rising in him. "You never did. But did that stop you? Not our hero, not for a minute. You charge around like a drunken bull, stepping on people's lives, throwing the pieces to the four winds. Then, *after* the damage is done, you slink in here and say you made a mistake. Sorry about that, old chap, a little mistake, just one of those things."

Buddy stared at the floor. "Henry already . . . he gave me hell. He talked to me, no holds barred."

"And I suppose, by way of thanks, you punched him in the nose. You are a walking disaster area, Mr. O'Hara. You leave a trail of broken spirits and bloody noses in your wake."

"I didn't punch him. I thanked him. I didn't want to hear that stuff about myself, but he made me listen. I deserved it. I deserve whatever you have to say to me. And Ma," he said, the word almost a cry.

"And Ma," Patrick said. "What about Ma? Going to put those pieces back together with a few pretty words?"

"Ma hasn't talked to me since . . ." Buddy broke off. He drank more water. "When I left here that time I began to wonder if maybe I'd been—wrong. I went to Ma. I begged her to tell me if I was wrong."

"And?"

"She was very angry. She said we'd better take a

398

while and just think about things. Look into ourselves. She said we'd have a talk, but not until I stopped acting like a baby. So I went to Henry. I told him the whole thing. He said I was crazy. He said a lot of things." Buddy took a tissue from his pocket, wiping at his eyes. "We went to see Julie. We heard her crowing to that guy. Henry laid into me then. He said—as a friend—he should have done it a long time ago."

Patrick rose. He poured a fresh cup of coffee for himself and put a cup in front of Buddy. "And you saw the light."

Buddy drank the coffee gratefully. "He didn't tell me anything I didn't know—inside. I guess I was always trying to see how far I could go before somebody said stop. If I'd had a father," he shook his head. "That's not true. I've been using him as an excuse. To myself, you know? Because all my life I've been so damn *scared*. It would get so bad I'd start to shake."

Patrick stared at Buddy, saying nothing.

"Well, these last months," Buddy went on, "everything was going along well. Then, before I knew it, everything started slipping away again. I couldn't take it, couldn't face it, whatever you want to call it."

Patrick returned to his chair. He saw Buddy's distress; he knew the distress was real, for Buddy had faced himself honestly and probably for the first time.

"It hasn't been a total loss. You've learned something."

"I've aged ten years, just in the last twenty-four hours."

"Aged, maybe. But matured?" Patrick asked.

"Yes, matured. I asked Ma about Thanksgiving and I *saw* the necklace, but I never stopped to—"

"No, you never stopped. Your mother spent Thanksgiving with me in Connecticut. Along with your Aunt Mae and Grace and her husband and the household staff. Grace and Rudy stayed the weekend. Your mother and aunt returned to the city the same night. The necklace was a gift to the woman I love."

Buddy's eyes were very round as he looked at Patrick. He'd heard the word love and he felt the hard ache of what he'd done to his mother, to everybody.

"I told you you had to learn to take responsibility for your actions. There is quite a lot of responsibility to be borne for your recent actions. Accept it, deal with it. There is no other way."

"I have accepted it. I'm trying to deal with it."

"I suggest you start with your mother. Tell her you've looked at yourself. Tell her what you saw. And tell her the kind of man you want to become, plan to become."

"Some man," Buddy said, wiping his eyes, "sniffling like a baby."

"It's been said a man without tears is a man without a heart. Open your heart, that's all you've ever had to do."

"You can talk to me like this, after what I did?"

"In all fairness, you had some help. Julie did, indeed, get the ball rolling. That doesn't excuse you, but you had help."

"The board . . . they're going to get you."

Patrick smiled slightly. "I very much doubt that. We are not going in there unprepared."

"I wish I could—undo—what I did."

"Settle what you have to with your mother. As for the rest of it, stay out," Patrick said firmly. "You are looking for things to come out even. It doesn't always work that way. *Lacrimae rerum*. Tears in the nature of things."

"It's hard to just sit back."

"Lots of things are hard. Life is hard. But believe it or not, many people manage to cope without the personal intervention of Buddy O'Hara."

"I wasn't—"

"Yes, you were," Patrick said, rising. "And I'm telling you not to."

Buddy stood up. "If there's anything I can do."

"I'll remember that."

Patrick came around the side of his desk and walked Buddy to the door.

"Restraint, Mr. O'Hara," he said, walking with him into the outer office. "Ask Dr. Potter for the crash course in restraint. Now get back to work."

Buddy nodded at Grace and then at Patrick. "Thank you, Dr. Dain," he said, leaving the office.

Grace looked at Patrick. "I was waiting for the shouting."

"Not today . . . Did you try David again?"

"I got the service. The operator said she had a pile of messages to the ceiling. He's not taking calls, Patrick."

Patrick sighed. "Will you get Lola for me? She can pick up some of the slack at the meeting."

"I tried. She left the hospital. They don't know when she'll be back."

Patrick stared at Grace. "That's dandy. And then there was one," he said, walking tiredly back into his office.

Lola Shay stood outside David's door. She pressed the buzzer, leaving her finger there until she heard footsteps rushing to the door.

"Yes, who is it?"

"William, it's Lola Shay. I have to see Dr. Murdock."

"I'm sorry, Dr. Shay, I can't let anybody in. If you want to leave a message?"

"No message. I *have* to see Dr. Murdock."

"Dr. Murdock won't see anybody," William said,

and she heard the agitation in his voice. "I'm sorry, but my instructions are—"

"William, I'm not going away. If Dr. Murdock wants to listen to the bell ringing all day, that's okay with me. I'm not going."

Lola turned, leaning against the bell. She heard the steady, grating sound ring through the apartment. "I can be as stubborn as he is and I'm not moving."

Lola heard the footsteps rush away. She took a folder from her bag and tossed the bag on the floor. She opened the folder and began reading, her shoulder leaning into the bell all the while.

After a few moments she heard a noise at the door. "Dr. Shay, Dr. Murdock says he'll call the police."

"Tell him to go ahead."

"Please, Dr. Shay," William said, distressed.

"I'm sorry to put you through this, William, but I am going to see Dr. Murdock if I have to stay here all day and all night."

"Yes, Doctor," he said and again the footsteps padded away.

Lola continued reading. She took a pen from an inside pocket and began making notations in the margin. Ten minutes passed, fifteen, twenty. The sound of the buzzer was beginning to hurt her ears, but she knew it was worse inside and so she didn't move. At the end of a half hour she heard the sound of metal scraping metal. The door opened a crack.

"Dr. Shay, Dr. Murdock asks if you will *please* stop this. He said to say he asks you as a friend."

"No. It's as a friend I'm here," she said, putting her shoulder back to the bell.

"In that case, Doctor," William permitted himself a tiny smile, "Dr. Murdock gives up. Will you come in please?"

"Delighted," Lola grinned.

She dropped her coat and bag on William's arm. "Where is he?"

"The bedroom, Doctor."

"Thank you, William."

Lola walked briskly through the hallway, passing through the handsome gray and blue living room into another, smaller hall. She turned to David's bedroom, throwing the door open.

"Good grief!" she said, looking at David, at the uncharacteristic mess of the room. "From Mr. Clean to a Collier brother overnight."

David sat up in bed. His hair was uncombed, falling onto his forehead; his face showed a week's worth of stubble. His pajamas were rumpled and stained and all around him were used glasses and cups, crumpled napkins and untidy stacks of newspapers. The windows were closed, the blinds drawn, and she saw his phone was unplugged.

Lola marched over to the windows. She raised the blinds, throwing open the windows.

"Don't," David cried, covering his bleary eyes with his hands.

"William!" Lola called and he came running. "Have we boozed it up this morning, or are we just having a hangover?" she asked, nodding her head at David.

"A hangover, Doctor."

"Get those glasses and bottles out of here. The place smells like a brewery."

"Yes, Doctor."

William took a tray from a table in the corner and set at his work. "Shall I bring coffee?" he asked, deftly loading the tray with the accumulated debris.

"Not yet."

Lola went to the bed, pulling back the covers, throwing them on the floor.

"*Lola*," David protested. "What do you think you're doing?"

Lola stared down at him. "You're a sorry sight. A sorry sight," she said, shaking her head. "William, come back when you're finished with that. I need you. Now," she looked at David, "what are we going to do about you?"

"How about leaving me alone? Why are you here? I'm in no condition for this."

"*That's* why I'm here."

Lola walked to the bathroom. She turned the shower on full, testing the water until it was cold enough. She walked back into the bedroom.

"Up," she ordered.

"*No.*"

"Up!"

"You'll have to carry me," David said, rolling over on his side, burying his head in the pillows.

Lola walked to the side of the bed and pulled the pillows out from under him. She threw them on the floor.

"Are you going to get up?"

"*No.*"

Lola turned, waving William into the room. "We're going to help Dr. Murdock to the shower," she said calmly. "You get his shoulders, I'll get his legs."

William looked at David. He looked at Lola. "Do you think—"

"Get his shoulders."

"Yes, Doctor."

David hollered and kicked, holding on to the sides of the bed. William and Lola, on a count of three, pulled him off the bed. They stood at either side of him, propelling him forward.

"*Stop* this," David insisted. "*At once.*" He wriggled around, looking at William. "If you value your job . . ."

"Shut up, David," Lola said, pushing him over the

404

threshold into the bathroom.

William moved the shower curtain back and he and Lola forced David under the water. They placed his hands on the safety rails and then quickly drew the curtain closed. David screamed as the icy water poured down on him.

Lola turned away. "William, I want tomato juice with a little Tabasco, soft-scrambled eggs, and lots and lots of coffee."

"Yes, Doctor," he smiled. "Good for you, Doctor, if I may say so," he said, bouncing out of the room.

"Lola," David called, "I want to come out."

"Throw your pajamas out and scrub. *You* smell like a brewery."

"Damn you," David grumbled, but a moment later a pair of sopping wet pajamas flew through the air. "I hope they got you right in the face."

"Your aim's none too sure today, pal," Lola smiled.

She kicked the pajamas out of the way and looked back to the curtain. She saw David's hand reach for the soap and she went to the door.

"I'll put out some clothes. Don't forget to shave," she said, laughing as she heard David mutter to himself.

Lola went to a bureau, opening several drawers. She collected underwear, socks and a shirt, carrying the clothing into his dressing room. She selected a suit and tie, hanging them carefully on a rack.

Lola worked quickly then. She moved the piles of newspapers into a corner. She wadded the used bed linen into a great ball, tossing it atop the newspapers. She straightened David's desk and moved several chairs into place. Finished, she sat down, tapping her fingers impatiently.

Fifteen minutes passed and David came out of his dressing room. He was neatly shaved and combed, immaculately dressed in the clothing she'd put out. His eyes were tired, a little red, but he looked much better; Lola was pleased.

"You look fine," she said.

"I *feel* rotten. I hope that makes you happy."

"It doesn't. C'mon," she said, rising. "Let's get some food into you."

"Food," David groaned. "Why do you torture me this way?"

Lola took his arm, pushing him into the hall. "Did you want to stay locked in your room forever? David, you're a grown man with grown-up responsibilities."

David glanced at her but said nothing. They walked into the dining room. The oval mahogany table was set with linen place mats and Spode china, crystal glasses reflecting prettily in the gleaming silverware. There was a large bowl of daffodils at the center of the table and David frowned at them.

"Flowers yet," he said.

"Sit," Lola said, going to open the windows.

"I should change my name to Rover," David said. "Up, she says. Sit, she says. When do you teach me to roll over and play dead?"

"You do that well enough on your own."

She sat down across from him. She stared at him for a moment. "Sorry," she said.

David unfolded his napkin on his lap. William transferred a pitcher of tomato juice and a platter of eggs and toast from a cart to the table. He placed a large pot of coffee on a trivet and looked around.

"Anything else, Doctor?"

"That's all. Thank you, William," David said. He looked at Lola. "What in *hell* is this all about?"

"It's about you, what do you think it's about? David, I'm sorry about Gail's death. I know it was a terrible shock . . . my heart goes out to you, truly."

"Thank you."

"Everybody has a right to mourn. Everybody has a right to mourn in their own way."

"But?" David asked, pouring coffee for them.

"But nobody has a right to destroy himself. Nobody has a right to hurt the people around him."

"I'm not destroying myself and I'm not hurting anybody."

"Think again. What about Patrick? He's going through a bad time and he's going through it alone."

"What bad time?" David asked, sipping his coffee.

"Ann. She's refused to talk to him, to see him. It doesn't look like she's going to change her mind."

David looked away. "I'm sorry, I thought that would be settled by now. I was sure—"

"You were wrong. And he's been handling the whole board meeting project. That's not a one-man job—especially when he has your duties at the hospital to see to as well."

"All right," David looked at her. "I've been selfish. I'm sorry, but there's nothing I can do about it now."

"Oh, yes, there is. I'm taking you back to the hospital with me. You're going to hold up your end at the board meeting, as planned."

"The board meeting? Is that . . . is that *today?*"

"Today. And you're going to be there. You owe it to Patrick, to all of us who've been working on this thing."

"I lost all track of time."

"I don't wonder. David, such self-indulgence, it's not like you."

"I had to get it out of my system," David said quietly. "You don't understand . . . did you know we'd broken up?"

"Patrick explained."

"The last time I saw Gail . . . I'd give anything to have it to do over again. I was cruel, deliberately cruel. It didn't have to be that way. Now there's no way I can say I'm sorry. There's no way I can take it back."

"If people lived their lives as if they were going to die tomorrow it would be a better world. But they don't and it isn't. Had you known what was coming you both would have been kinder. But David, with all the kindness in the world, whatever you said to each other would have added up to the same thing: goodbye. And while you're remembering cruelty, remember hers."

"I know. I'm not—glorifying—her, if that's what you mean."

"You'd be unusual if you weren't. We're doctors, we know that's a natural reaction. *At first*. It's when it goes on too long that people get into trouble."

"I'm okay. I had to get it out of my system."

"And did you?"

"She didn't love me, she needed me. Even at the end I refused to think about that too much. I refused to face the fact that I didn't love her . . . I loved the Gail I imagined, not the real Gail." David drank more coffee. "I went to Connecticut and mooned around but I never resolved anything. Then, with her death . . . with the newspaper headlines . . . I thought she'd be going through the same hell as I was. Instead it was business as usual. I had to face it then. I ran home and locked myself in."

"You locked the world out."

"Yes. And you'd be surprised how easy it is to forget there *is* a world outside. After a while you lose track of time—day is night, night is day—it might be Sunday or Thursday, December or April."

"I think I got here in the nick of time."

"I'd got to thinking that she'd left me with nothing. Nothing."

"The same people who loved you before love you now. The same people who needed you before need you now. That's not nothing."

408

"No," David said, taking a tiny bite of toast, "that's quite a lot. If you look at it that way. And I do."

"I'm glad."

"You should be. I might have stayed locked in forever. It was so easy. And then came Lola to the rescue."

He looked at her, a faint smile about his mouth. He remembered the good times they'd had—the laughter, the toe-to-toe battles, as comic as they were epic, the simple but clear happiness they'd shared.

"What are you thinking about?" Lola asked.

"This and that."

"There's no time for this and that. Finish your food and off we go. I owe Patrick. I'm going to get him the help he needs. It also gets you back to reality, so consider I'm killing two birds with one stone," she smiled.

"Are the reports—"

"Everything's ready. All we need is your sweet self. You have to hurry, we'll just about make it."

"Yes, ma'am."

Lola stared at him for a long time.

"David," she said slowly. "Is it really out of your system?"

"The truth is," he smiled, "my taste runs to women who throw me headlong into showers. Know anyone like that?"

30

"Well," Patrick said, stopping at the door of the conference room, "this is where I get off."

"Good luck," Grace said. "I'll keep my fingers crossed. And if I find Lola I'll send her in."

"Look hard," Patrick said, opening the door.

He strode into the conference room and looked around. Claven was seated at the head of the long table, several file folders before him. The members of the board had taken their places and were talking among themselves.

Patrick recognized most of them. Many of them were friends of his father, others he'd met at parties. They were men in their fifties and sixties, successful, wealthy men who served on many boards and committees and were always in a hurry.

"Good afternoon, gentlemen," Patrick said, taking his place at the other end of the table.

He nodded at a few of them, reaching to shake hands with others.

"I am Patrick Dain," he said, pausing as they laughed, for he knew he needed no introduction.

He saw Stuart stiffen at the easy familiarity he shared with the men and he smiled.

"I wish to thank the members of the board for allowing me to speak first. We are all busy men so I will be as brief as possible. Let's pass these around," he said, pushing a stack of bound reports to the center of the table. "You may read those at your leisure—I'll refer you to the salient points as we go along."

Patrick gazed around the table. He took a breath. "Dr. Murdock has been detained, he has asked me to relay his apologies. . . . This will not be a routine meeting, and I will not be speaking of routine matters. The purpose of the meeting is to approve the budget and in that regard both Dr. Murdock and I urge you to vote no."

Patrick stopped, watching as they looked at each other in surprise. "On page one of the proposed budget you will see the bottom line allocations for Larrimer Wing. They represent an increase of almost forty-five percent. You will also see only small allocations for the other hospital services. This means the other services would be operating at *below* last year's budget."

"Dr. Dain," Stuart said, "A word about that, if you please."

"I do not please," Patrick said. "Bear with me, gentlemen, my reasons will soon be clear. I will not bore you with the arguments, pro and con, about Larrimer Wing. We have all heard them before. But there is something about Larrimer you have not heard before."

Patrick looked briefly at Stuart. "Here I must give you some background. Dr. Murdock and I have learned that Stuart Claven planned to come before this board with a personal attack on our integrity. This in an attempt to discredit us. And this because of matters concerning Larrimer Wing."

Patrick heard the buzzing of voices as the startled board members exchanged words. Stuart jumped to his feet.

"Dr. Dain! Dr. Dain!" he said above the noise, "I object to this—"

"You will have your chance to speak, Stuart," Patrick said. "Please allow me to finish."

Stuart slowly lowered himself into his chair, his eyes fast on Patrick.

"I am speaking for the record," Patrick said to the stenographer. "As you know, the budget is prepared solely by Stuart. As you also know, Stuart gives Larrimer Wing vast financial preference in the budget. What you do not know is Stuart's reason."

Patrick saw Stuart start in his chair. He sat very still, his hands in small, tight, fists.

"His reason, gentlemen," Patrick went on, "is his own financial gain. Stuart instituted a kickback system in Larrimer Wing. It continues to this day."

"Lies!" Stuart shot up. "You lie. You can't prove—"

"Please sit down, Stuart," Patrick said. "I can—and will—prove it . . . Dr. Murdock and I looked at his budget carefully. We reviewed it line by line. I took the liberty of having the Dain financial managers look at it. There were many questionable areas. Dr. Murdock and I began talking to Larrimer Wing suppliers who, as you know, supply us under a separate requisition system overseen by Stuart. They confirmed our suspicions."

"More lies," Stuart shouted. "I can explain—"

"Sit down," a slim, graying member of the board orderd. "Go on, Patrick."

"Nothing gets into Larrimer Wing unless Stuart gets his cut. Not a bed, not a television set, not a plant, not a piece of equipment, not an aspirin. All of our suppliers admitted the kickbacks. Most of them were glad to sign statements and provide breakdowns. We estimate that Stuart's take—last year alone—was in excess of two hundred thousand dollars. That figure has been confirmed by the Dain accountants."

Patrick slid the folder across the table. The board members grabbed at it, riffling through the statements. They passed them to each other, nodding and pointing.

"Good afternoon, gentlemen," David said, walking into the room. "Go on with what you were doing."

He walked over to Patrick. They conferred briefly and Patrick sat down. David took his place at the end of the table. After a few minutes the members of the board looked up from the reports. They looked at Stuart and then looked away. Stuart tried to get the attention of Max Rhinelander and then gave up, sitting rigidly, his face very white.

"I see Dr. Dain has explained the situation," David said. "Gentlemen, our industry isn't automobiles, or cosmetics, or soft drinks," he said, looking from face to face. "Our industry is health care. You make a mistake in your industries and it costs you money. We make a mistake and it costs lives. There has been overemphasis on Larrimer Wing at the expense of the other services. Now we know why. And now we must deal with it."

David opened a folder. "Later on you will hear our recommendations for Larrimer Wing. We can run a private wing economically, and without jeopardizing the rest of the hospital. This we intend to do and we are prepared to discuss it. For now I suggest we take up the question of Stuart Claven. Perhaps Stuart would like to speak first? Stuart?"

"Before I reply to these lies," Stuart said, "I ask Dr. Maxwell Rhinelander—a member of this board—a member of the family whose name our fine hospital bears—to speak for me. We have worked side by side. Dr. Rhinelander knows my devotion, my deep concern for Rhinelander Pavillion cannot be questioned. Max?" Stuart smiled.

All eyes turned to Max Rhinelander. He stared down at the table, biting his lip, tapping his fingertips together. He didn't speak.

"Max? . . . Dr. Rhinelander?" Stuart asked weakly.

Max Rhinelander continued to stare at the table. "Stuart's . . . a hard worker," he said finally.

"Max . . . tell them, tell them the good things I do for the hospital," Stuart pleaded.

"He's . . . a hard worker," Max said slowly. "I . . . have nothing more to say."

"Dr. Rhinelander has nothing more to say. Please proceed, Stuart," David directed.

Stuart stared in shock at Max Rhinelander. His ally, his longtime friend, was not going to help him, he realized. He tried to catch Max's eye, but Max refused even to look at him. Stuart turned away, looking at each member of the board, his glance lingering on David and Patrick. They saw the hate in his eyes—enough hate for a hundred men, a thousand.

Stuart began speaking. He praised his record at Rhinelander Pavillion. He denied the kickbacks, describing them as the occasional gifts of grateful suppliers. He spoke of his rise from poverty to a position of respect and esteem. His words were angry and then tormented, tumbling one on another in incoherent rambling.

At the end it was Max Rhinelander, after brief caucus with the other members of the board, who gave Stuart his dismissal, effective immediately. It was Max who took Stuart's folders from the table, tossing their contents unceremoniously into the shredder.

For a long time Stuart refused to leave the room. He shouted at the board members; they fidgeted uncomfortably, staring at the table, or the wall. Finally, his anger spent, the truth of what had happened settling clearly in his mind, he left. He left without another word, looking older, looking smaller.

After a short, silent break, the members of the board proceeded to other matters. David led the discussions, Patrick occasionally joining in. The budget was defeated by voice vote. While certain areas of hospital policy drew heated debate, David and Patrick got most of what they'd wanted.

The meeting broke up some three hours after it had begun. The members dispersed quickly, silently. Max Rhinelander hung back. He hesitated at the door and then approached David and Patrick.

"I want you to know I think that was a terrible thing to do. You should be ashamed of yourselves."

"While you," David said, "were a prince about everything. 'He's a hard worker,' " David mimicked. "We have no use for Stuart, but he was *your* friend. Instead of defending him you left him there to die."

"The facts . . . spoke for themselves."

"You could have spoken up for him, Max," David said. "Whatever else he was, he was your friend. He deserved better from you."

"It's your fault. You started it."

"No," David said, "*he* started it. We finished it." He turned to Patrick. "Let's go."

They walked away from Max, walking into the corridor.

"I felt sorry for Stuart," Patrick said.

"He didn't feel sorry for the patients whose lives he risked. He deserved what he got, Patrick. It wasn't fun, but he deserved it."

They continued down the corridor, stopping at Julie's office.

"Feel like a visit?" David asked.

"The highlight of my day."

They walked through the empty outer office and stood outside her door. Patrick knocked and opened the door.

Julie was curled in her chair. She looked up. "Meeting over?" she smiled.

"Indeed," Patrick said.

"Anything important?" she asked with a malicious little smile. "Anybody get fired?"

"Indeed," Patrick said.

"Well, tell me. I'm dying of curiosity."

Patrick glanced at David. "Do you want to be the one?"

"No, you. You earned it."

Julie looked suspiciously at them. They seemed very confident; they seemed to be enjoying themselves and she didn't understand it.

"Stuart Claven was fired," Patrick said flatly.

Julie laughed. "Don't you wish."

"Stuart Claven was fired," Patrick repeated. "We caught Stuart with his hand in the cookie jar. Kickbacks, Julie, or didn't you know about those?"

Julie sat up straight. "I don't believe you. You're lying!"

"Don't you wish," David said. "He's gone."

"Which is a coincidence," Patrick said, "because so are you."

"This is ridiculous," Julie said. "I'll go find Stuart, he'll tell me the truth," she said, standing up.

"Sit down," Patrick said. "Stuart hasn't told the truth in so long I doubt he remembers how. Besides, if he's still here at all, he's clearing out his desk. He's through, Julie, finished. And so are you."

"No! I'll go see Max Rhinelander! He'll do something! He'll get this straightened out!"

"Max is the one who fired Claven," David said. "And I am the one who is firing you. As of now. The board put up a bit of a fuss about you, but they came around. We'll be generous about severance, but don't count on references. I want you out by tomorrow morning."

Julie fell back in her chair. She was stunned, for she realized they were serious. She saw her plans, her carefully made plans falling to ruin.

"Why, Julie?" Patrick asked quietly. "You're smart, you're beautiful. You could have gone far, playing it straight. Why did you do it?"

"I don't know what you're talking about."

"Your plan might have worked," Patrick said. "I would probably have resigned—as a point of honor. David's authority would have been eroded. Your mistake was involving O'Hara. He tipped us off. That gave us time to plan. And we planned well. It was a stupid mistake, Julie."

"It was no mistake!" Julie shrilled. "You're right, I *am* smart, I *am* beautiful. What a team we could have been! We could have had *everything*. But you . . . you . . ." she sputtered, her eyes sparkling with fury, "you had to take up with that . . . that . . . *drab*. With . . . that . . . *nothing*. I can't have you . . . but she can't have you either."

"Get your things and get out," David said. "I don't want to see you here again."

Julie scrambled to her feet. "Wait, you can't do that. I have a contract."

"Sue me."

"You're not going to do this to me. I'll find a way. I promise you I'll find a way!"

"You'll find nothing," David said curtly. "Except a new city. Because your name is going to be mud in every drawing room in *this* city. You're not playing with children, Julie."

Julie sat down. She stared at them. "What do you know about it? What do you know about any of it? You can't stand in my way. Nobody stands in my way."

"Make it a city far away," Patrick said.

They left then and didn't look back, walking swiftly

417

into the corridor. They walked in silence to their offices. Grace was waiting at the door.

"David, you made it!" she said. "Well," she looked at them, "what happened?"

"Mission accomplished," David said.

"Everything?"

"*Most* everything. Stuart and Julie are leaving. We have the go-ahead to reorganize Larrimer Wing. We get more authority over the budget. How *much* more remains to be seen."

Grace threw her arms around them. "I'm proud of you."

"No," Patrick said, "we're proud of you. Because without you . . . suffice it to say you will be rewarded," he smiled.

"I accept. Whatever it is," Grace laughed. "There's fresh coffee in your office, Patrick. I'm going home now. Rudy says this is like a soap opera. I can't wait to tell him how it came out."

"Good night," Patrick said as they entered his office.

Patrick went to his desk and sat down. He poured two cups of coffee, giving one to David.

"This is where I make my apologies for running out on you," David said. "It was a rotten thing to do."

"I'm not going to argue with that . . . Are you all right, David? What happened?"

David apologized again, telling Patrick about the past two weeks. He spoke of his feelings then and his feelings now, speaking freely, with the kind of detachment which signalled, finally, the end of the crisis.

"And you? Lola told me about Ann. I feel like a rat, deserting like that."

Patrick smiled. "Rat is one name for it. Believe me I called you all of them." He sipped his coffee. "Buddy's straightened out," he said, going on to explain his meeting with him. "As for Ann . . . if she's going to jump everytime Buddy pulls a string, then we don't have much. If we can be so easily parted . . ."

"You can handle Buddy."

"*I* can handle Buddy; Ann can't. There must be room for both of us in her life or it's no go. I couldn't take another bad marriage. Neither could Ann."

"You're jumping to conclusions," David said.

"She won't see me or talk to me. Draw your own conclusions." Patrick leaned back. "I kept myself so busy on the reports I didn't leave too much time to think."

"You're going to have to think about it."

"I know. The truth is I thought Ann and I had it all. I was certain. Now . . . But one problem at a time," Patrick sighed. "Tony's coming home tomorrow on spring break. I'm expecting a bit of a row."

"Why?"

"I . . . removed Catherine's portrait. I got rid of it. Tony's going to take it badly."

"Why don't I drop over tomorrow?" David asked. "Let me have a word with him."

"Thanks, but no. This business about Catherine must be settled once and for all. Tony will be seventeen this month, almost a man. It's time."

"Hallelujah."

"Don't count your hallelujahs before they're hatched. It's not going to be easy."

31

Patrick turned out the lights and left his bedroom, going into the hall. He felt refreshed, though he and Tony had had a long day. He'd met Tony at the airport late in the morning. After a brief stop at home, they'd spent hours shopping and walking and talking over a late lunch. They'd returned then, going to their rooms to rest and change clothes before dinner and the theater.

Patrick walked down the stairs, checking his pocket for the theater tickets. He reached the center hall and Hollis hurried to him.

"I'm sorry, sir, but Master Tony insisted. You were in the shower, sir, and I didn't—"

"Hollis," Patrick interrupted, "what is it?"

"Master Tony, sir. He's in the drawing room. He asked about Madam's portrait, Dr. Dain. He's very upset, he is."

"What did you tell him?"

"Nothing, sir. I told him I knew nothing about it."

"Thank you, Hollis. I'll take care of it."

"About dinner, sir?"

"This may take some time. Let's wait and see."

"Very good, sir," Hollis said, watching Patrick walk to the drawing room.

Patrick opened the door. He stood at the edge of the

room watching as Tony stared up at the Renoir which had replaced his mother's portrait.

"Tony," Patrick said quietly, walking into the room.

Tony spun around and the accusation in his eyes was clear. He said nothing, staring at his father.

Patrick sat down on a sofa. "I was going to tell you about the portrait. I thought it could wait until tomorrow. I'm sorry."

"Where is it?" Tony demanded.

"Gone. It's gone. I had to do it."

"Gone where?"

"I disposed of it, Tony. There's no way to get it back."

"How could you *do* that?"

Patrick closed his eyes briefly. He couldn't tell Tony the truth; it was too unbelievable, too horrible.

"Tony, it had to be done. There are things you don't understand. Please, sit down," Patrick said.

Tony did not move and Patrick looked at him. "Your mother and I didn't have a very good marriage. As a matter of fact it was a very bad marriage."

"Because you didn't *try*. Because you didn't *care*."

"No man could have tried harder or cared more. After the first few years the marriage deteriorated. The last years were hell, I can't put it more honestly than that. Fortunately you were away at school, you didn't have to see it."

"I felt the tension when I was home on holidays. And I heard Mother crying lots of times."

"That was for your benefit. They weren't real tears, Tony. Your mother didn't have tears . . . not even for herself."

Tony looked closely at Patrick. "Wait a minute. What are you trying to say? Are you trying to put the whole thing on Mother? When she isn't even here to speak for herself? That's pretty low."

"You already know—certain—things about your mother. I know you heard things. I know you had reason to believe them."

"Because she was *lonely*."

"No. Because she was too spoiled and too beautiful. She had a terrible need for attention. Almost pathological. She had to be the center of attention every waking minute of every day. She would do . . . almost anything to get her way."

Patrick watched the boy carefully. Dark red color streaked his cheeks. His face was taut, his body tightly coiled, as if ready to spring on Patrick.

Patrick ran his hand through his hair. "Given those circumstances the marriage didn't have a chance. That's the truth. You're old enough to understand. It was painful . . . too painful to keep reminders."

Tony turned his back on Patrick. Patrick stared at the fireplace for a moment and then looked up.

"Tony, this isn't about heroes and villains. It isn't about placing blame or taking sides. It's about truth. There comes a time when it's important to know the truth. It was a bad marriage, with mistakes on both sides. You didn't see your mother's mistakes, you saw very little of her. She was already running here and there by the time you were taking your first steps."

"Because you wanted her to," Tony wheeled around. "Because she had obligations to the Dain name."

"Is that what she told you? Not true. In a way, that was the beginning of our problems. She was seldom home."

"Were *you*? Mother told me you were so busy with your work she never saw you," Tony argued.

"Think about that awhile. Was there ever a time you needed me when I wasn't there? Did I ever miss an event at your schools, or your birthdays . . . or the times you weren't feeling well, or the times you merely wanted to talk? Yes, I worked, I worked hard. There are no playboys in our family, Tony. But I didn't work to the exclusion of all else."

"That's not what she said."

"I don't want to play she-said, he-said. Tony, I don't know what image you built of your mother and me, of our marriage. If you thought we were happy, I'm sorry to disillusion you. But we can't live with lies between us."

Tony was upset. He knew his father had always been there for him, his mother rarely, yet he couldn't let it go. He looked back to where his mother's portrait had been and his anger flared anew.

"You're twisting things around!"

"I'm not. And I won't go on feeling as if I must continually defend myself. I removed the things from your mother's rooms because there was no reason to keep them. I removed her portrait because it was—painful—to keep it."

"Is that it? Or did you remove it because of the woman you wrote me about?" Tony asked, his voice choked with emotion.

Patrick thought about Ann. He passed a hand over his eyes.

"Mrs. O'Hara has nothing to do with it. She was here once—the day of the Christmas party. I doubt she even noticed the portrait. Perhaps to notice how beautiful your mother was, but that's all. There is no conspiracy."

"Maybe there's guilt. Your guilt."

"My conscience is clear," Patrick said quietly.

"If your conscience is so clear, Mother's things wouldn't be so painful."

Patrick thought a moment before replying. "Tony, in your life you will love many people. Good people and bad people. Some of them will disappoint you.

Some will hurt you. But you will go on loving them. Loving them until the pain becomes too great. When that happens a kind of poison sets in. It destroys everything. The love dies. The memories are painful . . . and so we rid ourselves of as many memories as we can."

"Are you saying Mother was *bad?*" Tony cried, walking around in anguished circles.

"No. But she was very spoiled. She didn't think of anybody but herself. The closest she came to loving another person was you. She *did* love you in her way."

"You don't have to tell me that," he shouted. "I know she loved me. She loved me a lot. A *lot!*" he said, his voice nearly breaking. "It was you, you're to blame. And you are guilty. You're guilty about Mother's death. All those fancy stories about how she died. They were lies. You *lied*. Like you're lying now."

"I will tell you, now, exactly how your mother died. If I lied before it was to protect—"

"No!" Tony was beside himself with anger and confusion. "I don't want to hear anything else from you. All you'll do is lie again. You're not going to take Mother away from me this way. I won't let you! She loved me and that's all I need to know. She was *my mother* and you're trying to . . . trying to . . ."

Tony hurried out of the room. Patrick followed, watching as he ran to the door.

"Where are you going?"

"Out."

"Out where?"

Tony rushed out of the apartment, slamming the door. Patrick debated going after him and then decided against it. Tony needed time, he thought, time to sort out his emotions.

"Sir?" Hollis came up behind Patrick. "I'm sorry, sir, I heard some of that. Can I do anything, Dr. Dain?

Would you like a drink?"

"I'd like some coffee, if you will. I think it may be a long night."

"We've had a few of those, eh, sir?"

"We've had a few of those," Patrick agreed tiredly, walking to his library.

"Why, Tony," David said, opening the door. "What a nice surprise. Come in."

Tony hurried past David into the living room. He was flushed, out of breath, and David looked at him with concern.

"Do you feel all right?" he asked, turning down the music.

"Are we alone? I have to talk to you," Tony said anxiously.

"It's William's night off," David put his hand on Tony's forehead, "No fever."

"I'm not sick," Tony shook him off. "But I have to talk to you."

"All right," David said, sitting down. "But let's be calm, whatever it is." He stared at Tony. "What's the trouble?"

"It's about Mother. I want to know."

"Want to know what?"

"The truth. Dad said . . . some things about Mother. I want to know."

"I see," David was quiet, looking at the boy. "Since when don't you trust your father to tell you the truth?"

"It's not like that, Uncle David. Maybe he's too involved to know the truth."

"You don't believe that."

"She was my mother. I have a right to know about her. Dad said it was a bad marriage—okay, I guess that didn't surprise me that much. But he made it sound as if it were Mother's fault. He made it sound as if she

425

was . . . You knew Mother better than anybody. You grew up with her."

"Well, you're right. I knew her better than anybody. And you should know I tried in every way I could to discourage your father from marrying her."

"You're going to take his side!"

"Sit down, Tony, and don't look at me that way. You came here with questions. I am giving you answers."

Tony hesitated and then sat down, looking intently at David.

"Catherine was always too beautiful," David said slowly. "She was the most beautiful baby, the most beautiful child, teen-ager, woman. Her parents—my aunt and uncle—brought her up as if she were royalty. Royalty in a world of peasants. She got everything she wanted. She was flattered and praised outrageously. She was catered to beyond all reason. I remember as teen-agers, there wasn't a party where there weren't a dozen young men swarming around her."

David stared into space, remembering those times. After a while he looked back at Tony.

"She discovered that beauty was power. Power can build or it can destroy. She chose the latter course. She very nearly destroyed your father."

"*No*," Tony shook his head back and forth. "Even Dad didn't say anything like that."

"Of course he didn't. He's protected you from Catherine for years. I think he's wrong. You have an idea of what she was like, but you deny it. Every boy wants an idealized image of his mother to carry around, you're no different. But your conflicts are going to ruin your relationship with your father. I don't want that to happen."

"I shouldn't have come," Tony said, standing up, walking away.

David followed him, grabbing his shoulders, spinning him around.

"Tony, *why* did you come here? I think you've known the truth along. But you couldn't admit it. And you couldn't stand to hear your father say it. Tony, that's it, isn't it?" David shook him gently.

Tony rested his head against David's shoulder. He was breathing hard and when he looked up his eyes were wet.

"One of their arguments . . . I was about seven. Mother wanted Dad to send me away to school. Dad said I was too young. Mother—she said I was too *old* to have around. She said I made her feel like an old woman—it made her feel old to have a seven-year-old around. She said she didn't want to be reminded. She didn't want her friends to be reminded."

Tony walked to a chair and sat down heavily. "I opened the door a crack. Mother was looking into a mirror, fooling with her hair, talking about me as if I were a . . . *thing*. I never forgot that."

"And from that day on you made up your mind to win her over," David said quietly. "She's gone now but you're still trying. Is that it?"

Tony nodded. He took a handkerchief from his pocket and wiped his eyes.

"Pretty dumb."

"No," David said, "not dumb. Human."

"Dad held his ground. I didn't go away until I was ready for prep school. Even then I knew he was sending me away because he didn't want me to see what was going on. He always loved me. Mother . . ." he shook his head. "And then she died. How did she die, Uncle David? Some of the newspapers hinted that Dad . . ." he broke off.

"Your father's refused to discuss it. But I know him. I know he had nothing to do with it, despite enormous provocations."

"What was she like? Really like?"

"The details aren't important, Tony. Your father always said her upbringing ruined her. Maybe it did."

"I want to talk about her. I knew her for sixteen years but I didn't know her at all."

David looked at Tony. He smiled, for he saw the Dain will asserting itself in the boy's eyes, in the set of his shoulders. How many times, he wondered, had he seen that same look in Patrick, in Patrick's father and grandfather, in all the Dain portraits.

"My coffee isn't as good as William's," he said, "but I'm going to give it a try. What would you like? Coke?"

Tony nodded. "But—"

"Then we'll talk," David said, hurrying away.

Tony stood up, walking idly around the room. He thought about his mother. He stopped at a square oak table, looking at the array of framed photographs. He saw several of himself and several of himself with his father. He picked up one of the photographs and stared at it—he and his father in the pool at their Connecticut house.

Tony remembered all the photographs he'd seen—at his great-grandparent's homes, many years before, at his grandparent's homes, at his Aunt Betsy's, at the Connecticut house, here at Uncle David's. He remembered that not once had there been a photograph which included his mother. Yes, he thought to himself, he'd known; even way back then he'd known.

"Coffee's perking away," David said.

He gave Tony a soda and sat down.

"What was she like when she was young?" Tony asked, sitting across from David.

David shook his head. "Catherine . . . caused a lot of unhappiness, perhaps out of her own unhappiness. She had everything, but it was never enough. Her vanity, her jealousy . . . You never knew her brother, did you?"

"He died when I was young."

"Poor Charles. Charles was the forgotten one. He was younger than Catherine. An ordinary child—nobody paid the slightest attention to him. It was all for Catherine. Charles never had anything of his own. When he was about twenty he met a girl. She was from a good family, she had a sweet disposition, and she happened to be a knockout. Not as beautiful as Catherine, of course, but lovely. It was a surprise because Charles had always been a loner—and there he was in love with a wonderful girl who was in love with him."

David sat back, his eyes distant. He remembered Charles—quiet, self-effacing Charles—and he felt sad.

"Catherine was married to Patrick by that time. Her position was secure, she *really* had everything. Yet she was jealous of the girl. She couldn't stand to be around anyone who was remotely attractive . . . Personally, I don't think she could stand being around anyone who was happy. Anyway, she broke it up. Charles married the girl, but a year later it was all over."

Tony sat very still. "How?" he asked.

"It was very subtle, in the beginning. She just wore them down. She spread a series of very—nasty— rumors about the girl. Then she dug out an old family skeleton from her family's past. It was one thing after another."

David looked away, remembering how it was. He sighed, shaking his head.

"They moved to Boston but that didn't help. Catherine wouldn't stop. I don't think they knew what hit them. It turned bitter. They divorced. And Charles just seemed to . . . fade away. He was there, but he wasn't there. Your father and I tried to help but Charles was in another world. One day he drove his car through a guard rail into a ravine."

Tony's dark blue eyes locked on David. "How did Mother feel then?"

"She was quite upset. She didn't understand how Charles could have been so careless. I don't think she saw any connection between what she'd done and what happened to Charles. She was quite upset—and then she called one of her designer friends and got an outfit together for the funeral. I will never forget it because she was an absolutely stunning figure. In black from head to toe, except for the single white flower she carried."

David took a breath. He looked at Tony.

"I told you that story because it tells so much about Catherine. The intentional cruelty—the genuine surprise when it resulted in tragedy . . . She had an all-consuming need for attention. It devoured everyone. If you know that, you know the story of Catherine."

There was silence in the room. Tony was calm, thinking about what he'd heard. David watched him, relieved it was all over. The doorbell rang and David smiled at him.

"I phoned your father."

Tony nodded. "I'll get it."

David watched as Tony let Patrick into the apartment.

"I'm glad you came here," Patrick said. "Are you all right?"

"I'm fine, Dad," Tony stared at his father. "I'm . . . sorry for the way I behaved."

Patrick reached out, hugging Tony. They walked into the living room, Patrick's arm draped around Tony's shoulder.

"Sit down," David said. "I'll get the coffee."

Patrick sat next to Tony on the couch. He looked at his son.

"It's been rough for you. I'm sorry."

"Uncle David told me some things about Mother."

Patrick's mouth tightened. "He should not have done that."

"No, Dad, I'm glad. He said what he felt. Actually, I think I understand it now. I see how hard it must have been. I didn't make it any easier . . . The thing is, I never had to worry about your love . . . but Mother . . . I'd like to talk about it more at home."

"It's long overdue."

"I want to know . . . how Mother died."

David carried a tray into the room. "Am I interrupting?"

"No," Patrick said. "I want you to hear this, too. I'm not going to tell it twice."

David placed the tray on a heavy glass coffee table. He poured drinks for Patrick and himself and then sat down. He looked at Patrick. He saw his eyes grow quiet.

"The cause of death was pneumonia," Patrick began slowly. "That was true. But it wasn't all of it." He sat back, staring straight ahead. "Four days before Catherine died I came home unexpectedly. I had a bad cold, . . . a terrible cold . . . ."

32

Patrick closed the door behind him and sneezed. He was wet, soaked through by a blowing rainstorm, and miserable with the first stages of a heavy cold. He hung his coat in the closet, putting his bag on a shelf. He closed the door and walked toward the stairs.

Patrick trudged wearily up the stairs. He cursed the weather and off-duty taxis and his cold and the fact that it was Wednesday, the servants' day off, and Catherine would expect him to take her to dinner, cold or no cold. He walked into his bedroom, stepping out of his shoes, peeling off his jacket. He took a towel and sat on the bed, rubbing his wet head. He poured a brandy and sipped it slowly. He would, he thought, take a hot shower, have some tea and aspirin and sleep for a couple of hours.

Patrick was undoing his tie when he heard a noise coming from the direction of Catherine's rooms. He looked at his watch; it was three o'clock and Catherine wasn't expected until five. He stared at the door for a moment and then lay back on his bed. There was another noise, something fell to the floor, and Patrick sat up.

"Catherine? Is that you?" he called, walking across the room.

He was almost at her door when he heard laughter,

shrill, mocking laughter, Catherine's laughter. He tapped at the door.

"Catherine?" he called, as another wave of ugly laughter came from behind the door.

Patrick opened the door and then stopped, first shocked and then sickened by what he saw. Catherine's hair tumbled wildly about her face; her mouth was crudely layered with shiny, bright red lipstick. She wore a sheer black negligee, tightly fitted about her breasts, flaring out in yards and yards of chiffon from hips to floor.

Patrick recognized the man in her bed. He was Dr. Peter Lowry, one of the city's more prominent psychiatrists—Catherine's psychiatrist. He was naked, staring up defenseless as Catherine bent over the bed, her taunting laughter spilling over him.

Patrick took a step into the room and Peter Lowry turned. He grabbed desperately at the blanket, trying to cover himself. Catherine whirled around.

"What the hell are you doing home?" she shrieked.

Her eyes were bloodshot and Patrick saw the bottle of champagne nestling in a bucket by the bed.

"Ah . . . Patrick," Peter Lowry began, "this is a very embarrassing—"

"Is that what you call it?" Patrick asked quietly, his face white with anger. "How very civilized."

"What do you care?" Catherine asked defiantly. "It's not the first time . . . Anyway, Dr. Peter Lowry will not be coming back," she laughed, walking away. "The man is such a *fool*. He expects me to marry him. Can you *imagine?* He expects me to stop being Mrs. Patrick Dain . . . of the Dain millions and millions," she spun around, giggling, "to be Mrs. Peter Lowry, whatever that is. Now, I ask you, isn't that *incredible?* The poor boy has in*teg*rity. Why do I always get the ones with in*teg*rity?"

Patrick scooped up Peter Lowry's trousers and threw them at him. "Get dressed and get out! As for you," he looked at Catherine, "the party's over. I am going to instruct my lawyers to begin divorce proceedings. Immediately."

Catherine stretched herself out on the chaise lounge. She laughed, ugly, mocking laughter.

"What about Tony? Are you forgetting him? Mommies always get custody. And if you fight it, he'll be on page one in every paper in the country. You're spinning your wheels, Patrick baby."

"No! You've held that sword over my head long enough. If it takes a court battle, if it takes newspaper stories—I don't care anymore. Do you hear me? I don't care. Whatever it takes, it will be done. Because I'm convinced now that whatever you do to us—it's worth it to get you out of our lives. You're a sickness, Catherine, and we won't be infected with your poison any longer."

Catherine sat up. She looked at Patrick carefully. She saw the determination in his eyes; she heard it in his voice. She jumped up.

"You try it and you'll be sorry. You'll not only lose your precious Tony but you'll lose every cent you have. When I'm through with you—"

"It won't work," Patrick said flatly. "It won't work anymore. I'll get my son and you'll get what *I* choose to give you. And it won't be much," Patrick said, turning away. He went to the doorway. "Ain't love grand," he said, going into his bedroom.

Catherine followed him, weaving a little, stumbling once. Peter Lowry, half-dressed, trailed behind Catherine.

"Patrick," she grabbed his arm, "have you gone *crazy?* Dragging Tony through a custody mess—and for *what?* Because you found some man in my bed? Do you think he's the first?"

"I thought—at least—you ran your dirty little life with some discretion. I know what you are, I've known for years. I took it, for Tony's sake. But I didn't know you would *dare* to bring men into my home, into Tony's home. You're a filthy tramp, Catherine, and I'm through. Take your best shot. But remember, I *am* Patrick Dain. Of the Dain family. You can make it nasty for me, nastier for Tony . . . but by the time the Dain attorneys get through with you you'll be lucky if you have a dime, or a friend, or a boyfriend, to call your own. Go ahead, take the gloves off. We'll take the gloves off too."

"Now, Patrick," Peter Lowry said soothingly. "We're being a little—"

"Are you still here? I told you to get out. You, you son of a bitch, I've been paying you thousands for Catherine's therapy. Is this it? Bedroom therapy? You're a disgrace and by the time I'm through with *you* the closest you'll get to medicine again is dumping bedpans."

"Patrick, *please*. I loved her."

Patrick stared at him. "You probably did. You're not only a son of a bitch, you're a stupid son of a bitch. Now get out of here. Get out of my house."

Patrick turned toward the door. Catherine grabbed at him, hanging on to him as he walked. He stopped at the door and threw her off.

"You can take her with you," he said.

Patrick hurried into the hallway to the stairs. He was trembling but he forced himself forward, hanging onto the banister with all his strength. He heard Catherine and Peter exchange angry words but he didn't look back. He got to the bottom of the stairs and stopped, taking a deep breath.

"Patrick!" Catherine shouted. "This isn't over yet."

"Yes. It is."

He leaned against the banister, trying to push the ugliness of the last few minutes from his mind.

"I said it *isn't over!*" Catherine shouted, starting down the stairs.

"Catherine, give him a chance to cool off, for Christ's sake," Peter Lowry called.

She looked over her shoulder at Peter. "Go to hell!" she said, rushing down the stairs.

Patrick looked up. He saw the hem of her gown tangling under her feet. He saw her lose her balance. He saw her fall.

"*Catherine,*" he screamed.

There was a flash of black chiffon, a flash of golden hair, and then she was tumbling headlong down the stairs, smashing against the steps until her body came to a sickening, thudding stop at the bottom of the stairs.

"My God," Patrick said, kneeling over her. "Catherine, can you hear me? Catherine?"

Peter Lowry hurried down the stairs, "Is she . . . is she . . . Catherine, can you hear me? . . . Catherine? . . . Catherine!?"

Catherine moved her head slightly. She opened her eyes and then closed them.

"My bag. In the closet. Get it," Patrick ordered. "And then call an ambulance."

He peered down at Catherine. "You'll be all right. Don't try to move. Stay still. *Hurry*, Lowry. *Hurry.*"

Patrick paused, looking at Tony. He'd related a greatly edited version of that day's events; he'd used restraint wherever he could. Still he saw Tony fighting for composure; he saw the horror in his eyes.

"The ambulance came. The police came. One of the officers was young, kind of eager. Even in that terrible confusion it was obvious he was looking for more than an accident. He wanted to know how I happened to be home in the middle of the day. He wanted to know how Dr. Lowry happened to be there in the middle of the day. He wanted to know why Catherine was dressed that way in the middle of the day. Why was I without my shoes. Why Dr. Lowry was without shoes and socks," Patrick sighed. "The rumors began then and there."

Patrick took a sip of his drink. He sat back.

"The ambulance took her to Rhinelander. It was closest. I did *not* participate in her treatment, as was suggested in some newspaper accounts."

"I can pick it up from there," David said, for Patrick looked very tired. "There was concussion. There was a severe disc injury to her back. We called in the best men in the city—neurologists, orthopedic men. We stabilized her and proceeded with surgery. Catherine came through the surgery with no problem. We were sure our problems were over. But a pneumonia developed. A particularly virulent pneumonia. We tried everything, but she didn't respond. We flew in an expert on respiratory disease. Nothing. *Nothing* worked. There were entire medical teams with her around the clock. Nothing worked."

Tony stared down at the floor. "The pneumonia killed her?"

"Yes," Patrick said. "Though that young policeman was still nosing around. He'd spoken to detective division . . . I didn't want the circumstances of the accident spread all over the newspapers. Dr. Lowry certainly didn't. No purpose—except perhaps a prurient one—would have been served."

Patrick leaned forward, massaging the muscles of his neck. He sat up, taking more of his drink.

"Dr. Lowry and I met with a captain of detectives I'd met once. We told him the whole story. The truth, from beginning to end. I asked him for only one thing: discretion. He nosed around. He checked us *all* out. He was satisfied and the matter was closed. But the young officer had made a few comments and—some—of the press got onto it. Innuendos flew. Finally, the stories stopped."

"Where is Dr. Lowry now?" Tony asked.

"He's teaching in California. Don't look to put blame," Patrick said. "Because that's a big pie, a lot of people have a piece of it. I believe he did love your mother. Men were always falling in love with her. She was . . . so beautiful."

"On the outside," Tony said. He got up and hastily left the room.

"He needs to cry," David said. "I could cry myself."

Patrick finished his drink and reached for the coffee. He glanced now and again to the other end of the apartment, looking for Tony. Neither he nor David spoke, both of them remembering the Catherine they'd known, the many different Catherines she'd been in her lifetime.

"How terrible," David said after a while. "How really terrible. All of it."

"I hope we can lay it to rest now. I hope Tony can."

"You gave him a gentle account of that day. I can imagine what it was like—between the lines."

"A nightmare. I still feel sick when I think about it. Some awful things have happened in that house. I'll be glad to get out of it."

"What are you waiting for?"

Patrick shrugged. "There are other considerations. I want Tony to get settled at Yale first. By that time the Rutledge house should be on the market. It's a wonderful old house. Right on Gramercy Park."

"Sounds perfect."

"I wanted to show it to Ann first. Now . . . I don't know."

"Patrick, everything else is settled. Settle that."

"How? Should I abduct her and lock her in a room? If I can't *talk* to her I can't settle it."

"You're not going to give up that easily?"

Patrick sipped his drink. "It's funny, I thought once I'd exorcised Catherine's demons everything would be fine, no more obstacles. Now I see it's not that simple." He stared at David. "Have you ever thought that perhaps each of us is given only a predetermined quota of happiness? I mean, those early years with Catherine were a kind of perfect happiness . . . perhaps that's my quota. That's all there is, there isn't any more."

"Nonsense."

"Everything was wonderful for a while. Grace said she thought Rhinelander Pavillion was the best thing that had ever happened to me. And I agreed with her. I came out of hiding because of the hospital. I met Ann because of it. The whole business with Catherine came into the open because of it. I was dealing with my problems, living a real life . . . And then someone noticed I was over my quota and decided to make adjustments."

Patrick looked up as Tony returned to the room. His eyes were sad but it would take a while, Patrick thought, before the sadness went away.

"Are you all right?" he asked.

"Yes, Dad."

"Food," Patrick said to David. "We haven't eaten since lunch. Do you have anything around?"

David stood. "There are some steaks. I'll see to it," he said, going to the kitchen.

"Sit down, Tony. You'll feel better when you've eaten."

"I was wondering . . ."

"Yes?"

"Did Mother . . . was she conscious at all? Did she

say anything before . . ."

"No, she never regained consciousness," Patrick lied.

Catherine had indeed regained consciousness—only briefly and only once. It had been long enough to tell him she would haunt him.

And so she had, Patrick thought with a shiver. So she had.

33

The E.R. was crowded with teenagers awaiting medical attention. The youngsters were dishevelled and bewildered looking, some with cut, bloodied faces, others with bruises now starting to swell and discolor. Their tee shirts and jeans were caked with dirt and grass, souvenirs of a vicious fight which had brought the police running to Central Park.

"Thomas Breslin," Patrick called out.

A blond, skinny boy of about fifteen rose uncertainly. He held a wad of blood-soaked tissues to his face, drops of blood trickling down his hand.

"I'll see you now. This way please."

"How's it going?" Lola asked as Patrick turned back into the corridor.

"Making progress."

"Until next time."

"Next time?"

"We get this all through the spring and summer. Packs of kids go to the park, get boozed up, and start brawling."

"Doc, I don't feel so good," the boy said, coming up behind Patrick.

"I'm not surprised," Patrick said. He put an arm around his shoulder, guiding him along the corridor. "We'll get you fixed up, don't worry."

They entered an examination room. A nurse hurried forward, helping the boy up on the table.

"When will you kids learn?" she sighed, working quickly to disinfect the cuts on his face and scalp. "Hold on to the table," she ordered as he squealed in pain.

Patrick went to the sink. He looked at his hands, red and sore from the morning's repeated scrubbings. He turned on the taps and scrubbed again, carefully drying and powdering his hands before slipping on a pair of thin, surgical gloves.

"Let's see what we have here," Patrick said, standing at the table.

"Could you give me something for the pain? It hurts bad."

"Let's see what the damage is first," Patrick said, flashing a light in the boy's eyes. "Follow my hand, that's it . . . now this way . . . once more . . . okay, that's fine. How much have you had to drink?"

"I don't know, a few beers."

"How many is a few?"

"Doc, it *hurts*."

"How many is a few?"

"Maybe six, around there."

Patrick looked up at the clock. It was not yet eleven in the morning. "Have you had a tetanus shot recently?"

"Tetanus? The only shot I had was penicillin, for when I had the clap."

"When was that?"

"A couple a months ago."

"How old are you, Thomas?"

"Eighteen."

"How old?"

"I told you, eighteen."

The nurse opened a folder. "It's here, Doctor. He'll

be fifteen next month."

Patrick put a gloved finger to the boy's face, probing gently. His nose was smashed, a small mass of pulp and blood. Patrick felt out the bits of shattered bone.

"*Ouch*. Take it easy, huh?"

"Your nose is broken, Thomas."

"Yeah? What does that mean?"

"That means you're going to see Dr. Berkowitz now. Are your parents here?"

"The old lady's on her way."

Patrick stepped back from the table. "Take him to Berkowitz," he said to the nurse. "Make sure he checks with the mother about tetanus."

"Can I go now?"

"You're going to be here for a while." Patrick peeled off his gloves and threw them into the wastebasket. "V.D., drinking, fighting, why are you doing this to yourself? You're throwing away your life before it begins."

"We was minding our own business. These guys from Ninety-sixth Street came around, started hitting on our girls. We showed 'em good."

"Well, Champ, I hope it was worth it. Broken noses aren't fun."

"I can take it," the boy said, though his eyes were wide with fear.

Patrick put his hand on the boy's shoulder. "Take my advice," he said, "remember the pain. Maybe the memory of the pain will keep you from fighting again. Next time you might not be so lucky."

"What do you mean?"

"I mean one of your friends . . . John Napoli, is in Intensive Care with a bad concussion."

"You're lying."

"I wish I were." Patrick turned to the nurse. "Take him to Berkowitz. There's nothing more we can do."

"Come along, Sonny," the nurse said, easing the boy off the table. "Go ahead, lean on me."

Patrick watched them leave. He stared after the youngster, following his wobbly walk up the corridor. He felt sadness and anger at what he'd seen this morning. The bruised bodies and broken bones had been bad enough, but the real sickness was in the minds of these kids, he thought; these kids who, barely into their teens, routinely used alcohol and sex and drugs for amusement, and then dared you to tell them they were wrong.

"Dr. Dain?" an E.R. nurse stood in the doorway.

"Yes?"

"Dr. Ferris is here to see you."

"I'll be right out."

Patrick took his clipboard and hurried through the corridor. He saw Laura Ferris in the distance and smiled. She'd changed in the past months, he thought; she'd matured. Her spirit, her conviction was as high as ever, but she'd acquired a confidence in herself. She was able to handle disagreements as disagreements, not as confrontations. And she was no longer afraid of her beauty. She didn't flaunt it, but she didn't try to hide it either. She'd come into her own and Patrick was sure she was happier for it.

"Good morning, Dr. Ferris. Have you come to help?"

"I came to talk to you," Laura said, leading Patrick to an empty corner. "Dr. DeWitt just came out of surgery. He can use a friend."

"What happened?"

"He gambled once too often. This time he lost."

"Lost? Did his patient die?"

"Almost. They lost the heartbeat twice. DeWitt pulled him back but it was touch and go. It still is, it will be for a while. I was there. I watched the operation. I saw DeWitt's face. I think he finally realized what he's been doing. That's why I think he needs a friend."

Patrick glanced quickly around the waiting room. There were still half a dozen kids waiting for help.

"I can't—"

"Dr. Dain, Andrew DeWitt is in a bad way."

Patrick stared at Laura. "You're hard to understand. After all that's gone on, why do you care how he is?"

"You got the ball rolling. The hours and hours we spent in the film lab taught me things aren't black and white. You taught me there are gray areas."

"I'm glad."

"DeWitt and I still argue, but we argue as colleagues, not enemies. I've learned a lot from him . . . I'm saying I know he's not the bad guy I made him out to be. He convinced himself that what he was doing was right. He *believed* it. Today he realized he's been lying to himself."

Patrick looked toward the nurse's station where the afternoon staff was beginning to assemble. The interns and residents were busily scanning charts and admission records, girding themselves for the day ahead.

"Are you listening to me, Dr. Dain?" Laura asked impatiently. "Did you hear what I said?"

"I heard."

"Well? Are you just going to stand there?"

Patrick gazed into Laura's dark eyes. "If you feel so strongly about this, why don't *you* go to Dr. DeWitt? Why send me?"

"I'm the last person he'd want to see now."

"I don't know what I can say to him. We all knew this was coming. I warned him. Dr. Murdock warned him. There was nothing we could do about it while Stuart Claven was here. Now that he's gone we're formulating a new surgical policy, but we're too late to help DeWitt, or his patient."

"You can be a friend. You can help him that way."

"Doctors make right decisions and wrong decisions. They're accountable for both. If I haven't taught you that, I haven't done my job."

"You misunderstand me," Laura said angrily, bright color rising on her cheeks. "DeWitt's going to have to live with what he's done for a long time. And rightfully so. I'm not condoning him, but I don't want to see him destroyed either. I see enough destruction every day. Don't you see enough destruction? Don't you see enough waste?"

Patrick said nothing. He thought about the kids he'd seen in the E.R. this morning, about the waste, the easy destruction of their young lives.

He found himself thinking about Gail Parrish and about David. Catherine came into his mind then, quick, harsh pictures of their last months together. He thought about Buddy, about Ann. He thought about all the choices and decisions, some innocent, some deliberate, that had ruined so many lives.

"You don't ask easy questions," Patrick said quietly.

"Here's another one. Is it so bad to hold out a hand, to be a friend?"

"The first day I met you I knew you were something special," Patrick smiled slightly. "Justice *and* mercy. It's a worthy concept and you understand it. I'll go talk to him," he sighed. "I don't know what I'll say, but I'll give it a try."

"Can you go now?"

"Here," he handed his clipboard to Laura, "sign me out and I'll go now."

"Thank you."

Patrick stared at her for a moment. He started to speak, then changed his mind, walking through the E.R. doors to the elevator. He rode upstairs in silence, avoiding the other passengers, wondering what he would say to Andrew DeWitt, wondering if his presence would be welcome.

The elevator doors opened onto the bright whites and stainless steels of the surgical wing. Patrick hesitated before stepping into the corridor, blinking his eyes in the glare of the strong lights.

"Good morning," he said, stopping at the nearest nurse's station. "Where would I find Dr. DeWitt?"

"He hasn't been out this way. Try the locker room."

Patrick nodded. He turned into a long corridor, walking through a set of double doors into a shorter passageway. He stopped in front of thick glass doors marked MEDICAL PERSONNEL ONLY. Would Andrew want to see him, he wondered again, would he want to see anyone?

Patrick pushed the doors open and continued on his way, poking his head into the first of the surgeons' locker rooms.

"Andrew DeWitt?" he called out.

"Next door," a voice came from the shower.

Patrick went to the next room. He took a few steps inside then stopped abruptly. "Andrew," he said softly.

Andrew DeWitt was hunched forward, staring vacantly into his open locker. He was still in his surgical greens, his shirt soaked with perspiration and blood. His eyes were red-rimmed, hollow with exhaustion. His mouth was a jagged line, as if contorted with pain.

"Bad news travels fast," he said tonelessly.

"I'm here as a friend." Patrick pulled a chair over and sat down. "How's your patient?"

"Hanging on. No thanks to me."

"How does it look?"

"Fifty-fifty. No better than that."

"Do you want to talk about it?" Patrick asked.

"I should have talked about it months ago, a year

ago. I couldn't face what was happening to my life."
Andrew looked at Patrick. "I know what the rumors are . . . everybody thought I was doing it for the money. It wasn't the money."

"There's been talk that you're in debt."

"It's true. But I'm in so deep I'll never get out. Never. I did many of these operations at reduced fees, because money wasn't the point."

Patrick looked at Andrew, at the emptiness in his eyes, the tired pallor of his skin. "What was the point? You were the most conservative surgeon I knew. All of a sudden you're King of The Bypass. Why?"

Andrew stared at his hands. They were large, strong hands with long, tapering fingers, a surgeon's hands.

"Andrew," Patrick said softly, "why?"

"My life went to hell, that's why. The only place I had a life was in the operating room."

"I don't believe that. You had everything going for you."

"Once, maybe. Not for a long time. I left Jean, after all those years, to marry Erica. That was five years ago. That was when I thought I had everything going for me. I was happy. *Damn*, I was happy. I thought we had a great marriage. Then Erica left me to marry a stockbroker. Poetic justice, I guess. I did it to Jean; Erica did it to me."

"Andrew, you have a new marriage. You have Cheryl."

"Cheryl is twenty-two years old. Her interests are clothes, disco dancing, and Mick Jagger."

Andrew stood up. He walked slowly, stiffly, across the room, each step more labored than the last.

"Do you want anything?" he asked, opening the door of a small refrigerator. "We have soda and beer."

"No thanks."

Andrew opened a can of beer, tossing the metal tab

on the floor. He returned to his chair, sitting down heavily.

"The loneliness was terrible," he said. "And I was getting older. The world was changing, it wasn't the world I'd known. The message was: be young, be beautiful, have fun, look out for number one." Andrew sipped his beer, staring off into space. "I wasn't young or beautiful, so I married someone who was. I intended to spend the next years having a good time, looking out for number one. What a joke."

"I'm sorry," Patrick said.

"I bought a house near Sutton Place. I filled Cheryl's closets with designer clothes. I had plastic surgery. None of it meant a damn. It was an awful mistake."

"Does Cheryl feel that way?"

"Cheryl is young, beautiful, sweet, and incredibly stupid . . . But even she realized it didn't make any sense. It didn't even make sense in bed. We share a house, a name, that's all."

"That's when you stepped up your operating schedule."

"It started when Erica left me. I slowed down when I met Cheryl. But after a month of marriage, my work was all I had. We led separate lives. Cheryl took my credit cards and her friends and went on the town. Where was *I* to go? I needed my work. It was the only thing that made me feel as if I still had a life. It was the only dignity left in my life."

"Andrew, you must have seen where it was leading."

"You can talk yourself into anything, if you're desperate enough. I started taking on tougher cases. That led to impossible cases. After a while, other surgeons started sending me patients they didn't dare touch themselves. I was successful too. I was turning out miracles. Patrick, I felt valuable again. It no longer mattered that my wife would rather watch *Mork and Mindy* than talk to me. In the operating room I was a king. Hell, I was God."

Patrick saw the tears start in Andrew's eyes. He saw the anger and pain and raw despair of the man. He reached over and put his hand on Andrew's shoulder, not quite sure what he should say, what he could say.

"Patrick," Andrew said, rubbing his eyes, "my patient may die. Because I lost my way, because I couldn't cope, he may die. It's a nightmare. I must have been crazy. Laura Ferris tried to stop me, she tried to make me see what I was doing. I wouldn't listen to her. I wouldn't listen to anyone. *God*, Patrick," Andrew buried his head in his hands, "why didn't I listen?"

"Laura is the one who asked me to talk to you. She said you needed a friend. She very much wanted you to have a friend now."

Andrew shook his head. "She has every reason to hate me."

"She doesn't hate you. She understands a terrible truth . . . a terrible truth doctors hate to admit, even to themselves. Andrew, we're not special. We're fallible men and women with all the imperfections of fallible men and women. We have an obligation not to fail, yet we do fail soemtimes because all people fail sometimes."

"My failure may cost a man his life."

"I'm not excusing what you've done, Andrew. We deal in life and death, so of course we must be judged harshly. But there's more to it. There is the fantasy, that we are perfect beings, and there is the reality, that we are not. Doctors get sick, just like anyone else. The tragedy is that we deny our sickness. You were sick . . . you were falling apart. Yet nobody dared come right out and say so. Because you're a doctor, and doctors are supposed to be above all that."

"I always thought I was."

"We all think that. We know it's not true but we think it anyway. And that *is* the tragedy. People come to us to make them well. Most of the time we do, and feel damn good about doing it. We feel so good we forget about healing ourselves."

Andrew wiped his eyes. He drank the last of the beer and threw the can away. "It's too late for me."

"I don't think so. You've been a surgeon for twenty-five years. All the good you've done in those years counts for something. It's important."

"If my patient dies . . ."

Andrew got up and walked around the room. He stopped suddenly, pounding at the wall with his fist.

"Andrew!"

"The man has a family, Patrick. He would have had a lousy life without the operation, but he would have had a life."

"He may still."

"No. I should have heard by now. They should have stabilized him by now. If they haven't . . . he won't make it through the afternoon." Andrew looked at the clock. "In this case, no news is bad news."

"I'll stay by the phone, Andrew. Why don't you shower and get dressed."

"No, not yet."

Patrick glanced at Andrew's smeared, stained surgical garments. "You can't sit around in another man's blood all day."

"I don't want to leave the phone. Not yet."

"Don't worry about the phone," David said tersely, walking into the room. "I just came from Post-Op."

Andrew saw the look on David's face. He sank into a chair, clasping his hands together. "I knew it," he murmured. "I knew it."

"Your patient is stable," David said. "They think

he's going to be all right."

Andrew looked up slowly. "What? What did you say?"

"I said your patient is stable. It looks like he's out of the woods. How, I don't know. Your guardian angel must be working overtime."

"He's going to be all right," Andrew said, dazed. "I never thought . . ."

"The least you're going to get out of this is a rebuke from the Surgical Committee. That's the least, there'll probably be a good deal more. If there's any justice, there'll be a good deal more."

"David," Patrick said, "this isn't the time—"

"Yes," David snapped, "this is the time. I've had it with you, Andrew. I'm tired of hanging around Post-Op waiting to see which way the dice will roll."

Patrick went over to David. "Look," he said quietly, "it's been a rough morning all around. This isn't necessary."

"Don't tell me what's necessary. And don't tell me about rough mornings. It wasn't exactly laughs in Post-Op. I never saw a Post-Op team work so hard."

"Fine, there'll be time for that later."

"There's time for it now. Because any day Andrew DeWitt operates is a day I don't draw one easy breath."

"Andrew would be the first to agree with you."

David looked quickly at Patrick. "Oh? Since when?"

"Since this morning. That's what I've been trying to tell you."

"David," Andrew stood up, "my actions have been inexcusable. I deserve anything anybody wants to do to me."

"Well," David said slowly, "the epiphany of Andrew. What brought this on? And don't come any nearer with all that blood and gore on you."

"I'll fill you in later," Patrick said. "For now let's let

Andrew get cleaned up."

"I don't know what's going on here, but just because Andrew's seen the light, that doesn't mean he's off the hook."

"Come on, David," Patrick said tiredly, "Andrew's not on the hook alone and you know it. We knew what he was doing. We knew what he was doing was dangerous. We sat on our hands."

"Stuart Claven was here."

"Stuart or no Stuart, we should have made a move. We didn't, because doctors don't interfere with other doctors. Until it's too late. Sure Andrew's responsible but so are we."

David stared at Patrick. He smiled. "Is this going to wind up being my fault?"

"There's enough blame to go around. It took us a while to find our courage, if you remember."

"Direct hit," David said. "Yes, I remember."

"Patrick," Andrew said, "I appreciate you being here this morning. I really do. But let's not argue anymore. I'm going to take what's coming to me. If it's not severe enough, my own conscience will fill in the gaps."

"Okay," David nodded, "okay. But I'd like to see you in my office this afternoon, Andrew. Anytime after three."

"I'll be there."

Patrick walked over to Andrew. "Are you all right?"

"I will be. I'm going to shower and dress. I want to talk to Dr. Ferris. I want to see my patient. I'll meet with David. Then I have a lot of thinking to do."

"If you need to talk . . ."

"Thanks, I'll remember that. I'm grateful to you for listening to me this morning. More grateful than I can say. I don't know what it was . . . a breakdown . . . mid-life crisis . . . but it's time to put the pieces back together."

"Think it through carefully."

"The long night of the soul. I've heard of it, now I know what it is."

"Are you coming, Patrick?" David called.

Patrick turned and walked with David to the door. He paused in the corridor to look back at Andrew DeWitt. He was a lonely figure, haggard, drawn, pushed to the limits of his strength. He wondered if he would ever recover what he had lost; if, when he got his life back, it would be whole, would be worth having.

"Patrick," David said. "He's got to do this alone."

"I know," he said, as they walked through the corridor.

"As usual, I am a beat behind. What happened?"

"It's a long story. He's had a hard time of it."

"I figured that much out by myself."

"Let's get some coffee," Patrick said, stopping at the doctor's lounge.

David looked at his watch. "Ten minutes."

They walked into the lounge, empty at that time of day. A television set droned on in a corner. Patrick stared at it for a moment then switched it off. He sat down, stretching his legs out in front of him.

"Here," David said, putting two cups of coffee on the table. "You look terrible."

"It was a terrible morning. Kids beating hell of each other. Andrew . . . beating hell out of himself."

"I'd like to hear about that."

"Later. He may want to tell you some of it himself."

"You thought I was too hard on him."

"Well, all that righteous indignation. You're the one who told me he wasn't really doing anything wrong. Remember that?"

David smiled. "I like to think I've come a ways since that conversation. We had that conversation on your first day here."

"We've both come a ways since then," Patrick laughed. "God, we've been through it all."

"Any regrets?"

Patrick pondered the question. "No. Rhinelander Pavillion's been an education. It's been an education in people. People, in their infinite variety, ruining their lives in an infinite variety of ways. Big ways. Small ways. A wrong turn here or there, a right turn not taken."

"You're thinking about Ann."

"I'm always thinking about Ann. She's always there, in the back of my mind, in the front of my mind. Sideways, upside down. It all comes out Ann."

"That's no secret."

"Andrew could be me, ten years from now."

"Nonsense."

"It's not so hard to lose your way, David. A wrong turn here or there, a right turn not taken. Listening to Andrew this morning, I thought about the day we took our oath. Shiny new doctors, swearing by Apollo to keep our patients from harm and injustice . . . But what about us? A doctor's oath should include the injunction not to lose our way."

"Your way is with Ann."

Patrick smiled suddenly. "I'm going to make one more try at seeing Ann. One more try, with all my heart and soul. Because nothing makes sense without her."

"Do it. Do it before you lose your nerve."

"I'm not afraid of trying. I'm afraid of trying and failing."

34

Patrick searched around his desk for a letter. He glanced at it and looked at David.

"We're getting an excellent price for the Larrimer sculptures," he said. "They'll be shipped to the new owners later this week."

"What about the furniture? Is that set?"

"Our regular supplier will exchange the present furniture for standard hospital issue. We get a substantial credit to our account. And we get lowered maintenance costs right away."

"Good," David said. He pulled his chair closer to Patrick's desk, looking over a vast floor plan. "I'm wondering what we can do with the corner suites in Larrimer. They're such a waste of space. Lola suggested—" he looked up as Grace came into the office.

"Want to see how we're slicing away?" he smiled.

"Later. Pediatrics called. The CF baby they admitted last night isn't going to make it. They'd like you to take a look."

David shook his head. "She was doing all right this morning."

"It's pretty desperate now. The parents are there. Someone has to talk to them."

"Yes, of course. I'll go right up."

David went to the door. He stopped, looking back at

Patrick. "Can we get back on this later this afternoon? Say about three?"

"Make it four. I'll be at the medical school at three."

David left the office. Grace sat down, staring at Patrick.

"That baby's only sixteen months old," she said. "It makes you think."

"Terrible. It really tears you up when they're that little."

"And it makes you think. About not wasting life."

"What do you mean?"

"What are you doing for lunch?"

"Is that an invitation?"

"In a way."

"Would you care to elaborate," Patrick asked, "or is this a riddle?"

"I'm inviting you to lunch. But not with me. With Ann."

Patrick looked at her. "Ann! Did she call? Why didn't you put her through? Why—"

"Hold on, let me explain," Grace said. "I have a lunch date with Ann today. I thought it would be a good idea if you went in my place."

"I see," Patrick looked away. "Thank you but I don't think so."

"Patrick, you haven't called Ann in over a week. Why?"

"*Why?* Because for almost three weeks she refused to see me or talk to me. I tried every way I knew and the answer was no. It took me a while, but I got the idea."

"Give an inch," Grace said earnestly. "Ann's very unhappy. So are you."

"Ann was the one who broke it off."

"Maybe she had her reasons."

"Exactly," Patrick said quietly.

"Why don't you ask her what they are?"

457

"How? She wouldn't see me or talk to me."

"You have your chance today."

"No, not that way. Not an ambush. No, thank you," he said firmly.

"You're so damn stubborn. *Make* the first move; it won't kill you."

"I've made a hundred first moves. She's not interested."

"Don't be so sure. I've seen Ann a few times." Grace hesitated. She removed a folded piece of paper from her pocket, looking at it. "She had a good reason. And it wasn't Buddy. The day of the board meeting . . . Ann received a letter from Julie. An awful letter. Aside from its condescension, the essence of it is that Ann would ruin your career and your position if she continued to see you."

Patrick stared incredulously at Grace. "What did you say?"

"You heard me." Grace looked again at the paper in her hand. "Rudy and I had dinner with Ann. I took the letter when she wasn't looking. Here, see for yourself," she gave it to him.

Patrick read the letter, his jaw tensing with anger. He finished it and threw it down on the desk.

"I'll kill her. I'll *kill* her."

"Julie's long gone from New York. Forget about Julie. Think about Ann."

"Do you mean to tell me she *believed* this . . . this . . ." Patrick grabbed the letter and crumpled it into a ball. "She *believed* what Julie said?"

"At first. Patrick, she comes from a family which was very conscious of knowing their place. And she's always been conscious of knowing her place. After you spend a few years saying 'yes, ma'am, no ma'am,' to the upper crust, your place is very clear in your mind. The letter confirmed her fears . . . it confirmed what Mae had warned about."

"What do you mean *at first*?"

"Well," Grace smiled, "the O'Haras are a spunky lot. Ann thought about it. And thought about it. Finally she got mad. I know—she asked me where she could find Julie. She wanted to give her a piece of her mind."

"Find Julie? Why didn't she find me?" Patrick asked.

"She . . . couldn't."

"Why not . . . why not?" he asked and then sat back. "Don't tell me . . . her pride. Is that it?"

"The O'Haras are also a proud lot. I believe she was ready to make it up. And then you stopped calling. Terrible timing, Patrick. She figured it was too late."

"Incredible," he shook his head.

"Not really. Think of Ann's background. She *survived* on pride, pride alone. It's strong in her. There are some things you can't unlearn . . . See her today, Patrick. Get it straightened out."

"I can't do that."

"*Your* pride this time?"

"It's not that."

"Of course it is. Pride was a matter of survival to Ann. But you're Patrick Dain, pride is a birthright to you. Dains are not used to being turned down. Dains are not used to swallowing their pride."

"Awful people, Dains."

Grace laughed. "Look at it as a mark of character. You have to be big enough to swallow your pride and go to her."

Patrick thought about Ann, about seeing her again. Night after night for almost four weeks he'd pictured her in his mind, longing to be with her.

Grace smiled for she saw she had him. She saw the anticipation in his eyes. She saw the nervous excitement.

"Ann will be at the seal pond in Central Park at one. You have fifteen minutes."

"It's kind of a dirty trick," he said.

"It's love, and all's fair."

Central Park was bathed in sunshine, a soft breeze brushing the leaves of the trees. Children were all about, skipping and running, hurrying to see the animals. Gaily colored balloons bobbed up and down on long strings, and one small child held a bright red pinwheel to the wind, giggling as it spun round and round. The benches were dotted with people taking the sun or eating their lunch, leaving bits of bread for the pigeons.

Patrick approached the seal pond. There was a cluster of children at one side of the pond, pointing and laughing as a seal dove under the water and then reappeared, clapping its flippers together. He stopped, looking to the other side, and there he saw Ann.

She stood in profile to him, smiling at one of the smaller seals, a neat brown paper bag sticking out of her purse. He gazed at her. At that moment it seemed to him that he and Ann were the only two people in the park. He watched her a while longer and then walked to the pond.

"Ann," he said softly, coming up behind her.

She turned around. "Patrick," she stared up at him, her blue eyes wide with surprise.

"Hello, Ann. You're not going to start crying, are you?" he smiled.

"No."

"You look tired."

"So do you," she said.

"How are you?"

"Fair. How are you?"

"Fair."

Patrick touched her hair, caressing it lightly with his fingers. " 'Tis a proud woman you are, Annie O'Hara," he grinned.

She stared wordlessly into his eyes and he put his arms around her. He held her quietly, his head resting lightly against her soft blond hair.

"Patrick," she looked at him. "I'm sorry. I was silly, I was childish, I was thoughtless."

"And that's only the half of it," he said, laughing. "Ann . . . Grace told me about the letter."

"Coming on top of everything else . . . I panicked. I thought about it a long time. I *wanted* to call you. But by that time . . . "

"Where are we now, Ann?"

She turned away, looking back at the seals. "I had so much time to think. I didn't think just about the letter."

"What then?"

"I've been . . . independent . . . for so long. I'm not sure I can be anything else."

"Ann," he turned her to him, "I don't want your independence. I want your love. I don't want to take anything away from your life, I want to add to it. Is that so bad?"

"No. But my work—"

"Work as much as you like or as little. We're not children, Ann. We don't have to make the mistakes children make. We have nothing to prove."

"And the boys," she said doubtfully. "Buddy, and your Tony."

"I'm not promising it's going to be easy. They'll have a lot to get used to. We all will. But we can do it. Tony will get to know you and he'll love you. He has so much love bottled up inside him. He needs a mother. And Buddy's needed a father for a long time. It's not too late."

"Is it okay if I'm scared?"

"I'm terrified," he smiled.

Ann laughed. "I wonder if we know what we're doing."

"I love you."

"I love you, Patrick."

A great spray of water came their way as a seal dove off its rocky platform. Patrick took his handkerchief from his pocket and wiped at Ann's face.

"This," Patrick laughed, "isn't the setting I had in mind . . . but will you marry me?"

"Yes," Ann laughed too, wiping her wet hair. "Oh, yes."

Patrick took her hand, "I don't happen to have an engagement ring on me. Would you settle for a balloon?"

"A yellow balloon."

"And a hot dog?"

"And a hot dog," Ann laughed.

"And all my love?" Patrick asked, grinning, ducking as more water splashed them.

"And all your love . . . And mine."

FICTION FOR TODAY'S WOMAN

THE FOREVER PASSION (563, $2.50)
by Karen A. Bale
A passionate, compelling story of how a young woman, made hostage by a band of Comanche warriors, becomes captivated by Nakon—the tribe's leader.

THE RIVER OF FORTUNE: THE PASSION (561, $2.50)
by Arthur Moore
When the beautiful Andrea Berlenger and her beloved Logan leave their homes to begin a new life together, they discover the true meaning of love, life and desire on a Mississippi Riverboat and the great . . . RIVER OF FORTUNE.

BELLA (498, $2.50)
by William Black
A heart-warming family saga of an immigrant woman who comes to America at the turn of the century and fights her way to the top of the fashion world.

BELLA'S BLESSINGS (562, $2.50)
by William Black
From the Roaring Twenties to the dark Depression years. Three generations of an unforgettable family—their passions, triumphs and tragedies.

MIRABEAU PLANTATION (596, $2.50)
by Marcia Meredith
Crystal must rescue her plantation from its handsome holder even at the expense of losing his love. A sweeping plantation novel about love, war, and a passion that would never die.

Available wherever paperbacks are sold, or direct from the Publisher. Send cover price plus 50¢ per copy for mailing and handling to Zebra Books, 21 East 40th Street, New York, N.Y. 10016. DO NOT SEND CASH!

THE TEMPESTUOUS TOLLIVER SAGA

BY ARTHUR MOORE

THE TEMPEST (521, $2.50)
As struggling young America chooses sides in an inevitable Civil War, the passionate, strong-willed Tollivers, torn by jealousy and greed, begin their life-long battle for the magnificent Burnham Hill.

THE TURMOIL (490, $2.50)
While the Civil War ravages the land, the Tolliver men march to battle, and the women they leave behind fall victim to dangerous love and deception, uncertain if they'll ever see their loved ones again.

THE TRIUMPH (522, $2.50)
As the Civil War approaches its final days and the men, long separated, return home, the struggle between the Tollivers for possession of Burnham Hill is rekindled, with even more venom than before.

THE TAPESTRY (523, $2.50)
With the Civil War ended and Burnham Hill burned to the ground, the Tollivers who have scattered around the globe, reunite, continuing their fierce family feud as they rebuild their beloved plantation home.

Available wherever paperbacks are sold, or order direct from the Publisher. Send cover price plus 40¢ per copy for mailing and handling to Zebra Books, 21 East 40th Street, New York, N.Y. 10016. DO NOT SEND CASH!